Faggamuffin

John R Gordon lives and works in London, England. He is the author of three novels, *Black Butterflies*, (GMP 1993), for which he won a New London Writers' Award; *Skin Deep*, (GMP 1997); and *Warriors & Outlaws* (GMP 2001), both of which have been taught on graduate and post-graduate courses on Race & Sexuality in Literature in the United States. He script-edited and wrote for the world's first black gay television show, Patrik-Ian Polk's *Noah's Arc* (2005-6). In 2007 he wrote the autobiography of America's most famous black gay porn star from taped interviews he conducted, *My Life in Porn: the Bobby Blake Story*, (Perseus 2008). In 2008 he co-wrote the screenplay for the cult Noah's Arc feature-film, *Jumping the Broom* (Logo) for which he received a NAACP Image Award nomination. The same year his short film *Souljah* (directed by Rikki Beadle-Blair) won the Soho Rushes Award for Best Film.

As well as mentoring and encouraging young gay and lesbian and racially-diverse writers, he also paints, cartoons, does film and theatre design, writes afrocentric erotica under a variety of pseudonyms; and he is a student of Vodoun.

Faggamuffin

John R Gordon

TEAM
ANGELICA

Published 2012 by Team Angelica Publishing,
an imprint of Angelica Entertainments Ltd

Copyright © 2012 by John R Gordon

The right of John R Gordon to be identified as the
author of this work has been asserted by him in accor-
dance with the Copyright, Designs and Patents Act
1988.

Team Angelica Publishing
51 Coningham Road
London W12 8BS

www.teamangelica.com

A CIP catalogue record for this book is available
from the British Library

ISBN 978-0-9569719-1-3

Printed and bound by Lightning Source

Thank you to Rikki, Andy, Graeme, Baz, Zion, Diriye, Michael Pinnock and Nathan Clough for your wisdom, insight and support, and thank you too to Katie Goold for your time and advice.

Chapter One

Cutty twisted his head round and watched the island fall away into the night. Jamaica, JA, glittering jewel of the Caribbean. The place of his birth. His homeland.

Not any more.

Cutty was a man on the run.

The lights of Kingston receded slowly into the indigo dark. Then the plane banked and they were gone. For a long moment Cutty stared at his reflection in the curving glass of the airplane window. The eyes that gazed back at him were hard from lack of sleep, and bloodshot. His face looked ugly to him, as if the horror it had seen had twisted and permanently deformed it. He turned away and faced forward in his seat.

The Air Jamaica Kingston-to-London-(Heathrow) flight wasn't busy. There was no-one sitting in either of the two seats next to his, so he could sprawl out uninhibitedly. The few other travellers dotted about the compartment were mostly tourists and mostly white. It was a relief to be among strangers.

He stared ahead, trying not to think, monitoring the in and out of his breathing as if it was something that had consciously to be kept going. He hadn't washed or brushed his teeth or changed his clothes in forty-eight hours, and he felt sweaty and rank.

All he had with him were his ticket to London, his passport, the clothes he was wearing, a credit-card touching on its limit, and a roll of Jamaican fifty-dollar bills. At that moment, suspended high above the endless ocean, it was as if he had no past and no future.

If he allowed himself to think about what had happened he would start to cry and wouldn't be able to stop. *Don't think. Breathe.*

He knew he wouldn't be able to sleep on the flight.

Once the plane was at cruising altitude and the seat-belt signs were off he went to the bathroom to try and clean himself up. First he brushed his teeth with the complimentary toothbrush the airline provided, and spat into the sink. There was a little blood in his spittle and one tooth felt slightly loose. Then he used the toilet and had a bowel-movement of such shuddering intensity that he gasped aloud and had to brace himself against the walls of the cubicle with both forearms. A violent convulsion ran the whole length of his body as what seemed like an impossible volume of diarrhea sluiced out of his backside in noisy, shame-making spurts. Sweat broke out on his forehead and he began to shiver feverishly. His gut turned over repeatedly.

Even once he was finally empty he kept on sitting there, trembling and nauseated, his stomach spasticating, afraid there would be more internal chaos to come. When nothing came his body began slowly to regain its equilibrium. The sweaty chilliness passed from him and a little strength flowed back into his muscles. He stood up hesitantly, pulled up his track-pants and underwear, washed his hands and face, and returned to his seat feeling a little more human.

When the steward came round, Cutty spent some of the little money he had left on a double shot of rum. The steward, a pleasant-looking young white man with a cropped head and goatee, was polite, but seemed nervous of Cutty as he put the tumbler down in front of him.

A battybwoy, Cutty thought. *Him tink me Sizzla or Beenie Man or Vybz Kartel or one a dem murder musicians*. He raised the glass to his lips and swallowed as the steward moved away from him up the aisle. The tight navy trousers he was wearing hugged his butt. *Nice arse,* Cutty thought blankly. An image of himself fucking the steward roughly from behind flashed into his head. The rum tasted bitter in his mouth, and swallowing it made his stomach clench all over again, but it gave him warmth and took the edge off his thoughts.

He stared ahead, as if his gaze would somehow push the flight forward. In the dark it was as if they weren't moving at all.

Everything felt like an illusion, fake.

They didn't like him at Customs, this hard-faced young black man with no suitcases dressed raggamuffin-style in slightly soiled white Nike sportswear. This six foot Jamaican with a lean, sinewy, cane-cutter's physique, ornately-braided hair and a gold front tooth, who wore chunky gold chains around his wrists and neck, sovereign rings on the fingers of his large hands, and a miniature gold pistol in one ear. The hard, fuck-you expression on his face, the flat, bloodshot, unrevealing eyes, the large, full lips that seemed permanently twisted in contempt for all authority, angered the immigration officials and made them suspicious, as did his lack of luggage and his lack of deference towards them.

Yardie. Gangster. Benefit scrounger. Mugger. Nigger.

So much for the Mother Country.

'Is just a flying visit,' he told a short, fat, pasty white woman in a crumpled uniform. 'Scouting up talent for me record label back home.'

On previous visits that had been true.

They took him to a room and searched him for

drugs, though this time once he had stripped naked in front of them they were satisfied with shining a torch between his spread buttocks rather than forcing a rubber-gloved finger into his anus as they had on his previous visits to England. Loathing and hatred flooded through him at the repetition of this humiliation, and he thanked God he had discarded a small piece of cannabis resin that had been in his tracksuit-pocket before checking in at Norman Manley Airport.

Eventually, after examining every item of his clothing with forensic minuteness, they let him go.

Dawn was breaking weakly as he emerged from the Arrivals building at Heathrow Airport. The sky was grey and it was drizzling. The cold, damp air quickly penetrated his thin nylon tracksuit-top, draining him of energy, and he felt suddenly both very tired and extremely hungry.

Shivering, he re-entered the terminal building, found a Bureau De Change, and changed all his Jamaican dollars into UK pounds. The exchange rate was bad, but he held nothing back: what use would that money ever be to him again?

From a concession stand that was just opening he bought a latte and a croissant filled with hot, buttery scrambled eggs. Usually on his trips to England he enjoyed eating food that he didn't normally eat, but this time as he lifted the croissant to his mouth he felt a sharp nostalgia for his usual back-home breakfast of ackee and fried dumplings, even though it was only two days since he had last eaten it. Because this time was different. This time he wasn't going back.

After eating the scrambled eggs and drinking the coffee he felt a little stronger. He allowed himself to feel a thin sliver of relief that he had at least got this far: he had got past Customs and Immigration. He wasn't safe yet, nothing was solved yet, but at least he hadn't been bundled straight back onto the plane and sent back to Jamaica. He found a pay-phone and made a call.

Usually the first person Cutty called when he touched down in the UK was his cousin Dennis. It was Dennis who he normally stayed with whenever he visited England. But not this time. This time he didn't want Dennis to even know that he was in the country, never mind find out why he was here.

'Speak,' ordered a black male voice at the other end of the line.

'Buju? Is me, Cutty.'

Buju was a friend of Dennis's who Cutty had got to know a little on a previous visit to England.

'Cutty, mi idren!' Buju's voice became instantly warm. 'How you doing, man?'

'Me just reach England, you know,' Cutty replied, avoiding the question. 'London Heathrow. I just touch down.'

'Cool, man. You here for business or pleasure?'

'Business and a break.'

'Jamaica getting too hot for you?'

Buju's tone was jokey, but for a horrible moment Cutty thought: *he knows what happened*. But Buju couldn't possibly know. Or could he? Could Dennis have heard some news and passed it on to Buju already? *Now news can cross the world in an instant*.

'You speak to Dennis then?' Cutty asked warily.

'Not for like months, man,' Buju said, sounding offhand. 'Sides, ain't he off visiting your folks in Canada, is it?'

Cutty exhaled. *Him na know. Me just paranoid*. And he realised that Dennis being away made his next request more plausible: 'Him tell me say you might put me up for a night or two while him is away.'

It was a gamble, but it was an offer that would be in

character for Dennis to make on someone else's behalf without bothering to tell that person, even though Buju wasn't close to Dennis, and Cutty and Buju had met only a couple of times before.

'If you don't mind sleeping on the couch, though,' Buju said easily. 'Sure, no problem. Come over my drum whenever. You got the address, yeah?'

'Remind me, man. I lose mi organiser.'

Buju gave Cutty his address, a flat over in West London, on the White City estate. 'Just turn up, yeah,' he said. 'If I'm out my gal'll be there to let you in.'

'What shi name?'

'Cynthia.'

Cutty thanked Buju and hung up the phone.

Chapter Two

After making the call to Buju Cutty went and caught the tube into Central London. It was crowded, and he noticed that he was the only person in his carriage without heavy luggage who wasn't obviously an airport employee. Paranoia rolled over him again.

What if someone else notice?

He looked around suspiciously at his fellow-travellers but nobody was paying him the slightest attention: most of them were either in a jet-lag coma or else babbling away excitedly with their travel-companions. And what was there to notice anyway, he asked himself sharply. So what if he was travelling without bags? It wasn't a crime. The fear that had been saturating his head for the last two days was confusing his thought-processes, mashing the real into the unreal and making it hard for him to tell them apart.

It look bad to Immigration but not to anyone else. And he was past Immigration.

The train emerged from a long tunnel and began to run above ground. Cutty stared out at the passing suburban hinterland without really seeing it. The first time he had come to Britain he had been shocked by the dispiriting grey endlessness of the city's residential sprawl. Now he saw it as just what it was. As the train neared central London it sank underground again, and once more he had nothing to stare at but his own reflection, distorted in the grimy glass of the carriage window.

At Hammersmith Cutty changed and took the Hammersmith & City line two stops to Shepherds

Bush, then walked the short rest of the way up to White City. He found himself among commuters on their way to the row of BBC buildings that flanked the east side of the estate. They were, of course, mostly white. It always took him a little while to get used to being among white people.

The first time it had been almost like being in a movie.

All around White City there were signs announcing a huge project of urban renewal. Cranes rose skeletally against the skyline, and building work was aleady going on along the dual carriageways that bounded the estate to the north and east. The White City estate itself, however, seemed as yet untouched by any improvements.

Cutty headed into the estate along a curving road that ran past a succession of basketball courts, deserted at this hour. Buju's block was straight ahead of him. It was one of a succession of dirty concrete slabs that as he faced them were as flat and featureless as cardboard boxes. On the reverse sides were walkways, open to the elements, that connected all the flats on each floor with each other. None of them had lifts.

The security door to Buju's block stood open. Cutty climbed the stairs to Buju's flat slowly, his uneasiness now strong in him again. Could he really trust Buju, a man he hardly knew? But then that had been why Cutty had chosen him in the first place: Buju didn't know him well enough to be too much in his business. The stairwell stank of piss and bleach. He reached the third floor. Buju's door was the one at the end of the walkway, furthest from the stairwell. He went up it and rang the bell. A young woman answered, a pretty brownskin gal with large eyes, a button nose, a sulky expression and carefully-lacquered hair.

'Yeah?' she asked rudely. 'What you want?'

Cutty reckoned she was maybe eighteen, nineteen.

'I come to see Buju,' he said.

'He's out,' she said. She tilted her head back and looked down her nose at him, giving him attitude. She was wearing white ski-pants and pink trainers, and a baggy white jumper that slipped off one shoulder to show a silky pink bra-strap.

'But him tell you me coming, nuh, sistah?' Cutty said coolly.

'I ain't your sistah, man,' the girl said, pretending offence.

'But him tell you me coming,' Cutty repeated. A damp wind was blasting down the walkway that cut straight through the flimsy material of his tracksuit. He was feeling hungry again, and desperate and dangerous. He was bursting to go for a piss. His right hand started to tremble and his chilled fingers flexed convulsively.

'He did say something about it, yeah,' the girl conceded, her stance continuing to block his entrance to the flat, oblivious to the anger that was building in him, or wanting to provoke it further for some reason of her own.

'So what him say, then?' Cutty asked, trying to be patient, trying to keep aggression out of his voice. He fought a sudden impulse to strike her.

She shrugged.

'What him say, gal?' Cutty repeated, and this time his anger with her trifling was obvious.

She didn't reply, just rolled her eyes and reflexively hoisted the jumper back up over her bare shoulder. It slipped straight off again and he could see her mocha skin goose-bump in the cold air.

'Ya name Cynthia, right?' He tried to sweeten his voice a little.

She nodded suspiciously.

'Well, Cynthia, I is a friend of Buju, him invite me here, you and me is both freezing pon disya doorstep, so let me enter.' He forced a smile onto his face that he knew couldn't have looked pleasant.

Grudgingly she stepped back and let him in.

'You ain't got no bags,' she said as she closed the door behind him.

He ignored her remark and, seeing the bathroom, went in to go for a piss. He left the door half-open.

'So when Buju get back?' he called over one shoulder as he emptied his aching bladder noisily into the porcelain bowl.

'He didn't say,' Cynthia replied sullenly.

'Well den, fix I some tea, nuh, sistah.'

She didn't reply to that, but by the time he came out of the bathroom after washing his hands and face she had put the kettle on. The flat was pleasantly warm, and he began to feel less ill and drained, and more alive. He unzipped his tracksuit-top and slid it off in front of her, and her eyes were immediately drawn to his muscular arms and his leanly-muscled torso, which was, he knew, enhanced by the shimmer of the mesh vest he was wearing underneath the tracksuit-top.

Once he was sure of her desire the dynamic between them shifted. She realised it and at once became flirtatious, aiming to arouse a similar desire in him to compensate for her loss of power. He ran his eyes over her body briefly to show that he acknowledged what she was trying to do, then cut the contact by going over to the window and looking out at the view. Rows of low- and high-rise tower-blocks marched away in all directions. Rain began to lash the dirty glass.

'So you and Buju known each other long, then?' Cynthia asked.

'Couplea years.' He didn't turn to look at her. 'You?'

'We been going out for like eighteen months.'

'Pickney?'

She didn't answer. When he looked round he saw she was looking down and chewing her lip.

'Not yet,' she said. Then she turned and left the room.

Buju returned to the flat in the middle of the afternoon. Cutty struggled up from the sofa and they shook hands and hugged each other. Buju smelt sweetly of cocoa-butter, cologne and dope, and Cutty was reminded that he himself was unpleasantly sweaty and stale.

'Good to see you, man,' Buju said, smiling broadly, seeming not to notice.

Buju was short, looked younger than his twenty-one years, and had a cheeky, boyish manner that didn't conceal the streetwise toughness beneath it. He wore faun Timberlands, baggy jeans so low on his hips they were practically under his large, muscular arse, which was itself covered by snugly-fitting, snow-white Calvins, and a red-and-white leather biker's jacket. A tall red-and-white leather baseball cap was screwed onto the back of his shaved head at a jaunty angle. He was dark-skinned and very smooth, to the point of having almost no eyebrows, and his eyes were a hazy golden-brown. He wore a diamond in one ear, and gold on his fingers and wrists.

He pecked Cynthia hello on the lips.

'You been making my spar welcome?' he asked her.

'Course,' she replied flirtatiously.

'Good gal.' Buju turned to Cutty, grinning broadly again and putting an arm around her waist proprietorially. 'She's a good gal, my Cynthia.'

'I gotta go out though,' she said, pulling away from him.

'Where you gotta go?' Buju's grin froze in barely-concealed irritation.

'Just across to my mum's.'

'What, now?' His arm tightened around her waist.

'I been stuck here all day, ain't I?' she whined defensively. 'Waiting for your mate.'

'Okay,' he said coldly, letting go of her. She hesitated. 'Well, go then,' he said, an edge to his voice.

She bit her lip, then left the room. She was, Cutty could see, afraid of Buju.

'You got shi under manners,' he said, once Cynthia had left the flat.

'I keep all my women under manners, bruv!' Buju laughed, echoing the Jamaicanism. His own accent, like Cynthia's, was pure black Cockney. He went into the kitchen. 'You want a beer?' he called back.

'Sure.'

Buju returned with two cans of Red Stripe. He and Cutty cracked them, then sat on the sofa. It was white leather, and large, and dominated the room. Buju rolled a joint, sparked up, toked, then passed it to Cutty.

'So a wha gwaan?' he asked, as Cutty dragged deeply.

'Nothing much, man,' Cutty said, letting blue smoke trickle out of his nostrils like a Chinese dragon. 'Just a lickle business worries.'

'The studio ain't thriving?'

'Well, we had a fire, you know,' Cutty said carefully.

'You insured though?'

'Yeah, but dere is – complications.'

'What, like masters getting burnt up?'

'Dat, and other shit.' Cutty didn't elaborate, just toked again. 'What about you, man? Still running tings?'

'Course, man. Little bit of this, little bit of that.'

Buju pushed off his jacket. Underneath it he was

wearing a cut-off white tank-top that showed off his smoothly-muscled shoulders. On one shoulder a large 'B' was double-tattooed in gothic lettering. Cutty pointed to it, his fingertip brushing the raised outline.

'Looking good, man,' he said.

Buju seemed pleased that Cutty had noticed the tattoo, and twisted round so Cutty could see that there was a sun outlined on his other shoulder.

'You wanna see the rest, man?'

Before Cutty could answer, Buju pulled the tank-top up past his nipples to show off a leanly-muscled torso. Cutty could feel his dick start to stir in his pants as he admired a second sun around Buju's flat navel, and an automatic pistol angled up across one pectoral. Buju's nipples were large, dark and protruberant. Cutty found himself imagining tasting them, teasing them. Buju pulled his tank-top back down.

'You got any?'

'This.' Cutty showed an elaborate 'i' on one shoulder. The dot of the 'i' was an eye. 'Is di logo a mi record label, Informer Sounds,' he said. 'And this,' he went on, pulling up his mesh vest and pushing the track pants down to show his hip. A revolver was tattooed there, the line of the barrel following the angle of his pelvic bone and pointing down towards his crotch. On his right pectoral he had a scroll with the word 'raggamuffin' written in it in curlicue. He had some gothic text on his shoulderblades as well, but it seemed like too much effort to show that to Buju just then, so he left it.

'Cool,' Buju said, as Cutty pulled his vest back down. 'Cynthia don't check for tattoos,' he remarked.

'So why you have dem?'

'For myself,' Buju said. 'You can't do shit like get a tattoo or not get a tattoo cos of a woman says this or that, you know what I'm saying?'

Cutty nodded.

'You mind if I use your shower, man?' he asked, taking another drag on the joint.

'Go 'head,' Buju replied. 'There's towels in the airing cupboard.'

As Cutty showered he began to feel some sort of clarity returning to his mind. The beer and the dope had taken the edge off his fear, stopping panic from overwhelming him, and now the pressure of the hot water on his skin was re-energising him.

Money, he thought. Getting money had to be his first priority. Everything else followed from that.

He stepped out of the shower, dried himself with a large white towel, applied moisturiser and anti-perspirant that he found in the bathroom cabinet, put his jewellery back on, and was then forced to dress in the same dirty clothing he'd been wearing for nearly three days now. But still he felt better.

Money.

Few people in the West know what it's like to really have no money and no resources, to be in all but name a refugee. Few people here experience the desperation that that gives rise to. Fear rose in him again. How long could he sleep on Buju's sofa for? Not long. Cynthia would work on Buju to kick him out at the earliest opportunity: cah women don't like their man to have friends, he thought. Especially women who cyaan get pregnant. He went back into the living-room. An urban music video was playing on the flatscreen TV, on MTV Base.

'So she live wit' you?' he asked Buju as he sat back down next to him.

'Cynthia?' Buju answered. 'Nah. She lives with her mum.' He fired up another joint. 'She just hangs out here. I don't encourage it, though,' he went on. 'I mean, it ain't like I ain't got other gals, is it? And she knows it.'

'Babymothers?'

'Two. That I know of. Plus whoever. A man needs his space, you know what I'm saying? His privacy.'

'And here I am, man,' Cutty said apologetically. 'Cluttering up ya couch.'

'Don't sweat it, man,' Buju shrugged. 'You're welcome to crash in my drum as long as you need. You mi brudda.'

Cutty sensed a loneliness in Buju then, something he could use without using Buju himself, perhaps.

'So tell me the runnings, den,' he said, changing the subject before anything near sentiment could surface between them. His attraction to Buju was strengthening, his dick was once again tingling and lengthening.

'What runnings, blood?' Buju asked.

'To tell you the truth, blood,' Cutty said, 'Me no have no money to speak of and I must raise some any way I can.'

'And you don't mean minimum wage down KFC.'

'No.'

'How much you need?'

'Enough to get me set up and put a roof over mi head.'

Buju looked thoughtful. 'I might be able to arrange a little something something,' he said.

Cutty knew Buju dealt drugs, but had no idea of the scale of his operation, or how well-connected he really was. So many brothers talked themselves up, making themselves out to be gangstas or yardies when in reality they were just small fry who didn't know when to keep their mouths shut. Buju didn't talk himself up, which was an encouraging sign.

'I can front you pills,' Buju said. 'E and whatever. You can sell in clubs, blues and dances. Some street-selling on top. Whatever you get for 'em I get cost plus fifty percent of the profit. Deal?'

'Deal.' They shook on it.

'Safe,' Buju said. 'I can hook you up with some merchandise in a couple of days, yeah.'

'Cool.'

'Now, you wanna eat?'

Cutty nodded and, pulling their hoods up against
the cold night air, they left the flat and headed down to
a Caribbean takeaway on the nearby Goldhawk Road.
There Buju bought them a supper of curried goat,
oxtail, and rice and peas.

Cutty was no stranger to dealing: many of his initial
contacts in the music industry back in Jamaica he had
made through being able to provide the musicians and
their friends with a little smoke or a little snort. The
cash he had built up in that way became the seed
money with which he had started his recording studio,
Informer Sounds. Once it was up and running he had
quit dealing. It's not easy to walk away from the drug
business and it wasn't easy for him, but he had done it.

He'd been intensely relieved to get out of that violent, dangerous, unstable world. In his time he had
seen other dealers shot dead, by rivals or by the police,
or ratted out by paid informers and jailed for lengthy
terms, and he had twice been shot at himself. He had
seen men get framed and have to pay heavy bribes to
the police to avoid imprisonment. And he had seen his
own older brother dead in his coffin, shot in the chest
and the head on a street corner, a casualty of a turf war.

The name Informer Sounds he had conceived as a
joke, a play on words: taking the last thing you would
ever want to claim about yourself – being known as an
informer was a death-sentence in the world he had left
behind – and twisting it round and making it bold:
'Informing You Of The Sounds On The Streets' was the

fledgling company's slogan and its mission statement.

Being an informer: the last thing you would ever claim about yourself bar one, that is.

And now here he was, back where he'd been three years ago: on the streets, having to hustle just to put food on the table. To make it all worse, then he had a dream: now he had nothing. The dream was behind him, dead and burned. And the future was a blank, a grave, a trap-door.

But if I have a new studio I will call it Refugee Records, he thought. He slipped an oxtail bone from which he had sucked the marrow out of his mouth and set it down on the smoked glass coffee-table. But what artists would he record?

'You ever been to Jamaica?' he asked Buju.

'Only once,' Buju said. 'Back when I was a kid. To meet my granny. My mum's mum. I don't remember much about it except we had to like ford a stream to get there cos there weren't no bridge, and she had goats in the yard.'

He passed Cutty a dish for his oxtail bones.

Cynthia came by after they'd eaten.

'Didn't you save none for me?' she complained, seeing the empty takeaway containers and the platter of oxtail bones.

'Didn't say you was coming back, did you?' Buju replied carelessly.

Now Cutty knew that Cynthia didn't really live with Buju he could afford to be more relaxed around her: it wasn't her yard, and it wasn't up to her who stayed there or didn't stay there. And Buju had accepted him and was going to put some business his way. He was inside in a way Cynthia would never be inside, strengthened by that bond between men that is formed in part in opposition to women.

The three of them shared a spliff, then Cynthia announced that she was going to bed. To her evident annoyance Buju didn't follow her at once. Instead he and Cutty sat up for a while watching an old Jet Li movie on satellite while she clattered about in the bathroom. After the movie had ended Buju got a spare duvet, undersheet and pillows from the airing-cupboard in the hall.

'You must be crazy jet-lagged, man,' he said as he handed the bundle of bedding to Cutty.

Cutty nodded bleary-eyed as he took the bundle, and yawned like a lion. Buju went and used the toilet, then disappeared into the bedroom. The door clicked shut behind him and suddenly, almost surreally, for the first time in nearly three days, excepting being in a bathroom, Cutty was on his own. He felt a curious spasm of anxiety, then a strong sense of relief. He went and used the toilet, washed his face and brushed his teeth with the toothbrush he'd kept from his complimentary airline travel bag. Then he checked out his grooming in the mirror over the sink, patting his cane-rows carefully. They were still reasonably sharp and neat, and the cuts and bruises on his scalp had receded to near-invisibility. He went back to the lounge and undressed to his underwear, spread out the undersheet on the couch, lay back and put out the light.

Just as he was pulling the duvet up over his shoulder Cutty heard Buju mutter something through the wall and Cynthia giggle. He lay there listening intently, but no sounds of sex followed. He was almost disappointed.

He closed his eyes and tried to think about nothing except how exhausted he was. His head began to ache. The leather sofa squeaked every time he shifted on it even though there was a sheet between his body and its surface. The perpetually-lit lights on the walkway outside filtered prison-like through the partially-closed blinds, preventing the room from being truly dark.

London is never country dark.

Although he was certain he would never manage to sleep, at some point before dawn he sunk into a heavy grey oblivion.

He awoke with a jolt, his heart racing, sweaty, afraid, with no idea of where he was or what time it was, half starting up from the couch with a choking yell.

Buju was standing there in the gloom, watching him. Like a pornographic fantasy Buju was wearing nothing but a pair of black Calvins cut so high on the hip there was only the waistband. His compact physique was well-proportioned. His skin was dark and flawless. His shaved head glinted. Cutty felt an almost overwhelming desire to grip the full globes of Buju's buttocks in both hands and bury his face in Buju's bulging crotch. Why would sucking another man's cock help him right now? But it would. Hot pumping blood, the seed, the life. The thought of it made Cutty's dry mouth water.

'You was moaning and crying out and shit,' Buju said, by way of explaining why he was there.

'Yeah?' Cutty said guardedly. 'I was? What me say?'

'Not actual words or nothing,' Buju said. 'Just sounds.'

'I wake you?' Cutty asked.

Buju shook his head. 'I couldn't sleep anyway, man.'

'Sometimes it don't help to sleep,' Cutty said, rubbing his tired eyes. He sat up on the sofa, crumpling the duvet around himself to conceal his jutting erection, and gestured to Buju to join him.

Buju did so, sitting excitingly close. His need strong in him, Cutty groped for the next move. Cynthia evidently hadn't given Buju sex. Cutty knew that if a man was horny enough it was surprising how receptive he could be to a freely-offered mouth, whatever the sex of that mouth, if it was done without words, without the assertion of a sexual identity. It was surprising too how often such a man would then, wordlessly, reciprocate.

But Cynthia appeared in the doorway then, in a baggy tee-shirt, her face crumpled with tiredness and vexation.

'What's going on?' she asked, squinting blearily in the low light.

'Nothing, gal,' Buju said. 'My man here ain't sleeping so good, that's all. Go back to bed.'

'Come with me, Buju,' she wheedled, holding out her arms and pouting.

Letting out something that was almost a sigh, Buju got up off the couch and crossed over to her, and let her put her arms around him. Cutty felt his warmth retreat as if it was a solid thing.

'I'll see you in the morning, man,' Buju said. 'Try and get some sleep, yeah.'

Cutty nodded.

As Cynthia was leading him back to the bedroom Buju glanced over his shoulder at Cutty and the two men's eyes met intently for a moment. Cutty tried to read what Buju's look was telling him, if anything, but could not. Then Buju and Cynthia were gone. Cutty lay back down again, pulled the duvet to his shoulder, turned over and tried to sleep.

Chapter Three

Over the next few days Buju introduced Cutty to his click, a mix of black, mixed-race and white youth he ran with on the estate. At twenty-one Buju was the oldest of them and, to the extent that there was a chief, he was their chief. Despite his lack of money Cutty's greater age – he was twenty-five – and his wider experience combined with his obviously tough manner to give him an instant kudos with the click that offset his dependence on Buju's friendship for the roof over his head.

Maxie, a freckle-faced, mixed-race youth with short dreadlocks, was keen to show Cutty the ropes when it came to pushing. He reeled off a list of clubs that Cutty had never heard of, weighing up the pros and cons of dealing drugs in each: bouncers he knew who liked him; managers he was in with; bouncers he'd fallen out with; clubs with CCTV all over the place; what places were up for a police raid in the next couple of months; what places were off-limits because they were run by other crews.

'And then there's gay clubs,' Maxie continued, hitting the 'g' of gay aggressively hard. 'They're good.'

'Queers love pills,' agreed Gary, a thin white boy with sharp features. He wore a Burberry baseball cap and had lines shaved vertically through one eyebrow, a gold cuff in one ear, and sported a heavy gold chain outside his tracksuit-top.

'Me na check for no batty business,' Cutty said flatly.

'Course you don't, man,' said Maxie, laughing. 'Just check for them pink pounds, you know what I'm saying? You don't have to like someone to do business with 'em.'

'In fact probably better not to like 'em,' Buju said. 'Cos that way you don't sentimentalise, yeah.'

'But if you're gonna go psycho in that situation then don't do it,' chipped in Spin, a slim black youth with large teeth, cane-rows and long eyelashes. 'If you can't handle being around them people then don't go there, you know what I'm saying?'

'I can handle it,' Cutty said. 'Just, is different back home, you know.'

"Bun dem',' Maxie quoted, laughing again. "Batty-man fi dead!"

'Righteousness, man!' Spin laughed too. He and Maxie high-fived.

'But we ain't gonna start you in no gay club,' Buju interrupted. 'First things first, yeah? We get you set up with some gear. I'll pass you some contacts. Maybe we can go down blues Westbourne Park way and do some business over there. Let 'em know you're my peeps and shit, yeah? See how it runs, get so you feel the vibe, then work up to the clubs.'

Cutty nodded and they touched fists, sealing the deal.

That afternoon Cutty went down to Shepherd's Bush market and spent most of his remaining cash on socks, underwear, a pack of mesh vests and a knock-off Adidas tracksuit. Buju had lent him a thick silver puffa jacket with a funfur-lined hood. It was slightly too big on Buju and slightly too small on Cutty. But it was a relief to Cutty to finally feel warm enough as he tramped the chilly city streets.

On his way back from the market Cutty passed by a newsagent that he noticed carried the weekly edition of the Jamaican paper *The Gleaner*. He went inside and flicked through a copy under the unfriendly eye of the

Asian shopkeeper, his chest tightening as he turned the pages.

The story he was looking for was on page two, under the headline, *Studio Burns, Body Found, Proprietor Sought.* He paid for the paper and, hoping that no one would be there, and thanking God that Buju trusted him enough to lend him his spare key, hurried back to Buju's flat to study it in privacy.

No one was in. Cutty smoked a spliff to steady his nerves, then spread the paper out on the coffee table and read the article properly:

"Studio Burns, Body Found, Proprietor Sought

On the evening of Thursday, 10th February, the Informer Sounds recording studio, located in the Tivoli Gardens district of West Kingston, was burnt to the ground. Inside the remains of the building firefighters discovered the body of an as-yet unidentified young man. Despite the charred condition of the body the coroner stated that there was clear evidence the victim had been hacked to death, probably with a machete, as well as being shot numerous times. It was the opinion of the coroner that the majority of the gunshot wounds were inflicted post-mortem. Police are treating the fire as arson, either in an attempt to conceal the crime by burning the body, or to claim insurance on the business, and are seeking the proprietor of Informer Sounds, Cuthbert Munroe, whose whereabouts are currently unknown, for questioning in connection with the fire and the killing. Dental records have established that the deceased is not Cuthbert Munroe."

Cutty kissed his teeth. The phrase 'hacked to death' beat on his eyes like a physical thing, and his gut clenched so hard it was as if he had been punched.

Sonny. Hacked to death.

And now he, Cutty, was being all but straight-up accused of murdering Sonny, of hacking him up, butchering him and pumping bullets into his body, then torching his own studio in an attempt to cover his trail of murder. And/or get the insurance money, even though the two motives hardly fitted together in a way that made sense.

Tank God mi leave di country, he thought, pushing what was too unbearable to face down in his mind and focussing instead on himself, on his own needs. On survival. *Tank God me a leave.* But then he realised that his leaving only made him appear to be more of a suspect in the eyes of the law. *Becah why would a innocent man flee?* He wondered about extradition treaties. Could they drag him back to Jamaica to stand trial for murdering Sonny? He didn't know the law in the UK. Would they try? The police who had been there that night knew what had really happened. They knew he was neither the killer nor the arsonist. Would they bother to go that far to pursue a charge against a man when they knew that charge to be false? Would they really go to the courts to seek an extradition order against him?

Not a man, though: a battyman.

A battyman. And that would make a difference, oh yes.

And if they could get an extradition order, and if they succeeded in dragging him back home in chains, as it would have to be, for he wouldn't allow himself to be returned there any other way, what then? What would he have to admit to in order to exonerate himself from the charges they were laying against him? *Could* he exonerate himself, whatever he said?

The only corroborating witnesses for his version of events would be the police, and they had colluded in the crime, so they would lie. The perpetrators, those he could point out, those he could name, would alibi each other and deny everything. Or worse, maybe they would *admit* everything, and still he would face prison, ruin, disgrace, and possibly even death, because in the eyes of the law he would be to blame for what he had brought down upon his own head and upon Sonny's head. After all, he and Sonny had been committing a blasphemous criminal act, a blasphemous criminal act so disgusting, so outrageous, so much against God that it had roused the righteous wrath of his neighbours and compelled them to act in the name of Christian piety.

Boom Bye-bye.

He felt as if the room was pressing in on him, and his heart began to race erratically.

If any of Buju's click saw the paper, which wasn't that likely, they probably wouldn't connect the name Cuthbert Munroe with Buju's spar Cutty even though some of them knew that he worked in the music industry back home. But it was inevitable that someone somewhere would pick up on the story and tell Dennis, who liked to brag about his cousin being a music mogul in the making who ran his own studio. Dennis even had a large framed Informer Sounds poster hanging prominently in his front room. And of course it was through Dennis that Cutty had met Buju, so Buju would eventually find out about the killing and the fire that way. And what then?

Worse still, Cutty realised that his parents would inevitably hear about the fire and the murder too, if they hadn't already. He couldn't even begin to think what to say to them about it. At least they wouldn't think he was the burned, mutilated body that had been found in the blackened shell of his studio. And better for now that them think him a murderer on the run than what he was, a dirty, outcast battyman.

He imagined running, running until his legs gave out and he was in the middle of some great nowhere overlooked by nothing, and finding an oasis there.

An ugly thought occurred to him: Perhaps his

brother Robert, who lived and worked in Kingston, had heard the true version of what had happened. Robert was a policeman, and surely the sordid truth would already have been passed around the station and beyond:

Batty business.

Oh, woe is me, shame and scandal in the family.

Robert was Cutty's younger brother. He had joined the Kingston police-force shortly after their brother Joseph, oldest of the three, had been shot dead in a street-corner dispute. That was four years ago. Joseph's death had left Robert bitter and cynical, and with a desire for revenge far stronger than any impulse he might have felt to uphold justice. Even among his colleagues, men who were not afraid to break heads, Robert had a reputation for thuggishness.

Robert and Cutty had never got on. From their earliest years they had fought like cat and dog. Cutty still had a scar below his right eye where Robert had jabbed him in the face with a sharpened stick at the age of nine. And Robert still had a slight limp from the time when, aged fifteen, Cutty had dislocated his kneecap with a baseball bat. Now Cutty dreaded to think what Robert would tell their parents about what had happened. Assuming he knew the truth, would Robert allow them to think Cutty was a murderer, or would he get a more perverse pleasure from revealing that his popular and successful older brother was in fact a battyman? A cocksucker who took dick up his arse.

The thought came to Cutty then that if he was dead it would make things easier for everyone.

Quite calmly he got up and went through to the bathroom and ran a bath. Then he went to the kitchen and took a small, extremely sharp knife from the cutlery drawer and returned to the bathroom. All his movements were graceful, ritualistic. Steam covered the mirrors, hiding his reflection from him. That was good: he didn't want to see his face. He undressed but kept his underwear on, for some reason of old-fashioned propriety not wanting to be found naked even in death, then he stepped into the warm, reassuring water. It was like returning to the womb.

But before he could even sit there was a rattle and bang at the front door, and he heard Buju and the click roll in off the walkway, talking boisterously. Realising he hadn't locked the bathroom door, he stepped quickly out of the bath and slid the catch across. Just in time, as at once there was a thump as someone tried to push it open.

'Zat you in there, Cynthia?' a voice called. It was Buju's.

'Is Cutty.'

'Well, hurry it up, man. I'm busting for a piss out here, yeah.'

'Just give me a minute, man,' Cutty called back.

He placed the knife above Buju's sight-line on top of the bathroom cabinet, stepped out of his Calvins and dunked quickly in the tub to alibi what he'd been doing in there. Then he pulled out the plug and quickly towelled himself down. All the time he was thinking about the copy of *The Gleaner* he had left lying open on the coffee-table in the lounge. *Too late now. What's done is done.* He rinsed out the bath, tied the towel round his waist and exited the bathroom, his clothing bundled under one arm, giving Buju and the others a salutation of acknowledgement as he crossed through to Buju's bedroom, where he could dress in privacy. Once there he tried to push his rising anxiety levels down to a manageable level and, after a few deep breaths, succeeded. He moisturised and dressed in his cheap, clean new clothes.

No forget to get di knife and put it back in the

kitchen drawer later, he reminded himself matter-of-
factly as he sat on the edge of Buju's bed and tugged on
a pair of knock-off Nikes. He got to his feet and looked
at his face in the mirror. Beyond the marks of the
hardness of his life it gave nothing away of the thoughts
of self-murder that had just five minutes ago filled his
mind.

Once he had dressed he went and leant in the living-room doorway and watched as Maxie, who was
sitting on the couch with his thighs spread wide, bent
forward and studied the open *Gleaner*. Spin sprawled
in the armchair, fiddling with his iPod. Buju had gone
into the kitchen.

'Zat you, man?' Maxie asked casually, noticing Cutty and holding up the paper to show him the article, as
if to be a murder suspect was nothing.

'Is me,' Cutty replied.

There was a sudden awkwardness then. The immediate question on Maxie's lips was obviously, So did
you do it, man? But Maxie couldn't ask it like that, not
so raw. And young as he was, he knew enough to know
that you don't ask a man a question that will compel
him to either lie to you, or tell you something it might
be dangerous to both of you for you to know.

'Did you know they was looking for you?' Maxie
asked. That was a safer question.

'Not till I see *The Gleaner* today,' Cutty replied. And
it was true: until he had read the article it hadn't
occurred to him that he could be seen as anything other
than a victim, if he was seen at all. His fear had been
that the press would too-nakedly report exactly *why* he
had been a victim, and so put him in extreme physical
danger, and that fear had been real and extreme
enough to drive him out of the country.

Now he felt a different fear, and yet he realised that
if he was shrewd he could twist the situation in a way

that would be useful to him: for a man who is very likely a murderer is a man to respect on the streets. A man not to mess with.

A man to fear.

Chapter Four

So Cutty watched, and listened, and learned the ropes. It came easily to him. Drug business is the same everywhere, and he had plenty of experience from back home to draw on. He had the superficially easygoing but fundamentally hard-faced attitude you need to make sure you get paid, and the requisite steadiness of nerve. And he had a good contact in Buju, someone who looked out for him, who he knew would be in his corner if Babylon came knocking. Buju and the click filled him in on the nuances of UK law and current law enforcement policy as it related to drug offences, and within a month he was turning over a tidy amount of money from dealing at blues and house parties, and selling to friends and friends of friends.

He dealt principally in dope and pills – ecstasy, speed and ketamine – and mostly avoided the harder drugs: heroin, crack, crystal meth, cocaine. Those he associated with pure destructiveness in the community, and also, and more importantly, with his brother's death.

Cutty's brother Joseph had dealt exclusively in hard drugs and had become a user along the way, injecting his profits into his arm like a tragic cliché. As if he'd never been smart at school, as if he'd never seen some sort of legitimate future ahead of him that was worthwhile. It was a lethal failure of imagination on Joseph's part, but more lethally still he was injecting the profits of the men who employed him into his rapidly-collapsing veins. Their particular brand of product had no room for such a loss-leader, and Cutty believed with a cold certainty as good as proof that Joseph's street-

corner execution had been set up by his own employ-
ers, who had wanted rid of him at no cost or risk to
themselves.

Cutty was always scrupulous in paying Buju his
percentage. Cah business is business, seen, even if it is
criminal business, and a business partnership is a
business partnership.

Cutty needed Buju and he liked Buju, and he had been
deeply afraid that Buju would see him differently after
the revelations in *The Gleaner*. He worried that Buju
would see him as a threat and a liability, a magnet for
unwanted attention from the authorities, and personally dangerous to know.

Once the click had finally chipped that evening and
the two of them were on their own in the flat together
Buju did eventually ask Cutty, 'Well, so did you do it,
man?'

And Cutty had said, 'No,' and nothing more.

At the time Buju had seemed to genuinely accept
his denial, but Cutty hadn't been able to tell for sure. If
Buju had wanted to ask Cutty any further questions
about what had happened he hadn't been able to
because Cynthia had come round then and stayed over.

The next morning it was as if nothing had happened.

Two days after that Cutty rang his parents. By then he
had blagged a mobile phone off a friend of Spin's, but
he didn't want to use it to call them. He had acquired a
paranoid fear that the signal would get picked up by the
authorities somehow and used to track him if they
could associate that number with his name. So instead
he went to an international call shop down on Goldhawk Road that offered cheap call rates to the Caribbean. He entered one of the cramped glass booths, took

a seat, entered the code for Jamaica, tapped in one of the very few numbers he knew off by heart with stiff, numb fingers, and waited. After seven rings his mother answered.

'Mummy? Is Cuthbert.'

'Cuthbert?' the voice at the other end of the line exclaimed. 'Oh my Lord, is you!' She sounded breathless. She was a large woman, and he worried for her heart. 'Are you alright, son?' He could hear the tearfulness rising up in her voice, thickening it rapidly.

'I is alright, you know, yes,' he said, trying to sound easy, trying to bring the level of emotion down. Guilt stabbed through him both for the pain he had already inflicted on her by not calling her sooner, and for the pain that was coming that he would be unable to spare her.

'Oh, thank goodness!' she said, her voice throbbing with relief. 'Praise Jesus, thank goodness! Is where you calling from? Kingston?'

'England. Is London me reach.'

'London?'

'Yes.'

'And you is alright?' she asked again.

'Yes.'

There was a pause.

'I didn't know what to tell the neighbours, you know,' she said in a suddenly cooler tone.

'Is what you hear, den?' he asked, his heart sinking even though it was what he had expected, even though it was the whole point of making the call.

'What your brother tell us. Robert had the consideration to let us know before we haffi see it in the newspaper along with the whole rest of the parish. But why we have to hear that way? Why you don't tell us, Cuthbert? Why we have to find out so?'

'What did Robert tell you, Mummy?' Cutty interrupted, his whole body tense as he hunched over the phone, sweat starting in his armpits.

'Just what they was going to put in The Gleaner,' his mother said. 'That was all he knew. Cuthbert, who was that young man who die?'

'Him name Sonny,' Cutty said. 'He was a technician at mi studio, he work for me. Mummy, me na do nuttin' wrong, you know.'

'If that is so, shouldn't you come back here and sort things out and clear your name?'

If that is so.

'Me want to, but - '

'But what?' his mother asked sharply.

'Is complicated.'

'Robert could help you.'

'You know we don't get on, Mummy. We never have. He won't do nuttin' for me.'

'You are still brothers, Cuthbert.'

'No.'

He could hear his mother sucking her teeth in exasperation. 'Well,' she said grudgingly, 'if it is money for a lawyer you need, your father and I have a little put by that you can use.'

Tears started at the corners of Cutty's eyes at that. He knew his parents weren't well off. They were getting on in years and they would need that money for themselves. A slew of conflicting thoughts and feelings poured over him so rapidly that for a long moment he couldn't manage to even stammer out a reply.

Bless you bless you my mother, I am not worthy, Robert no tell you but I is a battyman. You still love me now you know dat? Me no kill Sonny but is cos a me him dead. Robert no tell you di truth cah him no want di association, di shame from di blood we share. His hatred is my shield but me no want a shield not from mi mother an' father, but me cyaan tell you alla dis, not now –

He took a deep breath. 'I is alright for money, Mummy,' he said, struggling to keep his voice level. 'Me earning a lickle here doing dis an' dat. Don't worry 'bout I.'

'If you need anything at all,' his mother said, 'you know you can ask us. Your father and I will help you and pray for you.'

'Tank you,' Cutty said. He glanced at his watch. There didn't seem to be anything else that needed saying right now, so he said, 'Mummy, I haffi go now.'

He hung up the phone and went and paid for the call. In other booths people of many different nationalities were calling home, and home was anywhere from Australia to Barbados to Bangladesh to Somalia to South Africa. As he stepped out onto the street he realised that he had forgotten to ask his mother how his father was. He almost turned back, but didn't.

The particularity of his guilt was worse than he had expected. He knew that his mother and father felt they had failed Joseph. However much they had denied it while he was alive, he knew they blamed themselves for his elder brother's slide into crime and addiction. And now here was he, Cutty, their supposedly successful second son, trading off their guilt and sense of failure. He knew his parents would refuse him nothing so long as they believed that their actions might save him from shame and disgrace and jail.

What made it worse was that he was the one they had been most proud of, the one who had tumbled into the mire and clawed his way up out of it to become a legitimate businessman. And although his success was in the raucous, bawdy, unGodly world of dancehall, they were prouder of him than they had ever been of their apparently more respectable third son Robert. Both of them had disapproved of Robert joining the police following Joseph's death because they had seen what Cutty had seen: that he was doing so not, as he claimed, out of a need for justice, but in a search for base, elemental revenge.

But they were traditional church-going people, his parents, a carpenter and a primary-school teacher who had been each others' childhood sweethearts, and if they resisted the lure of 'an eye for an eye' in the case of their oldest son's death, they were still largely Old Testament in their morality. They found it easier to believe in a wrathful God than a forgiving one. And throughout Cutty's childhood they had nodded tight-lipped in approval as the preacher at the church they had attended twice-weekly or more every week of their lives held forth from the pulpit on the sins of Sodom and the plague of AIDS, on the inviolability of the laws of Leviticus, and on the judgements and condemnations of Saint Paul.

Battyman, chichi man, anti-man sodomite bestialist blasphemer...

God seemed very far away that day.

As soon as he had a decent wedge in his pocket Cutty began looking for his own place to live. He enjoyed sharing Buju's drum but it wasn't practical as he didn't have his own bedroom. Members of the click would roll up at any hour of the day or night and end up staying till four in the morning or later, lolling idly on the sofa that was his bed, chewing the fat and smoking dope, playing videogames and watching movies, and he would have to rely on Buju noticing him getting increasingly vexed and sending them on their way.

Even then, more often than not one or other of them would end up staying over, nodding off in the armchair or sleeping under a duvet on the floor, corroding Cutty's limited privacy still further. Feeling claustrophobic and frustrated he would lie there listening to their dope-heavy breathing, his dick jutting painfully, his mind bursting with thoughts of sex, and feel like he was going insane.

To add to the tension he was becoming increasingly attracted to Buju, but like some tedious chaperone Cynthia was always there to prevent them being on their own together. She was forever hanging around Buju's gates, acting needy, repeatedly throwing her arms around Buju's neck to get his attention then pouting when she didn't get it. Cutty quickly grew bored of her continual presence, her alternate flirting and sulking, and he found it irritating that Buju seemed to find her a nuisance too but intermittently played up to her. He was also annoyed with himself for falling into competition with a woman for a man's attention.

If he had a yard of his own then he could have Buju round without Cynthia. If she wasn't there then things could flow more naturally between Buju and himself. It didn't mean that anything would happen – most likely it wouldn't as, as far as he could tell, Buju was a pure punani-hound – but at least there wouldn't be a girl there to inhibit that masculine flow.

It was Spin who put Cutty on to a place, a dodgy sublet on the fifth floor of the eastmost of one of a number of high-rise tower-blocks across the estate from Buju's block. It was grimy, with one bare bedroom, a filthy kitchen, a stained toilet, and damaged grey plastic flooring throughout, but it was cheap and below the radar of officialdom, so Cutty took it. The click helped him do it up, painting everything bright satin white, and he paid Maxie and Spin to lay cheap new laminate flooring throughout, which they did with unexpected speed and competence. Buju turned up in a van with a new cooker and fridge he'd got from somewhere in the back. Both lifts in the block were out of service, so he and Cutty had to lump the white goods up five flights of stairs, which they managed to do with grunting good humour. Gary provided a mattress still wrapped in its plastic, a small widescreen TV and a fern with slightly yellowing leaves.

Cutty was touched to receive so much help, all but unasked for, from the click in setting up his new home. Despite being only a few years older than Spin, Maxie, Gary and Buju, he had become a sort of father figure to them, or at least an older brother, and they were all keen to earn his approval by being, if for only a day or two, good sons.

None of them, he discovered, had fathers of their own.

'The cunt who knocked up my mum,' was how Spin described his, his tone matter-of-fact, as he drew a Stanley-knife across a strip of ash-blond laminate. But Cutty noted that he kept his cane-rowed head lowered, and his long lashes concealed eyes Cutty knew would be sparkling with hurt. He was seventeen, and still lived with his mother.

'He used to beat up on my mum,' Gary, the white boy of the click, said of his father. 'He walked out on us when I was four and I ain't seen him since. I wouldn't know him if I saw him, and I wouldn't piss on him if he was on fire.' And Gary shrugged as if it didn't matter much, then began rolling a wall with a rapidity and violence that sent a fine spray of paint flying, coating his flushing face.

Gary too was seventeen, and an inch shorter than Buju's five foot six. He stood very upright and reached as high as he could, but even with the extra height the roller gave him he couldn't quite reach the top of the wall, and Cutty could see fury building up in him.

'Chill, blood,' Spin said, noticing Gary's rage at the

same moment Cutty had. 'Mek I do the tops, yeah?
Trade you the tops for the skirting, yeah? I rather be
stretching than kneeling, you know what I'm saying?'

'Cos black man don't kneel?' Gary said, hovering for
a moment between anger and relief.

'Cos I ain't no good at glossing,' said Spin, taking
the roller from him. And Gary went off to get a tin of
gloss and a brush to paint the skirting-boards with.

Cutty asked Buju about his father.

'I seen him a couple of times since I was about ten,'
Buju said, shrugging carelessly. He had just got
through plumbing in Cutty's washing-machine. 'He
weren't nothing special though,' Buju went on. 'Just
some man who weren't there when my mum needed
him, you know? Just some next nobody man.'

Maxie's dad had been deported back to Nigeria
when he was very young, leaving him to be raised by
his white mother. He alone of the click allowed himself
a little romance about who and what his father had
been: 'He got so he was big in business,' Maxie said,
'and they couldn't stand to see a black man doing well
in this white world so they kicked him out the country
and never let him back in.'

The others nodded along to this, but Cutty could
see they did so more out of kindness than belief. And
Buju told him later that Maxie's mother hated Maxie
for having his father's eyes, his father's lips, and that
when she got drunk she would say she wished she'd
had the abortion. Or so Maxie said.

'Whenever I go round his yard she's nice, though,'
Buju said with a shrug, avoiding judgement.

Yet the four young men knew who they were and
where they were, and they knew what their lives were.
Despite having no fathers they weren't lost boys, not to
themselves: they weren't a lost generation from their
own point of view. It was their fathers who were lost,

these strange men who had impregnated their mothers and then vanished but were somewhere out there, and that somewhere wasn't some faraway place where lost fathers go, it was out on the same streets their sons walked in, and in the same houses and flats and shops and pubs and parks. They were around all the time, these invisible fathers. And they were hated.

The youths listened with undisguised interest when Cutty talked about his own father, about his parents and grandparents and their life back in Jamaica. Even Gary, the white boy, sat there attentively and let the joint go out between his pale, sovereign-ringed fingers, so caught up was he in Cutty's evocation of faraway family and home.

But even as Cutty spoke he could taste the irony in his mouth, taste what was suppressed in what he said like bile. Nothing he told the click was untrue, yet he knew he was a liar.

He continued to buy The Gleaner each week, needing to know for his own sake what fresh revelations were coming to light about Sonny's murder, and for his parents' sake how far the story was being kept in the public eye.

Sonny was identified the week after the story first broke:

"Body Named

The victim of the Informer Sounds fire has been named as Donald 'Sonny' Hilton, 22 years old, a recording engineer at the studio, which specialised in dancehall music. The youngest of five children, Sonny grew up in Negril, moving to Kingston in 2008 to train for work in the music industry as a technician. The owner of Informer Sounds, Cuthbert Munroe, is still being sought by police in connection with the fire, and with the death of Sonny Hilton."

Pushing down the terrible memories that threatened to well up and flood his mind, Cutty made some quick mental calculations: 1) The police didn't seem to know that he had left the country, and that suggested they weren't strongly motivated to find him. 2) The true reasons behind what happened that night hadn't become common knowledge, not so far, anyway. 3) The individual officers assigned to the case were almost certainly not strongly motivated to uncover the truth because they already knew exactly what had happened, having been involved in it. 4) They wouldn't want their involvement made public knowledge, however much battymen were despised, because it was still criminal business, and a death had resulted from it. Therefore, Cutty concluded, the truth would be unlikely to come out unless he himself was arrested and had to stand trial. But if he was arrested, it would. And that meant he couldn't return home, not now, perhaps not ever.

He sighed. If his reasoning was valid then that meant he could at least spare his parents one humiliation: Dem never need know 'bout di Sodomite business. Sonny's parents also would be spared the shameful arse-fucking truth.

Never to go home.

He closed the paper and wept.

By the third week the Informer Sounds Murder Investigation had ceased to be news altogether.

Chapter Five

There are crimes that are done for the money, and these are carried out in a businesslike way because they are business by other means. Most drug-dealing falls into this category. Then there are crimes that are done for the thrill of it, in which profit is secondary to the adrenalin rush. Street robbery, even when it is done to support a serious drug habit, usually falls into this second category, as does much burglary, as do most other crimes of violence against the person.

One day about a week before Cutty had moved into his own place he and Spin and Gary and Maxie were chilling at Buju's drum, smoking some weed and sipping some beers and talking robbery. It was the afternoon. Cynthia was at work. Spin and Gary were bragging about how they rolled queers on cruising grounds.

'It's like win-win, yeah,' said Spin. 'Cos most of the time they ain't gonna be belling the feds cos of what they was up to when they got done over.'

'Plus they're scared shitless cos they don't know what you're gonna do to 'em on top of just robbing 'em,' said Gary.

'You ever catch 'em like in the act?' Maxie flushed slightly as he asked the question, as if admitting to being curious about such things would make him somehow suspect in the eyes of his mates.

'It's more like you see 'em jumping up when you come up on 'em,' Gary said. 'Zipping up or pulling up their pants or shit.'

'And you're doing what you're doing,' said Spin.

'You're getting on with your business, not getting in theirs. So you see 'em but you don't.'

'Plus it's dark so you can't see that much anyway.'

'Straight away you got to get 'em under manners,' said Spin.

'Take charge of the situation,' agreed Gary.

'Sometimes you gotta give 'em some licks to show 'em who's boss,' Spin continued.

'Them ever fight back?' asked Maxie.

'Naw,' said Spin. 'They're pussies, man. They ain't real men, they ain't got it in 'em.'

'Less they've had it in 'em already,' Gary added, and laughed. He and Spin slapped palms and snapped fingers, and Spin, Buju and Maxie laughed too.

Cutty toked and watched, saying nothing, thinking about the lies men tell, especially young men.

So you never see nuttin' den, just movements inna di shadows? An' you only go an' look at man and man fi rob dem a dem money an' jewellery? And you study deseya cruising grounds for pure business, an' not for pleasure? You don't nevah curious 'bout batty business?

'So what you think then, Cutty, man?' Spin asked, suddenly aware of Cutty's non-participation in the conversation.

'Dem don't go to di law, you say?' Cutty asked.

'Well, they do more'n they used to,' Spin admitted reluctantly.

'The feds is supposed to be like friendly to gays now,' Buju said, speaking for the first time himself. 'They love 'em now, apparently.'

'And they sure as fuck don't love us,' Maxie added.

'Plus they all got mobiles,' Gary said.

'And they use them videophones,' Spin said.

'What you mean?' asked Cutty.

'Filming their dutty antics,' said Spin. 'So if you

ain't careful and you don't get their phone you could end up getting filmed too.'

'Yeah, but they ain't gonna show that to the feds, are they?' Maxie objected.

'They ain't got no shame,' Buju said. 'It ain't like back in JA, right, Cutty?'

Cutty nodded. He felt, at that moment, no solidarity with the rolled white queers of England, and while he felt solidarity with his click, with the youths and their wild quest for extremity, a sense of disgust was stealing over him at the whole conversation. It seemed small and dirty and mean.

'You ever seen any of that shit they film?' Maxie was asking.

'Why you so curious all of a sudden?' asked Spin, giving Maxie a sly look.

'Like seeing a car-wreck, innit,' said Maxie, shrugging defensively. 'Like you don't wanna look, but you got to.'

'You find it, you erase it,' said Gary. 'Can't sell on no phone with batty business on it, can you?'

'Hang on, though, blood,' Spin cut across him teasingly. 'What we got here?' And he pulled a Motorola from the pocket of his jeans jacket.

The others crowded round him as Spin scrolled through the search menu to access a video clip. Cutty pushed himself up out of the armchair and went and joined them: he would stand out if he showed no curiosity. And of course he was curious, if not for the same reasons the others were. They wanted to be appalled, disgusted. They wanted a freakshow that would affirm them in their normality. And Cutty? What did he want?

'Here we go,' Spin said, and the video-clip began to play on the inch-square screen. The image-quality was low: grainy and dark, with poor resolution. 'There's about thirty seconds of it.'

'Can't see nothin',' Maxie grumbled.

'Wait for it.' Spin was grinning in anticipation of the others' response.

'Oh my God!' Maxie burst out, laughing in shock as on the little screen a large, solid-looking pale erection swung into focus, apparently being filmed by its owner from above. A white skinhead, evidently kneeling, moved open-mouthed into frame and swallowed the entire length of it to the base in a single greedy thrust.

'Deep throat, man!' Spin laughed as Maxie, Gary, Buju and Cutty recoiled in seeming panic and alarm.

'That's raw, man!' Buju said, laughing too, and wincing, But Cutty noticed that he kept his eyes on the screen nonetheless. Him curious, he thought. 'Fucking raw,' Buju repeated.

'Cynthia suck cock that good, blood?' asked Spin.

'Fuck you, man,' Buju said irritatedly. 'Least I'm getting my dick sucked.'

The kneeling skinhead, now gagging, moved his head back with a belch, and disgorged the heavy, now shiny member to further shouts and groans from the click. As he lunged for it again the clip ended.

'Shit, man,' Maxie laughed, flicking his wrist and snapping. 'That was fucked up.'

Spin shrugged and pocketed the phone.

'People see that, they'll think that's what you're in-to, blood,' Buju teased.

'Fuck you, man,' Spin said in his turn. 'Any fool can see that ain't my dick.'

'Too big, yeah?'

'Too fuckin' small, man. So fuck you.'

They all sat back down. Gary relit one of the spliffs from the ashtray. 'Musta been just before we come up on 'em,' he said, and toked.

'Makes me think I seen this thing of this bitch getting fucked by a pig,' Maxie said. 'Sick, freak fucking - '

'You take weapons?' Cutty interrupted, addressing Gary and Spin.

'Just blades,' Gary said.

'Foolishness,' Cutty said, kissing his teeth. His mind was churning, his dick was half-erect in his track pants, but he kept his manner cold and flat.

'What you mean, blood?' Gary asked, flushing angrily.

'Cah AIDS is in di blood, mi bruddah. Either a you waan get AIDS?'

'It's just to threaten with,' Spin said defensively.

'We never cut no-one for real,' Gary added. 'Not like on the rob.'

Spin nodded agreement.

Cutty shrugged and took a spliff from the ashtray and lit it. He had to strike the lighter repeatedly to get a flame.

'Whatever, man,' Gary said furiously as Cutty toked. His right leg was bouncing rapidly up and down where he sat.

'My brother here's right though,' Buju said. 'Plus if you get caught with a shank by the feds it's serious shit.' He took the joint from Cutty's lips as Cutty blew sweet blue smoke out into the room.

'We ain't that careless,' Spin muttered, avoiding both Buju and Cutty's eyes.

They sat not talking for a bit after that, just smoking and drinking beer. Then the conversation started up again and quickly moved on to other, lighter subjects: music, football, good times and girls.

For the rest of that afternoon Cutty felt that Buju was watching him. Watching him in a way different to how Buju normally watched him. He felt that Buju was sizing up his reactions to whatever was being said by the others around him. Cutty reviewed his responses and decided he had said and done nothing that could be used against him. He wondered what Buju was watching him for.

That evening Cutty and Buju found themselves briefly alone in the flat together. The rest of the click had gone, and Cynthia hadn't yet finished her stint at the nail parlour. It was a rare window of privacy, and just being on his own with Buju gave Cutty an illicit thrill. He felt like some teenager trying to take advantage of the parents being out of the house to get it on with his girlfriend. The image of himself fucking Buju flashed into his mind then with thrilling vividness, realer than a memory, realer than real.

He remembered spying on his older brother Joseph as Joseph fucked some girl on the rug in the living-room of their family home, and being turned on by the sight of his brother's butt pumping between her spread thighs, the arse-muscles flexing concave, convex, concave, convex, and her excited gasps as Joseph rammed her hard for his pleasure. The memory of being turned on turned him on again now, and he shifted awkwardly on the couch to accommodate his lengthening dick more comfortably in his track pants.

Buju relit the joint they'd been smoking. He offered it to Cutty, but Cutty waved it away. Buju shrugged and dragged on it one last time.

'You're right, man,' he said, stubbing the roach out thoroughly in the ashtray. 'Enough is enough.' He was looking looking especially handsome today, it seemed to Cutty, with a dark blue bandana knotted round his shaved head. A cut-off white tank-top showed off his smoothly-muscled arms and gave tantalising flashes of his flat, toned belly, and he was wearing white Calvin Klein trunks, a good six inches of the body-hugging material of which showed above his baggy black jeans.

He sat in the white leather armchair opposite Cutty, his thighs spread, his feline eyes reddened and hazy.

'Cheap thrills, man,' he said, out of nothing in particular.

'What, star?' Cutty wrinkled his brow, feeling seriously stoned by now.

'Rolling queers.'

Cutty pulled a face and grunted. 'So what you do then?' he asked.

'What, me?'

'Yeah.'

'For thrills?'

'Yeah.'

Buju smiled a teasing, wicked smile. 'Whatever comes my way,' he said. 'I live for the moment, you know what I'm saying?' His hand lay loosely in his crotch. With apparent unselfconsciousness he tugged at himself there.

Cutty's heart started to pound. Was Buju finally making the move that Cutty had wanted him to make ever since he had spent that first night in the flat? He longed to kiss Buju's full, firm lips, kiss the bullets of Buju's protruding nipples, kiss his way down Buju's trembling stomach and take Buju's pulsing erection in his mouth and bring Buju to ecstasy with his lips and tongue.

But did Buju mean what he seemed to mean?

Now Cutty was in the most dangerous place of all, and so was Buju, if Buju was indeed trying to come on to him. It was like some stag-on-stag antler-clashing in the wild. You displayed your masculine prowess to impress the other male, to turn him on. Then the moment of greatest risk occurred when you had to open yourself to him to draw out his response, because if you got it wrong then you got gored. You suffered the particular agony of being attacked by the one you most desired, attacked psychologically and very likely physically as well, and that attack could escape from the private world into the public one, and destroy you there too. And Cutty needed this roof, this friend, these friends, this business contact: he couldn't risk all that, not right now, not just for –

And still Sonny was in his mind, Sonny who he hadn't loved, who he had liked and desired but no more than that, who had paid an even higher price than the one he, Cutty, was now paying for acting on that desire. Who had paid with his life.

Turned on and his mind in turmoil, Cutty sat frozen on the sofa, unable to do or say anything, for once willing Cynthia to come banging through the door with a bagful of moans and gripes about work, about her life, about her friends, about Buju.   About Buju. How could she complain about him? He was so fucking perfect.

She didn't appear.

'I got you something,' Buju said abruptly. He jumped up off the sofa and went through to the bedroom, a nervous bounce in his step. Cutty heard the sound of the wardrobe door opening, then some rummaging about, and a moment later Buju returned with a shoe-box.

'There you go, man,' he said, handing the box to Cutty.

'Prada?' Cutty said, noting the brand on the lid.

'It ain't shoes, bruv.'

Cutty opened the box. Inside, lying on crumpled lavender tissue paper like a wedding gift, was an automatic pistol. A 9mm. Its clip lay beside it, a bullet visible at the top. He reached in to take it out.

'Hang on a sec, yeah?' Buju went over to the window and swivelled the blinds closed so that no-one passing along the walkway outside could see in.

Cutty examined the pistol with the ease of one

who's handled guns before. It was in good working order. He up-ended the grip. The serial number had been filed off.

'Russian,' Buju said. 'I got it off this Polish geezer.'

'How much?'

'You don't arx how much a present costs, man,' Buju said, grinning shyly.

Cutty couldn't refuse it. He didn't even want to: the time might come when he would need it. He put the pistol back in the box, reached out his hand and he and Buju touched knuckles.

'Tank you, man,' he said.

'Don't tell Cynthia though,' Buju said.

Cutty nodded. It was like a bizarre parody of an affair.

'Don't carry it with you 'less you reckon you're really gonna need to use it, though,' Buju went on. 'Cos I don't need to tell you gun business is serious business.'

'You 'ave one?'

'Course, man. I got several. In like, different locations.'

'An' di others?'

'Spin and them? Nah, they ain't tooled up yet. I don't reckon they could handle it. They ain't got the perspective, you know what I'm saying? They ain't got the smarts.'

Cutty nodded.

'A tool is for business,' Buju went on. 'Not for thrills. And they ain't learned the difference yet, I reckon.'

'Rolling queers,' Cutty echoed.

'Exactly, bruv,' Buju said. 'Give 'em a tool and they'll be waving it about under the noses of them chi-chi men like it was a turn-on for 'em or shit.'

He laughed.

Cutty put the lid back on the box. 'You cyan keep it

for I till I sort out mi yard?' he asked.

'Course, man,' Buju said. 'No problem.'

And then there was a rattle of key in lock and Cynthia did come back. Buju took the shoe-box from Cutty's lap and slipped into the bedroom as she opened the front door and cold, damp air gusted into the flat.

Chapter Six

The first thing Cutty did once he had his own place was to change the locks and have a wrought-iron security door installed in front of the regular front door. Then he felt safe because unlike Buju's block there were no extended walkways, just regular internal hallways, and so there were no easily-accessible windows for an intruder to climb in through: the door was the one way in or out of the flat, and the flat was on the fifth floor. Only Buju and the other members of the click knew Cutty's new address. Only they knew his true last name, and that only because of the newspaper article. If he ever needed to give anyone else a last name he used Stevens, which was his mother's maiden name.

The next time he rang his mother was a fortnight after he had first called her. She told him that the police had been to the house to question her and his father but they had said they hadn't spoken to him since before the fire. His mother was a woman who hated to lie, and Cutty knew it had cost her something in self-respect to tell such an untruth, even though it was on her son's behalf.

Robert still hadn't told her anything about the circumstances of the fire and the killing of Sonny, although surely by now he must have heard the true story. Cutty assumed that his mother assumed it had been something to do with drugs, and he himself said nothing to make her think otherwise. *Better dat dan di truth.* He wondered about Sonny's parents, who he had never met. Sonny had a sister in Florida, he thought. He couldn't remember if he had ever asked Sonny what her name was.

Every night before sleeping he would drink whiskey or rum and smoke some sensi to deaden what his dreams would bring. He would sit up watching late-night trash TV until he slumped into unconsciousness, wake with a start a few hours later and drag himself through to the bedroom. But even once he was in bed he rarely slept unbrokenly, and hardly ever felt re-freshed on waking. Childhood stories of duppies and haints came unbidden to his mind, tales of spirits that haunted crossroads, and unlaid ghosts that stole into houses to trouble the sleepers within. Sometimes Sonny was the ghost, sometimes it was Cutty himself: he often felt dead these days.

The times when he felt most alive were when he was with Buju, hanging out at Buju's drum or his own, or just being out in the streets with him, waiting to see what the next turn of the card would bring. Then Cutty felt almost happy: when he was living as far as possible in the impulsive animal present, which required neither reflection nor planning to be enjoyed. And that was Buju's thrill too, Cutty learned: Buju planned, Buju was shrewd and smart, but he like Cutty needed moments of release from all that order; he needed to plunge from the brightly-lit, remorseless clarity of the world of the driven careerist into the hot-blooded, chaotic darkness of the impulsive thug. But even in his wildest moments Buju wasn't wholly self-destructive: he knew that he needed someone he could trust to watch his back, and he had decided that Cutty was that someone. And Cutty was honoured.

Buju was fearless in a fight. It didn't matter how much taller or heavier the other man was, Buju would lay into him unhesitatingly. *Tackle the biggest fucker first,* he would say, *then none a the others are gonna risk fucking with you.* Cutty first saw Buju fight at a house party in Westbourne Park, when an uninvited rival click forced their way into the house, a dilapidated Victorian terrace. The party was already seriously overcrowded, it was gone three a.m., and the interlopers were out to cause mischief. By that time the bloods who were supposed to be acting as bouncers had long since given up their role and gone and got pissed or stoned. It was Buju, backed up by Cutty and Spin, who had confronted the rival crew, who were causing friction, coming on to the girls and not taking no for an answer, threatening to break up the place.

Bold face, hard-faced Buju had stepped to the click's main man, a six-foot-two, musclebound, shaven-headed Nigerian named Ade who was pawing a frightened fourteen-year-old girl he had shoved up in a corner, repeatedly tugging her bra-strap down off her shoulder.

'Leave the sistah alone, blood,' Buju said, and something in his manner made the other man break off from what he was doing and turn to face him.

'Or what, little boy?' Ade asked, grinning sweatily. 'You better keep outta what don't concern you, though.'

'Or this,' Buju said, and fast as a snake he smashed a beer-bottle against the side of Ade's head and raked the broken bottle down his cheek. 'Tribal scars, bitch!' Buju spat. He threw the bottle-neck down.

As he turned away a member of Ade's crew, a skinny, mixed-race boy with an acne-rashed face, drew a gun on him. A glock. Before the boy could find his nerve Buju punched him hard in the face, breaking his nose, Buju's sovereign-rings cutting his cheek and lip. The boy stumbled back and discharged a shot into the ceiling.

At the sound of the gunshot the party collapsed into total chaos, with frightened guests shoving and elbowing and running in panic as the sound of police sirens drew near, the police surely called before the shooting by sleep-deprived neighbours irate about the noise and lateness of the event.

Somehow Buju, Cutty and Spin managed to escape the house and the police, clambering out of an upstairs window onto a flat-roofed extension, climbing down into the yard, then scrambling over a garden fence. They then stumbled through a neighbouring garden and over another fence, and soon they were back on the streets and in the clear.

They had walked back to White City on an adrenalin high, laughing and bragging and talking up the ruck into a legend. Once they reached the estate Spin headed home to his mum's. But Cutty went back to Buju's for a smoke, and to unwind. And there, as dawn broke, Buju told him the story of how he had lost his fear.

'This is way, way back in the day, like six plus years ago,' Buju began, his hazel eyes defocusing as he stared into the past. 'I was still living at home back then and my mum started seeing this bloke, this big, fat motherfucker. He was like six foot three and must of weighed like twenty stone plus. And I ain't no giant, you know? And I weren't no taller then, you know what I'm saying?' Buju was no more than five foot six now, for all that pumping iron had made his physique more beefy and sculpted. 'I was small and I hadn't started no weight-training or nothing back then, so I was like skinny, I was like this skinny little kid.'

'You was how old when alla this gwaan?' Cutty asked.

'Fifteen, man,' Buju replied. 'Just about fifteen. And this cunt, he was one of them jerks who reckons just cos he's sexing your old lady he's like all of a sudden the head of the household, bossing you this way and that way. And my mum, she was so desperate to have a man, she went along with it. When I called her on it,

she came up with alla this shit 'bout I'm a rowdy yout'
and he's a good influence and I need some discipline
and a male role model and alla that.' He pulled a
scornful face. 'Yeah, right. It'd of been one thing if he'd
like got a job or a career or shit, like brought some
dollars to the table, treated my mum to nice stuff. But
he didn't do nothing like that. He didn't do nothing,
period. He just come in our drum, sat his outsize arse
down on the couch and shouted for beers and burgers,
hogged the remote and sat there like a beached whale,
farting and belching. And when he weren't doing that
he was beating on me.'

'What him do dat for?' Cutty felt a sudden fierce
anger at the thought of Buju as a young boy being
mistreated by some brutal, idle thug.

'Cos he could,' Buju said. 'It started with him like
shoving me around, and he'd kind of pass it off as – he
called it rough-housing. Man, what a fucking phoney!'
Buju's eyes flashed as he remembered. 'That was right
in front of my mum, and when he saw how she sucked
it up and didn't do nothing he knew he could get away
with more. When she weren't there he'd really shove
me about, you know? Bounce me off the fucking walls.'

'And what you do, man?'

'Nothing to start off with,' Buju said. 'I mean, I was
a kid, I didn't have no money or job or nothing, and the
fact of my mum going along with it fucked with my
head so I felt like I was to blame for my situation, you
know? And maybe I was cos from day one I always
answered back. I never took no shit from him. But I
don't reckon that was what made the difference. If I'd
of been nice as pie he'd still of treated me like shit, just
cos he could.'

'Was you doing anyting pon di streets at dis point?'
Cutty asked.

'Bit a tieving, some street robberies, muggings and

shit,' Buju said. 'Mobile phones, whatever. It helped me let off steam and give me some spends, but I knew it weren't no solution to nothing. I did it but I was ashamed I was doing it, you know what I'm saying? Cos at the end of the day I weren't choosing it. I was just out the house running wild in the streets, and I didn't choose to be out the house, I was just sick of getting beat on. So it was more like a sickness.'

Cutty nodded.

'You get to a point where you got to do something or you're gonna go under,' Buju said. 'You got to take a stand in your own drum, you get me?'

'Seen.'

'So what I did was, I got this chisel what I lifted from a hardware store, right, and I sharpened it up prison-stylee till it was like a blade. Then I hid it in my room and I waited. That's where I learned patience, man. You lay a plan and you stick to it, you know what I'm saying? You don't lose control, you don't let your heart rule your head.'

Cutty nodded again.

'The night come up soon enough. My mum was at work, doing a double shift. She's a nursing auxiliary. It's shit money but it's a wage. He was in our yard, slobbed out on the couch as per normal, tits sticking through the mesh vest like some fat fucking sow, belly up like he's like fifty months pregnant, guzzling beers and watching the footie, family size bag of Walker's on one side, remote on the other, getting into it, grunting and shouting out shit like anyone cared. I was in my room, listening to it. Then it was the news, I heard the theme tune going. Flick flick flick with the remote cah he don't like to know nothing 'bout nothing. Ignorant fucker. Then comes some shit movie, shouting and shoot 'em ups. And I listened and listened cos I knew, I knew this was gonna be the night. Come midnight I crept down from me room with the chisel like hidden behind my back. I look in the front room and he's sat there, asleep on the couch. Mouth open, wheezing and snuffling. Fat wet lips, disgusting. I went in real quiet, man, creeping like a cat-burglar. I picked up the remote off the floor and turned the volume down on the TV, cos once I got started I didn't want no background noise to like interrupt the clarity of my flow.'

Buju's eyes were bright with excitement now, and his voice caught a little in his throat as he quickly went on:

'I went up to him like a ninja and I stood over him and I took the chisel and I brought it up level with the front of his adam's apple. His throat was fat and bloaty, like a big brown frog, and it quivered each breath he took like a jelly on a plate. So what I do is I rest the chisel on it, gentle-like. He don't wake up. I push on it a little. He still don't wake up. I push on it harder and it starts to make like a little red line on his skin. A little cut. He wakes up with a gasp and kind of a start. He sees me standing over him and it's like he's gonna jump up to give me some licks but then he susses the situation: if he moves he's gonna get cut and cut bad, so suddenly he's still. Funny, ain't it?'

'What?'

'The way all of a sudden cunts like him can control themselves when there's a straight-up bad consequence to losing it.'

He tapped out a cigarette and lit it with Cutty's lighter, which was lying on the coffee table in front of him.

'He looks this way and that way, like just with his eyes, looking for how he can shoot me a box and get me off of him without getting sliced up. Cos I'm standing right over him, right? And I can tell he'd like to knee me in the bollocks but he knows if he tries it I'm gonna go forwards and that chisel is gonna go right through his throat and into his fucking spine. He tries to say something but I just jab harder to shut him up cos he ain't got nothing to say what I wanna hear. There's like a long moment where nothing happens. And then I see it, man. I see what I've been looking for. What I been needing. You know what it was?'

Buju's eyes were dark and gleaming and wide. Cutty guessed but he shook his head.

'Fear,' Buju said. And he smiled a cold smile. 'I could see fear in his eyes. And I could *smell* the fear on him, man, all sweaty and disgusting. And that exact moment I knew I could do what I liked and he weren't gonna do nothing about it. I could piss all over him. I could piss in his mouth and he'd have to just take it. But you know the scary thing, man?'

And Buju caught Cutty's gaze then, and the smile left his face and suddenly he seemed very young, a boy not a man.

'What, mi idren?' Cutty asked.

'His fear come out of that he knew I could do it,' Buju said. 'He knew I could carve him up. He knew I could kill him. And *I* didn't know that, you know what I'm saying? I didn't know it till I saw it in his face. Like his fat stupid drunk face was a mirror. And then I did know it. And once you know something like that about yourself then you've changed, man. You're a different person.'

'But to know who you are, it is not a bad ting,' Cutty said carefully.

Buju shrugged. 'Maybe not, man.' He dragged on the cigarette, then ground it out in the ashtray. 'I said to him, "Don't speak, yeah. Don't even try. Just listen. You're a worthless, disgusting flabby sack of shit, and if you ever try and fuck with me again, if you ever even raise your voice round me, or if you get it into your fat head to go try and fuck with my mum, I'll cut your fucking throat. You get me, man? Cos if you're confused in any way I can make it like totally clear to you." And I give him another poke with the chisel to like underline what I was saying. He kind of gasped then cos that chisel was *sharp*, man, and he couldn't see what I'd already done. I didn't say nothing else. I said what I'd come to say. I swung off him careful-like, keeping the chisel where it was, just in case he was going to try some last-minute foolishness. Then I took the blade off his throat and I went outta that room backwards and fast.'

'Him try an' go for you?'

'I was sure he was gonna, but it turned out he was too freaked out. He like put his hand to his throat and it come away red and he shat himself when he saw it. I went up to my room, went in there, moved the chair so it was right by the door and turned out the lights. Then I sat up all night till my mum got off shift, waiting for him to try and sneak in and beat the shit out of me. But he never did.'

'What happened later on, though?' Cutty asked.

'He never tried nothing, man,' Buju said, smiling that smile again that was just a baring of teeth. 'I'd put the fear in him. He knew if he fucked with me one of us was gonna end up dead, and he knew he didn't have what it took to off someone so it was gonna be him. He was just some fat fucking bully waiting for a bigger bully to put the boot on his neck. He stopped tryna boss me around after that. In fact he stopped saying much of anything around me at all, which suited me fine, you know what I'm saying? My mum took it in and said she was pleased we was finally getting on better.' Buju shook his head, laughing softly but bitterly. 'She didn't understand why he pissed off a month later, but at least she didn't blame me.' His soft, mobile features hardened. 'And after that I was never afraid of nothing ever again, man,' he concluded. 'I mean, nothing that was like a actual physical fear.'

'That's some serious shit, star,' Cutty said, shaking his head in his turn.

'But I seen the same thing in your eyes though, bredren,' Buju said, looking at Cutty guardedly now. 'You been to the edge.'

'Yeah?'

'That's how I know I can trust you to cover my back.'

Cutty nodded, saying nothing to that, emotions roiling inside his chest and inside his head as they had on the day Buju gave him the gun. The intimacy between them now was so perversely parallel to the intimacy Cutty longed for that he was finding it hard to control himself. 'One love,' the youths in the click would say to each other, touching their fists to their own breasts. But it wasn't one love, was it?

'You up for something?' Buju asked abruptly.

'What, mi bruddah?' Cutty asked in return, trying to sound casual, his mind constantly on the alert for double meanings, for the secret signals he longed for Buju to send him.

'A job.'

'When?'

'Tonight.'

'Aright,' Cutty said with a shrug, casually reaching over for his lighter and pocketing it. 'What kinda job, though?' he asked.

'Burglary.'

'Burglary?' Cutty kept mild surprise out of his voice: he hadn't thought of Buju as a house-breaker. 'You scope out di place a'ready?' he asked.

'Yeah,' Buju said. 'I been keeping a eye on a couple of prospects lately.'

'Like a property investor.'

'But in reverse,' Buju agreed.

'A disinvestor,' Cutty said, pocketing his cigarettes. 'An' is disya prospect business or residential?'

'Residence.'

Cutty nodded.

Buju got up off the sofa and went over to the window. He looked out at the rising sun. He could see Cutty's block across the estate. In that light it looked clean and almost golden, almost like the architect had intended it to be.

'Who you want wit' you?' Cutty asked, allowing his eyes to roam over Buju's body as Buju stood there looking out at the endless glaring sky: his smooth mocha neck, his gleaming shaven head, his smooth bare muscular arms, the curve of his chest under his basketball vest, the firm fullness of his butt in his shiny black track pants, the jut of his crotch that promised size and fullness and made Cutty catch his breath.

'Just you, man,' Buju said. 'This is like a private thing, you know what I'm saying? Just between me and you. It ain't nobody else's business, you get me? But I need someone who's got my back.'

'So why tonight, star? Just for the hell of it?'

''Cos it's the first warm weekend of the year,' Buju said softly. 'People are gonna be out and about. But it still gets dark early on. Just right for a little early evening activity.'

'Where?' Cutty asked.

'Back a Hammersmith Grove,' Buju replied. 'There's a couple a two-up-two-downs round there set back from the street a bit with no burglar alarms, and hedges in front to keep shit private.' He turned his head and his eyes met Cutty's levelly. 'So are you in, man?' he asked for a second time.

'I tell you already,' Cutty replied. 'Me in.'

They brushed knuckles then palms in two leisurely

motions, locking fingers for a brief, tugged handshake followed by a finger-snap.

'Tonight, man,' Buju said. His face was expression-less, but there was a rising excitement visible in his eyes.

'Tonight, star,' Cutty echoed, knowing he was crazy to go along with Buju in this even as he knew that he couldn't say no to Buju in anything, pushing the risks and consequences down below the water-line, trying to match Buju's fearlessness with his own.

His heart was racing as he left Buju's yard.

Chapter Seven

They parked the van, a small white Ford, directly outside the house they were planning to break into. Buju, who had been driving, cut the engine. He and Cutty exchanged a look, then got out. They both wore dark hooded sweatshirts with the hoods pulled up, dark track pants and, despite the mildness of the evening, gloves. The house was semi-detached, narrow, and set back from the street as Buju had said it would be. It had a shingled porch and black gloss paintwork.

After glancing up and down the street to check that they weren't under direct observation from anyone they slipped through the garden gate and up to the front door. The house was in darkness. Buju rang the bell and stood there, balanced on the edge of the front step with only the balls of his feet on the stone, flexing his calves by raising and lowering his heels as he waited for someone to answer.

No-one answered.

Buju and Cutty moved across from the porch so they were standing in front of a large, old-fashioned sash window. From there they were shielded from the street by a tall privet hedge. Inside the window wooden blinds were down and half-tilted, obscuring the room beyond with confusing, slatted shadows. The sash window was secured by nothing more than an old-fashioned brass catch. Buju produced a six-inch metal ruler and slowly wiggled it up between the two frames of the sash. With more patient wiggling he was able to pop the catch back. It cracked sharply against the glass, making both men look round, holding their breaths.

Nothing happened. Buju began to carefully slide the

lower half of the window up. Wood shrieked noisily
against wood. He stopped. Then he continued more
slowly, his brow furrowed in concentration. The noise
was less. The first sign of sweat gleamed faintly on his
face. Eventually the window was raised enough for
them to slip in under it, but the blind was still in the
way. With slow-motion patience Buju reached in with
one hand and lifted up the corded slats. There was only
the softest clicking as he did so. He gestured to Cutty to
climb in first.

Cutty did so, stepping over the sill and putting one
foot down carefully on the polished wooden boards
inside. Then he bent low and moved his head and torso
over the threshold. As he pulled up his other leg and
drew it into the room after him he twisted round and
held the blind up for Buju, who followed him noiseless-
ly in the same way. Once Buju was inside, Cutty carefully lowered the blind. Buju found the rod that
adjusted the louvers and twisted them closed, shutting
out the night and prying eyes.

The room was warm and dark and airless.

They stood there for a moment, listening for the
slightest sounds of anyone else in the house, but all
they heard was their own hearts beating and the sound
of blood rushing in their ears.

'Torches,' Buju said huskily.

They had each brought a torch. They now turned
them on and played the beams around the room. It was
a wealthy-looking living-room: antique furniture and
lamps, a large widescreen TV, an expensive stereo,
framed art on the walls, the glass in front of which
flared into opacity as the torch-light hit it.

'Mek we put on di lights?' Cutty asked. Buju nodded.

'One second, though,' he added, and disappeared
through the open doorway into the passage beyond. A

moment later he was back. 'Nobody home,' he said, and clicked on a pair of dimmer switches, turning them up until the room was lit with a low, mellow light. He and Cutty turned off their torches and pocketed them.

'Bang & Olaffsen,' Cutty said, taking in the stereo. 'Top a di range.'

'Take it.'

'Di TV?'

'Zit plasma?'

'Just widescreen.'

'Leave it. Not worth the trouble. But we oughtta - '

Buju was about to say something more when he found himself staring at a large, framed photographic print that was hanging on one of the walls. It was numbered in pencil, *17/250*, and block-mounted, and was an image of a flawless male torso, marble-white against a black background, and twisted at an angle that highlighted the arching swell of the chest and the elegant bevel of the waist, and the curving-out of the top of muscular buttocks that were cut off by the bottom of the frame.

'Shit, man,' Buju said with a half-humorous snort of contempt. 'A chi-chi man pad.'

'A battyman yard,' Cutty echoed.

'Look for credit cards, yeah,' Buju said, looking away from the print. 'Queers always got lots a money.'

'How come so?' Cutty asked.

'Cah they ain't got no pickney or bitches to support,' Buju said. 'Lucky idle motherfuckers, you know what I'm saying?'

The two men moved quickly round the room, pulling open any drawers they came across and rummaging through papers, but they found nothing to steal.

'Shit,' Buju said. 'They must of taken 'em to the opera or ballet or whatever.'

Cutty looked round from opening an inlaid tortoiseshell box that had a handful of foreign coins in it and nodded. His eye was caught by a framed photograph on a mantelpiece above which hung a large antique mirror. He went over and looked at it more closely. The photograph's frame was silver and blocky with geometrical designs incised into its surface although the photograph itself was just an ordinary snapshot. It showed three white men standing together outside somewhere, all slightly dazzled by the sun. All had cropped hair. One was greying and wore a checked shirt, a second, who was blond, had on a skinny-rib vest. The third was topless, and a nipple-ring glinted on his not-especially-toned chest. All were smiling and happy-seeming. There was a rainbow flag billowing in the background, and other men milling about out of focus. One of them, barely visible behind one of the crop-headed men's shoulder, and with his back to the camera, was black.

Cutty looked up and found he was staring at his own face in the mirror. He felt terror, rage and excitement sweep over him. Did two of the men in this photograph live here together? Who did they think they were to live just like other people live, as if it was no big deal, as if it was their right, as if it wasn't some monstrous slap in the face to – to *something*?

To what?

God?

But Cutty barely believed in God any more. He believed in himself. His own face was ugly to him and it was handsome to him.

'Don't freak out on me now, man,' Buju said, noticing Cutty staring fixedly at his own reflection in the low light. Cutty grunted an acknowledgement and turned away from the mirror. He went to unplug the stereo.

'You ever been in a battyman yard before?' he asked Buju.

Buju was running his finger down a tower of CDs. 'Barbra Streisand,' he said, as if he hadn't heard Cutty's question. 'Liza Minelli. Kylie Minogue.' He looked round at Cutty with a smile. 'She *fit*, bwai.'

Cutty deftly unplugged the cables leading in and out of the stereo. 'So what you tink 'bout all dis batty business den?' he asked, trying to sound as casual as if the answer meant nothing to him one way or the other.

'Let's check out the bedroom,' Buju said, once again evading an answer, and Cutty felt like Buju was teasing him, leading him on. 'They must got at least a laptop or shit up there,' he added.

Turning their torches back on they went out into the hall and made their way up the narrow, creaking staircase as quietly as they could. Three doors opened off the landing. A moment's glance showed them that the first led to a small blue-and-white bathroom with a fancy stone sink and dried flowers in an urn, the second to a plainly-furnished study-come-spare-room containing a bed, desk and what Buju was looking for, a high-spec top-of-the-range Mac.

'Computer,' Cutty said.

Buju nodded, but rather than paying the Mac any more attention or getting Cutty to unplug and disconnect it, he wandered off into the third room. Cutty followed him. It was the main bedroom. A broad futon with solid, wood-block legs was covered by an unbleached cotton duvet. Beeswax candles were dotted about on shelves and surfaces. There were more physique prints on the walls, smaller than the one in the front room, and in black frames. All showed flawless white male bodies. In amongst them hung small, colourful abstracts on canvas, unframed blocks suspended on nails in the walls. White muslin hung in elegant folds at the window. Buju looked about him without a word. He seemed fascinated by the room.

'Queers love candles,' he said eventually.

He pulled out his lighter and started lighting them. Cutty said nothing. Instead he went and opened and closed drawers, shining his torch in at their contents, more to be doing something than because he was searching for anything in particular. He found neatly folded, colour co-ordinated designer clothes. In one drawer was a pile of Calvin Klein underwear, including the exact same style he himself was wearing at that moment. He found the coincidence perversely exciting and wanted to say something about it to Buju, but couldn't think how. In a wicker dish on a bedside table were condoms and sachets of lubricant.

'Fresh 'n' Wild,' Cutty said, reading off the label of one of the sachets.

'What, man?' Buju asked inattentively. He had now lit five of the candles. The mellow scent of beeswax began to fill the room. He turned off his torch. Cutty followed suit. In the candle-light Cutty was struck forcibly by how handsome Buju was. His smooth, dark skin glowed richly, and his eyes gleamed.

Overwhelmed, Cutty looked away from Buju and pointed to a small room leading off the bedroom that they hadn't checked out yet. A chrome towel-rail was visible. Buju disappeared into it and Cutty heard the sound of a bathroom cabinet opening. Buju's head reappeared round the door, a cheeky grin on his face that made him look about twelve.

'Here,' he said, and he tossed Cutty a bottle of Ck1. 'I'm going for the Issey Miyake.' Cutty opened the bottle, removed his gloves and dabbed a few dots of the fragrance on the glands under his neck. He felt almost as if the house, the room was somehow trying to seduce him. Or was it the room? Could it be Buju? Perhaps. He wasn't sure.

The air in the bedroom was blood-warm. Buju came

out of the bathroom. He too had pocketed his gloves to apply the scent. Cutty could smell it on him, and on himself. 'We haffi wipe the bottles,' he said with an effort.

Buju nodded inattentively, looking down at the bed.

'This is where they do their dutty business,' he said, a soft smirk on his face.

'You ever - ' Cutty began abruptly. Then he cut himself off equally abruptly. His mouth was horribly dry.

'What, man?' Buju flashed him an unrevealing look.

'You ever tink 'pon what it woulda be like to...' Cutty faltered.

'What?'

Cutty shrugged awkwardly

'What, man?' Buju repeated. He turned his head and looked at Cutty directly.

'Nothing, man,' Cutty said. "Llow it.' He felt excited and nauseated and afraid, all at the same time.

Buju moved across the room to where Cutty was standing as if transfixed, as if the candles, the perfume had hypnotised him.

They were facing each other now, just three feet apart, and gazing into each others' eyes. Their lips were full, their chests rising and falling in synch, their pupils dilated in the low light to discs of polished jet. Cutty could feel his dick expanding with alarming rapidity in his track pants, sliding to stiffness inside his briefs across one thigh.

If him na go for it I can always deny dat anyting ever happen, he thought. *I cyan call it a joke. Or a test.*

As if without willing it, as if in obedience to some ineluctable law of physics or chemistry, they moved closer to each other. Cutty could feel the heat radiating from Buju's face. He could feel the soft warmth of Buju's breath as he leaned in for the kiss. Buju closed his eyes as Cutty kissed him gently on the lips, and stood there still and passive as a statue. But Cutty could feel his lips respond. Then Buju's arms slid around Cutty's neck, and soon they were kissing hotly, embracing each other with what seemed like an ancient longing. As their stiffnesses connected through the flimsy, slippery nylon of their track pants both men gasped, and Buju opened his eyes.

For the length of a heartbeat Cutty waited for him to pull back, to go back on the longing that his kisses revealed so nakedly, to renounce and deny it, but instead he kissed Cutty again, this time brazenly pushing his tongue into Cutty's mouth.

It was a thousand years since Cutty had felt this human.

He broke the kiss long enough to pull Buju's hoody and vest up over his head and off, then quickly peeled off his own. Now they were both topless. They embraced again, skin and muscle against skin and muscle, their spirits fusing in the hot beat of blood as they kissed.

Buju placed a hand on Cutty's forehead and pushed his head back, arching his neck so he could kiss Cutty's adam's apple. Then he started to kiss his way down Cutty's lean, trembling torso, pausing to tease his stiffly-erect nipples on the way, nipping at them with his teeth.

'What if dem come back?' Cutty said hoarsely, trying to care about the possibility of being discovered, and failing.

Buju was now on his knees. 'Fuck 'em,' he said thickly. 'They ain't nothing but queers.' He nuzzled the oblique rigidity in Cutty's track pants, rubbing his cheek along its length, kissing and biting it gently through the material. Then he buried his face in Cutty's crotch, gripping the large, firm globes of Cutty's muscular buttocks through the shiny material of the track pants so he could push his face in harder, as if he wanted to smother himself in Cutty's maleness.

'Fuck 'em,' Cutty repeated as Buju grasped the waistband of his track pants and pulled them and his briefs down to his ankles in one fast movement. Cutty's erection sprung up and the air felt cool on it as it wagged heavily in front of his crotch. Without a word Buju took its head into his mouth and Cutty groaned with pleasure and relief as Buju began to suck hungrily on his dick, pumping his mouth rapidly back and forth on its rigid, throbbing length.

After a long, ecstatic minute Cutty lifted Buju up and, after kissing his shining lips, knelt in front of him, slid his track pants and briefs down to his ankles, gently pulled back his foreskin, and took Buju's hot stiffness into his mouth. Buju moaned and Cutty could taste his musk and his sweetness.

Soon they were lying on the bed, top to tail, going down on each other with greedy abandon. Cutty felt Buju's fingers brush between his buttocks, and Buju's forefinger linger tentatively on the dimple of his arsehole. Cutty broke off sucking Buju's dick just long enough to grunt, 'Yeah.' An extra thrill convulsed up through his body as Buju pushed a finger up inside him. Cutty could feel the cool curve of Buju's heavy gold sovereign ring pressing against his anal opening and he gasped throatily.

At that moment there was the sharp clack of a lock shooting back downstairs, followed by the rattle of what was surely the front door of the house being opened. With a gasp of shock Buju and Cutty broke off from what they were doing and rolled off the bed and onto the floor in a heap of knees and elbows, their pants tangled round their ankles, trying to pull them up in a panic as they struggled to their feet, spit-slicked erections still jutting and bouncing, skins still electri-

fied, chests heaving in panic, at the same time frantically tugging their knotted vests and hoodies on over their
heads as their dicks rapidly sank and shrank, clawing
the material down over their heaving, trembling bellies,
trying to do all of this in total silence.

The hall light clicked on and there was a murmur of
male voices. Buju snuffed the candles with the flat of
his hand in five sharp pats. Then he pulled up his hood
and gestured for Cutty to do the same. They stepped
out onto the landing as they heard the voices below
move into the living-room.

'You weren't doing anything with the stereo, were
you?' one voice asked the other, and Cutty flashed on
the Bang & Olafsen sitting disconnected in the middle
of the living-room floor.

'Go,' hissed Buju, and they both pounded down the
stairs fast, hoods up, faces hard and set as wooden
masks. They walked briskly to the front door, looking
straight ahead, breathing hard, saying nothing, preventing engagement, seeing only out of the corners of
their eyes two shaven-headed white men in their forties
in formal jackets and ties.

'Hey!' one of the men called sharply, half-stepping
forward as if to challenge the two black men now
opening his front door and walking out of his house,
then hesitating, pulling back from the confrontation as
the other man gripped his arm and in an urgent voice
hissed, 'Peter, don't!'

Buju and Cutty reached the pavement. Their hearts
were pounding, their fingers tingling with pins and
needles. The air outside was static, oppressive. Cutty
glanced back at the porch of the house. He couldn't see
anyone looking out. He assumed they were counting
their blessings that no violence had happened and
calling the police.

'We must split up,' he said.

Buju nodded. He ran off one way, Cutty the other. Cutty ran fast but not too fast, wanting to ensure that anyone he passed would take him for a law-abiding jogger, not a criminal fleeing the scene of a crime. He and Buju would have to come back for the van later. Taking it then would have been too risky: there would have been too many chances for them to be seen getting into it; too many chances that the number-plate would be noted down by someone and passed on to the police, and the van belonged to Buju's uncle.

Once he was back on the Goldhawk Road Cutty slowed his pace from a jog to a walk. The street was lively with drinkers standing outside pubs, black and white youths hanging out in front of the KFC with their hoods up, people of all races and nationalities going about their business or waiting at bus-stops. A gaggle of under-dressed Australian girls clattered past him in high heels, their mid-riffs bare, arguing boisterously. He pushed his hood back, dumped the torch and gloves he was carrying in a bin, and felt safe, and strange. It was as if what had just happened was a hallucination, as if he had had a particularly vivid dream, a wish-fulfilment, and then been woken from it with a start.

He pulled off his sweatshirt and knotted it round his waist. It wasn't really warm enough to be wearing just a mesh vest, but if the police came cruising around the area he didn't want to match the description they would have been given by the two men in the house. He caught his reflection in a plate-glass window and was surprised by the wildness in his eyes. He tried to push it down, make himself less vivid, less visible.

He stopped to buy cigarettes and a cheap lighter in a late-night supermarket. Back out on the streets he lit up, took out his mobile, and rang Buju.

'You aright, man?' he asked when Buju answered.

'I'm alright,' Buju said. There was a clattering, rumbling noise in the background.

'Where are you?'

'On the tube. I went down Hammersmith way and thought I better get off the streets for a bit, you know what I'm saying?'

'Meet me backyard den,' Cutty said. 'You have ya keys wit you?' He had given Buju spare keys to his drum.

'Yeah, man,' Buju said. 'Laters, yeah?'

'Seen.'

Cutty snapped his phone shut and started back towards his block. He walked as slowly as he could make himself walk: just a law-abiding citizen strolling home of an evening, someone with nothing to hide. Once he was on the estate he picked up his pace.

Chapter Eight

When Cutty got back to his drum he found Buju waiting for him in the living-room, sitting on the sofa and rolling a joint as calmly as if nothing had happened.

'Jesus fucking Christ, man!' Cutty said throatily. Now he was safely back in his own yard a violent shudder passed through him, and his knees felt weak as the adrenalin that had been keeping him going drained away. He laughed in relief as he locked the door behind him, shaking his head as he slammed the deadbolts across.

On the sofa, Buju sparked up.

Cutty went and dropped down beside him. 'Jesus fucking Christ,' he repeated. 'Dat was one piece a craziness, mi bruddah.' He tipped his head back until the base of his skull was resting against the cool plaster of the wall behind him. He closed his eyes and extended a hand languidly, waiting for Buju to place the lit joint between his fingers, which Buju didn't do.

'C'mon, bredren,' Cutty grumbled, keeping his eyes closed. 'Hit me up, yeah?'

Then Cutty opened his eyes wide because Buju was sliding on top of him and straddling his crotch. He looked up as Buju arched back, drawing deeply on the joint, then bent forward and kissed him on the mouth. Sweet, heavy smoke poured out of Buju's open mouth and down Cutty's throat and into his lungs, and came dripping out of both their nostrils until eventually they had to break off the kiss to cough.

Cutty looked into Buju's dope-reddened eyes and laughed, and there was joy in that laugh. He ran his hands over Buju's firm, muscular backside and felt all the desire that had been cut short by events back in the house surge up in him again, and his dick bucked in his track-pants with such violent suddenness that he almost came there and then.

They made love with a passion and intensity that was purely masculine, muscle thrusting against muscle, skin burning against skin, need bruising and answering need. Cutty swallowed Buju to the root, allowing the head of Buju's large, rigid dick to slide back and forth repeatedly over his gag reflex and deep down into his throat, the motion of Buju's hips against his face making Cutty's whole body buck and kick in excited response.

And later, and without a word, each knowing the other's need and his own, they greased each other with cocoa butter lotion, anointing stiff, throbbing dicks and massaging and relaxing eager, trembling arseholes with gently-probing fingers. It didn't matter that there were no scented candles, that there were no crisp new Egyptian cotton sheets on the bed. It didn't matter that the bed itself was a mattress on the floor, and the floor was bargain laminate not stripped and polished oak: at that moment they had everything they needed and more.

And Jah will provide the bread, Cutty thought.

They took it in turns to penetrate each other, to ride and be ridden. They both loved to fuck but even more, perhaps, they revelled in the ecstasy of being fucked, of giving up control, exulting in the relief of throwing aside masks and facades, in the defiance of breaking the ultimate taboo and doing what every mechanism of society had programmed them to resist as men, above all as black men: taking it up the arse and loving it.

Finally it was Buju who came first, sprawled on his

back with his legs lifted and thrown wide. Cutty was lying at right angles to him, driving his dick deeply and repeatedly into Buju's accomodating rectum. Every muscle was striated with sinew, every vein vascular as Cutty pumped his lean, flat hips against the muscular curves of Buju's butt. Buju's erection blurred in his fist and his face was tense with concentration as Cutty fucked him. Grunting sharply with each full insertion of Cutty's dick into his anal cavity he jerked himself off frantically, throwing his other arm up and covering his eyes as with a loud cry he came. The jism flew from his dick explosively, one drop even hitting his adam's apple.

'Me cyaan stop now,' Cutty grunted thickly, continuing to fuck the writhing, spasming Buju hard.

'Fuck me till you finish, man!' Buju gasped, now throwing both his arms up over his head and giving himself over to allowing Cutty his release. It came only thirty seconds later. And Cutty too cried out and the sweat flew from his face and body as he arched and drove his exploding dick into Buju to the root.

And if they didn't think of condoms or safe sex before, during or after; if they just did what they did with an animal simplicity, it was because they were not part of a world where any of that was thought about, where the virus was real. They were at that moment not part of any world at all. They were simply straight men who in secret preferred to fuck each other than women. Not dutty gays who had AIDS. And if being men meant they couldn't get pregnant why think of rubbers? And if that made no sense, so what? Most of life didn't make much sense.

After they had made love they lay side by side on the sagging mattress, staring up at the ceiling. Their cocks and their arseholes were soft and aching, and they felt, for once, simply human. Strange that that should be a rare thing, Cutty thought: to feel human.

'Man, I needed that,' Buju said, stretching his arms above his head and arching his back with a grunt.

'Me also,' Cutty agreed. He smiled to himself. 'What you tink woulda 'appen if dem queens back deh did catch we in di act?'

'Ah, they'd of probably wanted to join in, man,' Buju said lightly, amiable and accommodating now he had shot his load. 'It'd of been like a fantasy trip for 'em, you know what I'm saying? A taste of the jungle runnings. We coulda even got paper for it.'

'Yeah?'

'Dollars, man,' Buju said. 'I'm telling you. For the Mandingo thing.'

Cutty didn't ask Buju whether he had picked up that information off the TV or if it was something he knew from his own experience. Instead he asked:

'You reckon dis - what we just did now, you might want to do it again?'

'What, right now, yeah?' Buju mock-grumbled. 'I already got a arseful of jizz off of you, man.'

'Not right now,' Cutty said, though Buju's direct words made his soft dick twitch responsively. 'Just, whenever.'

'Whenever we wanna bust a nut?'

'Yeah.'

'Yeah,' Buju said. 'I could hang with that.' And he bent forward and twisted round and kissed the head of Cutty's cock with his firm, full lips.

'You waan stay?' Cutty asked.

'Yeah, but - ' Buju sighed. 'Cynthia's supposed to be coming over to my drum tonight.' He closed his eyes and snuggled up against Cutty.

'So you must leave?' Cutty asked, sliding his arm

around Buju's shoulders and pulling him closer.

'I suppose. But I don't wanna though,' Buju said, pouting.

'So stay.'

'I gotta keep up appearances, though.'

'But if you na go home she will jus' tink you is wit' one a ya baby-mothers, nuh?' Cutty said.

'I suppose. Truth is, though, I been stringing her along on that. There ain't no babymothers. Or none that I know about, anyway. I mean yeah, I was sexing some gals here and there, but... Truth is, I was larging up alla that – making out like I had a bitch in every port. It was just a way of getting me some space for – whatever, you know? Head space.'

'Becah a man must be his own man,' Cutty said, and he twisted round and kissed Buju on the forehead. 'Fuck Cynthia.'

'Fuck Cynthia,' Buju repeated, his voice muffled by Cutty's armpit. 'She don't own me. I ain't no slave to her pussy.'

'Better to die a free man dan live as a slave,' Cutty said quietly, his mind drifting back to the many girls he had had sex with back in Jamaica. At the time he had felt proud of his prowess, knowing that every pussy he fucked was another plate in the armour of his masculinity. Some of the girls he had even liked, though he liked them less as the years passed and his knowledge of what he really desired and really needed grew stronger in him. Now he saw all women except old women in terms of their endless cloying sexual and emotional demands on men and nothing else. It was their desire, which the world sanctioned, and his disinterest, which the world condemned, that made him see women in that bitter way. And some part of him, the part that didn't writhe in pain and anger, knew that that was a sad thing.

*

Buju and Cutty hooked up sexually at least three times a week after that initial encounter, almost always at Cutty's drum. Occasionally, when he was sure that Cynthia wouldn't be around, Buju would, out of bravado, try to bust a move with Cutty at his own gates, but Cutty always resisted him: the risk of being caught by Cynthia fucking with her boyfriend wasn't his idea of a turn-on.

Although Cutty and Buju never used the language of love or romance, only that of brotherliness and cameraderie, nonetheless something grew between them as the weeks passed that was more than just sexual healing, and something was set free in the world that others could see. It was like a crack of light breaking out between carefully-shuttered blinds, and it had many reverberations.

The most oblique of these was that for a while Buju, because he was happier, treated Cynthia better, so she too became happier and more bearable to be around. Also, and paradoxically, because he had a sexual secret to hide Buju was compelled to perform his relationship with Cynthia better, and to keep her sweet with romantic gestures that in some other, unimaginably free world he would have made to Cutty. He dropped talk of his babymothers and hinted that maybe he and Cynthia should formalise their relationship and get engaged. And if the sex between Cynthia and himself was increasingly abrupt and verging on the perfunctory, he imagined that she thought it was probably a worthwhile trade to get a man who seemed to genuinely care about her in every other respect.

Even so, it was difficult for Buju to live on two levels at once, and occasional spasms of rage would pass through him as he realised that he was pumping emotional energy that was rightfully Cutty's into his relationship with Cynthia because he had to release it somewhere. That realisation wounded him, and as a consequence at times he would turn on Cynthia and treat her badly. But even as he yelled at her and threatened to box her upside her head, and told her that she was too clingy and that a man must be free, the cold, calculating part of him knew that such actions served his purpose. Hinting at the engagement then keeping her on the back foot with threats of violence was the perfect way of making her reluctant to say yes to it. The ball was kept in the air.

At the same time Buju knew he was playing a dangerous game. His relationship with Cynthia wasn't a static thing; eventually it would have to go somewhere, up or down. He thought of breaking up with her but had a nagging, unreasonable fear that she would guess why. In any case, if he dumped her he would only have to find some other girl to be the emblem of his heterosexuality.

He admired Cutty for not feeling that need so strongly: Cutty's coolness towards women was almost a sort of courage.

Buju began to set aside a percentage of the drug profits to do something legit with, thinking perhaps he might get into some sort of business with Cutty, maybe something to do with promoting events or artists or tours, he wasn't sure yet. Cynthia was excited about Buju's plans, seeing them as symbolic of his desire to finally settle down and start properly supporting her.

'I could be your PA,' she said every chance she could. She liked her work at the nail parlour on the Goldhawk Road well enough, but she had larger dreams.

Cynthia even temporarily made her peace with Cutty, accepting that Cutty knew the music business and had contacts in that world.

Of course she didn't know that Cutty would be unable to draw on most of those contacts because of what had happened back in Jamaica.

Cynthia's best friend Sarah began hanging around Buju's drum. She was a sensual, fleshy, dark-skinned girl with a pretty face, a sharp mind and an earthy sense of humour, and it quickly became obvious that Cynthia was trying to set her up with Cutty.

Cutty flirted with Sarah in a careless way. Like Buju he knew it was essential that he do so in order to keep his heterosexuality beyond all doubt in the eyes of other men and women, and like Buju he had no particular objection to sex with a woman; it simply failed to penetrate to the core of him. When it seemed necessary to sex Sarah he did so, and if he was somewhat brutal about it it was because he was, fundamentally, indifferent. Part of him even despised Sarah for desiring him, for being so oblivious to the truth. The clinical, pragmatic part of Cutty's mind was secretly pleased when it got back to him from Buju via Cynthia that Sarah had found him 'too rough – but fuck, he can pump it, gal!'

Sarah's loose tongue combined with Cynthia's to spread the word around the estate that he was a roughneck punani-hound. Even his refusal to eat pussy reinforced his masculine rep: real men satisfy themselves; they don't worry about pleasing the woman outside of their own direct taking of pleasure.

Once that work was done Cutty dropped Sarah, saying that he needed freedom to play the field, and that a real man doesn't allow himself to be tied down by any one woman. His stone-cold dismissal of Sarah impressed the click, some of whom were having their own woman troubles at the time, especially Spin. It alienated Cynthia, however, and so Cutty ended up back where he had started, with her as an enemy.

Unwise though it was, he found himself unable to care.

Winter passed. Spring broke through, and the city turned from grey to green. Cutty was surprised how many trees there were: in winter there had seemed to be none. Gardens and parks became vivid with colour. There were more black people out and about, and white people looked less pasty and more attractive. In fits and starts summer arrived. Over the months Cutty's nightmares softened and faded. Although he still couldn't return to Jamaica, the police investigation against him there seemed to have fizzled out, and his fear of it reaching out to where he was living now receded. That seemed no more than justice: after all, those who knew what really happened, and that included the police, knew he was no murderer.

And the wrong done against him? He couldn't think about it, not yet.

Certain sounds and smells continued to give him flashbacks. One time he had been letting himself into Buju's flat with beers for the click, who were watching the Cup Final, and just as he opened the door a goal was scored and they burst out with throaty yells, roaring along with the crowd on Buju's widescreen TV, the sound of the mob on the television amplified by the powerful speakers Buju had wired into it. For a moment Cutty had been literally blinded by panic, terrible images flashing through his mind. He had staggered back as if he had been physically struck and dropped the six-packs he was carrying. Several of the tins burst on the concrete of the walkway, and for some reason that almost triggered tears. Fortunately he had managed to pull himself together before anyone saw.

Another time Cynthia had managed to burn popcorn in the microwave and the fatty, slightly woody smell had made his heart race and hysteria well up in him to the point where he had had to immediately leave the flat without any word of explanation: the feeling of lethal hatred arrayed against him was too intense for the possibility of words, even to Buju.

But just being in a country where pastors and Biblical moralists did not hold sway helped Cutty deal with those incidents, and the terror behind them. There were even laws in Britain supposedly making discrimination against men who preferred men sexually illegal, he heard, though he found it hard to imagine how that could work in reality, where it mattered, on the streets.

The idea of state protection was impossible for him to imagine.

In *The Voice* he read that the major music labels had agreed to stop distributing dancehall tunes with violently homophobic lyrics, and that made him feel strange. On one level he was, almost unexpectedly, elated, and yet on some deeper level he felt angry just as any other proud Jamaican might, that the voices of his countrymen were being suppressed by outside forces, by white gay men and their liberal allies. Moreover, the debate about so-called 'murder music' kept pushing homosexuality up into the public gaze, and any mention or representation of it, particularly in relation to black people, made Cutty deeply uneasy.

Buju was feeling the pressure too, and as a consequence both he and Cutty found themselves being more vocally homophobic than they had been before when they were hanging with the click, leading the abuse of 'dutty queers' to ensure that they themselves were as distanced from such deviants as possible. To act that way was a slow poison, and subconsciously they both knew it, but they couldn't stop themselves. There was a dead weight that pressed down on them both that was beyond their strengths to lift, that part of themselves that despised all out gay men for making a private matter public, for forcing a name and a judgement onto what did not need to be named and, without a name, could not be judged.

'Batty business,' Spin spat, kissing his teeth. He was reading in *The Voice* about the cancellation of a Vybz Kartel concert that had been scheduled the following month at the Hammersmith Apollo, following campaigning by the gay protest group Outrage.

'It say fear a violence di reason,' Cutty said, trying to sound disinterested, gesturing towards a paragraph to one side of the main article that listed a number of shoot-outs between concert-goers at other recent dancehall events.

They were sitting on a low wall in front of a 24-hour garage on the Goldhawk Road, waiting for Buju to pick them up. It was around two in the afternoon. 'They fuck up *everything*, man,' Spin grumbled, ignoring Cutty's observation. 'Fucking queers.'

'Yeah,' Cutty said flatly, feeling tired. 'Dem di problem wit everyting fi true.' The sun was glaring and it was humid and dusty and his throat was dry. 'You want a drink?' he asked.

'A Sprite, yeah? Thanks, man.'

Cutty wandered over to the garage shop to get some cans of pop. The wiry young Arab behind the counter watched him continuously as he drifted around the shelves. He took two cans, a Sprite and a pineapple Tango, paid for them, and went back out to the wall. He passed the Sprite to Spin.

'Thanks, man,' Spin said, popping the can and taking a swig.

'So you work tings out wit' Tracey den?' Cutty asked, more to be talking about something other than battymen and their wrongdoings than because he cared.

Spin kissed his teeth again, closing up the paper. 'She gives me a fucking brain-ache, man,' he complained. 'I mean you think going with a white bird is gonna be less trouble, right? I mean it's supposed to be easier cos they ain't put the same pressure on a black man a sistah will, you know what I'm saying?'

Cutty nodded.

'You don't check for white women though, do you?' Spin interrupted himself.

A small thrill of dread passed through Cutty's chest at the question, but he acted indifferent and shrugged. 'Is all good, man,' he said. 'Pussy is pussy.'

'Yeah, but I seen you don't look at 'em though,' Spin persisted. 'Like they don't do it for you.'

'But me no make no judgement 'bout what anyone else does though,' Cutty said coolly.

'That ain't what I meant, man,' Spin said.

'No?'

At that moment, and with the bass tube pounding loudly enough to make the street shake, Buju pulled up in front of where they were sitting. He was driving his latest purchase, his new pride and joy, a fat-tyred white Sportrak with ultraviolet underlighting, and was looking gangsta-lean in a white Nike basketball vest and three-quarter-length shorts, and his eyes were hidden by Raybans. He wore a navy bandana on his shaved head beneath an angled white leather baseball cap, 50 Cent style. Maxie had been sitting in the front seat alongside Buju, but automatically clambered into the back so Cutty could take it, squeezing in between Spin, who had just climbed in himself, and Gary.

Buju turned in the garage forecourt and they sped off up towards the West End. The sky was blue and vast, the sun was bright, the roof was off, Beenie Man was blasting from the speakers, and for a brief time they all five felt like the world was theirs.

They drove as far as Marble Arch. Buju found a meter on a nearby side-road, and they ambled up Oxford
Street to do the department and sportswear stores. The
pavements were choked with tourists and weekend
shoppers out with their kids, and the air tasted metallic
from traffic fumes. The click gave Selfridges the once-
over, taking in the usual designer stands – Tommy
Hilfiger, Armani and the rest – and the scent counters.

They had a silly, joking argument about underwear
at the Calvin Klein counter:

'A thong is *gay*, man,' Spin was saying. 'Going up
your arse like that.'

'Nah,' Gary said. 'A jock is gay. Cos it don't cover
your hole.'

'Fuck that, man,' Maxie said. 'I wear jocks.'

'So you know what that makes you.'

'Fuck you, man! You want a smack?'

'Boxers ain't gay,' Buju interrupted.

'What, you wearing boxers then?' Spin said, tugging
cheekily at the waistband of Buju's low-slung three-
quarter-length shorts.

'Trunks,' Buju said, slapping Spin's hand away.

'What 'bout you, Cutty, man?' Spin asked.

'What you wanna know for?'

'No reason.'

'Cos he's a queer, that's why!' said Maxie.

'Fuck you, man!' Spin spat back, real anger flashing
on his face.

'A brief, cut high on the hip,' Cutty said abruptly,
hoisting up his basketball top as if to reveal a concealed
weapon, to show the line of the waistband of his Calvin
bikini-brief raised high above the top of his baggy
shorts along one hip.

'Not boxers, then?' Gary said.

'Me need di support down dere,' Cutty said, grabbing the heft of his crotch. 'Cos a di weight.'

'So what the ladies like, you reckon?' asked Gary, flushing slightly.

'Is about what make you feel good about yourself,' Cutty said. 'If you feel attractive den dem will pick up pon it and respond.'

The others fell quiet then, uncomfortable at any mention of the fragility of male self-esteem, and went back to browsing the underwear section. Cutty was thinking of briefs he'd like to see Buju wearing: tight, low-cut, skimpy and constraining. He wanted to buy Buju a pair and see him wearing them. *Fi please me.* Cutty felt his dick stirring at the image his mind was creating, and tried to push it out of his head. His mind flashed on the idea of him and Buju getting matching tattoos.

'Let's do NikeWorld,' Buju said.

The others nodded agreement, and they left the store and made their way along to Oxford Circus. There was a press of mostly black youths milling around outside NikeWorld under the observation of beefy, uniformed security guards in mirror shades. Buju, Cutty, Spin, Maxie and Gary passed into the store to scope the new trainers, greeting a few familiar faces as they entered.

This was what they did most Saturdays. Afterwards they wandered down to the Trocadero, a mall located between Leicester Square and Piccadilly Circus, and hung out in front of its busy entrance. There they perched on the railings and chatted and fixed deals with the other mostly black youths who loitered there from the middle of the morning to gone midnight despite the constant police presence. They could move on, of course, but why bother? Wherever they went the police would follow, so why not at least be exactly where you wanted to be? And while they hung out they watched the tourists who constantly passed back and forth between Piccadilly Circus and Leicester Square, sizing them up for business.

Unlike most of the clicks who hung out around the mall Buju and his click never dealt drugs in the Square or the backstreets around it. There were too many surveillance cameras, and the police presence was too overt. Sniffer dogs were routinely employed by police-officers on foot, cute golden retrievers trained to simply sit down next to anyone on whom they smelt dope. That person would then be searched and arrested. Even so it was tempting because tourists, cheerfully believing the stereotype that all black men were drug dealers, while at the same time feeling invincible because they were on holiday, would come right up to members of the click and brazenly ask them if they had any dope or pills for sale. But Buju had judged that dealing in such an environment was a mug's game, and the others went along with his judgement. Still, they made contacts to cut deals with later, away from the most obvious streets, and they also hung out there because they enjoyed the buzz, the feeling that at any moment something extreme might happen: a raid that would send everyone scattering; a fight breaking out and leading to arrests; a street-robbery gone wrong leading to a knifing; a flirtation with some Dutch or Italian girl away from home and eager for experience. Sometimes, later in the evening, such a girl, by now extremely drunk, would be prepared to be fucked front and back by two youths simultaneously while standing in the shadows of a side-alley with her knickers round her ankles.

Buju preferred to deal further up in Soho around pub kicking-out time, to young people on their way to the many clubs in the area. Mostly he and the click sold E and ketamine, as well as some dope. The clientele they serviced depended on what night of the week it was. As tonight was a Saturday night the big clubs were G.A.Y. at the Astoria, and Heaven, which meant they would be selling to a predominantly gay crowd. For the first time Buju was taking Cutty into a gay environment.

After stopping at the Leicester Square KFC for chicken, fries and Cokes, they wandered up through a thronging Chinatown into the heart of Soho and an equally busy Old Compton Street. In addition to tourists, theatre-goers and bikers, overtly gay men were everywhere, provocative in tight tops or flamboyant open-necked shirts or even bare-chested, their talk loud, their hair gelled or shaved, sitting at cafés or wandering up and down the street, spilling out of bars and pubs onto the pavement, some cruising, some passing through, some in couples holding hands. They were all nationalities; some, Cutty noted, were even black.

On reflex the click magnified their swagger, seeking to assert their heterosexuality by giving off an atmosphere of threat, even though they knew they would have to turn their aggression down later to make their sales to these same homosexuals they so needed to despise.

It was the first time that Cutty had ever seen such overt displays of gayness out on the streets. Back home it would have been suicide. Back in Jamaica he had himself either made extremely discreet pick-ups on the streets of Kingston, always in an agony of anxiety that he was somehow misreading the other man's signals, or else, more usually, he had gone to house-parties. These were run by wealthy but of course still extremely closeted gay men he had got to know through the music business. The parties often degenerated – or evolved - into orgies, which were enjoyable and cathartic, but

always in the back of everybody's mind was the dread
of a police raid: the fear that the host hadn't paid off
the right officers, or had, without realising it, become
some political pawn who the opposition wanted to
bring down. And if that fear intensified the sex it also
corroded the humanity of those involved.

Many times at such parties he had heard the quee-
nier boys talking about snagging a British or American
or German boyfriend, a white partner who would take
them away from Jamaica, and with whom they could
settle in another country and feel safe as gay men, and
have wider options. It was understandable to Cutty that
these effeminate young men would be anxious to get
away from the island. It had never occurred to him that
he would end up having to flee himself because there
was nothing in his manner or appearance that gave
away his faggotry. He had watched the camp young
prettyboys fluttering around the few white men who
were invited to those house-parties high up in the hills
and despised them for being both unpatriotic and
deluded: he hadn't believed that things could really be
better anywhere else.

Even his previous visits to Britain hadn't changed
his opinion. But on those occasions he had never stayed
long, and he had always hung with straight, mostly
black men and women on the dancehall-bashment
music scene, and had gone to straight, mostly black
clubs and bars. He had avoided even the thought of gay
bars or clubs, and had resisted finding out if there were
any black or predominantly black ones he could go to:
just to know they existed might have been too strong a
lure, and the dread of going to one and then being
recognised there hung over him like some persecuting
Old Testament Jehovah.

When he wasn't doing business he was at his cousin's drum, spending time with his cousin's straight

mates and gals. Looking back at it now, he could see that his experience of London had been even more trammelled in than his life back in Jamaica.

Now, looking at these men holding hands out on the street as if it was their right, these male-male couples who were even able to sign partnership registers like normal man and woman, these gay men who could, he'd read, even complain to the police if they were harassed for their sexuality, made Cutty think that the prettyboys had been right all along: there could be a better life out there.

But even as he thought it he missed his homeland all the more sharply. He felt no freer here than he had there. This freedom he was looking at was for other people, not him; it was for the prettyboys who had to make a stand because they couldn't hide what they were. For a moment he hated them and he hated himself and he longed for the excuse for violence against somebody, anybody. For a moment a word, a glance could have set him off. But then the anger passed from him. He looked at the white boys with their bright marble skin under the sodium glare of the streetlamps, their hair glued up into glittering faux mohicans. Different skin colour, different hair texture, but underneath it they were the same as the boys back home. Strange to realise that he understood them so easily.

A fey, good-looking and very dark-skinned black youth with a shaved head and a steel rod through one eyebrow caught Cutty's eye. He was wearing a skin-tight, midnight-blue vest scattered with sequins, and low-cut combat fatigues that showed a band of Armani underwear and above it a flat, sculpted belly.

The youth gave Cutty a look that was hard to read, then looked away. Cutty felt both fear and anger at that look. Fear, that the youth would see him for what he

was, see through his façade and give him away to the
click. And anger because if he didn't, if he failed to see
the truth of Cutty, then he would surely see him as an
enemy. And Cutty could feel the sharpness with which
the eyes of other queens cut across his path, knowing
that they were waiting for the heterosexual him to
judge them, curse them out, maybe even physically
attack them. At that moment, despite having Buju at
his side, Cutty felt utterly alone: community is not
nothing. And he remembered the dark-eyed boys he
would smile at in those private rooms back home, and
the brief sense he would feel of freedom and belonging.

It was at one of those parties, in some pilastered,
marble-floored colonial mansion high up in the cool
hills above the city, that he had first met Sonny Hilton.

And now, on this street where men held hands with
men, the memories he had been repressing came
flooding back: Sonny, all in red, bandana knotted
floppily around his short, bleach-blond dreads, handing him an ice-cold beer. The two of them winding it up
in the middle of the vast tiled living-room, beneath
slowly-revolving fans, to the music of artists who
wished them dead. That had seemed like a small thing
then, behind those high walls and the other walls of
protection and privacy that money can buy. And that
particular evening they had felt a perverse sense of
double safety, because present at that same party was a
singer who had recorded one of those murder tracks to
which they were all then dancing, and he was currently
grinding his butt excitedly against the crotch of a
muscular youth who was known to be extremely well-
hung and exclusively a top. The world outside seemed
an artificial thing then, full of struck poses and empty
of reality.

Later, after they had given each other a hot and
sweaty release beneath orange trees and a vast, star-

strewn sky, Cutty had discovered that Sonny was a trainee sound engineer and had invited Sonny to work with him at Informer Sounds, his studio, which he was then just getting started. It was the first time he had worked with another man who he knew preferred men, and it was strange and exciting. Both of them had a laid-back, masculine style that was taken for straight, and both of them were adept at monitoring their interactions to keep any giveaway homosexual slippages at bay. As with Buju now it was an unspoken game that was both gratifying to play well and ultimately impoverishing to the spirit to have to play at all. And as with Buju the effort of repression generated a perverse side-effect: a growing desire to take risks.

At that time Cutty lived in a small, three-room apartment on the top floor of a two-story block that extended along three sides to enclose a gated courtyard. His studio, which was where he spent most of his time, was just around the corner, two minutes' walk away. The studio was a single-story concrete box of a building and sat directly on the street. Opposite it were a rum shop, an electrical goods store and a fish-shop. There were also several stalls from which higglers sold soft drinks, snacks and cigarettes.

The front of Cutty's studio was painted a vivid sky-blue, with the Informer Sounds logo, which was a large black-and-white 'I' filled in with red, next to the front door. Inside there was a small office space with a desk, phone, computer and refrigerator, and behind that the recording studio itself. A side-door opened onto a passage leading to an outhouse toilet and a neglected back garden dotted with banana trees. Around the garden was a high briese-block fence topped with coils of razor-wire. The front of the studio had a steel shutter that Cutty kept pulled down and chained when there was no-one there, though because it was a popular place for the local young bloods to hang out there was little danger of him being robbed: any thief would have to answer to the Lick Shot Posse, and they were more than happy to beat, stone, shoot or chop such a transgressor.

Cutty enjoyed having the young bloods around. They respected his hard man past as a drug-dealer, and even more than that they respected the fact that he was getting up out of a criminal situation and into a legitimate one. They knew the runnings, after all; the likely end of any man who got too deeply involved with gun and drug business and didn't know when to get out. And music seemed to them the key that could open a door into some other, better life, almost the only key – apart from sport - that they could imagine. And so they gravitated to Cutty's studio, and he would give them try-outs and cut demos for them, often on the never-never. They would protect his business, and he would give them hope.

The more reliable of the youths he gave work to: sweeping up or running errands; fly-posting new releases and events at which his artists would be appearing. It was often the only legitimate money they had ever earned. And he and Sonny found that they worked well together, gaining an increasing understanding of the way running a recording studio worked, and growing as they did so. Everything seemed to be going well for them.

Almost everything.

The one thing they lacked was privacy, and the absence of personal space was becoming increasingly exhausting and frustrating for them both. The young bloods of the Lick Shot Posse hung around the studio from the time it opened until Cutty pulled the shutter down in the small hours of the following morning. Back at home the fact that his apartment faced into a small courtyard meant that the neighbours in the apartments opposite his had all too clear a view of any goings-on in both his living-room and his bedroom. And even when blinds and shutters were closed windows tended to be left open, and sound-proofing was non-existent.

Sonny's situation was even worse: perpetually short of money, he was renting a room a few streets away in the house of a pastor and his wife, friends of his parents, and so had no privacy at all. Ironically Cutty and Sonny had sex more often at house-parties than in their own homes. And yet they meant something to each other. It wasn't exactly love, but it was something.

The night of terror that drove Cutty from the district, the city and ultimately the country took place the week after there had been a running gun-battle in the street in front of the studio. A posse from the neighbouring district, the Bruk Up Crew, had decided to challenge the Lick Shot Posse for ownership of the area, and had made an aggressive foray into the heart of Lick Shot territory one sweaty weekday evening, driving through fast in a cavalcade of black-windowed SUVs and pumping off bullets at random in the direction of any young male on the streets. Rankings in the Lick Shot Posse had returned fire as non-combatants dived for cover. Several of the posse had been wounded in the ensuing fire-fight, and one youth from the Bruk Up Crew was left dead on the still-warm tarmac not fifty feet from the front of Cutty's studio. After half an hour of sporadic exchanges of gunfire the police had arrived in force and the youths had melted away into the night.

Cutty had sheltered one of the wounded youths, a lanky lad named Dalton, dragging him quickly into the studio, pulling down the steel shutter just as the police arrived. Cutty turned out the lights, ignored the rattle of police batons on the grill and kept Dalton and himself out of sight of probing torch-beams. Dalton had left his revolver lying in the middle of the street, where the police picked it up. There was blood spatter from where he had been shot, but fortunately no conclusive trail to Cutty's door. Cutty bandaged the youth's wounds as best he could and, once the police had finally left, drove him over to Kingston Infirmary. He dropped Dalton on the corner to stagger up to the emergency room alone, and there tell whatever lies he would have to tell about how he came to be shot, and have a bullet extracted from what turned out to be his spleen.

Things had been tense after the fire-fight. Machetes were laid ready and guns were carried more frequently. The weather turned humid and heavy. Storms were forecast, possibly reaching hurricane strength. Tin roofs were roped down, shutters fastened and windows boarded. The police added to the tension in the district by suddenly appearing in force, descending on the area and conducting random searches, interrogations and beatings. This was politically motivated: there was the tourist industry to protect, and tales of gunfire in the streets of the nation's capital did it no favours. Action had to be seen to be taken, both at home and abroad. The weight of the weather, the threat of further gang violence, and the weight of the police presence pressed down on the sufferers.

Something had to give.

Then came the day when Cutty was due to record a track by a local youth about the ructions in the streets called *Pop Pop (Nigga Fi Dead)*. It was catchy, anti-police and anti-authority, and Cutty knew it would be a hit. He would take flack for producing it, but it would help put Informer Sounds at the cutting edge of the reggae scene. The singer's name was Baretta, and he was an associate member of the Lick Shot Posse. He had been performing the song at local dances to lively response from the audience, and recent events had increased its topicality.

The studio was hot and crowded with rankings. Sweat was running down the walls as Baretta, skinny and red-eyed, growled his lyrics into the mic, and the air on both sides of the glass was blue with ganja smoke. Most of the youths were at least a little drunk as well as extremely high by the time the track was recorded, and anticipation of the coming storm made everyone nervy and excitable.

Down the street a mobile sound-system had set up and a crowd had gathered to dance their troubles away, at least until the storm drove them inside and under cover. Behind the pulse of the music there was a suppressed stillness to the air. Youths from the posse would drift back and forth between the recording studio and the dance, barely-concealed guns tucked into the backs of their baggy, knee-length shorts.

Trouble was anticipated.

Finally the track was done. Cutty burned some CDs for Baretta to give away at the dance, slipping them into card sleeves with the song title and artist's name on the front, and the Informer Sounds logo and details on the back. Baretta and the rest of the youths headed off in the direction of the dance in high spirits. Cutty and Sonny said they would join them over there once they had locked up. A minute later and they were, suddenly and unexpectedly, on their own in the studio. The time was a little before midnight. They moved around each other in a businesslike way, not needing to say anything as they went through the routine they went through every night when they closed up. Then Sonny brushed past Cutty, playfully pushing his crotch against Cutty's butt as he did so. Seizing the moment Cutty turned and kissed Sonny hotly on the mouth.

'Me need a good hard fuck, man,' he said breathlessly, breaking off the kiss and staring into Sonny's hazy brown eyes, his dick thrusting to instant hardness in his shorts.

'Here?' Sonny asked, glancing round at the unlocked door to the front office, his voice thickening with fear and desire.

'Pull down di shutter an' turn out di office-light,' Cutty said. 'No-one will come in.'

Sonny vanished from sight. Cutty heard the metallic clatter of the shutter coming down. Then the office light went out. Then Sonny was back, and they were kissing again, hands exploring each others' bodies, caressing and gripping each others' butts as they ground their crotches together. They too were feeling the tension of the last few days, and both of them needed a release that was more intimate and intense than that to be had from dancing, drinking and smoking. They could have gone to the dance and hooked up with some girls and got some relief that way: pussy was better than nothing, after all. But tonight they wanted – needed – the real thing.

Sonny lit a joint and they shared it, blowing smoke into each others' mouths, letting curls of it slide lazily out of their nostrils as they kissed deeply. Cutty turned and flicked a few switches on the mixing desk and the raunchy beat of Baretta's *Pop Pop* filled the small room. Sonny laughed and they ground their hips together to the music, winding it up to the rhythm. As one they pulled off their string vests and danced chest to chest, heart beating against heart as hot skin connected with hot skin.

'Fuck me,' Cutty said throatily, turning and grinding his butt against Sonny's crotch. He tugged the buttons of his fly open and let his shorts fall to his ankles, then pushed his briefs down as Sonny reached round for a jar of Vaseline they kept on a small shelf along with a medical kit and other bits and pieces, supposedly for chapped lips or dry scalps. His stiff cock wagging, Cutty pushed his buttocks out and held them open, making his already receptive anal opening available to Sonny as Sonny greased his own erection. Sonny smeared a gobbet of Vaseline between Cutty's buttocks, sending a thrill through Cutty's body and making him groan aloud as Sonny's fingertips slid over his puckering sphincter. Although they sometimes used rubbers with strangers at the house-parties they attended – if the host provided them - they didn't use them with each other, not least because even to be known to possess rubbers – to be denying a woman your seed – could seen as suspect by the hyper-macho youths of the Lick Shot Posse.

Sonny placed the head of his large, stiff dick firmly against Cutty's greased arsehole and pushed his whole length up into Cutty's body in a single greedy thrust. Cutty gasped and his own cock bucked between his legs repeatedly, beading pre-cum as Sonny began to pump his hips against Cutty's butt. With one gold-ringed hand the grunting Cutty reached over to the mixing-desk and turned up the track until the walls were shaking with each thud of the bass-line.

Which was why neither he nor Sonny heard the studio's lowered but unlocked security shutter being slid up.

Which was also why Baretta and another youth had come back to the studio in the first place: to hear Baretta's hot new track being played full blast after the deejay at the dance had told them that he wouldn't play it for at least another hour. Hearing the music from the studio and realising it meant that there were people still in there, Baretta and the other youth had pushed the shutter back up and entered the darkened office.

And now they came into the mixing room, and

there was Cutty bent over the mixing desk being fucked up the arse by Sonny, his shorts round his ankles, his heavy erection wagging brazenly between his sinewy thighs as he took another man's cock up into his rectum and loved it.

'Battyman!' Baretta spat in hard-faced shock, mouth twisting with disgust, suddenly an absolute stranger. Cutty straightened up so abruptly that Sonny was knocked back against the wall behind him, his erection sliding out of Cutty's body with a shocking suddenness that made Cutty grunt and momentarily close his eyes.

'Raasclaat chichiman! Battyman fi dead!' Baretta snarled.

The blood drained from Cutty's extremities. Immediately the situation was a nightmare: what could he – could they – do? Run? To where? Kill? Could he kill? He was stronger than Baretta, stronger than the other youth too, and Sonny was tough, Sonny was a fighter, but there they were, stripped, with their shorts round their ankles, their flagging dicks exposed, caught in their shame.

'Go,' Baretta ordered the youth standing goggle-eyed next to him. Wordlessly the youth nodded and hurried out of the room. Cutty and Sonny could hear him shouting in the street as he sprinted off in the direction of the dance, yelling as if there was a fire: 'Battyman in di studio! Battyman in di studio!'

Baretta stared at Cutty contemptuously then lifted one hand and cocked a finger and thumb, making a pistol which he aimed at Cutty's head. He mimed pulling the trigger, then stepped back, and was gone from the room. *Pop Pop* ended. Outside a hubbub was already becoming audible above the sounds from the dance.

With frantic haste Cutty and Sonny pulled up their

shorts and buttoned them, and pulled on their vests. They had only moments to decide what to do. They had no guns, no machetes, just one baseball bat. Sonny took it.

'Di backyard?' he suggested.

'Razor wire pon di fence,' Cutty said. 'An' is too high anyway.'

'Lock di shutter?'

'Den dem a bun we out. Plus it haffi done from outside wit' padlock.'

They were already moving into the front office, which opened directly onto the street. 'We must run,' Cutty said, and they stepped out onto the tarmac.

Already youths were standing there in front of the studio, five or six of them, eyes both blank and bright with excitement. Two of them dangled machetes from their hands. One held a baseball-bat. Cutty didn't know them, but knowing them would have made no difference; in fact those who knew him would feel all the more betrayed and enraged by the revelation of his and Sonny's true nature as abominations.

People were milling down from the dance, keen to see who had been caught violating God's law, the law of the land, and the tenets of Leviticus, eager to see punishment meted out Old Testament style. Under the burden of that carnival of hate, under the burden of a single word, Cutty and Sonny were changed from people into objects, things that could be ill-treated without guilt, things that *deserved* to be ill-treated, broken, destroyed. One of the youths kicked at Cutty with a sandaled foot, catching him on the hip. It hurt, and Cutty was almost knocked to the ground, but he knew that if he fell he was dead and he kept his balance.

'Disya is bullshit, man!' he said loudly. 'Pure lies and foolishness!'

'Why Baretta lie so?' one of the youths challenged, and Cutty knew there was no answer he could give that would satisfy him.

Sonny, the baseball bat held out defensively in front of him, tried to make a dart for it, but a youth with a machete barred his way, spitting 'Get back, chi-chi man!'

A crowd was building now.

Sonny moved back, his eyes wild, neck and arms striated with sinew and pumped veins. He and Cutty now had their backs against the wall of the studio. Their chests were heaving, their hearts thudding.

'Bun dem!' a woman's voice shouted hysterically from some way back in the gathering crowd, and a bottle of spirits flew over Cutty's head and exploded against the bright blue front of the studio, sending shards of glass and whiskey raining down on him.

'Bun dem!' The cry was taken up and people began to press forward, surrounding Cutty and Sonny four or five deep on every side. Their once-familiar faces were now the faces of strangers, sharply etched in the yellow street-light with a laughing contempt, distorted with hatred, filled with a fascination that could only be expressed in violence.

'Bun di battyman!'

For all the strident urgency of the cry it was as if they were stoking themselves up, as if still there was a moment where no-one might cast the first stone that would make the rest so easy.

Then a youth Cutty knew came pushing through the excited crowd, a revolver in his hand. Alphonse, who sometimes swept up in the studio, who had a pretty smile and a shy manner.

Not tonight.

'Cut dem up!' a man's voice shouted.

Alphonse shoved his way to the front of the mob

and stood facing Cutty and Sonny, his face blank. He
raised a lanky arm, pointed the revolver up towards the
sky, and fired a shot heavenwards. Immediately the
front row of the mob surrounding them fell silent and
drew back a pace, opening up a circle where breath was
once again possible for Cutty and Sonny, uncertain of
which way things were going to go, alert to the fact that
they could be in the line of fire if any more shots were
let off, aware that the stakes had been raised from a
beating to a killing. Was it Alphonse who was ap-
pointed to be the executioner of God's law?

The silence radiated out across the crowd so now
no-one was shouting. A woman laughed, but her laugh
was cut short. Cutty and Sonny instinctively moved
forward a pace so they were no longer pushed up
against the wall. This brought them face-to-face with
Alphonse. His face was sweaty and his eyes were red.

'So you is a battyman fi true?' he asked Cutty in a
loud voice, as if he was a spokesman for the crowd. But
the question was rhetorical: Cutty could see there was
no doubt in his mind. Because why would anyone make
such a heinous accusation against a man who wasn't an
enemy unless it was the truth? But still he needed to
hear Cutty say it, still it seemed that there might be a
chance and Cutty knew he had to say – what? Something. Anything.

'Alphonse, mi bruddah,' he began, with no idea
what words were going to come out of his mouth, just
the sense that if he spoke, if they heard his voice they
might remember that he too was a human being, that
he was their neighbour, their friend -

'No use mi name you dutty-raas chi-chi man!' Alphonse interrupted, closing down the human connection between them with a curse.

The air was more humid and heavy than ever. The
storm was coming. Cutty fell silent. He and Sonny

stood still as statues, as if if they were still enough they might become absent or at least invisible. Could Alphonse shoot them, execute them, commit a double-murder in cold blood in front of a hundred witnesses?

There was a moment where perhaps the situation might somehow have blown itself out, but some youths further back began to chant a lyric by Elephant Man and the crowd took up the chant, and then Baretta came shoving his way through to the front like a boxer being cheered to the ring. He was holding a machete in his right hand and his right arm was tensed and ready. He gave Cutty and Sonny a look of venomous contempt, then he turned to face the crowd.

'Me did see dem at dem dutty business!' Baretta yelled. Then he turned back to Cutty and Sonny and killing was in his eyes. Alphonse watched him excitedly, as did the youths in the front line surrounding them.

'Cut dem!' voices called excitedly. 'Kill dem!'

Without hesitation Baretta drew back his arm back and, amidst a chorus of excited shouts and cat-calls, chopped at Cutty. The space was tight but moving fast as a boxer Cutty managed to jump back and evade the slicing blade. The weight and momentum of the machete-blow dragged Baretta off-balance, and before he could draw his arm back for another strike the youths behind him surged forward eagerly, and he, Alphonse, Cutty and Sonny were shoved up hard against the concrete front wall of the studio in a confused crush of sweaty, heaving bodies.

Punches and kicks rained down on Cutty and Sonny and a bottle was smashed over Cutty's head, cutting his scalp, concussing him and soaking his cane-rows in spirits. His vision blurred and he bit his tongue hard enough to taste blood but adrenalin surged and pounded through him in crashing waves, driving out pain, pitching fear to a place beyond fear. He flung up both arms to shield his head. Rocks clattered against the shutter above him, some dropping and striking him, most falling on his assailants, and the close press of attackers meant that there wasn't space for anyone to use a machete or even a baseball bat.

There was the sound of more bottles being smashed and as his head was twisted sideways by the press of bodies he saw between shoving arms and shoulders the glittering movement of a broken bottle being repeatedly thrust into Sonny's face, Sonny's beautiful face that he had kissed and caressed on this and other nights.

Cutty's sight went red as blood poured down into his own eyes from what turned out later to be a minor if messy cut on his scalp, and he fought back with renewed violence, elbowing and bucking against the hands that were trying to lay hold of him, knowing for sure that once they held him fast he was dead.

Somehow a fire suddenly flared up just to his right: someone had lit the whiskey that had been flung against the wall of the studio a few minutes earlier. Several people's clothing caught at once and they tried to pull back and beat out the flames but were unable to make the space to do so due to the shouting, laughing mob behind that was still pressing forward excitedly, eager to beat and kick and cut the battymen. The weight of the hatred was dizzying. Shots were fired, why or by who or at who Cutty couldn't tell at that moment, though later he would realise that they were triggered by the appearance of members of the Bruk Up Crew further up the street, and some of the youths at the back of the mob had peeled out to see the intruders off.

More shards of glass rained down on Cutty as further bottles smashed against the wall above his head. The kicks and punches of the men pressed up against him were ill-aimed but more and more of them were connecting, bruising and battering his sides, his thighs, his shins, his arms, his face, his chest. He didn't know if he could keep standing much longer. He tried to punch and kick back but there was no space to draw back an arm or a leg to get in a proper blow, and even if he did there were too many of them for it to do much good.

Then more shots were fired, and closer, and there was the sudden sound of several police sirens blaring at once and the rip of vehicles pulling up. Almost instantly the whole mob fell still. The chanting and shouting stopped. The blows stopped. The youths who had been beating Cutty pulled back from him and Sonny. Cutty leant back against the wall, his chest heaving, trying to claw breath into his lungs. Sonny was kneeling on the ground, his hands covering his face. Blood ran in scarlet rivulets between his fingers and down over the dark, dusty skin on the backs of his hands. Cutty wanted to go to him but he couldn't. He couldn't make the slightest gesture. He could barely breathe. His hands and arms were numb and heavy and his whole body ached.

Three police officers in uniform, all of them wearing sunglasses even though it was by now gone one in the morning, pushed through the silent crowd with batons. Behind them came an officer in charge, also wearing sunglasses, and he held a revolver up across his chest, cocked and fully visible. Beyond the crowd Cutty could now see that two police cars and a van had pulled up along the street from one direction, and a third car was blocking it from the other. Two officers stood by the third car, their hands resting easily on their holstered revolvers, monitoring the situation. The only hope Cutty and Sonny had now was that the policemen would arrest them: even if the officers dispersed the mob, if they simply let Sonny and Cutty go it would be almost impossible for them to escape the area alive.

'What is going on here?' the officer in charge demanded, shoving the front line of youths aside to reach
Cutty and Sonny. Those youths with guns quickly
shoved them into the waistbands of their shorts,
concealing them with basketball vests, moving back
into the crowd so as to be out of the officer's sight-line.
Sullen resentment was on their faces.

'Help us,' Cutty said thickly. 'Dem attack we.'

'Why?'

'Cah dem is battymen!' someone shouted from way
back in the crowd. There was a general noise of assent.

'Bring us in, mistah officah, sir,' Cutty said in a low,
urgent voice. 'Otherwise dem will kill we.'

'So is not gang business?' the officer said. 'You is
not members of di Bruk Up Crew?'

'No, sir. Me is a businessman.'

'Becah we will not tolerate gang runnings in this
district.' The officer was raising his voice so that
everyone in the crowd could hear.

'Take we in, mister officah, please,' Cutty repeated.

The police officer looked at him then as if for the
first time. Cutty saw his own tense, ashen face reflected
in the man's mirrored shades, saw the terror and
desperation there. He smelt the man's bitter aftershave
and his own rank stench. He smelt rum and wood
charring and blood.

'How you know dem is battyman?' the officer asked
loudly, keeping his hidden eyes on Cutty.

'Man catch dem in di act!' voices called in response.

'You is a battyman?' the officer asked Cutty.

Cutty's tongue clove to the roof of his mouth. His
bladder was clenched so tight he could feel a spasming
in his dick, itself wrenching back into his body in
agonising retreat. He couldn't answer. What good
would it do? None. And there was nothing he could
offer this man. 'Bring us in, mistah policeman, sah,' he

said again. 'Or dere will be murder so.'

'We is di gang unit,' the officer said. 'Disya is not gang business.' Without another word he turned and started to push his way back through the crowd. Cutty went to reach after him but the youths closed in instantly behind him, hard faces now triumphant.

The mob waited in a strange state of stillness as with swaggering leisureliness the policemen got back into their cars and the van. This took no more than a couple of minutes, but it felt like an eternity to Cutty. He stared ahead blankly. He had no thoughts in his mind. Not even death was a thought. But he sensed that if there was going to be a moment where something might be possible it would be at that exact moment when the engines revved and the cars started to pull away into the thickening night, in that handful of seconds where the mob would have to watch to be sure the police were really going, and before it could refocus its attentions on the two beaten battymen it had feared the policemen were going to remove from its reach.

Car-doors slammed. Engines started up.

The van went first, the three cars, sirenless but with their lights still rotating, peeling out a second later, turning in loops in the street. And it was as they turned that Cutty propelled himself forward with all his strength into the youths in front of him, most of whom were still craning their heads over the mob behind to see the police go and so not looking his way, punching and kicking and elbowing his way through them, adrenalin surging wildly again as he struggled at a slant towards where he thought the mob was thinnest. He could feel Sonny trying to get to his feet to follow his lead but in that moment's delay the advantage was lost and Cutty knew Sonny had no chance at all.

He could hear no individual voices or words, feel no

individual bodies, just the close, surging heat of the
mob as it flared up with instantly-rekindled rage. He
shouted and yelled his rage too as he thrust his way on
and staggered forward. He elbowed a youth wielding a
broken bottle in the face, breaking his nose, and the
youth's swing went wide and the jagged teeth of the
broken bottle slashed across the bare upper arm of a
girl in a sleeveless gold pantsuit. She screamed as her
smooth brown flesh opened like an eyelid to show pink
and white fat. A heap of people fell over each other in
the confusion. Some of those who had been further
back in the crowd hadn't seen Cutty or Sonny properly,
and so didn't know which of a number of possible men
were the battymen in question. They momentarily
turned on the youth with the bottle, shoving and
kicking him to the ground, and it was for that reason
that Cutty was able to force his way through to the
fringe of the mob and collapse on his hands and knees
onto the still-warm tarmac of the road beyond.

A split-second later he was up and running, sprint-
ing straight along the road away from the still-confused
mob as fast as he could. Then, as his brain started to
work again, he flung glances left and right, looking for
cover, for concealment. He knew Sonny had not
escaped; he knew the feet slapping on the tarmac
behind him did not include Sonny's feet. His heart was
pounding wildly as he staggered off down a side-street
and pelted down an unpaved alley without streetlights
lined by tin-roofed shacks. People who had heard the
sounds of shooting earlier stood about speculating as to
what was happening up on the main street, but he was
past them long before they heard the news. Not knowing whether he was fleeing gangsters or the police,
whether he was hero or villain, no-one tried to bar his
way. And then he was past the last few shacks and into
the darkness beneath the trees beyond. His blood

roared in his ears. He didn't slow his pace until finally he tripped and fell headlong into a shallow stream.

For a moment he was stunned. All the fight was knocked out of him and he sprawled like a dead thing, totally limp. The water forced him awake, however, and coughing and spluttering he dragged himself upright, took two uncertain steps across to the far bank, and collapsed again among the bushes there. He mustered just enough strength and sense of self-preservation to drag himself out of possible view, and lay still.

There was no sound of pursuit.

He peered out between the bushes. An orange glow was lighting up the sky. He knew it was his studio. His studio, his pride and joy, his baby, was burning. And Sonny? There was the sound of further gunshots. Was Sonny running?

Get outta di country, he thought. *Go a foreign.*

To do that he would need his passport and credit card and bank-books. They were back at his apartment. Would it be possible to get back there unseen? Had anyone who lived in the block gone to the dance? If they had, would they think to lead the mob back there to search for him? To wait for him?

He would have to take the chance: without passport and credit cards he could do nothing, go nowhere.

He felt sick and exhausted, but there was no time for anything but action, and the slightest delay could be fatal. His limbs were heavy with weariness and weak and trembling now that the adrenalin was draining away from them, but he dragged himself to his feet and started off at once, keeping as far as possible under the cover of the trees and bushes as he went.

Most a dem no know is me get attack, he thought as he left the shelter of the trees and slipped round to the deserted street he lived off, keeping to the walls and listening for the slightest sound of activity from the direction of the nearby main road where his studio was located. From where he was he could see smoke under-lit orange against the black night sky. He encountered no-one.

He unlocked the wrought-iron gate that led into the courtyard of his block and passed inside. As he was crossing the courtyard an old woman's voice called out from one of the ground-floor apartments, 'Cuthbert, is you?'

'Yes, Mrs Cumberbatch,' he answered, trying to keep his voice level. He prayed that the old lady wouldn't be able to see in the low light how he had been beaten, cut and dirtied up by the mob.

'Is wha' gwaan?' she asked. 'I hear gunshots and I can smell fire.'

'Is di Bruk Up Crew,' Cutty said. 'Dem did bust up di dance, you know.'

'Lord have mercy.' Mrs Cumberbatch pulled her baggy pink cardigan around her ample bust as though the night was chilly. 'Anyone killed?'

He answered with difficulty: 'Me na know. Is more dan possible though.'

'Di police come?'

'Come an' gone.'

She sucked her teeth. 'Once this was a decent neighbourhood,' she said, shaking her head. 'Well, goodnight, young man.'

She turned and went back inside. Cutty quickly climbed the steps to his apartment, slid the key into the lock and let himself in. He took a minute to change into a new white Nike tracksuit and trainers, then shoved all the cash he had to hand into his pockets, along with his passport, credit card, bank-book and other papers. Then he left.

Checking constantly that no-one was watching him, he went back up the road the way he had come and disappeared under the cover of the trees again. Once hidden in darkness he took a few minutes to gather himself, and to plan a way out of the immediate area. Once he was away from anyone who knew him he was reasonably safe. But he couldn't remain in Kingston: he was too well-known. And if he couldn't remain in Kingston then he couldn't remain in Jamaica. Cuthbert Monroe, the owner of rising music label Informer Sounds, had a face that was just that bit too familiar to remain at large and survive as a publically-beaten battyman.

Go a foreign, he thought. *Get away from alla dis. Dem cyaan touch me a foreign.*

Of course he didn't know then that within forty-eight hours he would also be the prime suspect in Sonny's murder.

The rare smell of wood charring in a barbecue or bonfire, the chanting of a football crowd drifting over from the White City stadium, images of bloody violence in films, these were the things that had given him flashbacks since he came to England. But this street, this London street of parading, unashamed battymen, took his emotions in a very different direction. He felt his heart breaking.

For himself. For Sonny.

Chapter Nine

'So what you think, man?' Spin asked. 'Seeing alla this batty business right out in the open like it's normal?'

'Me don't comfortable 'bout it fi true,' Cutty replied, clutching his real feelings to him and keeping his expression blank as two young Chinese men with bleach-blond spiked hairdos swished past him giggling, arm-in-arm in tight tank tops and platform sneakers. 'But dem de punters we sellin' to, right?'

'Yeah,' said Spin.

'And the customer is always right,' Maxie said facetiously.

'That's what professionalism means, yeah,' Buju said. 'Keeping your eye on the bottom line. On the dollars,' he added, seeing the smirks on Spin and Maxie's faces. 'So you reckon you can hack it in queertown, Cutty, my man?'

Cutty nodded. 'Yes, mi bruddah,' he said. 'I can handle it.'

Cutty wondered why Buju had brought him here, what game Buju was playing. Perhaps it was a game Buju was playing with himself. Perhaps he was playing out his own pain on this street just as Cutty was: seeing what he was, what he wasn't, and what he could become if he didn't resist this thing that beckoned to him: faggotry.

Just the idea of finding himself once again on the other side of the stares, on the other side of the savage judgement behind those stares, filled Cutty with horror and loathing and squirming dread.

He would rather kill than that.

'Is just business,' he said.

'See,' Buju said, clapping his hand on Cutty's shoulder and gripping it briefly, audaciously. 'My man here gets it. He don't let his moral judgement cloud his business judgement, you know what I'm saying? My bredren got *acumen*.'

'What's that,' asked Maxie, 'a skin disease?'

'Nigga is *hignorant*!' Spin laughed, tossing a styrofoam fast-food container into the gutter.

'Fuck you, man!'

'Why we no sell inside di club?' Cutty asked.

'They're CCTV'd out,' Buju said. 'Plus they don't let you wear baseball hats or hoodies or nothing in there no more. New regulations. Ain't practically nowhere you can deal they don't got your face on file.'

'So we get the punters on their way to join the line to get in,' Spin amplified. 'They like it cos they can get their buzz on before they even get through the door and we skip a whole heap a messy situations.'

Cutty nodded.

'Everyone cool?' Buju asked. The others nodded. 'Maxie, you take the queue for G.A.Y., yeah?'

'A'ight.'

'Spin and Gary, The Village then Heaven. You can go in The Village. And me and Cutty's gonna hit Kudos before it closes.'

'Kudos?' Cutty asked.

'Gay bar down Charing Cross way.'

The click touched fists and split up.

'Dem does ever arx you?' Cutty asked, as he and Buju made their way through a crowded Leicester Square down towards Charing Cross.

'What, man?'

'Why di focus pon gay clubs.'

'I tell 'em with queers there's less violence, less aggro. Except for the new shit about hats and hoodies there's no dress-codes cos whatever you're wearing it's a look, you know what I'm saying?'

'What 'bout us, man?'

'We're straight, man.'

'But.'

'But if they was doin' the look we're doin' it'd be like faggamuffin, yeah?'

'Faggamuffin?'

'Like raggamuffin. Dancehall stylee, you know what I'm saying? But faggot. Plus I tell Spin and them if they try and deal in straight places there's too much distractions, you know what I'm saying? Gals and that wanting freebies for favours. Then their boyfriends looking for a fight. I tell the click, keep it businesslike, yeah? Don't let no pussy lead you by the nose. We're here, man.'

Kudos was a glass-fronted gay bar that stood on a street-corner round the back of a church, St-Martins-In-The-Fields, just off Trafalgar Square. A little way along from it, on a stretch of pavement next to a covered market, stood a small statue of Oscar Wilde. Because of the warm weather the glass fronting of the bar had been pushed back along one side. A Beyoncé track was playing over the speakers. Patrons spilled out onto the pavement and stood in clusters, drinking and talking. Cutty was struck by the fact that perhaps a third of them were black.

Again he flashed back to the house-parties he had attended in Kingston. Again he almost felt a connection, but the publicness of the space blocked that connection.

'Let's get a beer, yeah?' Buju said. Cutty nodded and Buju wormed his way into the crowded bar while Cutty loitered outside, uncomfortably aware that the bouncer on the door was eyeing him intently. The bouncer, who was also black, was tall and burly, with a shaved head.

Cutty's hackles rose and confusion descended on him. Was he being scrutinised by this man as a), a dirty fag letting down the race or b), a potentially trouble-making heterosexual drug-dealer plying his criminal trade in a law-abiding gay bar? Violent thoughts flared up in Cutty's mind, but he pushed them down and worked to control his body-language so that he gave away nothing of what he was thinking and feeling.

And did these men, black and white and Asian, laughing and chatting and flirting with each other, seemingly oblivious to the bouncer's stare, did they feel they were – free?

As Cutty was wondering that, Buju returned with two ice-cold bottles of beer. He handed one to Cutty and moved him along so that they were out of the bouncer's sight-line. They clinked glass against glass, and drank.

It was a strange evening for Cutty, one of the strangest of his life: to be among these gay men, these black gay men and the rest, but not be part of them. To make eyes and return guarded looks that signified not sexual attraction but the hustle of business, the sale of small packets of illicit pills. One shaven-headed brotha in his fifties with a moustache and prison buff had come on to him, and Cutty had had to say, 'I ain't gay, man, just doing a lickle business, you know?' He had said it as easily as if it was a statement of plain fact, and he had felt hot and excited and cold and hollow all at the same time. But nothing had showed on the surface: through an act of will so ingrained in him that he was scarcely aware of it, he held his performance together.

And he believed that the mask was the truth, and that there was no face behind the mask.

By 12.15 the last loiterers were leaving the bar to hit the

clubs or catch taxis or night-buses home, with pick-ups or alone. Buju signalled to Cutty that it was time to move on: what business they were going to do there had been done. He texted the others and the five of them met up fifteen minutes later in front of the Leicester Square McDonald's.

By then the mood and composition of the crowds thronging the streets had changed: the older people and obvious tourists were gone, and a drunken hysteria had taken over. Low-lifes were more in evidence – junkies, prostitutes, rent-boys and derelicts; late-night crazies decked out in wild outfits that should have raised a smile but didn't because of the hardness of the faces of those who wore them; raucous girls and leery lads stumbling about pissed out of their brains, suburbanites on a drunken bender in London's legendary West End. The pavements ran with urine.

'Sometimes I reckon them Shariah motherfuckers got a point,' said Buju, pointing out a tearful, busty girl in a short skirt who revealed blotchy thighs and no knickers as she bent over and vomited wetly into the gutter, her equally drunk girlfriend trying to hold her hair out of the way. 'Drunk ain't pretty.'

'Got any skunk?' a skinny, German-sounding youth with dark eyes and tousled hair asked Cutty.

'We look like drug dealers to you?' Buju responded belligerently. 'Go on, fuck off! Fuckin' sket!'

The youth turned away with a bleary-eyed shrug of apology.

'Let's get out of here, man,' said Maxie. 'This shit is *tired*, you know what I'm saying?'

'So what, then?' asked Spin. His eyes were bright. None of them were ready for bed. Work was done: now it was time for play.

They ended up driving over to west London and going

to a blues off Westbourne Grove that was being dee-jayed by a cousin of Spin's. Soon they were alternating hanging by the bar, where they sipped beers, smoked weed and chilled to the music, and winding it up with a posse of fit, easy-going, scarlet-lipped sistas who wore nothing but skimpy bra tops, tight battyriders and spike heels, and who had jewels glittering in their ears, round their necks and in their navels.

Usually Cutty felt totally relaxed and at home at a blues. He knew what was expected of him, and how to perform his masculinity. But tonight he couldn't shake off a feeling of dislocation, and the horror of exile was strong in him. The familiarity felt like a fraud. He was aware that he was drinking and smoking more than he wanted to, more than was wise.

The deejay put on a crowd-pleasing track by Bounty Killer. A pretty girl with a long, straight, golden-brown weave who had caught his eye earlier grabbed at his hand with glinting talons. Fastened into each of her elaborately-detailed nails was a miniature gold ring.

'Dance with me, man,' she ordered.

Buju was already grinding with another girl, so Cutty let himself be pulled away from the bar and began to wind it up too. The girl was fit and firm-bodied. She wore plunging black lycra trunks embroidered with a spider's web of shimmering black sequins, knee-high boots, and a black sequinned bra that barely contained her full, thrusting breasts. Hazel contact lenses that could not dilate made her feline eyes look alien in the low light.

'So what's your name?' she asked him, leaning in close to be heard above the noise of the music. She smelt of vanilla and musk. Her lips were plum-dark and large, and they brushed his ear.

'Cutty,' he said.

'Well, hello, Cutty,' she said, pushing her voice

down low. 'I'm Estelle.'

'Estelle,' he repeated.

'That means 'star' in French,' she said.

He didn't reply to that. Her firm, hot body was giving him a hard-on. She kissed him on the mouth and he responded. If he fucked her tonight, he thought, it might make him feel better, it might silence something that was roaring inside him.

She wanted something too, he could tell: she had her own grief to blot out. After they had danced she didn't ask him to buy her a drink but instead took him by the hand a second time and led him from the blues. Not a word was spoken between them. The air outside was warm as blood. Nearby, almost directly under the vast flyover of the Westway beneath which the club was situated, a small park ran alongside a canal. There were iron steps running down from the bridge that rose over the canal to the towpath that flanked the park. Hand-in-hand Estelle led Cutty to those steps. Hand-in-hand he followed her down them and into the shadows below.

The gate to the park had been left unlocked. She pushed it open and they slipped inside. The outer part of the park was open grass and lit by the streetlights beyond the railings, but nearer the water it was bushy and tree-lined and dark. Estelle turned and looked at Cutty and her eyes were wide.

'I need a man,' she said. 'A real man.'

He didn't answer her. Real men don't justify. His dick was hard. He turned her round and pushed her ahead of him into the bushes. Then he stepped up behind her, gripping her waist and grinding his crotch against her full buttocks. After a while he reached round and tugged the front of her bra down, baring her breasts. She gasped. He fondled them curiously. They were firm for breasts but had none of the energy of a man's pectorals under his hands.

'Don't be so rough,' she complained breathlessly.

'You need it rough,' he said. He broke off from toy-ing with her breasts and tugged down her shorts. Embroidered beads and sequins snapped and fell from the skin-tight material. He took a moment to push his track pants and thong down to mid-thigh. His erection sprang up. He gripped it in his fist and guided it up into Estelle's hot wetness. She moaned as he pushed his rigid length into her vagina, and he began to pump his hips against her buttocks. He was both aroused and not. His dick was hard but he was elsewhere.

He was struck by the dully mechanical nature of what he was doing, and as he continued to fuck Estelle he became increasingly detached from what should have been an intensely intimate act. After what seemed like an unbearably long time he sensed that he was pushing her towards a climax. Or she was pushing herself towards a climax, with his body, his dick as the conduit for her need. He pounded his hips harder, faking a rising excitement in himself in order to get it over with as quickly as possible. He put his hand over Estelle's mouth as she began to cry out excitedly, frustrated to realise as he faked his own orgasmic grunts that fucking her hadn't answered his need.

Afterwards he pulled up his thong and track-pants and she tugged up her shorts and rearranged her bra, and they made their way back to the main road.

'So where you live?' he asked her once they were back on the bridge and standing under the streetlights again. It was the first words he had spoken to her since they had fucked.

'Harlesden,' she said.

He took her to a minicab office and waited with her.

'You got dollars?' he asked.

She nodded. 'I think I got enough,' she said. She

opened her bag and rummaged. He offered her a twenty but she shook her head without looking at him. 'I'm alright, yeah,' she said. 'Don't worry yourself.' She kept her head down, her long weave concealing her features, and angled her open bag away from him, shielding its contents from his gaze.

They wouldn't meet again, he knew. She had a man who she didn't want to leave, and even if she did leave him, she wouldn't want some roughneck raggamuffin like Cutty who didn't want her. She had just needed a moment of release with someone who didn't care, who was a stranger, who would vanish into the night.

He understood that. Normally he didn't understand women, at least not from their own point of view. It made him almost like her. In some other life he could have liked her a lot.

Half an hour ground by in silence. Then a short, plump Nigerian man came in. The controller, a heavy-set, bored-looking Indian woman, nodded in the direction of the waiting Estelle, and she and Cutty struggled up from the sweaty, uncomfortable shell chairs on which they had been sitting. The Nigerian man pointed to where his car was parked at the kerb outside. Cutty noticed the man trying to keep from eyeing up his provocatively and scantily-dressed fare, obviously afraid that any sign of interest on his part might incur the wrath of the man she was with.

Cutty saw Estelle to the waiting car like a gentle-man, taking her hand and helping her into the back seat, even pushing the passenger-door shut behind her once she had drawn her bare, smoothly muscular legs inside. The car pulled away. She didn't look back.

Once she had gone he began to walk slowly in the direction of White City and the estate. The streets were mostly deserted now. He wondered about Buju. Had he too copped off with the girl he'd been winding it up with at the blues? Had fucking that girl satisfied Buju any more than fucking Estelle had satisfied him? He glanced at his watch. It was nearly 3 a.m. He felt tired but restless. Would Cynthia be waiting up for Buju, he wondered, imagining her face set in hard lines, her eyes burning with resentment. Sometimes, Buju told Cutty, he deliberately allowed dramas to happen, letting Cynthia smell the pussy on him just to big up his rep as a cocksman.

'U still up?' Cutty texted him.

'Y,' came the reply a second later.

'U got compny?'

'N.'

'U want compny?'

'Y.'

Cutty was now at a bus-stop. By great good fortune a night-bus was speeding down the road towards him.

'C u n 20,' he texted Buju, flagging the bus down as he pressed Send.

Cutty climbed the stairs to the third floor of Buju's block and made his way along to Buju's front-door. He knocked on it softly, then, without waiting for an answer, let himself in with the spare key he still had. The hall was in darkness but a low light was visible under the living-room door. Cutty opened it and went in.

Buju was waiting for him, sprawled out on the white leather couch wearing only a Calvin Klein thong and Nikes, a red headscarf tied round his shaved head. His mocha skin gleamed with body-heat and his eyes were as deep and darkly open as Estelle's had been lacquered and inaccessible. They were fixed on Cutty as he put a joint to his full lips and dragged on it, all the while toying idly with one of his dark, protuberant nipples. He had heavy gold round his neck and wrists, in his ears, and glinting on his fingers. He smiled wickedly, letting smoke pour from his nostrils and between his teeth. The shape of him – his outlines defined by muscle not flesh – pleased Cutty. The smell of him – male musk and spicy cologne, not pussy and perfume – pleased Cutty. And the distended, jutting bulge in Buju's thong pleased Cutty most of all.

Cutty kissed Buju as he hadn't kissed Estelle: with genuine desire. He gripped Buju's chin and was sharply, excitedly aware of its masculine angularity against his fingertips. Their lips met hungrily. Buju's tongue pushed confidently into Cutty's mouth. Cutty's cock bucked painfully inside his own thong and he moaned with excitement. To let go of performance, to drop the façade, to finally just be himself, was a relief so intense it made something soar inside his chest.

They made violent love. Cutty tasted the pussy on Buju's dick just as Buju tasted the pussy on his. And he could taste that Buju hadn't come any more than he had come, that Buju hadn't gained his satisfaction from fucking a girl either, and that added to Cutty's excitement at being with him.

Curled around each other like an interlocking African carving they hooked back each others' knees to the armpits and ate each other out, tonguing each others' tensing sphincters greedily. Then they pulled back, each bending the other's heavy erection stiffly upwards, and began to pump their mouthes greedily on each others' aching rigidities, writhing and bucking on the edge of gagging as they repeatedly took each other's crowns to the back of their throats and beyond. And as they did this they slid greasy, Vaselined fingers up into each other, magnifying the oral pleasure as each man opened receptively to the attention of the other's hand. Cutty pushed his arse back eagerly onto Buju's probing fingers, and was surprised and excited to find he could take three of them to the knuckle without discomfort. This encouraged him to push a third greased finger up Buju and Buju grunted sharply but didn't resist, and a second later he too was accommodating three rapidly thrusting fingers as he pumped his mouth with increasing rapidity on Cutty's hot and pulsing erection.

They came almost simultaneously, Buju a second or two earlier, flooding Cutty's mouth with his hot, sharp-tasting excitement and relief, cutting off Cutty's breathing with his rigid, thrusting dick and flat, pumping hips, the constriction pushing Cutty over the brink too. Kicking and gasping he shot his load straight down Buju's throat. Then they slumped in a sweaty, exhausted heap on the slick, sagging leather sofa, finally able to breathe properly now they no longer had dicks filling their mouthes.

Carefully they withdrew their hands from each other. Cutty felt a sudden sense of loss as Buju's fingers slid out of his body, and he missed the warmth inside Buju's body against his own fingers as he too withdrew them. But finally he felt good.

They went to bed without showering or even brushing their teeth.

Outside birds were beginning to twitter. It was dark, but dawn was coming.

Chapter Ten

It was the first night Cutty had ever shared Buju's bed. After making love both of them had been too tired, and were taking too much pleasure in the simple fact of each others' physical closeness, for Cutty to ruin it by forcing himself to get up, pull on his clothes, and walk back to his drum alone beneath the heartless early-morning sun. So for once they risked being discovered: they gave in to defiance.

Still they had not been able to escape self-consciousness. Fear of an unscheduled breakfast visit from Cynthia – always on the alert for any evidence that Buju was cheating on her - forced both of them out of bed hours before they would rather have got up. And even though they shared a shower, and felt unexpectedly child-like and innocent in doing so, what should have been leisurely and romantic was rushed and perfunctory.

After they had showered and dressed Buju hurried to put the sheets in the wash while Cutty wiped down the leather of the sofa with a face-towel soaked in Dettol. The image of a criminal concealing a crime flashed into his mind.

No past no present no future, he thought as he wrung the towel out in the sink. At that moment he existed precisely nowhere.

Cynthia hadn't come knocking that morning, although later in the day she had turned up and picked a fight with Buju over the girl he had fucked after the blues. Apparently a girlfriend of hers had seen Buju and the girl winding it up and then leaving together. The girlfriend had texted the scandal to Cynthia right then and there but Cynthia had run out of credit on her mobile, so hadn't got the text until the next afternoon when she got a top-up.

'Or I'd of come round right then!' Cynthia had shouted at Buju. 'I'd of kicked in your fucking door in and fucking marked her! Fucking bitch, tryna steal my man! And you letting her lead you on like you got a ring through your nose!'

Cutty had witnessed the row impassively, but a chill ran through him at the thought of Cynthia turning up on the doorstep while Buju had three fingers pushed up his arse on the couch, shrieking to be let in. Even had they not answered the door, what if she had managed to peep in through a chink in the blinds and see a glimpse of the batty business going on inside? Just the slightest glimpse was all it would take to build a whole new hell for them.

He could see from the fixed inexpressiveness of Buju's face that the same fear was in him too.

For a second Cutty's mind flashed on grabbing Cynthia by the throat with both hands, pressing his thumbs down crushingly hard on her larynx, and choking the life out of her. The police, the courts, the social workers and the newspapers would all ask why but he would never tell them, and Buju would never tell them.

We would be safe.

He pushed the thought from his head and resolved to be more careful in the future. And yet even after that warning sign he and Buju continued to take risks. There was a masculine bravado to it, perhaps - a defiant assertiveness that both of them were secretly proud of. A covert proof that, as Cutty liked to say, 'We run tings. Tings no run we.'

But did he and Buju run things? He had to ask himself that question after they had carried out two more burglaries because, even though they had managed to pick unoccupied houses both times, and had come away with credit-cards and lap-tops, they had also felt compelled to fuck in every house they turned over. The obvious recklessness of what they were doing became too much for Cutty.

'We run tings, man,' he was forced to repeat to Buju during the second burglary, while fucking Buju hard, face-down on an antique four-poster bed. 'Tings no must run we.'

'What you mean, man?' Buju had asked, looking round hazy-eyed over his smooth, bare shoulder.

'Disya burglary business, it runnin' us, man. Is time we finish it.'

Reluctantly Buju had agreed.

Since that night when he had stayed over at Buju's drum Cutty had also insisted that from then on they go to his gates when they wanted sex. Buju had fallen in with his insistence easily enough: in Buju's drum they performed heterosexuality. At Cutty's they could be a little more themselves. But even there neither of them could put aside for long the pose they had spent their whole lives perfecting, any more than the other youths in the click could, even though they were straight.

Because underneath the pose they had nothing real to be.

It was a month later, a grey, overcast day in July, dull and humid, with spots of rain pricking the air. Dry gusts blew grit in Cutty's eyes and, despite it being supposedly the height of the British summer, the wind was chilly. He was heading down to the International Call Shop on Goldhawk Road to make his fortnightly call to his mother back in Jamaica.

There was a strangeness to his calls home because his mother never referred to the reason he was in England, treating his exile as if it was just an extended version of his previous business trips. However she did tell him, as if there was no direct connection, that the supposed investigation of Sonny's murder seemed to have fizzled out. After the first few visits the police had stopped coming to the house, and Robert had told her that because it wasn't gang- or drug-related the case was no longer considered a priority.

No other rumour seemed to have reached his parents about the truth of what had happened.

Yet.

Cutty's mother told him that Robert was bitter because he had been passed over for promotion for the second year running.

'He says it is because he is too dark-skinned,' she said. And it was true, Robert was extremely dark, taking more after his father than Cutty, who was slightly lighter. But neither Cutty nor his mother believed that that was the real reason Robert had been passed over.

'Well, perhaps next time,' Cutty had said diplomatically on their last call.

He closed the door of the booth behind him, sat, and punched in the number. After a couple of rings an unfamiliar woman's voice answered.

'A who dat?' Cutty asked, surprised and instantly uneasy.

'Well, who are you?' the woman asked in return.

'Well, I did want to speak wit' Mrs Monroe,' he said evasively.

'Cuthbert?' the woman said. 'Is that you?'

'Auntie Pearl?' he said, suddenly recognising the voice.

'Yes.'

Pearl was his mother's half-sister, but they had never been close: Cutty's mother had always considered her too worldly. Married three times, she was now living in sin with a younger man and worse than that, supporting him. The last Cutty had heard they had set up house in Negril, which was several hours' drive from the village where his parents lived. So why was she there now?

'Is your father,' she said.

'What about him?'

'Him did have a heart attack last night.'

'A heart attack?'

'Your mother is at di hospital with him dis morning.'

'It serious?' Cutty asked, a sinking feeling in his chest.

'Well, him collapse, your mother tell me. But apparently they will discharge him later today, so he can return home.'

At least him no dead, Cutty thought, feeling powerless and frightened and ashamed that there was nothing he could do to help. He gave Auntie Pearl his mobile number. It suddenly seemed ridiculous that he had been afraid for his parents to have it, or to call their home using it: childish paranoia. If he had given them his mobile number then his mother could have called him the moment his father collapsed. But what difference would that have made? None. Except that for a moment she might have felt less wholly alone.

'Tell mi mother she can reverse the charges,' he told Pearl. 'Arx her fi call me when shi get home. And tell she me a go wire she some money towards di medical expenses.'

He paid for the call, then went to the nearby international money transfer shop and sent his mother £200, which was all the cash he had to hand. After that he wandered the streets in a daze, his head full of thoughts of his father dying while he was thousands of miles away. This was the truth of his exile.

Cast out like a demon.

Eventually, needing company, he headed over to Buju's drum.

Mek me just see Buju.

He climbed the steps to Buju's floor. He had no idea who would be in, if anyone. He hoped it would be Buju on his own, but most likely either Cynthia or Maxie or Spin or Gary would be loafing about on the sofa as well, or maybe the whole lot of them. Sometimes Cynthia would even bring Sarah along. The idea of finding Cynthia there with Sarah was almost enough to make Cutty turn from Buju's door without even knocking. But then he thought better of it: if it did turn out to be just those two he would force himself to play nice with them and try to build a few bridges.

And right now any company was better than none.

He still had Buju's spare key but he knocked anyway.

No answer.

As he was hesitating on the step, half-thinking of letting himself in and waiting for whoever to turn up, there was the sound of feet in the stairwell. A moment later Buju appeared. His tall white leather baseball cap was riding high on the back of his head, he had a red bandana tied low and knotted dancehall-style over one eye, his biker's red-and-white leather jacket was pushed back off his shoulders to show off the smooth chocolate muscles capping them, and baggy, patch-covered jeans were belted under his arse, forcing a bow-legged roll into his stride. His smooth face was boyish today, and his lips split into a broad smile when he saw Cutty standing there. His manner was boisterous as he greeted Cutty with their familiar high-five lock finger-snap routine.

'Cutty, my man!'

'Buju, mi bredren!'

'Come in, yeah,' Buju said, unlocking the door. 'Come hang wit' me.' He pushed the door open and let Cutty enter first. 'You want a beer, man?' Buju asked, disappearing into the kitchen.

'If you got one,' Cutty answered, passing into the lounge. It was a relief to be off the streets. Reflexively he picked up the remote and flicked on the TV. The channel was Base. R&B was playing. Cutty watched as Christina Aguillera swivelled her hips to the beat in low-cut jeans and a sequinned bra-top. He didn't want to think about his father. 'So where di click at?' he called through to Buju, raising his voice as he raised the volume of the music.

'Maxie's visiting his mum, Gary and Spin prob'ly getting fucked up somewhere,' Buju called back. 'They supposed to be coming round later, but it's strictly BPT, you know what I'm saying? So it's like whenever whenever.'

He came through with two cans and handed one to Cutty.

'And Cynthia?' Cutty asked.

'Gone to the fucking sales, man,' Buju said, sounding irritated. 'That gal loves spending money on clothes and shit, man! She texted me she's gonna go over Sarah's after to show off what she blown her dollars on, then they're off on some girls' night out shit. So I guess she's gonna pitch up pissed come kicking-out time, looking to get sexed up.' He kissed his teeth and shook his head, popped the can he was holding, and took a sip. ' "Bitches ain't nothing but money and trouble," ' he added.

'Ice-T,' Cutty said, registering the quotation.

'The master.'

'Old school.' They touched cans.

They sat side by side on the sofa, neither close nor apart. The blinds on the walkway side of the lounge

were open. The sky beyond was leadenly grey but there
was a glare to it.

'Hurtin' my eyes, man,' Buju said. He got up and
went and swivelled the blinds closed. He returned to
the sofa and without another word or the slightest
hesitation straddled Cutty's crotch. His feline eyes met
Cutty's. His need was strong in him.

'Fuck me,' he said urgently.

Behind him a lithe, well-oiled Christina Aguillera
was now draping herself around a pole and tossing her
head back, straight blonde weave hanging heavy,
flanked by two other skimpily-dressed girls doing the
same.

'Fuck me like a bitch,' Buju said hoarsely.

'Dutty talk.' Cutty smiled broadly, caressing Buju's
large, firm backside through his white Calvin Klein
trunks, his erection lengthening rapidly inside his own
briefs as he did so. His need was strong in him too. He
knew this would help. He knew this was all that would
help. Buju reached back for the TV remote and turned
up the volume until the bass was pounding loud
enough to make the window-glass jar in the frames.

'Now no-one can't hear none of it 'cept you, my
bredren,' he said huskily, his eyes bright with desire.
'Fuck my arse deep, man. Slide that dick right the way
up me and fuck me till I come screaming.'

'Me jook you till you beg me fi stop,' Cutty answered
him. 'Den mi jook you some more.'

'I'll never arx you to stop, man!' Buju challenged
him excitedly.

Cutty peeled his vest off in a single movement, then
shoved his three-quarter-length shorts and briefs down
to his ankles. His erection sprang up and slapped
heavily against his lean stomach. This was what he
needed. This absolute involvement in the continuous
present that freed him from the horror of the past and

dread of the future. He sprawled back on the couch as Buju stood and quickly stripped, leaving on only his baseball cap and his old-school Hi-tops. He strode from the room, erection wagging, returning a moment later with Vaseline from the bathroom. Within a minute he was squirming his butt down onto Cutty's large greasy erection. Grunting and gasping Buju reached back with both gold-ringed hands and pulled his arse wide open, needing to take every last inch of Cutty's dick up inside his body, his own cock bucking and kicking and oozing precum as he did so.

In the humid half-light of the room they moved against each other to the heavy beat, groaning and gasping for breath as they rose up together towards ecstasy and release.

The building excitement of pumping blood, of arse pumping on dick, and the pounding of the bass enveloped them so completely that Cutty and Buju were barely aware of a block of chilly air moving forward into the lounge from the direction of the front door. It seemed like nothing, almost a relief in the closeness of the room, an unexpected flush of coolness and oxygen. But then behind the beat they heard the sound of the front door banging shut and a second later there was Cynthia, standing in the doorway of the lounge, her eyes open wide, her mouth open wide, bulging bags from her shopping trip hanging loose in both hands.

Buju pulled himself up off Cutty's cock with a sharp gasp and a grunt. There was an audible slurping pop. Cutty's cock slapped greasily up onto his belly, making him gasp too. Baretta's face exploded in Cutty's mind then, shattering his thoughts. And suddenly Buju was him and he was Sonny and a broken bottle was being jabbed repeatedly into his face. The exactness of the repetition of what happened before nauseated him like prophecy.

'You give she a *key*?' he growled incredulously the moment he could pull his thoughts together, struggling up from the sofa to a standing position, turning away from Cynthia to shield his greasy dick from her while he pulled up his briefs and buttoned his shorts, unable to think of anything better or more meaningful to say.

Buju's dick was already starting to sink down as he shifted nervously from one foot to the other, his eyes flicking between Cutty and Cynthia.

'A fucking key!' Cutty repeated.

'Just to let in the plumber one time, you know what I'm saying?' Buju said defensively. 'She never give it back, though,' he added, glaring at Cynthia accusingly.

'You're a fucking queer!' she burst out. 'All this time I was with a fucking gay and I didn't even notice!'

'I ain't no queer,' Buju snarled, bending down to tug on his briefs and jeans.

'Excuse me, but taking it up the arse looks pretty fucking queer to me!' Cynthia continued angrily as Buju pulled up his jeans and buttoned them.

Breathing heavily through his nose Buju didn't reply, but concentrated on buckling his belt.

'I told you, man, I ain't queer,' he said once he was done. His voice was more level now. Now he had some clothes on he was less afraid of her. 'You didn't see nothing,' he continued, trying to take control of the situation through sheer force of will, through the force of his voice. 'None a this never happened, yeah.'

'It fucking *did* happen,' Cynthia said. 'My man a battyman! Fuckin' hell! It's pure fucking *Jeremy Kyle*, man!' There was a look of contempt and bafflement on her face and a tone in her voice that oscillated between laughter and hatred. 'And you - ' She turned on Cutty. 'You ain't no better! Shoving your cock up where it don't belong! What a fucking joke!' she spat. 'Big man on the estate, the Don and his gangsta mate nothing but chichi men! Just a pair of cocksuckers taking it up the arse!'

Her voice was getting louder and louder. Behind her on the TV screen Christina Aguillera had given way to Lady GaGa. Cynthia's voice was loud enough to be heard over the music, loud enough to be heard outside the flat. Fear was in Cutty's chest, heavy and painful, an iron spike rammed into a lump of raw meat. He could only breathe with difficulty. Within that fear a rage was spinning, dazzling his eyes. He was aware of the slenderness of Cynthia's arms, the delicacy of her thorax. She was at least six inches shorter than him, maybe forty pounds lighter. He could lay hold of her and lift her up by the neck and -

'You better quieten down, sistah,' he said grimly, his face expressionless, his eyes stone.

'Or what, mister arse-fucker battyman?' she taunted, not yet feeling her danger. 'You'll hit me with your handbag?'

With a sudden violence that shocked him as much as it shocked her he punched her hard in the face, knocking her back onto her backside on the floor, sending her sprawling like a rag-doll. Tears of hurt and fury sprang into her eyes and he could smell the fear in her rising up as she struggled to her feet.

'Beating on a woman!' she shouted defiantly, her voice cracking but still loud. 'You think that makes you a man or something, Mister Cutty cocksucker?'

'Shut it, Cynthia,' Buju snapped.

'I ain't gonna shut it for you, Buju battybwoi!'

Then Buju had her by the throat, his face a sweaty mask of fear and hate as he saw everything he had slipping away from him fast. The veins in his forehead throbbed as he tightened his grip. Cynthia's pupils dilated and she started to choke. But then she kicked out, her sharp heel scraping down his shin, making

Buju cry out and momentarily loosen his hold on her. Still she was trapped in a corner, and had nowhere to go. She tried to beat him off as he grabbed at her arms, but he was too strong for her. He broke one of the spaghetti-straps on her top as he caught hold of her and closed his sweaty, muscular arms around her, pulling her too close to him for her to kick or claw.

'Make her silent!' Cutty ordered hoarsely.

'How, man?'

'Battybwoi!' Cynthia shouted in Buju's face.

'Fucking shut it,' Buju warned her through bared teeth. She spat in his face. 'What we gonna do, man?' he asked Cutty breathlessly, tearfully.

'Mek I tell you - '

Cutty strode from the lounge and through to the kitchen. A moment later he returned with a small, sharp knife, the same knife he had taken into the bathroom with him shortly after arriving in England, when he had planned to cut his wrists. His mind was blank and filled with redness.

Cynthia's eyes widened with fear when she saw the knife. With a strength born of a massive adrenalin surge she struggled and writhed in Buju's grip, getting herself just free enough to elbow and shove Buju away from her. Thrown off-balance, he stumbled backwards into Cutty, sending the knife flying from Cutty's grip and skittering under the sofa.

'I'm gonna tell everyone!' Cynthia shouted, darting out into the hall while Cutty, on all fours, groped about under the couch for the knife.

'Stop shi!' he snarled at Buju.

But Cynthia was already clawing the front door open by the time Buju leapt into the hall, and before he could reach her to drag her back inside she was out on the walkway. For a moment she was on all fours. Then she was up and running.

Buju hesitated on the threshold. Every nerve in his body was electrified. His chest was heaving. His heart thudded suffocatingly. But what could he do if he chased after her out into the streets? If he caught up with her and she started shouting shit out, what could he do about it? Shoot her a box? How would that help? What short of killing her would do any good at all?

And it was too late for that.

He looked along the walkway towards the stairwell. None of the neighbours had come out to see what was going on. At least that.

Torn by indecision, he turned uncertainly and went back inside.

He found Cutty pacing manically up and down in the lounge, the knife back in his hand. Cutty shot him a look so wild that for a moment Buju was afraid of him. The music was still pounding from the speakers that flanked the plasmascreen TV.

'You let shi go?' Cutty asked angrily.

'I couldn't drag her back in here in front of people could I?' Buju protested, picking up his vest and pulling it on. 'They'd of called the feds for sure.'

'So you let shi go to spread shi dutty lies!' Cutty snapped.

'What was I supposed to do, man?' Buju came back at him hotly.

Cutty shrugged irritably.

'Yeah, well,' Buju went on, his own anger flaring up too. 'And what was you gonna do, man? Put a blade in her? You was gonna do that for real? How was that gonna turn out?'

'Me na know, me na know,' Cutty said, still pacing. 'She don't must talk, man!' He gestured with the knife in Buju's direction. 'She must be silenced.'

'Yeah, yeah, she's gotta be shut up for real, I know that, man,' Buju agreed, putting up both his hands. 'But it's easier to say it than do it, you know what I'm saying?'

'And now shi gone!'

'It's fuckeries, man,' Buju said. 'Pure fuckeries. Her using that fucking key, man. Trust a sket.'

'Is you give her di key in di firs' place,' Cutty said coldly, coming to a sudden halt.

'Yeah, but – '

'So where shi go?'

'How the fuck do I know, man?'

'Use your mind, mi bruddah.'

'Sarah's,' Buju said. 'She'd go Sarah's.'

Cutty's eyes hardened. 'Den go dere, man. An' do what you can to shut shi mout'. Go now!'

Buju nodded, and ran from the flat.

Once Buju had gone Cutty began to pace backwards and forwards again, feeling the smallness of the room constraining him like a cage, trying to bring his breathing and heart-rate back under his control. His right hand, the one he was holding the knife with, began to tremble uncontrollably as the adrenalin started to drain from his body, and tears pricked at his eyes, hazing his vision. He blinked rapidly to clear them. Then he looked down at the knife and felt disgusted with himself for having even thought about using it. *Me no a killer.* Feeling suddenly profoundly weary, he went back through to the kitchen, returned the knife to the open cutlery drawer, then closed the drawer carefully. When he re-entered to the lounge he turned off the television. Silence closed about him in a fuzz of static. His nerve-endings felt raw.

What could Buju do or say that would shut Cynthia up, he wondered. He couldn't think of anything that would work, just as he hadn't been able to think of anything that would have worked that night when he and Sonny had been surrounded by a circle of hate-carved, moonlit masks that had once been the faces of their friends and neighbours.

Lord help me.

But God wasn't there to hear the prayers of chi-chi men. Cutty knew that. The divine rejection toughened him. He held up his right hand and stared at it until the trembling passed from it.

He needed to call Buju.

He fished his mobile out of his shorts' pocket but its screen was grey and blank, its fascia cracked from where he had fallen heavily onto it when Buju knocked him over during the fight. The battery fell from the back of it and hit the floor with a clatter. He picked the battery up and tried to press it back into place, but even when he eventually managed to clip the two pieces of the phone back together it still wouldn't work. It was fucked. He was fucked. He could feel sweat breaking out on his forehead. *Cyaan reach Buju.* What could he do?

Run.

He shoved the broken mobile back into his pocket and left the flat, yanking the door shut behind him but not pausing to double-lock it. His heart was pounding erratically again, and his head was buzzing. *Home,* he thought. *Go home.* In his own drum he would be safe. In his own drum he could think. Buju would come there.

Buju would come there.

Chapter Eleven

Once Buju was out on the streets his pace slowed. Nausea kicked at his gut and he stopped to lean against a lamp-post, sure he was about to throw up. He dry-heaved several times, tasting the acid tang of vomit at the back of his throat, but nothing came. He wiped a hand over his sweaty face, feeling ugly.

How could I of been so fuckin' stupid, though? He cursed himself for his recklessness. *What the fuck did I think I was doing? Right in my own fucking drum. I knew she had that fucking key. Why did I act like I didn't care, like it didn't matter, like nothing could happen?*

And now what?

He had said to Cutty that he was sure Cynthia would go straight to Sarah's but would she? She might go to her mum's, or her cousin's, or to some other friend's yard. And when she got to wherever she was going she would tell whoever was there what had happened: why wouldn't she? Buju's brain was whirling. All he could see was the edge of a cliff and beyond it a plunge down into endless darkness. Marked as a queer, a faggot, a chi-chi man, how could he live? How could Cutty live?

Sarah's yard was ten minutes' walk from Buju's block. She lived in a raised ground floor flat in a terraced house on a street that flanked the estate to the west. Buju found himself wishing that Cutty hadn't fucked Sarah over so nastily when he was seeing her. He wished – but what was the point of wishing now?

He arrived at Sarah's door without having managed

to think of anything to say to shut Cynthia up. It made no difference. He did what he had to do: he pressed the buzzer. Maybe Sarah would turn out not to be there. Maybe Cynthia had gone somewhere else. But that would solve nothing. Maybe other people were in there and they already knew the news. Other sisters, other brothers; other dons. Maybe she'd already texted everyone on her mobile and it was already too late for him to do anything. Maybe he was already a pariah.

He banged on the door impatiently. 'Sarah?' he called. 'You in there, gal?'

'Is that you, Buju?' Sarah's voice was muffled. She was apparently standing just the other side of the door.

'Let me in, man.'

'Is Cutty there?'

'No, he ain't. Let me in, yeah.'

There was the clatter of bolts being drawn back and the clunk of locks being turned. Then Sarah opened the door a crack and peered out, looking scared but feisty in a raspberry silk dressing-gown that showed off her generous cleavage. Her hair was up in a wrap, priestess-style.

'Let me in, man,' Buju repeated. 'I gotta see Cynthia.'

'She ain't here.'

'She *is*. C'mon, Sarah, man, I gotta see her.'

'The thing is - ' Sarah began. Then Buju heard a woman's voice from further inside the flat say something. He couldn't make out the words but he could tell it was Cynthia speaking.

'Cynthia!' he called, trying to look past Sarah. Sarah nodded in response to whatever the voice was saying, continuing to block Buju's way.

'Okay,' she said. 'If you're sure.'

'C'mon, man,' Buju said. 'Let me in, yeah.'

'Alright, then.'

But she didn't let him in at once. Instead she pushed her head out and looked up and down the street. Only once she was satisfied that Cutty really was nowhere to be seen did she stand back and open the door a little wider so that Buju could squeeze in past her. He stood in the hall while she locked and bolted the door behind him.

'So where is she?' he asked.

'In the front room,' Sarah said. She turned to him. 'Buju - ' She touched his arm. He looked at her then, and her expression was hard to read, but her touch was gentle.

'Yeah?'

'She told me what happened.'

Buju opened his mouth but no words came out.

'You do *know* what happened, yeah?' she asked, seemingly puzzled by his expression, her brow furrowing.

'Course I know, gal,' he said blankly, his mind increasingly confused by the way Sarah was acting towards him. 'But I still gotta see her.'

'I'll go first,' she said.

He followed her into the front room. Two pink-shaded lamps gave it a rosy intimacy. Cynthia was sitting on a striped yellow and pink sofa hunched over a mug of tea. She held the mug in both hands as if she was chilled to the bone even though it was July and the air was sweatily humid. He was struck by her physical delicacy, by her prettiness, by her disarrayed weave, by the iridescent bruise on her cheekbone, unexpectedly small, from where Cutty had punched her in the face less than ten minutes ago. Shame flushed through him. *She don't deserve this*. She didn't look up when he appeared in the doorway, and he was relieved not to have to try and meet her eyes. He didn't go into the room, but hung back in the doorway.

'That bastard,' Sarah said behind him. She slipped past him and went and sat down beside Cynthia, putting one arm round her and hugging her.

'What you mean?' Buju asked, not moving from where he was standing, the urge to run strong in him.

'I thought you said you knew,' Sarah said, looking up at him sharply.

'What you saying, man?' Buju pushed anger into his voice to cover his confusion. 'Don't yank my chain, yeah. Whatever you got to say, just say it, yeah.'

Sarah didn't answer him. Buju switched his gaze to Cynthia.

'Cynthia?' It was the first time he had addressed her. 'What you coming out with, gal?'

Cynthia kept on looking down at the mug she was holding.

'Your best mate,' Sarah said abruptly, and her voice was now angry too, 'your so-called best mate, he come round your drum this afternoon, didn't he?'

'So?'

'And Cynthia was there on her own, waiting in for you, wasn't she? And cos he was like your mate she let him in, didn't she? And – he raped her.'

Buju's jaw dropped. Cynthia looked up at him then with eyes as blank as a doll's.

'What you mean, he raped her?' Buju was still addressing Sarah although he was staring at Cynthia.

'What you think she means?' Sarah said, speaking for her friend. 'Look at her. He knocked her about and then he – '

'Don't, man,' Cynthia interrupted. 'Please.'

'Sorry, man,' Sarah said. 'But he's got a right to know.'

Cynthia nodded a brave little nod. 'I suppose,' she said. 'You got any more tissues, gal?' she asked, squeezing the one she was holding into a sodden ball.

'Sure,' Sarah said kindly. She patted Cynthia's hand and disappeared off to the bathroom in a rustle of raspberry silk.

'What you doing, gal?' Buju hissed. He knew they would only have seconds before Sarah was back.

'What you think I'm doing?' Cynthia snapped back, her voice compressed, her face tight and hard, her eyes bright.

'I don't fucking know, man,' he said. 'Spreading lies!'

'You want me to tell the truth then?'

Before Buju could reply Sarah returned, carrying a box of multi-coloured tissues. She handed it to Cynthia, who lowered her eyes again immediately. 'We were just about to call the police when you got here,' Sarah said, sitting back down beside Cynthia.

'No,' Cynthia said quickly, shooting her a look that might have had fear in it, or something else.

'Gal, I know it'll be rough,' Sarah said. 'But you've got to do it or he'll get away with it, and you know that ain't right. Am I right?'

Cynthia didn't reply at once. She was looking down once more but Buju could see the flicker of her eyeballs as she tried to think what to do. Sarah handed her the phone. Cynthia took it but didn't press in the number.

'Do you want me to do it?' Sarah asked gently.

'You ain't got to do this, Cynthia,' Buju interrupted, his thoughts flying in all directions at once. 'We can sort this without the feds being in on it, yeah. Between ourselves, yeah?'

'I don't believe this,' Sarah said, turning on him angrily. 'Your mate rapes your girl and you don't wanna do nothing but talk about it?'

'I didn't say nothing 'bout talk, did I?' Buju said sharply. 'I didn't say "Do Nothing", did I? I just said don't be bringing the feds into it.' He locked his gaze on

Cynthia then. 'So what you saying, gal?'

She looked up with flashing eyes. 'I ain't *saying* nothing,' she answered boldly. 'I'm telling the truth.' And she looked down at the phone and tapped in 999.

'Hello? Yeah, give me the police, yeah. My number? Um - ' She looked over at Sarah, who told it to her. Cynthia repeated it down the line, then waited. 'Hello? Yeah. My name is Cynthia Mitchell and – and I been raped.' Her voice cracked on the word. 'Yeah, it was someone who is known to me. No, he ain't, he's not in the immediate vicinity. I mean I don't think he is. Yeah, I got a friend with me so I ain't in actual danger right now, but – yeah. Okay. Okay.' She gave Sarah's address, and ended the call. 'They're sending someone over straight away,' she said coolly. 'To take a statement and that.'

'And do like a rape kit,' Buju said.

'What you mean?' Cynthia asked, fear flashing on her face for sure this time.

'Like for forensics, like for evidence in court an' alla that.'

'Oh, shit,' Cynthia said, turning to Sarah. 'Gal, I can't do nothing like that.'

'You got to be brave, Cynthia,' Sarah said. 'If they don't get evidence they can't prosecute.'

Cynthia nodded and fell silent, this time avoiding Sarah's eyes as well as Buju's.

They sat there, not speaking, waiting for the police to arrive. The seconds dripped by. Buju felt a kind of madness raging in his head. How long would it take the feds to show up, he wondered, and what would happen when they did? His bladder felt painfully full, and his guts churned from Cutty having fucked him earlier.

'I need to piss,' he announced abruptly, pushing himself away from the door-frame. He went through to the bathroom, locked the door behind him and called

Cutty on his mobile. It defaulted instantly to ansaphone. Buju was about to leave a message but then he thought better of it: if the feds got hold of it, it could be damning evidence of – what? Something suspicious, at least. No evidence was better.

He didn't leave a message.

He dropped his shorts, pushed down his underwear, sat and opened his bowels. He farted loudly and couldn't help visualising Cynthia sitting on the sofa in the next room, hearing the sound and thinking about the cause of it; remembering seeing her boyfriend, the man she had often said she loved, being poled up the arse by another man. If it had been him fucking Cutty, Buju thought, it wouldn't have been quite so bad.

He pushed the image from his mind and tried to think things through logically. Cynthia was accusing Cutty of raping her. That meant she couldn't tell anyone about Buju and him being battymen. That was good. Any evidence that there had been a fight, and that she had been beaten up, would be put onto the rape. That was good for him, but bad for Cutty. But then Cutty couldn't be convicted of rape when he hadn't had sex with Cynthia, and Buju hadn't either, not for at least a fortnight. If Cynthia obviously hadn't even been sexed up by a man lately, never mind raped, which he was sure was the reason why she didn't want to be medically examined, there couldn't be a case against Cutty. Although Cutty had hit her hard in the eye, to Buju's relief there didn't seem to be much swelling: it seemed a minor thing. A domestic. He could even cop to it himself. And without even thinking about it Cynthia had begun reflexively pulling her hair into some sort of order, making it look less of a state. Yes, the weave had become dislodged, but there didn't look to be any actual hair torn out of her scalp.

When the feds arrived Buju would have to play the

caring boyfriend. Cutty would spend a few nights in jail, but then he would get out and they would continue their relationship. It would be harder than before, of course, and they would have to be a lot more careful. He would have to be around Cynthia a lot more too, to make sure she didn't go running on at the mouth to Sarah or any of her other friends. He wasn't so worried about what his mates would think: in a dropped case of sexual assault the click would be more likely to side with Cutty, who they liked, than with Cynthia, who they thought was a drag. They would assume she led him on as she had led some of them on at various times, and had got her come-uppance for being a prick-teaser.

But in the meantime Buju couldn't reach Cutty to tell him what was happening. If the feds found Cutty before Buju could speak to him there was no knowing what Cutty might say to them. Buju couldn't imagine Cutty telling them the truth, not even to get off a charge of rape, but –

He stood, pulled up his underwear and shorts, and flushed. Could he get away with slipping out and trying to find Cutty to warn him? He could just go. But he didn't know where Cutty was. He might have gone back to his drum, he might be wandering the streets, or he might even have disappeared altogether.

The thought of that tore at Buju's heart, and per-haps for the first time he realised that he was in love with Cutty. *I gotta go to him*, he thought. But just as he arrived at that decision he heard the brief whoop of a police siren in the street outside. Peering through the tiny bathroom window he saw two police-cars pulling up in front of the house, their lights flashing. He called Cutty's number again. Again it defaulted to ansaphone.

'The feds are in on it,' he said, then hung up.

There was the sound of police radios crackling out in the street, then Sarah's buzzer sounded loudly. Buju rinsed his hands, splashed water on his face.

Cutty had thought he would feel safe back in his flat, with the door locked and bolted and dead-bolted behind him, but he didn't, he just felt trapped. He showered quickly and changed his clothes, trying to put a psychological distance between himself and what had just happened.

Suppose Cynthia hadn't got away, he asked himself. What then? Grim images of himself and Buju trying to work out ways of disposing of her body flashed through his mind. Could they have got away with it? Perhaps. But then he would have become what the Jamaican police had accused him of being: a murderer. His degradation would have been complete.

Suppose Cynthia ain't got away.

Could he have killed her? Could Buju have killed her? In the heat of the moment, perhaps. Perhaps everyone can kill in the heat of the moment. If he had had a gun in his hand he might have pulled the trigger when she started yelling, 'Battyman!' But afterwards? Clinically, pragmatically, like an executioner? He didn't think so.

Still, better a killer than a chi-chi man. Better a mortal sinner than an abomination. Soliders kill. War can be righteous. You can go to war for God. Man that lies with other man is nothing but an abomination. An enemy of God, of righteousness.

It was time to go. He didn't want to leave his new home, his new life. He didn't want to leave Buju, but what choice did he have? Once the news got out, and it inevitably would, he and Buju would have no reputation, and on the streets your rep was all you had. He had no other status, no other resources. He would have to go somewhere else, become someone else.

Brixton, he thought. *Me go a Brixton.* South London was big enough for him to hide in.

And when he was seen by someone who knew him - as he inevitably would be, in the end – with every week that passed it would matter less. It would slowly become some old rumour that he could push aside; a false accusation made by a spiteful girl he had once rejected. In England this would be possible in a way it wouldn't have been back in Jamaica. But for now he had to disappear.

And nobody know mi name.

It was as if the mark of Cain was upon him.

Again, he thought. *Again me run.*

With a crawling sense of nightmare repetition he shoved some clothes into a sportsbag and dug out his passport and bankbook from where he kept them hidden under one corner of the wardrobe in the bedroom. He threw some toiletries into the bag on top of the clothes and zipped it up, then shoved the passport, a roll of cash, some weed and a bag of pills into various pockets of the tracksuit he was wearing. He hesitated for a moment. Then he took the passport and bankbook out again and went through to the kitchen. Next to the cooker was a small air-vent. He carefully levered the grill covering the vent out of its frame with a knife, knelt and peered into the shaft beyond. Two copper pipes ran vertically up and down its length. He wedged the bankbook into the passport and slid the bulging document carefully between the pipes so it was held fast. Better that he couldn't be identified if Babylon caught up with him: that way they wouldn't be able to connect him with the murder back in Jamaica. They wouldn't be able to drag him back there. The only other identifying thing he had brought with him, the credit card, was long since maxed and discarded. He replaced the grill.

Back in the bedroom he pulled out his broken mobile and fiddled around with it again, trying to get it to work. This time he managed to get the battery to connect, and the screen lit up. The reception signal and power levels rose, and the symbol showing that a message had been left appeared on the cracked screen accompanied by a polyphonic flush of music. He scrolled to the number of the caller who had left it: it was Buju. Cutty tried to listen to the message but at that point the connection failed and the phone went dead. Cursing, he tried to get it going again, but this time he couldn't even get the screen to light up. He gave up, pocketing it to try and fix later.

He knew the message wasn't going to be anything good.

Time to go, he thought. He looked round the bare living-room one last time, and felt a tightening in his chest: he had been happy here. It had been a refuge. It had been home. And now he was a wanderer again. A refugee, working his way through the circles of hell. But was he working his way in or working his way out? He picked up his bag.

At that moment there was a loud thump at the front door, as if it had been kicked hard. Alarmed, Cutty stepped out into the hall.

'Police!' a muffled voice shouted from beyond the door. 'Open up!'

There was a second thump, heavier and more solid-sounding than the first, and the centre of the door split. The frame juddered and one of the bolts broke off and fell to the floor.

No no no.

The door was the only way in or out of the flat: no windows opened onto the internal corridor that led to the lifts and stairs.

Bag in hand, Cutty ran back through to the bed-room and wrenched open a French window that gave onto a tiny balcony, a joke balcony three feet wide and two feet deep that had rusty, waist-high iron railings around it. He slammed himself against the railings and looked down. Behind him the front door burst open, twisting off its hinges as it did so, and two officers in riot gear staggered in after it, carried forward by the weight of the pneumatic ram they had been using to break it down, the momentum sending them crashing to their knees. For a moment they blocked the corridor, keeping the other officers behind them from getting in.

Looking down, Cutty felt giddy: the flat was on the fifth floor, the ground at least fifty feet down, and there was nothing to break a man's fall except asphalt and concrete. A couple of kids were cycling about aimlessly in formless figure eights. From that height they looked like tadpoles milling in a pond. Cutty's mouth was dry as cotton. He heard a voice from the corridor outside the flat shouting, 'Go go go!' and the sound of four or five officers in riot gear shoving past their colleagues with the ram. He had only an instant to do whatever he was going to do.

Looking up and down the tower-block's height he saw that each flat on each floor had a balcony identical to the one he was leaning over now. They descended in orderly lines from the topmost floor to the ground like rungs on a giant ladder. If he clambered over the rail and let himself hang down as far as he could it might be possible for him to drop from one balcony to the next, and so work his way down to ground-level. If he took risks he might even be able to get to the ground before the feds could.

Without giving himself time to think he swung his legs over the rail, twisting his body round so that he was facing inwards, bracing himself with both feet on the balcony's edge on the wrong side of the railings.

The bag slipped from his grip and tumbled away into space. He glanced round at it as it spiralled down and felt instantly nauseous. He missed his footing on the balcony's edge, slipped, and had to wrap one arm round the top rail to stop himself following the bag's plunge, kicking out panickily as he did so. After a long, stomach-churning moment he realised that he would have to unfold his arm and get a grip on the railings with both hands to be able to lower himself down to the balcony below. He took a breath, unhooked his arm, and did so. Once the railings were in his sweaty hands he managed to get both feet firmly planted on the wall beneath the balcony and brace his body outwards. Then he began to move down slowly, keeping his movements controlled. Rust and corrosion tore at his palms and his arms ached. He inched his feet down the wall as far as he could while still holding onto the upright rails of his balcony, which was now above his head.

His heart pounding, Cutty glanced down. The drop to the next balcony was at least eight feet, more than his own body-height. The drop to the ground beyond if he missed the balcony was at least fifty feet. The balcony extended out only two feet from the wall. He would have to swing himself inwards as he dropped to make sure he didn't miss it. A kid's tricycle and a plastic chair had been wedged out there, along with some pots with dead plants in them; even if he did manage to land in that confined space he would probably break an ankle.

He had to try. In any case he probably didn't have enough strength left in his arms and fingers to pull himself back up to his own balcony.

At the heart-stopping instant he let go two pairs of strong, gloved hands laid hold of him, one gripping his right wrist, the other the collar of his tracksuit. For one stomach-turning moment he swung out slowly into the void, with only the counter-weight of the two men above him preventing him from falling. He kicked and struggled reflexively.

'Stay still,' one of them ordered breathlessly.

'Go limp or we drop you,' snapped the other.

Cutty closed his eyes and went limp. He let the two men drag him back over the railing. Already he was regretting running. Why hadn't he just stood there and fronted it out? This was Britain. Being a chi-chi man wasn't a crime in Britain. So he had hit Cynthia and threatened her, so what?

She must have told them about the knife, he thought: the feds wouldn't have turned out in force for a minor domestic incident like a box. He would deny using the knife and Buju would back him. She was jealous. It was understandable she would exaggerate under the circumstances.

It was painful being dragged back over the iron railings. The two policemen took little care and Cutty's right knee was banged sharply as they hauled him onto the balcony. They dragged him into the living-room and pushed him face-down onto the floor. Cutty grunted with pain as one officer knelt heavily in the small of his back while the other wrenched his already-aching arms round behind his back and cuffed him. The cuffs bit into his wrists, one of which, the one the officer had grabbed hold of as he'd been about to drop, felt like it was dislocated.

'Get the bag,' someone ordered someone in response to something he didn't hear. His head was twisted so his face was pushed into the side of the sofa and he could see nothing. The knee was removed from his back, but he could feel that a hand was gripping the links of the handcuffs and twisting them, forcing him to stay where he was.

'Let me up, man,' he growled.

'You'll stay exactly where you are,' the officer behind him said flatly.

'You are known as Cutty, and resident at this address?' another officer asked. The tone of voice was studiedly neutral.

'Me na say nuttin' to no rasclaat Babylon,' Cutty spat angrily, his voice muffled by the sofa fabric.

'You have the right to remain silent,' the voice went on. 'But if you do so and you come before a court then a jury may draw the proper inference from your refusal to answer questions when they are put to you. Do you understand?'

Cutty didn't reply.

'Do you understand?'

'What is di charge?'

'Sir, do you understand what I have said to you?'

'Yes, mistah officah, and me arx you, what is di charge?'

'Rape.'

Chapter Twelve

Despite the stifling heat of the July night, the walls of the cell they put Cutty in were clammy to the touch. There was a window but it was small and high up, had mesh in the glass, and couldn't be opened. Cutty stared up at it blankly. No thoughts were in his head except that he was now where he had most dreaded to be: in the belly of the beast. It had an inevitability to it somehow. He lowered his gaze to the door that was the only way in or out of the cell. It was iron, and painted a pale blue. In its centre was an observation slot. The slot was closed.

The feds had offered Cutty a legal aid solicitor when they brought him in two hours ago, and he had taken them up on the offer. Now he was waiting for the solicitor to show up. He was in no hurry, though: it wasn't like the solicitor could set him free.

Whatever happen dem no release I.

At first, in all the panic and confusion, his brain had shut down. But now, stuck on his own without distractions, he slowly began to think his situation through. And it was bad.

Rape.

So why Cynthia say he rape she? It didn't make sense to him. And had Buju found her, he wondered, and did Buju know about the accusation? Presumably Buju hadn't found her, and in the meantime she had come up with her lie and taken it to the police out of spite, knowing that Cutty would never exonerate himself by telling the authorities the truth about what he and Buju had really been doing.

Better jail dan dat.

He realised her true motivation then: she was getting him out of the way so that she could really get her
hooks back into Buju, who of course could not tell the
police the truth either.

How long was the sentence for rape? Five years?
Seven? With maybe a third off for good behavior. If he
behaved. And if they didn't change the rules in the
meantime. He would have to ask the solicitor.

A more troubling possibility entered Cutty's head:
had Buju in fact found Cynthia and told her to make
the accusation against him so that she couldn't accuse
Buju of committing batty business in the future? Would
Buju go that far to protect his rep on the streets?

Buju no betray me so.

But how many lovers had believed that, and been
wrong?

He got to his feet and went and banged on the cell
door. 'Mistah policeman! Mistah policeman!' he called.
'Me waan make phone-call!'

The officer on duty took his time over unlocking the
door and leading Cutty to a pay-phone right next to the
custody sergeant's desk.

'You got three minutes,' he said grudgingly.

'Me na have no money,' Cutty said, trying a helpless
smile.

The officer shrugged and turned back to his paperwork.

Cutty tried to make a reverse-charges call to Buju's
mobile, but it defaulted instantly to ansaphone, so the
operator couldn't gain permission from Buju to put
Cutty through so he could leave a message. Cutty
wouldn't have known what to say anyway: he needed to
actually speak to Buju.

The officer led him back to his cell and locked him
in again.

'Where's mi solicitor?' Cutty asked when the officer

drew back the observation slot for a final glance at him, allowing a belligerent tone to creep into his voice now the man was of no further use to him.

'He'll be here when he gets here, sir,' the officer replied.

And slammed the slot shut.

The solicitor, a smartly-dressed, diminutive Indian woman with a short bob and a brisk manner, eventually turned up at the station around one a.m., and was taken through to Cutty's cell by the same custody officer.

'I'm Jasmina Jalwar,' she said, extending her hand for him to shake.

'Cutty,' he said, taking it. It seemed tiny in his. She was pretty, he thought, though slightly puffy round the eyes from the heat and likely from working a long day. She looked round at the officer, who was hovering in the doorway.

'You can let the custody sergeant know that we won't be ready for him for some time,' she said.

The officer gave her a look of thinly-veiled contempt. 'You know what he's in here for, don't you?' he said. He had a fat, pasty face and his sleeves were rolled up to reveal pale, hairy forearms.

'Naturally I know what the charges are,' Jasmina Jalwar said crisply. And she waited, not moving a muscle, keeping her eyes on his, until the officer withdrew.

Once he had gone Cutty scooted his butt along the bunk to give Jasmina Jalwar room to sit alongside him as there wasn't a chair in the cell. She sat. From her briefcase she produced a pad on which she had already made a number of notes, and a pen. These she set on the blanket between them.

'Well?' she asked.

'Well?' he echoed.

'Let's start with your name.'

'Cutty.'

'Full name.'

'I don't waan disclose it.'

'Right,' Jasmina Jalwar said. 'Okay. But the thing is, unless you can prove your identity to the satisfaction of the court the magistrate won't grant you bail. You'll remain in custody – in prison - until the trial, assuming the police press charges. And that would be a matter of several months, maybe longer.'

'But dem could drop di whole ting.'

'It's possible. It depends on the evidence. What is the evidence?'

'Nuttin'. Cah me na do nuttin'.'

Jasmina Jalwar glanced down at her notes. 'According to her statement, Ms Cynthia Mitchell was beaten and raped by you earlier today.'

Cutty snorted derisively but made no other comment.

'So you're saying her claim is untrue?'

'If it 'appen she musta arx for it,' Cutty countered.

'What do you mean, "if"?' Jasmina Jalwar asked sharply.

'What I say.'

Jasmina Jalwar put down her pen. 'Okay,' she said carefully, 'the situation is, I'm here to represent you legally. To offer you legal advice during your interview with the police and to make sure that that interview is carried out appropriately, and also to represent you when you're charged, which will probably happen here later tonight. What I'm not here to do is play games. I'm not here to tease a story out of you. I'm not a journalist and you're not a celebrity. It's past one a.m., I'm extremely tired, and I'm not going to beg you to let me help you as if you're the one doing me the favour.

I'm on a salary. You're being charged with rape.'

Cutty looked at her thoughtfully, weighing up this woman who was being so direct with him. 'Well,' he said eventually, 'if you call mi friend him cyan produce ID.'

'Give me his number,' Jasmina Jalwar said. 'I'll call him first thing in the morning. What form will it take, this ID?'

'Passport.'

Will he be able to bring it either here or straight to the magistrate's court by nine a.m.?'

'Yes.'

'Do you understand what will happen at the magistrate's court?'

'No.'

'The magistrate will confirm the charges the police have made against you. You will enter a plea, presumably of innocent to those charges. That's all a formality, but the magistrate will also decide whether to grant you bail or not, and that isn't. Do you have a UK passport?'

'No.'

'Do you have assets here?'

'No.'

'Is there anyone who can stand surety for you?'

Cutty hesitated. Could he count on Buju? 'Me na know,' he said uneasily. 'But is possible. Dere is someone.'

'And this would be the same friend whose number you're going to give me?'

'Yes.'

'And you're here legally?'

'Yes.'

Jasmina Jalwar made a few brisk notes in her pad. 'Now,' she continued. 'You knew Cynthia Mitchell before she made the accusation against you?'

'Yes. She di girlfriend a mi bes' friend Buju. Is his

number I give you 'bout di ID an' alla dat.'

Jasmina Jalwar frowned. 'So if, as you say, nothing happened between you and Ms Mitchell, why do you think she's made this very serious accusation against you?'

'Cah she come on to me an' me turn shi down,' Cutty said. 'And when me tell Buju 'bout how she carrying on so right in front a she, she get vex an' attack I.'

'And so you - ' Jasmin Jalwar flicked back to the notes she'd made before coming to Cutty's cell. 'Punched her in the face.'

'I ain't proud of that, you know.'

'But you didn't have sex with her?'

'No.'

'Either then or at any previous time?'

'No.'

'And when the police question your friend Buju, who you've just told me witnessed the entire scene, he's going to confirm your story?'

Cutty hesitated, cursing himself for not having thought faster in the first place: if only he'd worked his story out quicker then he might at least have been able to leave it as a message on Buju's ansaphone. Then Buju might have heard it before speaking to the feds, and then he and Buju would be coming out with the same answers to the same questions when the police interviewed them. They would be off the hook. He pushed his jaw forward and didn't reply to Jasmina Jalwar's question.

'If your friend's not going to confirm what you're telling me,' she said, 'you might as well come clean about it here and now because he's being interviewed by the police as we speak. There's no point in you telling them something in the course of your interview that your friend will have already contradicted.'

'He will confirm it,' Cutty said.

'Are you sure?'

'If him tell di truth.'

'Okay.' Jasmina Jalwar flicked back a few more pages. 'There's also the secondary matter of the drugs possession charges, although they won't be the focus of this interview.'

'What you talkin' about, drug charges?'

'You were seen to throw a bag containing quantities of marijuana, ecstasy, mephadrome and methamphetamine sulphate from your balcony when the police entered your flat.'

'Dem kick down di door!' Cutty interrupted angrily. 'Bruk it down!'

'And the drugs?'

Cutty kissed his teeth. 'Me na know nuttin' about no drugs,' he said. 'Maybe someone did chuck di bag off a higher floor an' it fall down di same time me come out pon di balcony. Pure coincidence, man.'

As he was saying this Cutty was trying to recall whether anything personal to him had been in the bag along with the drugs and clothes that were just clothes that could belong to anyone. He didn't think so. 'Your friend's number?' Jasmina Jalwar asked. Cutty gave it. 'His surname?'

'Staples.'

'And your full name?'

He hesitated, but there was no use in concealing it now, murder investigation back in Jamaica or not. 'Cuthbert Stevens Munroe,' he said.

Jasmina Jalwar made a note of it. 'I should warn you right now, Cuthbert, that because of the seriousness of the charge, even if you can prove your identity and have someone to go surety for you, you're unlikely to make bail.'

'Cutty.'

'I'm sorry?'

'Cutty,' he said. 'Not Cuthbert.'

'Right. Well. Are there any questions you want to ask me at this stage?'

'I waan fi speak wit' Buju before me rap wit' di feds.'

'That won't be possible.'

Cutty kissed his teeth again.

'Anything else?'

He shook his head.

'Then I think we're ready for the interview.' Jasmina Jalwar stood up and banged smartly on the cell door with the flat of her hand. A few moments later the officer's pasty face appeared at the slot.

'My client is ready to be interviewed,' Jasmina Jalwar said.

Chapter Thirteen

C utty's face was a mask as he took his seat opposite the two detectives who were going to interview him. They were both heavyset white men in cheap suits that had sagged in the heat, and they looked tired. One was dark-haired with a moustache, the other fair, balding and clean-shaven. Jasmina Jalwar took the seat next to Cutty's. The detective with the moustache set down a folder he had been flicking through and pressed the 'record' button on the tape-machine that sat on the desk between them.

'July 27th,' he began, leaning forward slightly towards the microphone. 'I'll start that again,' he corrected himself. 'July 28th. Interviewing Cuthbert Stevens Monroe in connection with a complaint of rape and assault by Miss Cynthia Annette Mitchell. It is now...' he glanced at his watch. ' 1.17 a.m. Present are detectives Foster and Collins and duty solicitor Ms Jalwar.' He sat back slightly in his seat and looked Cutty over. 'Well, then,' he began.

'Is you Foster or Collins?' Cutty interrupted.

'I am Detective Sergeant Foster. This is DS Collins.'

'So.'

'Now, Cuthbert - '

'My name is Mistah Monroe. You cyan call me dat.'

Foster sighed. 'Alright, then, *Mister* Monroe, why don't you tell us your version of what happened this evening.'

'No version. I will tell you di truth.'

'Everyone's telling us the truth tonight,' DS Foster said drily.

'Cynthia lie,' Cutty said angrily. At once he felt Jasmina Jalwar's hand on his arm, a light warning touch that said, *Volunteer nothing.*

'That would be Cynthia Annette Mitchell, would it?'

Cutty didn't answer. If only he knew what Buju had told the feds. 'So what she say, den?' he asked evasively. He at least needed to know what exactly she had accused him of doing.

'She said you assaulted her and raped her in the flat of her fiancé.'

'She don't got no fiancé,' Cutty said sharply.

DS Foster opened the folder in front of him but didn't look down at it. 'A Mister Brian Staples,' he said.

Brian. Cutty had never know Buju's given name. *Fiancé?* 'And what does Mistah Staples say 'bout alla dis bullshit?' he asked.

'Never mind what *he* says,' DS Collins broke in, speaking for the first time. 'What have *you* got to say?'

'Me no rape she.'

'Yeah, well, we're going to need a bit more than that,' Foster said, tapping his pen on the table.

'You did have sex with her though, didn't you, Mister Munroe?' said Collins. 'Yesterday afternoon?'

'No-one have sex wit' she,' Cutty said.

'Not according to the medical evidence.'

'Is what you saying?'

Foster leafed through the folder. 'The fact is that you did did have sex with Miss Mitchell, didn't you, Mister Monroe?' He looked up and fixed his bright blue eyes on Cutty's.

Cutty started as he realised: *someone sex shi dat afternoon.* 'No sah,' he said emphatically. 'I was not intimate wit' she.'

'Oh, you may have used a condom, but you had sex with her alright,' Collins said. 'No question.'

'So you found the condom that you're claiming my client was wearing during the alleged assault?' Jasmina

Jalwar queried.

'We have Ms Michael's statement that a condom was used,' Foster said smoothly.

'So that's a 'no', then.'

Jasmina Jalwar made a brisk note. Irritation flickered over the two detectives' faces.

The realisation flashed into Cutty's mind: *Cynthia was cheating on Buju! But who with?*

'If we could swab Mister Monroe's genital area that might resolve - ' Foster's voice trailed off as he lent forward again and took in Cutty's clean smell. He sniffed theatrically. 'You showered?'

'Yes.'

'After you saw Ms Mitchell?'

Cutty shrugged.

'Note that interviewee shrugged assent in response to my question,' DS Collins said. The tape in the recorder spooled slowly on.

'Showering in the afternoon on this exceptionally muggy day is hardly probative,' Jasmina Jalwar said drily.

'We'll be taking an oral swab for DNA comparison in any case,' said Foster.

Cutty was hardly listening. His mind was whirling. Someone had fucked Cynthia just before she had turned up at Buju's flat. He, Cutty, had punched Cynthia in the face, and that must have marked her. The rape charge might stand up. And if they found out that he was the subject of a murder enquiry back home then he was really fucked. But what was Buju's story? Buju's story would make all the difference.

Maybe, Cutty thought, *I could say Buju find out shi cheat pon him wit dis whoever-he-is man. Den is Buju punch shi in di face cah him lose him temper cos a dat. And me say in front a shi dat he should dump shi. So she accuse me a raping she so she cyan get me outta di way and win Buju back.*

He was tired, the room was airless, and he couldn't work out whether that was even a plausible account of what could have happened. It certainly wasn't the one he had told Jasmina Jalwar ten minutes earlier. But then she was working for him not the feds: wasn't she honour-bound to be on his side whatever he came out with?

But what *had* Buju told the police? Did Buju know that Cynthia had had sex with another man that day? And if he did, did he find that out before or after he had spoken with the police?

'So what exactly did happen at Mister Staples's flat then, Mister Monroe?' Foster asked.

'Well, it was a domestic situation, you know,' Cutty said carefully, avoiding the detectives' eyes.

'Between?'

'Mister Staples and Ms Mitchell.'

'Carry on.'

'I went to visit Mister Staples. He is my friend. And when I arrive they was having a argument.'

'What sort of argument?'

'Well, dem did raise dem voice.'

'But not physical?'

'Not at dat point.'

Both detectives leant forward slightly now he was telling them what they wanted to hear. He wondered what would happen if he stopped right now and refused to say anything more. Would their case just collapse in a jumble of conflicting accounts?

What did Buju tell them?

Another thought occurred to him then. Had Cynthia said he raped her in the bedroom or the living-room? If she'd said the bedroom, fine, there was no possible evidence there. But if she'd said the living-room then the police might have swabbed the couch for samples of DNA, and they might have found – well, something - some fluids from his love-making with Buju they could somehow use against him.

But if they had found anything like that then they would have already said so, wouldn't they?

Wouldn't they?

'So when did things become physical?' Collins prompted.

'Arx Mister Staples.'

'I'm asking you.'

Cutty wavered. He could tell the story he had told his solicitor back in the cell. He could tell the story he had just thought up. Both of them made sense on their own terms. But what had Buju said? If he guessed right then Cynthia would be discredited and everything would work out fine. But a mis-match would look worse than saying nothing at all. Eventually he decided that he just couldn't take the chance.

'Me na have nuttin' more to say,' he said.

'Your client understands that his refusal to answer our questions and account for his actions satisfactorily may be used against him in court?' Foster asked Jasmina Jalwar. Evidently he assumed that Cutty's sudden stonewalling was part of a pre-arranged strategy on his solicitor's part.

'May I have a moment alone with my client?' she asked.

Foster considered for a moment then nodded. 'Of course.' He checked his watch. 'Interview suspended 1.47 a.m.'

'What are you doing?' Jasmina Jalwar asked once the two detectives had left the room. Her tone was sharp.

'Me no rape di gal,' Cutty said. 'Me no sex shi. Is someting else a gwaan.'

'What?'

'I cyaan tell you.'

'And the story you told me before?'

Cutty shrugged.

'Look,' Jasmina Jalwar said, 'if you don't account for what happened last night then you will be charged with rape, no question about it.'

'So what Buju say 'bout di situation?'

'I don't know. But even if I did I'm not allowed to coach clients, so I couldn't tell you.'

'Den me cyaan say nuttin' more to di feds.'

Jasmina Jalwar informed the detectives that Cutty would refuse to answer any other questions they might put to him, and the interview was abandoned. DS Collins and DS Foster took him from the interview room to an office on an upper floor where several other policemen in plainclothes worked at computers. Bar one light-skinned black officer, all of them were white, and all of them were men. The lighting in the room was fluorescent, and cruel. They looked him over as he stood there.

'So this is him, then,' said one.

'Let's get it over with,' said another. 'I should've been off an hour ago.'

'Where's the sarge?' asked a third.

'On his way.'

They fell silent. Something started to grind out of a printer in one corner of the room, but no-one attended to it. Cutty was glad to have Jasmina Jalwar at his side.

In one corner a fan on a desk whirred, slowly turning back and forth on its stand. The thick air smelt of sweat.

'My client would appreciate a seat,' Jasmina Jalwar said.

'He can stand,' the shortest of the officers said flatly, not even looking at her. He was the one who had spoken first.

A uniformed officer in his fifties came in through swing-doors behind Cutty and came up so he was standing just behind Cutty's right shoulder, out of his line of sight.

'You are Cuthbert Stevens Munroe?' he intoned.

Cutty glanced back. The man had cropped hair and was looking down at a clip-board. 'Yes,' he said.

'Cuthbert Stevens Munroe, you are charged that on Wednesday, 27th of July, you did rape and feloniously assault Cynthia Annette Mitchell.'

'I am not guilty.'

'That will be for the court to decide, Mister Munroe. You will be taken to the local magistrate's court in the morning, where a trial date will be set and the matter of bail will be discussed. Do you understand?'

'Yes.'

Cutty was then fingerprinted and photographed, and a swab was taken from his cheek. A swab from the tip of his penis was requested, but he refused to submit to it once his solicitor had told him that he didn't have to.

'Your refusal may be used as evidence against you,' one of the officers reminded him. Still he refused. He was returned to his cell.

There he made arrangements with Jasmina Jalwar. She tried several times to reach Buju on his mobile, to arrange to go with him to Cutty's flat in the morning to collect Cutty's passport, and to see if he would be prepared to stand bail for Cutty. Each time she was sent straight to ansaphone, and eventually Cutty had to ask Jasmine to go to his flat herself and get the passport. That meant he had to tell her where he had hidden it, which made him feel foolish and look guilty, but with it he could at least establish his identity and thus have the possibility of bail.

It must have been after 3 a.m. when she finally left him. He lay back on the bunk and closed his eyes, hoping to snatch a few hours sleep before dawn rolled around. He was exhausted, but his churning brain refused to let sleep come for at least another hour.

He was woken at 6 a.m. and, after being given a greasy breakfast of bacon and eggs in his cell that he was unable to face eating, he was handcuffed and led to a police van standing in a covered yard at the rear of the station. He was put inside the van along with six other men, each of them silent, introspective and unshaven, and driven to what turned out to be the local magistrate's court. He felt unwashed – he had only been given a couple of minutes to empty his bladder and splash water on his face before being taken to the van - and was hard-eyed from lack of sleep. Shame was strong in him. What would his mother and father think if they could see him now? He hadn't had a cigarette since before he and Buju had had sex the day before, and he found himself drumming his fingers restlessly from nicotine withdrawal.

After a journey of about fifteen minutes they arrived at the courthouse. They were unloaded from the prison van and led to cells in the basement of the building. There they were uncuffed. They sat three to a cell. No-one said a word to anyone else. After an hour had inched by a short, hefty woman in the uniform of a prison official came to Cutty's cell door.

'Cuthbert Munroe?'

Cutty looked up.

'Solicitor,' she said, unlocking the door. 'Follow me.'

It was a relief to get out of the cell. One of the other men in there, a drunken derelict, had stunk so strongly it had turned his stomach. Cutty was led to a stuffy, featureless room with No Smoking signs on every wall.

Jasmina Jalwar was there waiting for him. She looked rumpled, as if she too had slept badly. She told him that she hadn't managed to reach Buju, but had sent her assistant round to Cutty's flat, and had got hold of his passport.

Cutty was returned to his cell. To his relief the drunk was gone. After a further hour's wait he was taken up and brought before the magistrate.

To his surprise no-one wore gowns or wigs, and the procedure, which he had expected to be somehow ritualistic and long-winded, was brief and peremptory in tone. His name was called, he gave his address to the magistrate's clerk, and was told that he was being charged with rape and actual bodily harm. He entered his plea: Not Guilty. He was then informed that, due to the seriousness of the charge, the case would be heard in a crown court. He would be expected to attend the crown court in a week's time. There a date for the trial would be set.

'I am now prepared to hear applications for bail,' said the District Judge, looking over at Jasmina. 'Miss...' he hesitated.

'Jalwar,' the clerk supplied blandly.

'Miss Jalwar.'

Jasmina made what Cutty could tell was a formulaic bail application. She had Cutty's passport, and could therefore prove his identity, but it didn't help. It was possibly even counter-productive, as it enabled the representative from the Crown Prosecution Service to argue that since the charge was serious, and Cutty was a foreign national who had no assets in the UK and no-one to stand surety for him, he would be likely to flee.

'Moreover,' the CPS lawyer went on, even if Cutty didn't try to evade justice by absconding, he knew where his accuser lived and was well known to her, and so was likely to pose a threat to her safety. 'There is every reason to believe that as well as intimidating her he may attempt to dissuade by threats or bribes other witnesses from testifying against him. Therefore bail should be denied.'

The District Judge concurred, and Cutty was remanded to Brixton Prison until the case was brought to trial. No trial-date was scheduled at that point: that would happen at the crown court a week later, but Jasmina told Cutty that he would certainly be in jail for three months, quite possibly more.

Alone and friendless he was handcuffed and taken down. He was led to an underground parking area where other detainees waited, and put into a secure van. The air inside was sharp with despair and tainted with fear. A slender black boy with baby dreads and vertical lines shaved through both eyebrows was trying to look tough and hold back tears, his jaw moving restlessly. Cutty wondered what manner of foolishness he had committed to wind up in there. A shaven-headed white youth in a tracksuit who stank of whiskey and had small cuts all over his face stared down wordlessly at his sovereign-ringed hands. His knuckles like his face were cut and chipped. Other older men, black and white, sat in silence, passive, emoting nothing: they knew the drill, and wasted no energy on fear or hope. Cutty nodded to the black men although he didn't know them, and they nodded back at him. The black youth shot him a nervous look as he settled in his seat and Cutty gave him a nod too. Gradually the van filled up. Once it was full they waited there for a further hour without any explanation why. Then a driver and two guards appeared and the van set off.

It was surreal to drive through the city a prisoner. He felt himself capable of great evil.

Chapter Fourteen

Brixton Prison was a vast, grim, brick-built Victorian edifice. It sat surreally among streets of regular houses, as if it was as ordinary and unremarkable as a shopping centre or leisure complex. Perhaps to the people living in those streets it had become invisible, being the preserve of the damned alone, and nothing to do with themselves, the law-abiding. Cutty's spirits sank to zero as the tall gates swung open and the van passed inside. It was like being swallowed alive.

The van pulled up. The two security guards who had been sitting up front got out and unlocked the rear doors. Cutty and the other prisoners clambered out awkwardly, their hands still cuffed in front of them. They were led through to a reception area, where they were finally uncuffed. Along with the others Cutty was formally inducted into the prison and signed forms saying that he wasn't suicidal or otherwise mentally ill, nor was he a drug addict. Then he was strip-searched. He had to spread his buttocks but he wasn't searched internally. His clothes were searched for drugs and concealed weapons then returned to him: being on remand he didn't have to wear prison uniform. His jewellery he did have to hand over, however.

After that he and the other new inmates were taken to the hospital wing. There he had to give urine and blood samples to a stolid Nigerian nurse. These, she informed him, would be tested for the presence of drugs and sexually-transmitted diseases, including HIV. Finally he was taken to his cell.

There, having nothing else to do, he studied a booklet of prison regulations he had been issued with at his induction. To his surprise it included advice on how to make a formal complaint if a prisoner felt he had been ill-treated by the prison staff.

Cutty found his whole experience of entering the prison oddly neutral and bureaucratic. Unlike in Jamaica, where a punitive, thuggish mentality tended to be overt among the guards, in this jail the staff were almost solicitous in manner, more like social workers than warders. But the locked doors were the same. The petty rules were the same. And behind their apparent manner the guards were the same mixture you would get anywhere: the few who meant well and the rest; the jobsworths, the outright sadists. The prisoners too were the same as prisoners everywhere: a random assembly of the lost and the weak, the cunning and the stupid, the amiable and the vicious, the guilty and the innocent, the redeemable and the truly evil.

Cutty's cell-mates arrived, both of them also on remand. One was a burly white man with a shaved head, bright, staring blue eyes and a Union Jack tattooed on his chest. The other was a scrawny white youth with a severe stammer and a heroin twitch. Being on remand, and so supposedly just passing through the system, they were given little consideration by the authorities, and were packed in three to a cell. Those who had been convicted slept two to a cell, while lifers got a cell of their own.

In addition to space and privacy, work was a privilege those on remand were not entitled to, so they had nothing to do to kill the time until their cases came before the courts. Mostly they sat in their cells, bored and frustrated, brooding on their upcoming trials. Mingling with the convicted was discouraged.

Cutty's cell-mates alternately depressed and appalled him, so he spent as much time out of the cell as he could. He was, however, careful to keep himself to himself when he was out on the wing, and he told no-one what he had been charged with. He knew that rape was not a crime that brought a man kudos with other inmates. Because of the many years he had spent around drug dealers, addicts, and the hard-faced youths of the Lick Shot Posse he knew how to carry himself inside, and he showed no fear of either the other prisoners or the guards. He had mastered the cool ease of a hard man, and both inmates and guards recognised that quality in him and treated him with a certain amount of circumspection.

Even so, fear was with him always. It was a fear larger and more all-encompassing than the simple fear of physical harm. It was the fear that this was his future: years, possibly even decades of rotting away behind these walls and bars for a crime he didn't even commit. And what then, once his sentence was served? Inevitable deportation back to Jamaica. And once he was returned there perhaps he would even have to stand trial for Sonny's murder and even be convicted of it. And in Jamaica life meant life. Or death.

Unlike the Mother Country Jamaica still had the death penalty for murder. Or would that charge be dropped but he would still find himself pointed out as a battyman pariah, an anti-man with the faggot mark of Cain upon him and no money to build protective walls around himself? Either way his parents' shame would choke him like a physical thing.

Of course his parents didn't know he was in prison. Not yet. And he would do anything he could to stop them learning that he was behind bars. But his mother would already be wondering why he hadn't called her to see how his father was doing after his heart-attack. If she had tried to call him on the number he had given his aunt then she would have been diverted straight to ansaphone because the number was for the phone that had got wrecked in the fight with Cynthia. His mother might have left any number of messages on that phone already, Cutty thought, messages which he couldn't access, and be sitting there wondering why he was failing to call her back. She would certainly be wondering why he hadn't yet sent her any money towards the medical bills beyond that first £200, as he had told Aunt Pearl he would.

For all he knew his father was dead.

He remembered Pearl saying that his father was going to be discharged from the hospital later that day, which made it sound as if his heart-attack had been comparatively minor. But sometimes people went into hospital for what sounded like nothing and never came out again. And sometimes people were sent home to die.

He remembered a wooden fort his father had made as a Christmas present for him and his two brothers when he was seven years old, complete with crennelations along the tops of its walls, and a keep with a drawbridge that could be raised or lowered by winding string onto a little spindle. There was a great generosity of spirit in that gift: to pick up his lathe and chisel after a long day's work as a carpenter night after night to make a gift for his sons. He couldn't imagine his father not being there.

After a day's painful indecision he appealed to one of the prison officers on compassionate grounds to be allowed to make a call home to his mother. The deputy governor let him use some of his bankroll to buy a phone-card to use in one of the prison payphones even though it wasn't the usual day for such purchases.

Although there was always a queue for them during Association, once you got to the front of the line the phones themselves were glassed in and fairly private. If Cutty was careful about it then his mother and father needn't realise he was calling them from jail.

Cutty called his solicitor briefly first, arranging for her to visit him the following morning to discuss his defence and the evidence against him. Then he rang his mother. She answered on the very first ring, as if she had been waiting by the phone for his call.

'Mummy? Is Cuthbert.'

'Cutty? I tried to call you - '

'Yes, I know Mummy. I dropped mi phone and it did broke. I couldn't answer or hear my messages.'

'So where you call from now?'

'Pay-phone. Mummy, how is Daddy?'

'Lord be praised, he's doing alright. The doctors say the attack was not too serious, thank you Jesus. He's home now but he's very tired.'

Relief flushed through Cutty like ink through a cut flower. 'I sorry me no send di money yet,' he said. 'I have had a few difficulties here. But I will send it inna di nex' few days. Is Auntie Pearl wit' you?'

'She is,' his mother said grudgingly.

'Well, is someting, you know. Mummy - ?'

'Yes, Cuthbert?'

'Is Daddy awake? I cyan speak wit' him?'

'Hold on. Him in di guest room.' There was a pause, then Cutty heard the clatter of his mother dragging the phone on its lead through to his parents' guest bedroom, which was on the ground floor of their house.

'Hello?' His father's voice sounded weak and remote. 'Cutty?'

'Is me, Daddy. Still inna England, you know.'

'Your mother tell me.'

'How you doin', sah?'

'Tired, you know.'

'I will send money.'

'Cuthbert,' his father said. 'Tell me. A wha gwaan? Wit di studio an' alla dat?'

'Well, I was in a situation, you know, sah,' Cutty said evasively, glancing down at the credits clicking off his phone card and wishing they would go faster, or slower. Give him all the time he needed or no time at all.

'Drugs?' his father asked.

'No, sah.'

'Your mother, she worries, you know,' his father said. 'And I worry too.' He lapsed into silence, then after a long moment asked, 'So you a go come back home?'

'Soon, I hope.'

'Yes. Come home soon, Cuthbert, my son.'

'Yes, sah.'

The next voice Cutty heard was his mother's: 'Your father haffi rest now.'

There was a pause as at either end of the line they groped for words.

'Robert a help you?' Cutty asked eventually, just to be saying something.

'Yes,' his mother said. 'And Annette says she will help out too, but of course there are the children.'

Annette was Robert's wife. They had three young children, two boys and a girl.

'I will send money,' Cutty said again.

'We would both like to see you, my son.'

'Me haffi go now, Mummy.'

'We pray for you.'

He hung up the phone. The bell for lunch began to clang. He joined the other zombies as they shuffled into the dining-hall. The stink of boiled cabbage, rancid fat and cheap cuts of meat was strong. The food, so different from anything he would normally eat, drained him of energy and constipated him.

That lunch-time there was a fight. One man threw a mug of boiling water into which sugar had been stirred into the face of another man. The molten sugar stuck to the victim's skin, worsening the scald. Cutty sat there watching, not moving a muscle, not even tense, as three prison officers rushed in to subdue the man who threw the water with mace and batons. He was a large, ugly black man with dreadlocks. The victim was an Asian skinhead. His skin bubbled and peeled, showing raw pink under the brown.

I am in hell, Cutty thought. *Di lowest circle a Hell*. He wished he could pray.

The following afternoon Jasmina Jalwar came to discuss his trial, and for the first time Cutty heard the evidence against him in detail. Cynthia's statement was, of course, the centrepiece of the prosecution's case. She alleged that she had found Cutty alone in Buju's flat, for which the police knew he had spare keys. She claimed that he had propositioned her for sex and, when she refused him, had dragged her kicking and screaming into Buju's bedroom, tearing her clothing and dislodging her weave in the process. He had punched her in the face to shut her up, she said, and she had thereafter been half-stunned and too frightened to resist. He had then held a knife to her throat, removed her undergarments and raped her while she was 'paralysed with fear'. Her paralysis at that point would be used by the prosecution, Jasmina explained, to account for the fact that the medical examination, while confirming that she had had sexual intercourse that afternoon, did not prove actual rape.

Cutty's supposed use of a condom to prevent DNA evidence being left in Cynthia's vagina would allow the prosecution to argue premeditation on his part, though of course the condom he was supposed to have used had not been found, which helped the defence.

'And no condom packaging, no opened foil packet or condom box was found at the scene either,' Jasmina Jalwar added. 'Which is good for us, obviously. Also the knife - '

'What about di knife?' Cutty asked, his mind flashing back to going to the kitchen drawer and getting it out.

'No knife was found on you when you were arrested or in your flat when it was searched.'

'What if she say I did use di kitchen knife?'

'She didn't say you went to the kitchen to get a knife in her statement.'

'No.'

'She said you had a knife ready to hand.'

'Yes.'

'But you couldn't have known, by her own account, that she was coming round then, or that Buju would be out at that time, because those weren't planned events. And even if you did know, you wouldn't have known that – according to her story – she would reject your advances.'

'Me na make no advance-dem.'

'So you wouldn't have gone and got the knife from the kitchen beforehand, would you?'

Cutty managed a lop-sided smile. 'Ya smart, you know, sistah,' he said.

'Just attentive to details,' Jasmina Jalwar said with a slight shrug. 'So that's all broadly helpful to us. However - '

Just as Jasmina had predicted, Cutty's refusal to properly account for his own whereabouts at the time of the alleged rape made him look very guilty. He found himself regretting not having said more at the police interview when he had had the chance. He should have gone with the first story that came into his head, he thought: that Cynthia was making a malicious and false accusation against him out of spite because he had turned her down for sex and then told Buju she had propositioned him.

Then he read Buju's statement and it rendered that regret obsolete and made him relieved he had kept his mouth shut after all.

Buju claimed that he had never even been in the flat that afternoon/evening. He had been returning home, he said, when he had seen a dishevelled Cynthia running away from his block. Naturally he had run after her, calling out to her to stop. Evidently thinking it was Cutty pursuing her, Cynthia hadn't stopped, but had run on faster out of fear. Buju hadn't caught up with her until after she had already reached the home of her best friend, Sarah. There she had told Buju and Sarah that Cutty had raped her, and they called the police.

Sarah's statement confirmed the latter half of Buju's story.

Cutty scowled as he handed Buju's statement back to Jasmina. So Buju had sided with Cynthia to protect his rep after all. He had sacrificed Cutty for that. And now Cutty was caught between the hammer and the anvil. For a moment he hated Buju.

But even as that hatred slid down the core of him like a spike of ice, Cutty understood: Buju was silencing Cynthia forever. By pushing her accusation forward he was preventing her from ever revealing his secret. He was protecting himself, and in a fucked-up way he was protecting Cutty too. And would he, Cutty, have done any better if their positions had been reversed? Buju had had to think on the spur of the moment as Cutty had had to do in the police station, and he would have done whatever it took to make sure that Cynthia didn't tell Sarah the truth. And there was this: the charge

against Cutty made his heterosexuality iron-clad, and
there was a sort of power in that, and a sort of armour.

And surely Buju he was working on Cynthia even
now to make her drop the charges.

Cutty had to believe that to survive this ordeal.

But in the meantime he had to protect himself. He
now told Jasmina he wanted to make a formal statement, and for want of a better idea repeated a slight
variation of the story he had come up with at their first
interview: Cynthia had come on to him, he had re-
buffed her and subsequently, in her presence, told Buju
all about it and advised Buju to dump her for being a
slag. She had attacked Cutty in a rage, (him punching
her in self-defence), and run off, and come up with the
accusation against him later out of spite. Cutty added
one further detail: When the medical examination
showed that Cynthia had definitely had sex with
another man on the afternoon of the supposed rape,
Cutty suggested to Jasmina that Buju had most likely
assumed that man was him, and so had supported an
accusation he knew to be false out of anger at his
former best friend's apparent betrayal of him.

'In fact,' Cutty said, 'di medical evidence, it prove
she cheat pon him, yeah? An' dat fit with what I am
saying: dat di gyal is a slut, man. A pure slut.'

'But the prosecution will want to know why you
didn't say all this to the police in the first place,' said
Jasmina.

'Well, me know I no rape she,' Cutty said. 'So me
know dere cyaan be no evidence pon me. And I didn't
want to make no trouble or disclose personal business
or tings dat was a private matter between Buju and
Cynthia, you know?'

'Because Buju is your good friend?'

'Mi best friend.'

'But once you realised that the accusation was being

taken seriously you decided that you had to speak up?'

'Yes.'

'Okay,' Jasmina said. 'Well, at least that doesn't actually contradict anything you said to the police in your previous statement.' She checked her planner. 'Your section one crown court hearing is set for next Wednesday.'

'Section one?'

'Another formality. It'll be almost exactly the same as the magistrate's court, but this is the crown court. They'll just reiterate the charges and set a trial date.'

Wednesday rolled around eventually and Cutty was handcuffed and taken to the crown court, where he was once again charged with rape and assault. The courtroom was larger than the one he had been in before and the setting more formal: here the judge wore a red robe and a wig, and the barristers too wore wigs and gowns. But otherwise, as Jasmina had said, the procedure was much the same. A trial date was set for Wednesday, 2nd November, and Cutty was returned to Brixton Prison. As the gates clanged shut behind him for the second time he felt suicidal.

'So shi no drop di charges, den?' was the first question he asked Jasmina Jalwar when they met the following day to discuss his defence, although of course it was already clear that Cynthia hadn't.

'No.'

Cutty kissed his teeth and wondered if Buju had betrayed him totally.

'There's still a possibility the CPS may drop the case even if she doesn't,' Jasmina said. 'They know it could be stronger.' She tapped her pen twice on her pad. 'It's a shame you punched her in the face.'

'No,' Cutty said. 'Is Buju punch she.'

'You said before that you punched her.'

'No. It was Buju.'

Jasmina Jalwar gave him a look. 'Are you sure that's what you want to say?' she asked.

'Yes.'

Jasmina Jalwar fished out Cutty's statement and amended it. Immediately she had done so he realised he had made a mistake: if it was Cynthia's fiancé who had punched her in the face, why would Cynthia accuse his best friend of raping her? Cutty almost changed his statement back again, but didn't. After all, he thought, everyone knew that women could be capricious and spiteful. Also, if he changed his story any more times it would start to turn Jasmina against him, and he couldn't afford that.

'Sarah don't like me neither,' he added. 'She would lie pon me too.'

'Why?'

'Well, we was involved for a time, you know.'

'And it didn't work out?'

'She say me treat she so bad she must break up wit' me. She *bitter*, man. Bitter cah she fail to hold onto a prospect like myself.'

Jasmina gave Cutty a sceptical look and made a note in his file. She scheduled their next appointment for a week's time and left him alone with his thoughts.

Every day he was stuck rotting in prison Cutty fantasised about being summoned to the Governor's office and told that Cynthia had dropped the charges against him and he was free to go. Every day no such summons came. He had no visitors except Jasmina, and so the minutiae of his case became his whole world. Ever more elaborate and far-fetched defences rotated through his head in an endless futile spiral. Even dope, which was freely available to any inmate with the spends, barely muted the constant synaptic babble.

One encouraging development centred around Cynthia's torn clothes: Only her outer clothing had been in any way ripped or damaged; her underwear had not.

As the weeks wore on he was relieved to find that no-one in authority seemed to have made any connection between himself and the Cutty Munroe who was wanted for questioning back in Jamaica in relation to the Sonny Hilton murder inquiry. Perhaps it was no-one in particular's job to check up on that sort of thing, although that seemed unlikely. More likely was that the glacial nature of complex bureaucracy, so often punitive to those caught up in it, was working in his favour for once.

He called his parents once a week, and arranged with a social worker in the prison to send some of his dwindling roll of cash back home to his mother. It wasn't much, and he wouldn't be able to keep doing it, but at least it was something. His father was slowly recovering, and his sister-in-law Annette had turned out to be more helpful than his mother had expected her to be.

Cutty managed to keep from his parents the fact that he was in jail, although his refusal to give them a phone number on which they could reach him inevitably strengthened their suspicions that something wasn't right in his life.

It was strange and disorientating to be in a situation where his surroundings were so viscerally, stinkingly present and yet know that his real life was elsewhere: his meetings with Jasmina, his phone-calls to his mother, his thoughts of Buju, these were his reality, as were his dreams. And his nightmares.

Thoughts of Buju made Cutty hard whether Buju had betrayed him or not, but he rarely had a moment's privacy to masturbate. One of his cell-mates, the burly white thug, jerked himself off uninhibitedly, whenever he felt like it, filling the cell with the sour smell of his sweat and the tang of the jism he pumped out and mopped up with his blanket. It turned Cutty's stomach.

Why must him reek so?

One time he came in the cell and the thug and his other cell-mate, the scrawny white junkie, had abruptly moved away from each other and glanced at him with sharp, glittering eyes. Cutty had thought they were planning to attack him – the thug was a member of the British National Party, a racist Nazi organisation, and the junkie was easily led. But later it struck him that actually he had caught the thug trying to press the junkie into blowing him. If Cutty had been on the phone to his mother for five minutes longer that day the thug would probably have succeeded.

Still, Cutty didn't sleep that night. And thereafter he performed his heterosexuality more rigidly than ever.

Although each minute Cutty was in jail dragged by with excruciating slowness the weeks slipped by in a monotonous flow that was almost scarily rapid. He both longed for and dreaded the arrival of his court date, but neither longing nor dread made any difference to the count of days. By the time it came he had long ago done everything he could to prepare for it, and he had felt everything he was going to feel about it. All that was left was the event itself.

On the morning of Wednesday, November 2nd, Cutty showered, shaved, and was led through to reception to collect his personal effects. Then he was handcuffed, bundled into a van with several other prisoners, and taken to court. It was strange to have his rings back on his fingers and the gold ropes back around his neck.

Wearing his gold made him feel like a real person again.

As the prison gates swung shut behind him he suppressed the hope that he might not be returned there. Through the van's reinforced-glass windows he watched the city pass and it seemed unreal.

He was assigned to the same holding cell he had been put in at his section one hearing. This time there were two other prisoners in there with him. One was a large Rastafarian with a barrel chest and a gold tooth, who greeted him with an easy, 'Bruddah man,' and with whom he touched fists. The other was a pudgy white man in a rumpled suit, who had lank hair, a black eye and bruises on his face. The pudgy man kept his eyes on his hands, which were knotted in his lap.

'Kiddy fiddler,' said the Rastafarian, giving the man a baleful look. 'We give him some licks.'

Twenty minutes later the alleged kiddy fiddler was taken away. A Bengali boy in a hoodie was led in to replace him. He gave Cutty and the Rasta guarded nods, but said nothing.

After a further hour an officer came and took Cutty through to the interview room, where Jasmina was waiting for him. She was on her own. Cutty was instantly uneasy: he had expected his barrister to be there as well. Jasmina looked annoyed about something.

'Where's Mistah Petherbridge?' Cutty asked. This was the barrister Jasmina had arranged to represent him at the trial.

'He doesn't need to be here.'

'Why not?'

'Because just as I was leaving the office to come here a fax came through from the CPS saying they're discontinuing the case.'

'Discontinuing di case?' Cutty asked, a sudden hope

soaring up in him.

'Dropping it.'

'So - ?'

'So you'll be free to go. We just have to go through the formalities.'

'Why you sound vex so?' Cutty asked. 'Is good, nuh? Is a result for we.'

'I'm angry because the CPS apparently decided to discontinue ten days ago, and had they bothered to tell us their decision promptly we would have been spared a lot of preparatory work and you would have been spared a good deal of worry. They really can be shits sometimes.'

Cutty smiled. 'Whatever dem pay you, you deserve more,' he said.

'So I have to keep reminding the partners,' Jasmina Jalwar said drily. 'Right.' She stood and checked her watch. 'Time to go, I think. You should be up shortly.'

Cutty was returned to his cell. Inside he was churning. He wanted to shout out. He wanted to laugh aloud, but he pushed all that down: time enough for joy when he had been released, when he was beyond the windowless walls and locked doors. The part of him that couldn't trust half-believed he was being conned, that there would be some reversal in the court-room that would put him back behind bars. That this was one last attempt to break his spirit. The final torture: hope.

Half an hour later he was handcuffed and led up to Court 3. It was almost identical to the courtroom he had been in the last time he was there, all golden wood panelling, with a latticed white ceiling high above. His barrister, Mister Petherbridge, and the CPS barrister were sitting side-by-side behind desks exchanging inaudible remarks. Mister Petherbridge looked round and gave Cutty a brief nod of acknowledgement as he took his seat in the dock. The policewoman who had escorted Cutty uncuffed his hands, then sat behind him to his left. Cutty rubbed his wrists. The jury box was empty. A clerk and a few other court officials were present.

Cutty looked round at the spectators' gallery, half-hoping he would see Buju up there, half-expecting to see Cynthia, eyes filled with venom, but there was only an old white lady in a brown coat and a pink knitted hat.

'Be upstanding in court,' ordered the clerk, standing as he spoke. Everyone got to their feet as the judge, a short, elderly man wearing half-moon glasses, shuffled in and made his way to his chair, which was central, and elevated.

'Please be seated,' he said. They all sat and waited as he examined some papers in front of him. 'The Crown versus Cuthbert Stevens Munroe,' he read. 'The charge is rape and assault. Mister Tippett?'

The CPS barrister, a slender, fair-haired, fastidious man in his fifties, rose. 'Your honour, the crown wishes to make an application for discontinuance. We offer no evidence.'

'Thank you, Mister Tippett. Mister Petherbridge?'

'We would make the usual claims for costs incurred, your honour,' said Cutty's barrister, getting to his feet in his turn. 'There is also the related matter that has been brought to our attention, which is that the prosecution decided to discontinue this case ten days ago, but only notified us this morning. We would seek a compensatory sum for Mister Munroe for the suffering this delay has caused him.'

'Thank you, Mister Petherbridge,' the judge said. 'I will consider an appropriate sum. Mister Munroe?'

Cutty rose from his seat. 'Yes, your honour?'

'You are a free man.'

Chapter Fifteen

Cutty stepped down from the dock. Everything seemed heightened and unreal, as if he was in a film. His hands were so clenched with pins and needles that he couldn't straighten his fingers. An officer of the court guided him gently from the courtroom by the elbow and left him in the corridor outside. For a moment it felt wrong to be on his own like that, unguarded, uncuffed. He looked round for Jasmina but she was nowhere to be seen.

Di trial over, Cutty thought. *Me no haffi go a jail.*

He fished a crumpled pack of cigarettes out of his tracksuit pocket but realised as he fumbled the lid open that he had no lighter or matches. Anyway there were No Smoking signs everywhere.

No get busted for dat.

James Petherbridge came up to him looking pleased. 'I know,' he said. 'It must feel very odd.'

'Why dem no drop di case in di firs' place?'

'I know,' the barrister repeated. 'It puts both accused and accuser through the most possible stress while wasting the maximum amount of everyone's time. But that's the CPS for you.'

'So why dem drop di case at all?'

'If they reckon there's less than a fifty percent chance of obtaining a conviction then they rule it not in the Crown's interests to take a case forward. Obviously it takes them some time to arrive at that decision. Hence what happened here today. At least they didn't prevaricate.'

'"Prevaricate"?'

'Well, they could have asked for the trial date to be

put back while they continued to consider the evidence. You would have been stuck back on remand, and they would still have dropped the case, just three or four months further down the line. Anyway - ' he glanced his watch.

'Dere is one more ting I must know,' Cutty said.

'Sure.'

'Dem did drop di case cah Cynthia Mitchell drop shi accusation, right?'

James Petherbridge gave him a curious look and shook his head. 'Neither Cynthia Mitchell nor Mister Staples withdrew their statements,' he said. 'Ms Mitchell certainly didn't drop the charges. It was entirely the decision of the CPS.'

'Tank you.'

They shook hands briefly, then the barrister hurried off down the corridor to meet his next client.

Cutty wandered out into the weak autumn daylight. The last time he had walked free under the sun it had been the height of summer. Now the leaves had fallen from the trees and there was a rawness to the air. He wondered if the CPS had told Cynthia they were dropping the case. He supposed they had. After all, she would be expecting to be called as a witness. The thought that they could have kept him rotting in jail for another four months chilled his heart.

It was strange to walk freely past uniformed officials and police officers and out unchallenged onto the street where office workers and business people passed to and fro, oblivious to the dramas going on behind the courthouse walls. Traffic waited at the traffic lights, then surged forward aggressively to the next jam as red flicked through orange to green.

Despite the weakness of the light everything had a brightness to it that made Cutty want to squint. He felt disorientated. He hardly knew where he was, except that it seemed to be a sort of legal or business district. He looked up and saw he was on High Holborn. Above the sign bearing that name was a City of London crest. Below it a second sign pointed towards an Underground station. He followed the sign and a few minutes later found himself at Holborn tube station.

He took the tube to Shepherds Bush and made his way to his favourite Caribbean takeway, The Roti Hut, on the Uxbridge Road. There he ordered saltfish and ackee, rice and peas, and a can of sorrel pop, a drink he had loved as a small boy.

'Ain't seen you around for a while, man,' said the browning girl behind the counter. Her hair was pulled back in a mass of corkscrew curls. She had a round, pretty face and a flirtatious smile.

'I been away,' he said, handing over his last fifty-pound note. 'On business.'

'What business?'

'Di mind your own kind.'

'Whatever.' The girl rolled her eyes and entered his order on the till.

The Roti Hut had seating, and once she had given him his change Cutty went and took a seat. A minute later the girl brought his food over to him. He nodded his thanks. He ate quietly, enjoying the familiar food and the familiar accents around him, and thinking about what to do next.

Me haffi see Buju.

He had originally planned to go back to his own flat first, but had then remembered Jasmina Jalwar telling him that the police had bolted a steel panel over his stoved-in front door 'to make the property secure.' That meant he would need to apply to his local police station to get it opened up again. All he would need to get that done, Jasmina had assured him, was present them with some sort of proof of address: 'a council tax bill, an electricity bill, a bank statement, whatever.' But since Cutty wasn't the legal tenant, had no UK bank account, and had rigged the electric meter, he had no proof of address. Once again he was homeless. It was painful, but it made things simple.

He finished eating and made his way up to White City and Buju's block. It seemed like a lifetime since he had last been there. The grey chilliness of the weather reminded him of the first time he had come to Buju's drum with nothing in his pockets and nowhere else to go. That had been seven months ago. Was it really only seven months? He climbed the stairs feeling like an old man.

As he stepped up to Buju's front door he felt as though he was caught up in a re-run on TV. *Except dis time me 'ave keys.* He pressed the buzzer and waited. No-one came. He knocked loudly. Still no-one came. He took out his bunch of keys. Would they have changed the locks while he was inside? He slid the key for the mortice-lock in and turned it. The lock clicked back. Then he tried the Yale. That worked too, and he pushed the door open and went inside. He guessed that Buju and Cynthia probably hadn't heard about the charges being dropped much before he had, and so hadn't had time to arrange a locksmith.

The flat was pleasantly warm and seemed little different from when he had last been there, except for the presence of two white upright chairs and a small round table in one corner of the lounge, apparently positioned to suggest a dining area. Cynthia's idea, he assumed. He was irritated, but what did he expect? Of course she would try to take over the space while he was away. He closed the door behind him and relocked the mortice. That way if either Buju or Cynthia came back while he was in there they wouldn't be alerted to his presence in advance.

He would have the drop on them.

He went through to the bedroom. The bed was made. The duvet was stretched smooth and tight across the mattress in a way that Cutty knew Buju would never bother to do, and the pillows were carefully plumped. There were female beauty-products on top of the chest-of-drawers, and some of Cynthia's clothes were draped over the Lloyd loom chair that sat next to it.

Cutty crossed to the wardrobe, opened it, knelt, and rummaged among the trainers and boots until he found what he was looking for: a Prada shoe-box. He opened it.

Inside, still lying on lavender tissue paper, was the automatic pistol Buju had offered him as a gift, the Russian 9mm that Cutty had accepted but had asked Buju to keep safe for him until he had things sorted. Next to it lay a full clip of bullets. Cutty had handled similar guns back in JA - they were popular with the Lick Shot Posse – so he knew how to slide the clip up into the pistol's grip, clicking it into place with the palm of his hand. Then he pulled back the housing, lifting a bullet up into the breach and making the gun ready to fire.

He thumbed on the safety-catch and tucked the pistol into the back of his track pants. Then he put the shoe-box back in the wardrobe and wandered through to the kitchen, where he helped himself to a beer from the fridge.

His mind was pulling in two directions at once. One way he simply wanted to reconnect with Buju and somehow carry on as they had before; just forget the whole thing with Cynthia getting him thrown in jail. Because in the end she had failed, and now she couldn't expose their relationship and they were safe. He missed Buju strongly. He missed his company and friendship

and understanding. And, of course, he missed the sex:
Buju fulfilled him better than any other lover he had
ever had. In prison he could have had sex, of course:
there were youths available to be fucked or give you a
blow-job for drugs or drink or cigarettes. But that
would have felt like putting down roots in somewhere
he didn't want to be; making ties that strangled even as
they gave release. And if it became know that you
sucked dick or took it up the arse yourself, as Cutty
enjoyed doing too, then you would be marked out as a
punk.

Buju never made him feel like a punk whatever they
did together.

Also Buju supplied Cutty with drugs, and Cutty
needed drugs to raise money, now more than ever. And
Buju put a roof over his head when he first came to
England. Cutty couldn't just forget and reject that,
whatever had happened since.

Those were all strong reasons for trying to reconcile
with Buju. But the other part of Cutty's mind saw Buju
and Cynthia as two enemies who had banded together
against him, who had tried to destroy him, who had
colluded in framing him for a serious crime. It was that
part of Cutty that was so careful to re-lock Buju's front
door after himself once he had entered the flat. It was
that part of Cutty that sent him to the wardrobe to get
the 9mm.

Traitors and haters, he thought, pulling the gun
out and stroking his thumb reflexively over the safety-
catch. *On off, on off, on off, on -*

Suddenly he felt extremely tired. He went through
to the bedroom, lay back on the bed, and stared up at
the ceiling. He thought he could smell Cynthia on the
bed-covers, her perfume at least. He knew he could
smell Buju, and his dick stirred slightly in his pants at
that, but only slightly: today he was on another mis-

sion. Cutty closed his eyes. Unconsciousness swept over him.

He woke with a start. It was still light out, but beyond that he had no idea how long he had been asleep. He checked the bedside clock. It read 3.17 p.m. He had been asleep for nearly forty minutes. He sat up and rubbed his face. His breath was stale from the beer he had drunk earlier and he was bursting for a piss. He got up and went and emptied his bladder, placing the gun on top of the cistern while he urinated.

Just as he was about to flush he heard the soft sound of a key sliding into the lock of the front door. With a stifled curse he snatched up the gun and slipped back into the bedroom. Had the bedroom door been open when he came into the flat? He thought it had. He left it open and positioned himself behind it, out of sight.

Cool air flowed into the flat, and a moment later he heard the rustle of shopping bags being carried in. The front door banged shut and the bags rustled through to the kitchen.

'Don't put that there, man,' a voice said. It was Buju's voice, and it had a complaining edge to it.

'Whatever, man,' a girl's voice replied flatly. *Cynthia*. At the sound of her voice Cutty felt his hackles rise. Without thinking he thumbed the safety catch of the pistol to the off position. There was more rustling and the sound of shopping bags being unpacked.

'Stick that in the lav, yeah,' Buju's voice said.

Through the crack in the hinges of the bedroom door Cutty watched Cynthia as she slouched past to the bathroom carrying a six-roll pack of toilet paper. 'Shit, man,' she called back complainingly to Buju. 'Don't you never flush?'

'Course I do, man.'

Cynthia pushed the handle down. 'Men,' she muttered. 'Why you always gotta train 'em?' She went back to the kitchen.

'Put the kettle on, yeah,' Buju said.

'You do it.'

'I'm putting this away, ain't I?'

Cynthia sighed. A moment later Cutty heard the kettle being filled. 'So what we gonna do, then?' she asked.

'I don't know, man,' Buju said, sounding tired.

'Did you call the locksmith like I said?'

'No.'

'Why not?'

'Cos I didn't.'

'Fucking hell, Buju! This is serious shit, you know.'

'Don't fucking sweat me, Cynthia,' Buju said angrily. 'I know what it is.'

'We gotta have a plan, though.'

'I got a plan.'

'Yeah, right,' Cynthia scoffed. 'So what is it, then? This plan?'

'I'm gonna deal with the situation as and when,' Buju said. 'Like, play it by ear.'

'You call that a plan?' Cynthia was scornful.

'What you call it, then?'

'Making it up as you go along.'

'So what, you got a plan, then?' Buju asked coldly.

'You got a gun?'

'Yeah, I got a gun,' Buju said.

'Where?'

'It's in the bedroom, innit,' he said. 'In the wardrobe.'

'Well, get it then.'

Cutty stiffened behind the bedroom door. His finger tightened on the trigger of the 9mm. *Yeah, man,* he thought, *come and get it.*

'Later, yeah,' Buju said. 'I mean, it ain't like he's

gonna come shooting the door down, is it?'

'But he'll come here though,' Cynthia said. 'He ain't got nowhere else.'

'Cah them padlock his yard.'

The kettle clicked off.

'You know what I fancy?' Cynthia's tone was suddenly flirtatious.

'Leave it out, man.' Buju said sharply.

'It's been over a month, man,' Cynthia complained. 'Almost two.'

'You don't like it, you run back to that man what was sexing you back in the day,' Buju retorted. 'Oh, I forgot,' he added spitefully. 'He's already got a wife an' kids.'

'Fuck you, man.'

'Fucking cheating on me.'

'Oh, right. Like *you* wasn't cheating on *me*!'

'Say that again and I'll shoot you a box you won't forget.'

'Yeah, that's right, punch a girl! You put a mark on me I'm gonna go to the police, yeah.'

'What you fucking want from me, Cynthia?'

'You know what I want, man.'

'What? We got engaged like what you wanted. You moved in like you wanted. What more could you possibly want outta this situation?'

'What you think I want, Buju?'

'I think I been asleep, man, that's what I think,' Buju said. 'I think I been a mug. Cutty's out and it changes everything, you know what I'm saying? *Everything*.'

'Why?' Cynthia asked hotly. 'Why's it gotta change *anything*? We was doing good, and – and now - ' She sounded suddenly tearful. Cutty's back began to ache from having to stand so still and hold himself so upright behind the bedroom door. 'I wish he'd never come here,' Cynthia said thickly. 'I wish he was fucking dead. If he was dead we could go back to where we was before he ever come here.'

'Gal, get real. We was never all that, you know what I'm saying?'

'So why you arx me to be your fiancée, then?'

Buju didn't answer.

Cutty tried to make sense of what he was hearing. Was Buju on his side, on Cynthia's side, or just out for himself?

'He's gonna come round here, I'm telling you, man,' Cynthia said, once it became obvious that Buju wasn't going to answer her question. 'And what you gonna do then? Kiss and make up?'

Buju kissed his teeth. 'I told you, man. Don't even be saying shit like that, you get me?'

'It was just a joke, man.'

'No it weren't.'

'Yeah, well, I'm gonna get changed,' Cynthia said, ending the conversation abruptly. She came slouching into the bedroom. She was wearing a powder-blue tracksuit, pink trainers and a pink baseball hat. Her hair was straightened and scraped back into a ponytail. She looked tired and puffy-faced. Her dressing-gown was hanging on the back of the bedroom door. She swung the door round to get to it and found herself face to face with Cutty. Wordlessly he raised his right hand and aimed the gun at her chest. Her eyes widened with fear. She seemed like she was about to say something, but didn't.

Chapter Sixteen

Wordlessly Cutty gestured to Cynthia to step back. Her eyes were fixed on the gun he was aiming at her chest. She backed out of the bedroom and into the hall. He moved with her, not knowing yet what he was going to do.

Cynthia backed into the kitchen, where Buju was standing at the sink, staring out of the window, holding a mug of tea. He was as handsome as Cutty remembered; as smooth, as dark, as flawless. On his head was a red bandanna. A diamond glittered in his ear. He was wearing a white basketball vest over a blue tee-shirt, baggy, sagging jeans and retro hi-tops.

Still Cutty didn't know what he was going to do.

Buju turned. His lips parted but he didn't speak. With a wave of the gun Cutty gestured that he join Cynthia, then waved them both through to the lounge. Once all three of them were in the lounge Cutty crossed over to the window and twisted the blinds closed so that no-one could see in. He was careful to keep his eyes on Buju and Cynthia as he fumbled for the rod that closed the blinds. Then, keeping the gun trained on them, he slowly sat down on one of the new hard-backed chairs next to the small, round dining-table. Cynthia and Buju remained standing, staring at him. He felt the power of the performer then, magnified by the eyes upon him. He realised that Buju and Cynthia believed he could kill. But did *he* believe he could kill?

'You want a smoke?' Buju asked, breaking the silence, breaking the moment.

'Sure,' Cutty said. His voice sounded surprisingly casual even to himself.

Buju reached carefully into his jeans' pocket and produced Rizlas, a pack of cigarettes and a small baggy of grass. 'You mind if I sit down, man?' he asked. 'It makes it easier to roll.'

'Siddung.'

Buju sat on the sofa, bent forward and began to roll a spliff on the smoked-glass coffee-table. Cynthia remained standing. Ready to run. She had learned her lesson.

'So you're out, then,' Buju said, glancing down to run his tongue along the Rizlas, joining them together.

'Me out.'

'I knew you weren't going down, man.'

'Did you?'

'Course, man,' Buju said, trying to sound easy. 'I mean like, there weren't no evidence, was there? I mean, proper evidence, you know what I'm saying?'

'You never hear about miscarriage a justice?'

Buju didn't reply to that. He split a cigarette open and tipped the tobacco out in a line along the two Rizlas. Then he sprinkled a line of herb onto the tobacco. Buju didn't like to smoke pure herb. He rolled the joint up, ran his tongue along its length to seal it, put it to his lips, and sparked up. He took a long drag. Then, at extreme arm's length, he passed the joint to Cutty. The tips of their fingers brushed. Cutty felt a current surge through him. A song-lyric flashed into his mind: *It's a thin line between love and hate.*

For the first time since his release the idea of love was in his head. His finger eased a little on the trigger of the pistol. He dragged on the spliff and felt the fast lift of good herb.

'Why don't you put up the gun, blood?' Buju said carefully. He met Cutty's eyes for a moment then looked away, as if he was afraid that too much engagement would trigger something bad.

Cutty bared his teeth in a feral, humourless grin and toked again. 'Why you back shi lies, man?' he asked, in a voice rapidly made creaky by the dope.

'It was that stupid bitch Sarah what done it, bruv,' Buju said.

'What you mean, Sarah done it?'

'You musta read the statements, man,' Buju said. 'Cynthia run over to Sarah's yard looking like she's been beaten - '

'I *was* beaten,' Cynthia broke in sharply.

Buju shot her a warning look. 'So Sarah wants to know a wha gwaan, you know what I'm saying? Cynthia weren't saying nothing at that point, but then Sarah goes, Was you raped?'

Cutty turned his gaze on Cynthia. She looked back defiantly, but he could see the chords in her neck stand out from where her throat was tensing, and her chest was trembling as it rose and fell.

'Cynthia was pissed off with what had happened,' Buju continued, 'so she nods along with what Sarah said. And by the time I get there Sarah was already belling the feds.'

'So alla dis was Sarah's idea?'

'What was I supposed to say when she said it, man?' Cynthia asked. 'Tell her the truth?'

'You was suppose to keep your mouth shut,' Buju said angrily, and now Cutty glimpsed the trap that Buju had found himself in.

'Fuck you, man!' Cynthia replied to Buju, her temper flaring too. 'You're making out like I'm the villain, yeah, but I ain't. I ain't the villain, man, I'm the victim!'

'You ain't the one what spent four months inside,' Buju said hotly.

'And *he* ain't the one what lied to the gal he was seeing!' Cynthia spat back.

'You better not start talking 'bout lies, gal,' Buju

said. 'Cos you're the queen of lies, as it goes.'

'So I was seeing someone, so what?' Cynthia's voice was getting louder. 'You sure as fuck weren't doing the business, were you? At least,' she shot a bold-faced look at Cutty. 'Not with me. Not with me,' she repeated.

She started to cry then, standing there small and delicate and vulnerable for all the hardness of her words and manner. The two men watched her impassively. After a while, seeing that her tears were achieving nothing, she stopped.

'You never make shi drop di charges,' Cutty said, turning his attention back to Buju.

'I never thought you'd go down for it,' Buju said defensively.

Cutty's head began to ache. They were talking in circles.

'You look weary, man,' Buju said.

'Cyaan get inna mi gates,' Cutty said. 'Dem is lock up by di feds.'

'I can help you out, though.'

'Yeah?'

'Course, man,' Buju said. 'Spars fi true, yeah?'

But what was Buju really offering him, Cutty wondered. A step backwards into being mates, into being business partners, into what their old life had appeared to be?

Buju was holding out his hand.

Now profoundly weary, Cutty put the gun down on the small, round dining-table. He reached out and brushed Buju's hand first back-to-back, then palm-to-palm. Then they briefly locked fingers before pulling back and ending with a snap. It seemed to seal something. Cutty didn't give Cynthia a glance. Nor did Buju. This was man's business, and she would have to wait on their decision.

Buju pulled out a roll of notes and counted off five

twenties.

'Here's a pony, yeah,' he said, handing the money across to Cutty. 'Just to hold you till we can get you proper set up again.'

Cutty took the money and pocketed it. 'And she?' he asked, indicating Cynthia with a nod.

Buju didn't answer at once. Cutty could see he was torn. Could he disavow Cynthia to her face? Could he end it with her right then and there? Kick her out? Could he be that bold, take that much of a chance? Did he even want to? And anyway, didn't her silence depend on their constant proximity?

'Well?' Cutty prompted.

'I can't speak to that now, man,' Buju said eventually. 'I've got to ponder on it. But you can stay here tonight.'

'Buju - ' Cynthia started to object.

'What I'm suppose to say, man?' Buju snapped at her. 'This my spar, yeah.'

'I suppose,' Cynthia conceded grudgingly, her eyes darting back and forth between him and Cutty.

'So chill, yeah,' Buju said. 'What's gonna be is what's gonna be.'

'What about me, then?' Cynthia pouted. 'I mean, how's it gonna look with him staying here?'

'Maybe you ought to go stay over at your mum's tonight.'

'No way, man,' Cynthia said immediately. 'I ain't going nowhere with *that* one round here.' She indicated Cutty with an electric-blue talon. 'Trust me on that.'

'Whatever,' Buju shrugged.

Dusk had fallen while they were talking, and the lounge was now plunged in gloom. Buju reached out and turned on a lamp that stood by the sofa. Cutty switched on a smaller lamp that sat on the dining-table, and the room was lit with a mellow glow.

'You know what?' Buju said. 'I'm starving, man.'

At that moment there was the sound of several footsteps approaching along the walkway outside. Then the buzzer sounded harshly and at the same time there was a loud banging at the front door.

'The click,' Buju said. Cynthia rolled her eyes. 'Well, let 'em in, yeah,' Buju said, his manner as easy as if nothing out of the ordinary had just been happening. Cynthia sighed and slouched off to do as she was told. Buju gestured at the gun on the table and Cutty snatched it up and slipped it into the waistband of his track-pants, pulling down his basketball vest to conceal it.

As he was doing that he heard the front door open and Spin's voice say, 'Cynthia gal, you looking *phyne.*'

'My man hear you talk so, he'll cut ya,' Cynthia replied jokingly.

'Gal, if you was mine I'd keep you locked down like them muslim gals,' Spin said cheerfully. '24-7, you know what I'm saying?'

'Like you got what it takes,' Cynthia scoffed. She came back into the lounge, followed by Spin, Maxie and Gary, all of them boisterous and high-spirited. Then they saw Cutty sitting there. Abruptly they fell silent.

'Fuck, man!' Spin said after a few uneasy seconds had passed, trying to recover his previous good cheer. 'I didn't know you was out, man!'

'Me just get out today,' Cutty said.

'Cool.' Spin batted his knuckles against Cutty's then touched fists with him. 'That's cool, man.'

The others stood awkwardly in the middle of the room, not sure how to act.

'Maybe we shouldn't be here, yeah,' Spin went on, speaking to no-one in particular. 'We don't wanna like – intrude.'

'No, man,' Buju said. 'Is aright. We was just sorting

a lickle business, but is done now.'

'You sure, yeah? Cos we can just piss off, you know what I'm saying?'

'It's alright, man,' Buju said. 'Stay, yeah.'

Spin glanced over at Cynthia. She nodded, barely perceptibly.

'Cool,' he said.

'We brought beers.' Maxie held up a blue carrier bag heavy with cans of Red Stripe.

'And rum,' Gary added, brandishing a bottle of Cockspur.

'Then we can celebrate the release of a sufferer,' Spin said, turning his back on Cynthia. 'Right, Cutty, man?'

'Yes, mi bruddah,' Cutty said. 'A black man must be free,' he added with an effort, forcing energy into his voice. 'Resist di downpressor. Battle di shitstem.'

Even as he said this he was fighting a strong impulse to escape the situation, to just get up and leave and be on his own again. But would he really be happier on his own, wandering the cold night-time streets with nowhere to go? No. And he knew he should take this chance to reconnect with the click, to claw back the ground he had evidently lost to Cynthia while he had been locked up.

'So how you doin', man?' Spin asked him half-confidentially as he took the spare dining-chair and turned it back to front, straddling it as the others found themselves seats on the sofa or in the armchair.

'Well, just surviving, you know,' Cutty said. He relit the spliff, which had gone out, puffed it back to life, then passed it to Spin. Spin took it, at the same time removing his baseball cap and setting it on the dining-table, and Cutty saw that he had braided his formerly cane-rowed hair into an elaborate spiral. Spin dragged deeply on the spliff with full, pouting lips. Cutty had never really thought about him sexually before, but he was a pretty youth and, Cutty now decided, very fuckable. Possibly out of a subconscious desire to make Buju jealous, Cutty found himself giving Spin all his attention.

'So what happened, man?' Spin asked him, smoke pouring from his nostrils.

'Di CPS drop di charges.'

'All of 'em?'

'Well, except dem say dem did find a lickle drugs in my yard, you know. But dem no charge me wit' dat.'

'The CPS, yeah?' Spin looked round awkwardly at Cynthia. Evidently he'd assumed that she had dropped the charges against Cutty or Cutty wouldn't be here now.

Buju, who had been watching the conversation intently, caught their shared look. 'Get us some ice for the rum, yeah,' he ordered Cynthia. Her eyes flashed, but then she lowered her gaze and went and did as she was told.

Spin started to ask Cutty something but then seemingly remembered that Buju was still in the room even if Cynthia wasn't, and didn't. Instead he asked, 'So, what you gonna do now, man?'

Cutty shrugged. 'Sort a new drum,' he said. 'Get back into business.'

'But ain't there gonna be like – awkwardness, man?' Spin asked, unable to help himself. He glanced at Buju.

'What is past is past,' Cutty said, taking the joint from between Spin's fingers, putting it to his own lips and drawing on it deeply. 'Right, man?' he asked Buju as he passed Buju the spliff.

'Can't bring nothing back,' Buju agreed, toking in his turn.

'So I hear that jail is *rough*, man,' Maxie said, breaking into the conversation.

'Well, you need a correct mentality,' Cutty said, avoiding his eager eyes.

'Or you get fucked,' Gary snickered as Cynthia came back in with a bowl full of ice-cubes. She set it down on the coffee-table.

'Glasses, yeah,' Buju said. Cynthia trailed off to the kitchen again toget them.

'Piece a piss compared with them Jamaican jails though, I bet,' Spin said. 'Right, man?'

Cutty shrugged.

'I heard they was gonna give out rubbers in one a them Jamaican joints cos of AIDS and shit,' said Maxie. 'And there was a fuckin' riot, man!'

'Why, man?' asked Gary, twisting the cap off the bottle of rum.

'Cos they thought it was like the authorities saying they was all queers.'

'So what happened, then?'

'They go on the fuckin' rampage, man!' Maxie said excitedly. 'Kill and torture up any suspected battyman in the place, slice 'em up and - '

'That's harsh, man,' said Spin, half-laughing.

'You reckon?'

'Well, yeah. Cos say you was banged up for life, you tell me you ain't gonna need some a them cocksuckers, you know what I'm saying?'

'Man, you're so gay.'

'Cept I'm the one gettin' a trailerload a pussy.'

Cynthia set down hastily-wiped glasses on the coffee-table with a clatter.

'You're making that shit up, man,' Gary said, dropping ice in the glasses and pouring the rum. 'He's making this shit up. Ain't he, Cutty?'

'What him tell is di truth,' Cutty said quietly.

They toasted freedom and drank. Cynthia put on some R&B in the background. Buju clicked the TV on with the sound muted.

'So tell me 'bout di runnings,' Cutty said, finally beginning to relax as the rum warmed his heart. 'A wha
gwaan while me gone?'

As it turned out little had changed since Cutty had been
imprisoned, though he gained the impression that Buju
had had trouble holding the click together in his
absence. Buju had, it seemed, become used to having
Cutty as his general, and without him being there
everything had evidently become less exciting to Buju,
and less worthwhile. But the click continued to do
business around clubs and at parties and blues. No
serious busts had occurred, though a rumour was going
around that the feds were planning a major crackdown
on the estate in the near future. Buju was considering
renting a flat down Shepherds Bush way as a temporary
relocation until the crackdown had come and gone.

They talked and they drank and they smoked and
watched TV until the small hours. After the unrelenting
routine of prison Cutty found himself luxuriating in the
unstructuredness of it all. Cynthia went to bed around
one, but Buju stayed up with Cutty and the others,
getting drunk and stoned with them until they all
finally dozed off, one after the other, sprawled around
the lounge, Buju, Spin and Gary on the sofa, Cutty in
the armchair, and Maxie on the floor, curled up like a
cat on a large scatter-cushion.

Cutty had no dreams. That night.

Chapter Seventeen

The door-buzzer sounded jarringly, jolting Cutty out of a deep, leaden sleep. He glanced blearily at his watch. It was 9.20 a.m. The lounge was still in darkness, with only a dim grey light framing the blinds in the windows. *Not my yard, not my business*, he thought to himself. His neck was stiff from having slept slumped all night in the armchair and his head ached. Spin, Maxie, Buju and Gary were all in the positions they had been in when he had finally dozed off around 4 a.m. the night before. All of them were still asleep. Or, if the buzzer had woken them, they were pretending it hadn't and were keeping their eyes shut. Cutty closed his eyes too.

The buzzer sounded again, more lengthily this time. Cutty forced his eyes open and watched an equally bleary-eyed Buju push himself up off the couch and go to answer the door. He felt a thin satisfaction on realising that Buju had spent the whole night in the front room with the click and himself. He thought of Cynthia waiting for Buju in the bedroom, unsatisfied and afraid. The thought pleased him.

Cutty heard Buju shoot the bolts back and open the front door. A voice announced itself as belonging to Ranjit Sharma, from Elliot & Markby. Cutty's ears pricked up at that. Elliot & Markby was Jasmina Jalwar's law-firm, and he remembered that Ranjit Sharma – who he had never actually met - was Jasmina's assistant.

'I'm actually trying to trace Cuthbert Munroe,' he heard Ranjit Sharma say. 'I apologise for coming to you, under the circumstances.'

'Circumstances?' Buju's voice was slurred by lack of sleep.

'Well, your fiancée.'

'Oh. Yeah. That. Well, you know, whatever, man,' Buju said blankly. Cutty could visualise his dismissive shrug.

'The thing is,' Ranjit Sharma went on, 'we don't have an address for Mr Munroe. Well, we do, but it's been boarded up by the police. So we don't know where he is. His mobile phone isn't working. You and he were close and we were wondering if you might have any idea where we could find him. It is rather important.'

'No.'

'"No"?'

'I don't know where he is, man,' Buju elaborated. 'I don't got no ideas 'bout where he's gone.'

'Oh. Well, if you do happen to see him...'

'Yeah, I'll tell him.'

'Ranjit Sharma from Elliot & Markby. It is important.'

'Yeah.'

Buju shut the door and rammed the bolts back into place. Cutty was wide awake now. He struggled up from the armchair and went out into the hall.

'Cup of tea?' Buju asked him, wandering through to the kitchen. Cutty followed him. 'Zat your lawyer, then?' Buju asked, filling the kettle at the sink, switching it on, and taking down a couple of mugs from a shelf.

'Shi assistant,' Cutty said.

'Who was that, then?' a sleepy voice asked behind him. Cutty looked round and to his extreme annoyance saw Cynthia leaning there in the doorway, wearing nothing but an oversize man's tee-shirt. Her legs were smooth and firm and a rich mocha colour. He wanted to tell her to cover them up.

'Just someone for Cutty,' Buju said, not looking at Cynthia.

'How come they know he's here?'

'They don't.' Buju dropped tea-bags in two mugs.

'Is one of them for me, then?' Cynthia asked, looking at the mugs.

Wordlessly Buju took down a third mug from the shelf and dropped a tea-bag in that one as well. He added milk from the fridge as the kettle came to the boil. Once he had made the tea he handed the mugs to Cutty and Cynthia. Cynthia took hers and mooched around the kitchen aimlessly, lightly touching things, half-singing to herself, enjoying the fact that her presence silenced Buju and Cutty, apparently oblivious to the waves of hatred building up around her.

'Me need air,' Cutty announced abruptly. He scooped the tea-bag out of his mug with a spoon and flicked it into the bin, then went out into the hall. He unbolted the front door and stepped out onto the walkway. It was chilly outside, and the sky was grey as lead, but the fresh air cleared his head a little. He looked out across row upon row of terraced houses, low-rise tower-blocks and, further off, slab-like high-rises. In amongst them were scattered trees with bare grey branches. The view depressed him intensely. Back home the sky would be azure, the plant life would be a vibrant green and the heat would be intense, and he would understand the meaning of everything he saw as he knew he did not understand the meaning of everything here.

He decided he would go and see Jasmina Jalwar straight away. Let the axe fall. Get it over with, whatever it was. He couldn't face going back into the flat, not even just to say where he was going, so he left his half-finished mug of tea steaming on the brick ledge opposite Buju's front door and headed for the stairwell.

Maybe whatever Jasmina's news was would make sorting things out with Buju and Cynthia irrelevant.

Only once he was on the streets did it occur to Cutty that he didn't actually know where Jasmina Jalwar's office was. Sure, he had the address – it was on the card she had originally given him at the police station, a number on Gray's Inn Road - but he didn't know where Gray's Inn Road was. He was forced to go into a newsagent's and consult an *A-Z*. He felt oddly stupid at having to do so.

Gray's Inn Road turned out to run down from King's Cross station to the Crown Court where the case against him had been discontinued. Cutty took the Hammersmith & City line round to King's Cross, a journey of about twenty minutes. The butt of the gun he had walked out of the flat with still jammed down the waistband of his track-pants pressed against his belly as he sat on the underground, the barrel poked down uncomfortably into his ballsack, parting his testicles. He knew it was pure foolishness to be carrying a gun in public when he wasn't even in fear of being attacked but it was too late to do anything about it now: he had left Buju's without thinking anything through, and this was the price he was paying. He couldn't even get rid of it by dropping it in a bin for fear of being caught doing so on CCTV.

The Tube was stuffy and airless, and he found himself wishing he had taken a shower before setting out.

The firm of Elliot & Markby was five minutes' walk from the station. Its offices occupied two floors above an estate agent's. He passed several other lawyer's offices along the way, one of them African, and wondered how they compared with Jasmina Jalwar's. There was a side of him that distrusted Asians.

Still, she had kept him out of jail so far. And he

didn't trust Africans either. Or whites. Or Jamaicans.

He pressed on the buzzer, announced that he was there to see Jasmina, and the door clicked open. He felt a plunging sensation as he climbed the steep, musty steps to the reception area on the first floor. A pleasant, plump blonde white girl behind a desk asked him if he had an appointment. He replied that he didn't, but that Ranjit Sharma had told him that Jasmina wanted to see him urgently. The girl rang through to Jasmina's office, told her that Cutty was there to see her, and asked him to wait.

'She's with a client now, but she should be with you shortly,' the girl said. 'Please take a seat.'

Cutty took a seat and flicked through the dull magazines set out on a low table in front of him, his mind a blank. He regretted not having got something to eat at the train station, both to mute down the wrenching in his gut and to give him some energy. The pistol was warm and hard and heavy against his belly. *Madness*, he thought. *To bring a loaded gun to your lawyer's office. Pure craziness.*

'You 'ave a toilet?' he asked abruptly.

The blonde girl indicated a door by the entrance. Cutty got up and went into the cupboard-sized room beyond. He locked the door behind him and looked around, but there was nowhere to hide a gun except in the cistern. But to dump a gun in the cistern of the toilet was as crazy as bringing it to the law-firm in the first place. And he might need it later. He felt suddenly tearful and overwhelmed and alone. He struggled to push his weakness down, to be a man. He pushed the pistol back into his track-pants, adjusting it so it sat more comfortably and less obtrusively, flushed the toilet, and went back to the reception area.

Just as he was sitting back down a dispirited Middle-Eastern-looking woman in a headscarf came out of

a side-door. She led a sad-eyed toddler and was followed by Jasmina Jalwar. Jasmina showed the woman
to the door without acknowledging Cutty.

'So you must bring in photocopies of all those documents by the end of the month, Mrs Ghodessi,' she
was saying. 'Otherwise we'll lose the chance to appeal
the council's decision, okay?'

The woman nodded.

'Don't forget or there'll be nothing we can do to
help you.'

The woman nodded again. She shuffled out with
her child and Jasmina turned to Cutty. 'Come through,
please.'

He followed her into an open-plan work area where
secretaries and admin assistants sat at computers. A
photocopier was rattling and humming and pumping
out documents.

'This way.'

Jasmina Jalwar led Cutty into a small office just off
the main area. He noticed that the office had a glass
door so that you could be seen at all times by whoever
was in the main area. On Jasmina's desk sat, in addition to a computer, phone and fax, a pile of bundled
case-files two feet high. On one wall hung framed legal
certificates. Through the window opposite the tops of
double-decker buses were visible as they passed by in
the street outside, and there was the constant noise and
vibration of traffic even though the window was firmly
closed.

Jasmina gestured to Cutty to take a seat. He did so.

'So you spoke with Ranjit?' she said.

'Him speak wit Buju an' Buju tell me say you want fi
see me.'

'Right. Well, what it is is, the police intend to prosecute you over the drugs they found in your flat.'

'But dem no bring di charge inna di courtroom,'

Cutty objected, his heart sinking.

'The CPS hadn't made a decision at that point,' Jasmina said. 'I think that if the rape case had gone ahead they would have let the drugs charge drop as a waste of public money. But since the rape case was dropped because of lack of enough solid evidence to convince a jury rather than because of solid evidence that no rape had taken place, or because the alleged victim withdrew her statement, they're trying to nail you for whatever they can. So they're charging you over the drugs.'

'Is persecution.'

'The drugs *were* found at your place of residence.'

'A frame-up.'

'Why?'

'Cah me is a black man.'

'They also say that you threw a bag containing substantial amounts of Ecstasy, Ketamine and cannabis resin out of the window when they broke into your flat,' Jasmina said. 'Ecstasy is a Class One drug considered to be on a level with heroin and cocaine.'

'Someone trow it down from a higher floor. Is nuttin' in dat bag dat connect it wit' me.'

'But they also found small amounts of Ecstasy, Ketamine and marijuana in your flat.'

'Someone else leave it dere.'

'If it's in your property the law says it's your responsibility.'

Cutty's eyeballs twitched. 'So what you sayin', den?'

'The amounts the police found in your flat were small enough to be considered for your personal use, rather than for dealing. Possession for personal use is a comparatively minor offence, though the range of drugs in your possession won't impress the court. However, if you then add in the amounts in the bag it becomes dealing and that's a much more serious charge. The police intend to charge you with dealing.'

Cutty's mind went blank. He felt the usual desire to run, but what good would that do? 'So what we a go do?' he asked.

'You and I go to the police station and you give yourself over to be charged.'

'When?'

Now wouldn't do, not when he had a loaded 35mm pistol in the waistband of his track-pants.

'I'll call them and tell them we can go in tomorrow morning.'

'No.'

Going to the police station of his own free will seemed like suicide in slow motion.

'There's really no other choice.'

'Dem a send me back a Brixton.'

'Probably not, if you give yourself up voluntarily. If they have to issue a warrant for your arrest, then certainly you would be remanded in custody, yes.'

'And den what?'

'As before you'll be charged in the Magistrate's Court the following day. Your bail application will be heard and the date of your committal hearing will be set.'

'Me cyaan go back a jail,' Cutty said hoarsely.

'I think that can be avoided,' Jasmina Jalwar said. 'I'll argue in the Magistrate's Court that you already spent four months in prison for a charge that was dropped by the CPS, and that to confine you further is unduly harsh.'

'So den me free, nuh?'

'Till the committal hearing, yes. But of course if you don't appear on the date the court sets for that a warrant would immediately be issued for your arrest.'

Cutty sighed. This was all worse than anything he had expected, although in retrospect it should have

been obvious that he would get done for at least possession. He wondered if Jasmina believed he had raped
Cynthia. If she did then maybe the advice she was
giving him now was bad.

'I have a suggestion,' she said.

'Tell me.'

'If you're found guilty of dealing you're looking at
maybe a three-year sentence and at the end of it
deportation back to Jamaica.'

Cutty winced.

'However the prosecution may have trouble connecting you with the larger amounts of drugs in the
bag. As you say, there's nothing to connect you con-
cretely with the bag itself. If you're prepared to plead
guilty to the smaller amounts found in your flat, for
which you'd almost certainly only get a fine and not a
custodial sentence, then we may be able to persuade
the CPS to drop the dealing charge.'

'Why would dem do dat?'

'Because it would save time and money and still be
some sort of result for them. If they prosecute you for
dealing and fail to connect you with the bag sufficiently
to convince a jury then they've wasted a lot of court-
time and public money and got nothing out of it at all.'

'Me haffi tink about it,' Cutty said uncertainly. It
went against his grain to give the authorities anything,
and pleading guilty even to the lesser charge seemed
like folly. But he understood too that it was about
strategy. *In di shitstem justice nuttin' but a game*, he
thought.

'Aright,' he said. 'I will confess.'

They arranged to meet at Jasmina Jalwar's office at
8.30 the following morning so she could go with him
when he gave himself up to the police. This he was
going to do at the police station on the Uxbridge Road,
where he had been taken after his first arrest. In the

meantime Jasmina pressed him to get his mobile fixed, or get himself a new one, so they could contact each other when necessary.

That gave the next part of Cutty's day purpose, and he got the tube back to Shepherds Bush to hunt a new mobile down.

The easiest way to do that was to go straight back to Buju's drum. It had just gone twelve. He and one or more of the posse would most likely still be loafing around there. One of them would almost certainly have a spare phone they could give Cutty right away, or would know of someone trying to offload one who he could go and see. Cutty resigned himself to returning there, although the prospect of being in the same room as Buju while Cynthia fluttered around him sent cold rage coursing through his chest.

Cutty felt a sudden spasm of lust then, a pumping need for hard, raw sex. Buju couldn't give him that, not now, maybe not ever. But maybe some stranger could. He dug back through his mind for anything anyone had ever told him about where men met men for sex in London, but he could remember nothing. And then a memory flashed into his mind of a conversation he had had with Spin and Gary about robbing queers. Where had they said they went to do it?

Hampstead Heath.

Now where the fuck was that?

And the mobile?

Fuck the mobile.

He slowed, turned, and headed back towards the tube-station.

Chapter Eighteen

C utty kicked himself for not having bought the *A-Z* he had looked at in the newsagent's earlier. Rather than go back there he went and stared at the tube map in the Underground station. Eventually he found two stations in North London that sounded about right, Hampstead on the Northern Line and West Hampstead on the Jubilee Line. He decided on Hampstead as he didn't know whether the Heath was to the north, south, east or west of it and didn't want to find himself in totally the wrong place. He took the Hammersmith & City line back round to King's Cross, feeling as he did so that he was getting nowhere with his day. But then he changed lines, and as he headed north on the Northern line anticipation began to build up in him. What would the Heath be like? Would he be able to connect with anyone once he found it? The train drew into the station. The doors juddered open and he got out. A chill draft of air flowed down to meet him as he climbed the escalator to the surface.

His first impression as he emerged from the station was that he was in a different city from the one he had left half an hour ago. To his left the road fell away steeply and there was a panoramic view across London. Directly ahead of him a main road ran away on the level. To his right it slanted sharply uphill, as did several smaller lanes branching off it. Unlike in Shepherds Bush or Brixton or even the West End the people on the streets were almost all white, and they had the particular confidence of the wealthy. The parked cars that lined the street running downhill were uniformly expensive: Bimmas, Mercedes, Saabs, Diahatsus. All-terrain vehicles were perversely popular in this wealthy, well-paved urban village. The shops – bar a generic Starbucks - were quaint and the buildings were old, older than anything around where he lived, but picturesque and well-maintained: antique, not run-down.

No-one was paying Cutty any attention but he began to feel self-conscious standing there looking around like a tourist. Where was the Heath?

He went back into the tube station and saw on one wall what he had only subliminally noticed before: a local map. It took him a moment to align the map with the streets outside, and then he realised that any of the roads running uphill would bring him to the Heath, which was much larger than he had expected, four square miles or so. He wondered where the cruising ground would be.

Feeling his nerve starting to drain away, Cutty pulled up his hoodie, left the station, and set off up the first side-road he came to. It was steep, and quickly dwindled into a pavementless lane. He passed brick cottages with well-tended lawns, quietly elegant Georgian terraces with pilastered porticoes and closed shutters, and a high and curving garden wall above which the branches of long-established pear- and apple-trees showed black against the pearl-grey sky. Sitting atop the wall a grey cat watched him pass by with opaque yellow eyes. Further along the lane Cutty's attention was caught by a great rose-bush trained on a trellis around a slate-roofed porch, and all of a sudden he found himself in the England of his childhood primers, the picturesque Mother Country so many of his parents' and grandparents'generations had believed in, and honoured, and found to be an illusion.

He reached the top of the hill and started down the

other side. Ahead, across a curving main road along
which cars were parked, was woodland. The Heath,
surely. A slim blonde woman in a long black leather
coat was urging two muddy red setters into the back of
a Range Rover. Two hefty, rosy-cheeked girls in shorts
jogged heavily past her, following a track parallel with
the road. Further on a man and a woman walked arm-
in-arm across a grassy area, their golden retriever
frisking around them.

Just as Cutty was reaching the conclusion that he
had come to the wrong part of the Heath he saw a skin-
headed white man wearing a military green bomber
jacket and leather trousers emerge from where the
trees fringing the grassy area were densest. The man
crossed casually to where his car – a Daihatsu Sportrak
- was parked a few spaces up from the Range Rover, got
in and drove off. Cutty crossed the road and headed for
the exact spot where the man had emerged from under
the trees.

The long, damp grass quickly soaked the ankles of
his tracksuit bottoms and the ground was muddy and
slippery underfoot, forcing him to tread carefully, but
once he got under the trees it was drier. Golden leaves
were strewn on the black, peaty earth and above his
head the bare branches created a greyish-green haze.
All colours were muted to earth tones. Despite the chill
and dampness in the air Cutty felt there was a certain
peace and beauty to the place that he hadn't come
looking for.

He noted used condoms lying here and there
among the roots of the trees, and thoughts of sex
returned to his mind and he made his way further into
the wood. He hadn't really given any thought to what
sort of men he might encounter here, but now it struck
him that they would most likely be white. Back home
he had never had any desire to have sex with white

men, but now he was here in Britain, where they were the natives and numerous, it seemed more natural to do so. He was even a little curious, as he knew from the pornography he had seen that white men were prepared to do almost anything sexually.

The sky darkened ominously overhead and colour drained away from his surroundings. Dark things sunk into blackness and light things took on a silvery, pellucid quality. Cutty felt the pressure drop slightly and shivered, hoping the rain would hold off as there was no shelter nearby other than that offered by the mostly leafless trees. His skin prickled as he looked about him.

Now he noticed men moving along the tracks and pathways among the trees and masses of dead furze and dry bracken. They walked at a particular slow pace that marked them out from those who had somewhere to get to. Some wore tight gay clothing, others Cutty wouldn't have been able to tell from their appearance that they liked sex with other men. He felt out of his depth. Back home he would have known what to say. Here he did not, and none of the men particularly attracted him. He moved on, avoiding meeting any glances that were sent his way.

Soon he found himself at a crossroads. He hesitated and looked around him, having no idea which way to go.

'Hey.'

He turned and saw a man leaning against a tree, watching him. He was blond, in his late twenties maybe, and studiedly unshaven. His long hair was pulled back in a ponytail and he had gold earrings in both ears. His face was angular, his mouth was wide, his lips were full for a white man's, and he had bright green eyes. He was slightly taller than Cutty, just over six foot, and lean-bodied, with strong-looking legs. He wore close-fitting black jeans, bike-boots and a black leather biker's jacket, and Cutty immediately pegged him as a roadie. The man held up a cigarette. He had silver rings on his large, square hand.

'Got a light, mate?' he asked.

Cutty didn't. He had left his cigarettes and lighter at Buju's. 'I don't, mate,' he replied, echoing the man's Cockney accent, making himself more anonymous.

The man shrugged and slipped the cigarette behind one ear. 'You got the time?' he asked.

'Sure.'

Cutty stepped off the path and went over to where the man was standing, raising his left arm as he did so. The man reached out and took hold of Cutty's wrist to bring the watch closer to his face. Cutty let him. He smelt of tobacco and deoderant.

'Thanks, mate,' the man said. He released Cutty's wrist. Cutty remained standing close to him, wondering what to say or do next.

Rain began to patter on the dry leaves. The man looked up at the bruised sky. 'I know somewhere,' he said.

Without another word he started towards the crossroads. When he reached it he looked back at Cutty. 'You coming, then?'

Cutty nodded, and followed him. The path they took curved round and up onto a raised area of scrub. Above it, further up the hill, were buildings of some sort. A large brick wall twenty feet high ran away to Cutty's right, curving gently down and out of sight. On top of it Cutty could see arbors and colonnades around which climbing plants had been trained. He and the other man followed the wall for a hundred yards or so and came to a long set of tall railings extending off from it to define a square or courtyard. Set into one side of the wall of railings was a wrought-iron gate that was ajar. The square was made up of empty flower-beds set out geometrically among orange-brown gravel walk-ways. At the back of it the high brick wall ran on. Arches were set into it, recessing into shadow.

The sky opened, the rain began to fall heavily, and without a backward glance the man broke into a run, forcing Cutty to run to keep up with him. A moment later they had both passed through one of the arches into the gloomy cloister within. It smelt strongly of soil and damp. Cutty laughed, breathless, afraid, exhila-rated, as the rain fell in a rushing grey-and-white curtain outside.

'What is dis place?' he asked, once he had got his breath back. 'We trespassin'?'

'Some big landscaping project,' the man said, wan-dering over to look out at the rain. His butt was high, and compact. 'They've been doing it up for years,' he went on. 'Ever since I been coming here. Renaissance gardens, Italian gardens, whatever. You can just walk about in 'em. But they lock this bit up at night. Not that it stops people climbing in if they've got a mind to,' he added.

He looked over at Cutty then.

Cutty swallowed nervously, excitement rising in his chest. Despite the cold his dick started to stiffen inside his briefs. Although it was gloomy he could see enough to see fear and excitement in the other man's face, and that gave him courage. After all, he had been chosen by this man. This man desired him.

'So what's your name, mate?' the man asked him.

'Steve,' Cutty replied, using a shortened version of his middle name.

'Jacko.'

They shook hands and didn't let go. Cutty's heart was pounding and his mouth was dry.

'So what you like doing then, Steve?' Jacko asked.

Cutty didn't reply.

'You like sucking?'

Cutty nodded. Jacko drew him back into the shadows. Wordlessly Cutty sank to his knees and buried his face in Jacko's crotch. The denim smelt freshly-laundered and he could feel Jacko's hard-on solidly diagonal against his nose and lips. This was what he had needed all day. He reached up and unbuttoned Jacko's fly and pulled Jacko's jeans down to mid-thigh. Underneath Jacko was wearing black lycra trunks. His dick jutted sideways along the line of his pelvis, held in place by the elastic material. It was large and thick. Cutty peeled the trunks down. Kneeling on the hard stone wasn't comfortable, but right then he didn't care. Jacko's skin was pale but smooth, and his stomach was flat. His pubic hair had been trimmed back to a neat fair patch and his circumcised dick bobbed in front of Cutty's eyes. It was buttery-peach in colour, with red undertones.

Cutty took Jacko's erection into his mouth. There was, somehow, a difference in taste, but it wasn't unpleasant, just different, and whether it was Jacko's whiteness or his particularity as a human being Cutty had no idea. His dick was hot and hard and it was what Cutty needed. He began to pump his mouth greedily back and forth on it, and Jacko gasped with pleasure above him.

After a few minutes Jacko gently took hold of Cutty's head and withdrew his dick from Cutty's mouth. 'Now I wanna suck you,' he said.

He sank to his knees in front of Cutty as Cutty rose to his feet.

Jacko reached up and took hold of the waistband of Cutty's track-pants with both hands. As he began to slide them down over Cutty's butt Cutty's pistol, which was still jammed into the front of the waistband, tipped forward and fell with a clatter onto the stone-flagged floor. Jacko looked down at it, then looked up with a startled expression on his face. Before Cutty could make a movement or say a word Jacko had scrambled to his feet and stumbled over to the archway, clawing up his jeans as he went. With only the most momentary backward glance he vanished into the still-bucketing rain.

Cursing his own stupidity and carelessness, Cutty snatched the gun up and shoved it back into his track-pants, jabbing the still-swollen head of his own dick painfully as he did so.

By the time he reached the archway Jacko had vanished from sight.

Cutty decided he had better return to the tube station directly and leave. It wasn't likely that Jacko would go to the police – not when he'd been out chasing dick on a gay cruising ground - but gun business was serious business and it was possible that he would alert the authorities, especially if he believed that Cutty had been planning to rob him at gunpoint.

Hunching his shoulders and wishing he had a proper jacket to wear rather than just his unlined tracksuit-top, Cutty hurried out into the downpour. He tried to retrace his steps but in his haste and worry missed his way and got lost. He criss-crossed the wooded area in a state of increasing panic. Eventually he came out at the main road where he had first entered the Heath, but further along, and for a while he trailed along in the wrong direction.

By the time he was fumbling for his travelcard at the ticket barrier of Hampstead station he was soaked right through. His feet were sodden, his trainers muddy and flooded. Despair and red madness filled his head as the escalator returned him underground. Under. Ground. The grave. The underworld. He seemed checked and defeated at every turn. He imagined shooting himself. And then he imagined shooting Cynthia.

Chapter Nineteen

By the time Cutty got back to White City he was shivering and feverish. Hood up, head down and shoulders hunched, he made his way back to Buju's block. The rain had passed but the temperature had dropped sharply. The wind cut through his still-damp clothing, draining him of energy and making his teeth ache. He stumbled up the steps to Buju's floor as exhausted as if he had run a marathon, buzzed on Buju's door, then let himself in without waiting for it to be answered.

'Is Cutty,' he called as he went inside.

He found Buju and Spin lounging on the sofa watching TV. Spin's X-Box was sitting on the coffee table: they had evidently been playing video games earlier on.

'You look terrible, man,' Buju said, getting to his feet as Cutty came into the room.

'I did caught in di rain,' Cutty said breathlessly, his skin prickling now he was out of the cold.

'You better take off them wet garms, bruv,' Buju said. 'I got some stuff you can wear while they're in the wash.'

'Tank you, man,' Cutty said, unzipping his sodden tracksuit top and peeling it off. He tried to read Buju's face as he handed the garment to him, but it was a mask. And since it was a mask worn in part because Spin was there, there was no way Cutty could get behind it and see the real Buju.

At least Cynthia wasn't around.

'You should have a hot shower, blood,' Spin said as

Cutty sat by him on the sofa and tugged off his water-logged trainers to reveal stained, muddy socks.

'He's right, bruv,' said Buju. 'Go shower, yeah. You know where the towels are.'

Cutty nodded. He got himself a towel from the airing-cupboard in the hall, then went through to Buju's bedroom and undressed. It was a relief just to be out of the wet clothes. He left them lying on the floor. The gun he placed out of sight on top of the wardrobe. He tied the towel round his waist, went through to the bathroom, and had the hottest shower he could bear. He felt better for it even though just standing upright under the pressure of the water was exhausting, and the artificial raising of his body temperature made it impossible for him to tell how feverish he really was. When he went back to the bedroom to dress he found that his wet, dirty clothing was gone. In its place, carefully laid out, were white socks, white Calvin Klein trunks, grey jogging pants and a loose white tee-shirt. Touched by Buju's gesture of consideration, Cutty put on the fresh, clean clothes. The gun he left on top of the wardrobe.

For di present.

He checked himself out in the wardrobe mirror and saw in the reflection that Buju was watching him from the doorway. Without a word Buju came forward and kissed him full on the mouth, a hot, urgent kiss. Buju's hazy eyes were wild. Behind him the bedroom door was wide open. Beyond it the lounge door was wide open. If Spin came out into the hall at that moment, or even just lent over on the sofa and looked out, he would see his don and his general eagerly pushing their tongues into each others' mouthes.

Buju broke off the kiss, turned, and left the room.

Cutty's dick had thrust to such instant and full erection in response to Buju kissing him that he had to wait several minutes before it softened enough for him to be able to go back to the lounge, and Spin, without his arousal being obvious. Buju was in the kitchen. Cutty watched him for a moment from the hallway, his head bent over the kitchen table, grating ginger root. The vivid smell of fresh ginger pricked the air. Behind Buju the washing-machine was churning and the kettle was boiling.

'So where you vanish off to this morning, man?' Spin asked when Cutty re-entered the lounge. 'Cos Buju was freaking out, blood, I'm telling you. *Freaking.* Like he thought - '

'I did haffi go see mi lawyer,' Cutty said, cutting Spin off. He lowered himself into the armchair. His joints were aching. It was flu for certain.

'Bad news, yeah?'

'Yeah. Dem wan' charge me over di drugs dem find inna mi yard.'

'Shit, man. What, possession or dealing?'

'Di lawyer shi reckon I cyan plead to possession and dem will drop di other charge.'

'Well, possession ain't a big deal, bruv,' Spin said. 'Not so long as it's just like for personal use only.'

'So di lawyer tell I.'

Spin nodded. Then, after glancing at the doorway to check that Buju was still in the kitchen, he lent forward and asked in a low voice, 'So what's the deal with Cynthia, man?'

'She make a mistake, mi bruddah.'

'Yeah. But - '

'No trust she,' Cutty interrupted. 'She lie. Di bom-baclaat bitch lie.'

'Hey,' Spin said. 'She ain't say jack about what went down to me. She ain't tell me nothing 'bout nothing, you know what I'm saying? So that's why I was arxing, you know? To get like the true picture.'

'Well, dat is all mi haffi say pon di subject, seen.'

'I ain't wanting to pain you, man. Just it's been the subject of 'nuf vexation with the click, you know?'

'Cah you like Cynthia?'

Spin looked down, embarrassed. 'It ain't that, man,' he said awkwardly. 'Yeah, she's fit and that, but she's Buju's matey and anyway even if she weren't the click comes first, I know that. Just - '

'So Buju no tell you wha'appen?'

'Well, yeah, he did,' Spin said. 'Well, kind of. But what I wanna know is - '

Spin cut himself off as Buju came into the lounge with a hot mug of lemon, honey and grated ginger. He handed it to Cutty, who took it from him and held it in both hands, inhaling the steam gratefully. Buju went back to the kitchen and returned a moment later with two mugs of tea, one for Spin, one for himself.

The three of them sat in silence for a while. An old Technicolor Western was playing on the TV with the sound down. Cutty sipped his drink and wondered what Buju had told the click, and what Cynthia had told Spin. It suddenly occurred to him that it was Spin who Cynthia had been cheating on Buju with. It was Spin who had fucked Cynthia the day of his arrest. If that was so, then Spin was an enemy. But what had Cynthia told him? A bunch of lies? Or the truth? Or, as Spin himself said, nothing? When Cutty looked over at Spin Spin met his eyes easily enough. Cutty didn't believe Spin could sit alone in a room with two battymen and act normally.

Cutty began to feel very sleepy. But there were things that had to be dealt with, and he pushed himself upright in the armchair and tried to focus on them. He cleared his throat and told Buju what he had already told Spin about the drugs charges, adding that he was going to the police station with his solicitor the following morning, and to the magistrate's court probably the day after that.

'Cah if I don't plead to possession for personal use when it go to di court proper, and dem do I for dealing and convict I, den me lookin' at serious jail time an' den deportation afterwards.'

'Your solicitor reckon you get bail this time, though, yeah?' Buju asked.

'Yeah, probably,' Cutty said. 'Cah it a minor charge and I was stuck in jail for months di time before and dem finally just drop di charge. But if dem need a bond, den me na have no money.'

Buju met his eyes, then looked away.

'They probably won't, though,' Spin said, trying to sound positive.

Cutty grunted. He was sure they would demand a bond, why wouldn't they? He wanted, needed, Buju to offer the money. He couldn't ask him for it. But Buju didn't offer it.

Cutty's head began to whirl.

There was a rattle at the front door.

'Cynthia,' Buju said tonelessly as they heard the door judder open and cold air gusted round the flat. A moment later Cynthia appeared in the doorway in a long quilted coat with a white fun-fur hood. She smiled at Spin. Then she noticed Cutty.

'You look like shit,' she said coldly.

'My man got caught in the rain,' Buju said, giving her an unfriendly look.

Cynthia crossed the room and kissed Buju on the cheek anyway, clearly determined to claim him in front of Cutty. Cutty watched Spin checking Cynthia's backside as she bent over Buju. He wondered if Buju had guessed that Spin and Cynthia were fucking each other. If he had, wouldn't he just kick Cynthia to the kerb? But of course if he did that, then what would stop her from telling Spin the truth?

He tried to imagine a world without complications, a world where you could just be yourself, but it had no form and no texture.

'I cyan crash here tonight?' he asked Buju with an effort.

'Course, man,' Buju said easily. 'Long as you like.'

Cutty nodded his thanks and lay back in the armchair. Sleep came over him rapidly. As his eyelids fluttered closed he watched Spin watching Cynthia as she watched Buju.

When Cutty awoke he was on his own. Someone had put a duvet over him while he was asleep. The blinds were closed and one lamp was on. He looked at his watch. It was 10 p.m. His head was aching and he was bursting for a piss. He dragged himself to his feet and went through to the bathroom. As he emptied his bladder his head began to throb so intensely that he thought for a moment that he was going to faint. He flushed the toilet, then dug some Panadols out of the medicine cabinet above the sink. He closed it and stared at his reflection in its mirrored door. His eyes were red, his skin was greasy, and he looked haggard.

Buju's bedroom door was half-open. He looked in. No-one was there: the flat was deserted.

He stumbled through to the kitchen, poured himself a glass of water, and swallowed four pills. Then he went back to his chair in the lounge. The TV was still on with the sound muted. Some British cop show he didn't recognise was showing. Squad cars were pulling up, police-officers in riot gear peeling out. There was an explosion in a building. He closed his eyes and tried to go back to sleep but his aching body kept him awake. After a while he went and stretched out on the couch, which was a little less uncomfortable.

Eventually he drifted off, but his sleep was troubled by broken-up, confused fragments of dreams. He dreamed he was back in Jamaica, but it looked like Hampstead Heath. In its centre was a church, and the church had a cloister with arched entrance-ways, and these led down into dark pits he was drawn to but did not dare to enter. He seemed to be seeking sanctuary. Sometimes he was himself, sometimes he was watching himself, as if he was a character in a film. Then he was watching an image of Sonny's erect dick being pro-jected onto a vast screen. It was perfect and flawless and enormous and full of throbbing masculine energy, but it was also laced with blood. In the background men were talking about which type of gun was best for an execution, and Cutty had the sudden image of Buju kneeling with blood running down his face, his hands tied behind his back, and a gun in his mouth. At the same time he, Cutty, was tasting the metal of the barrel of the gun in his mouth as if he was Buju.

He woke abruptly. The room was in darkness: the lamp and TV had been turned off, and the door to the hall closed. Buju and Cynthia must have come back and gone to bed, he supposed. His watch told him it was 1.30 a.m. He was half-minded to go and peep in on them, to see if Cynthia really was there in bed with Buju, but just sitting upright made his head pulse.

He would get Buju on his own eventually.

He set the alarm on his watch for 7.30 a.m. and tried to go back to sleep.

Chapter Twenty

At 7.30 a.m. Cutty's watch-alarm went off, nagging him from sleep. Outside it was still dark. Cutty felt drained but the fever had passed from him, and when he got to his feet only the slight resonance of a headache remained. He shook out the duvet, folded it, and put it away. Then he showered away the night's sweat. Buju had draped his freshly-washed clothes over the radiators in the lounge and hallway, and they were now dry and warm and ready to wear. His trainers hadn't fully dried out, but his feet were two sizes bigger than Buju's, so he had to resign himself to wearing them slightly damp. He gulped down a pint of water to rehydrate himself, then left the flat. It was 7.50 a.m. He knew he should eat something but he had no appetite.

The tube to King's Cross was packed with commuters so he had to stand the whole way, which tired him more than it would have done if he'd been well. It was a whole other world, this early-morning world of salaries and pay-packets, careers and bonuses and paid holidays, suits and daily papers and grumbles about delays and Never Getting A Seat.

At King's Cross he bought some popcorn chicken from a KFC opposite the station and forced himself to eat it as he made his way to Jasmina Jalwar's office. He had said he would get there for 8.30 but ended up not arriving until just after 9. He could tell Jasmina was unimpressed with him turning up over half an hour late for their appointment, stuffing his face on fast food, but felt too flat to care.

They went through to her office and from there

Jasmina called Uxbridge Road police station to explain that Cutty was coming in voluntarily to be charged. Then they got the Tube back round to Shepherds Bush, which took half an hour. Cutty sat in silence for most of the journey, beaten down by the judder and rattle of the train. Jasmina worked her way through two files she had brought with her. Cutty wondered what her husband was like – he had noticed she wore a wedding ring - and if she had children.

The police station was only five minutes' walk from the tube station. It felt extremely strange to Cutty to be walking of his own free will into the same police station he had been dragged into, battered and handcuffed, four months before; where he had been charged with rape.

This time it was very different. There was no attempt to intimidate him, and everything proceeded in a civilised, bureaucratic fashion. He didn't even have to give his fingerprints or be photographed, as his prints and his face were already on file from his previous arrest. The only change was that he now gave Buju's address as his place of residence. He was charged with possession of controlled substances with intent to supply and instructed to appear at the designated magistrate's court the following morning. He was warned that should he not turn up a warrant would be issued for his arrest. Then he was free to go. The whole procedure took just under half an hour.

It felt stranger to walk out of the police station than it had to walk in. Almost good, were it not for the two court appearances looming. But at least they hadn't locked him up. Not yet.

He walked Jasmina back to the tube. She chided him for failing to sort out a mobile phone, suggested that he wore a suit for his court appearance, and stressed that he had to be on time or the magistrate might rule that he had failed to appear as instructed and issue a warrant for his arrest, which would without question land him back in jail. He told her to chill out. She gave him an annoyed look and went to get her train.

It was 10.30 a.m.

Uppermost in Cutty's mind was the question of how he was going to get the money to give over for his bail. In a previous conversation Jasmina had guessed it would be set at around £2,000. Which wasn't much if you had money, but a fortune if you didn't. That had been for rape. Was drug-dealing worse than rape in the eyes of the law? Probably. Then he would need more than £2,000.

'Yo, blood!' a voice called from across the street. 'Blood!'

Cutty looked round and saw Gary, the white boy of the click. He was wearing a white baseball hat at the same jaunty angle as Buju did, an outsize white Nike sweatshirt with a gold rope worn outside it around his neck, sagging blue jeans and Timberland boots. He swaggered across the road, forcing a bus to slow and a cyclist to swerve. He came up to Cutty and they gripped hands Centurion-style and embraced momentarily.

'So what you doin'?' Gary asked as they stepped back from each other.

'Just been dealing wit di feds and di law,' Cutty replied. 'Me haffi go a magistrate's court tomorrow morning.'

'Bad news, man.'

"Llow it,' Cutty said with a shrug. He didn't want to talk about it. 'Ya up earlydoors, blood,' he remarked.

'JSA, innit,' Gary said. 'Jobseekers Allowance,' he added, seeing the blank look on Cutty's face. 'Social. The dole. Welfare.'

Cutty nodded.

'They made me come in for a interview, man. They want me train up go work in some shitty call-centre for minimum wage somewhere. Can you believe it? Course I told 'em to fuck off. Fuckers.' He shook his head in disbelief at the presumptuousness of the state.

Although he was white, Gary had always very much reminded Cutty of the lost boys he had known in the Lick Shot Posse. He had the same anger and aggression as they did, covering the same deep sense of worthlessness. Perhaps because of his encounter on Hampstead Heath the day before with a white man who he'd found attractive, Cutty was also for the first time aware of how intensely blue Gary's eyes were, and that for all the sharpness of his features he was a good-looking youth.

'You know anyone dat want rid of a mobile?' he asked him.

Gary was tapping out two Marlborough Lights from a packet. 'You want a mobile?' he asked, handing Cutty one of the cigarettes.

'I need one today,' Cutty said, taking it.

'No sweat.' Gary lit Cutty's cigarette then his own. 'Come by my drum and I fix you up, bruv.'

'Now?'

Gary shrugged. 'If you ain't doing nothing else.'

Side-by-side they set off for Gary's yard.

Gary lived with his mother in a moderately well-to-do estate made up of low-rises and subsidised housing just west of White City. She had had to fight to get herself and her son into a small block that contained just six flats. It was modern, well-maintained, the lobby was carpeted and the intercom always worked. A well-tended pot-plant stood by the front door. The downside of living there for Gary was that he wasn't supposed to bring his friends round because the other residents had made a formal complaint to the managing agency about youths loitering intimidatingly in the halls and stairwell. They had meant the click, and Gary's mum had been threatened with eviction as a result. So she had barred Gary from having Buju, Maxie, Cutty or Spin to visit. But right now she was out at work, at the part-time job she had as a receptionist at a nearby dentist's. In the afternoons she further supplemented her income by cutting and styling local women's hair in her own home.

Cutty had never been in Gary's flat before. The front room was simply furnished and very clean, but cluttered with scissors, razors, clippers, brushes, an over-head hair-dryer, rows of bottles and bowls of Caucasian hair-care products. Magazines full of pictures of the ways Euro hair could be cut and styled were fanned out carefully on a coffee-table. The room smelt like a salon, a not unpleasant smell.

Cutty followed Gary through to his bedroom. It was small, and very much a boy's room, with posters of Fifty Cent and Tupac on the walls, surrounded by pictures of hip-hop honiez torn from magazines. There was a wardrobe, a single bed, a chest-of-drawers with a portable TV on it, and a small blondwood desk with a computer on it. Clean and dirty clothes were strewn about mixed in together. Gary pulled open the bottom drawer of the chest-of-drawers. It was full of mobile phones still in their packaging. Gary pulled one out and held it out to Cutty.

'Blue tooth, video messaging, the works.'

'How much?' Cutty asked.

'Compliments of the house,' Gary said with a grin.

'I owe you one, yeah,' Cutty said, taking the phone from him.

'They're all enabled and ready to use.'

'Whey you get dem from, blood?'

'They was kind of in transit,' Gary said evasively, still grinning. 'Now they're just even more in transit, you know what I'm saying?'

Cutty nodded and prised the packaging open. He didn't much care where the mobiles had come from so long as they worked. If Gary wanted to be mysterious about it that was his business. Cutty had kept the chip from his old phone in his wallet. He opened the new phone up, lifted the battery and slid the chip into place beneath it, then clicked the casing shut.

'Let's get it charged up, yeah,' Gary said, taking the phone off him. Cutty followed Gary through to the galley-kitchen. There Gary placed the mobile in a charger that was sitting on a work-surface already plugged in.

'You want something to eat, man?' he asked.

'What you 'ave?'

'Microchips.'

'Sure.'

After Gary had heated the chips in the microwave and he and Cutty had eaten them he rolled a joint and they smoked it together. They didn't talk much. Cutty imagined Gary probably wanted to ask him about what had happened between him, Cynthia and Buju, but couldn't find a way in. Cutty didn't offer him one. Once the phone was charged Cutty called Elliot & Markby and left his new number with the receptionist.

Around 12.30 Gary began to get edgy.

'Sorry, man,' he said. 'But I gotta kick you out now. My mum'll be back any time now and you know she don't check for my bredrens.'

Cutty shrugged and got up. Gary saw him to the door of the building. There they gripped hands and embraced again.

'Bell you later, man,' Gary said.

Cutty nodded. Gary went back inside. The security door swung shut behind him and locked.

Cutty wondered what to do next. At least it wasn't raining. His thoughts returned to bail money. If Buju would front him some gear he might be able to hustle something up by tomorrow morning. Or, if that wasn't practical, much as he didn't want to he would have to ask Buju to loan him the money outright. He rang Buju's mobile to find out where he was but the call went straight to ansaphone. Defeated, he trudged back to the flat.

No-one was in.

He was just helping himself to a beer from the fridge when there was a clatter at the front door and someone let themselves in. It was Cynthia. She was carrying a bulky carrier bag. He glared at her.

'Making yourself at home, I see,' she said, glancing down at the can in his hand, then returning his hard look coolly.

'Me na di only one,' Cutty replied, moving his eyes down to the carrier bag she was holding. In it was a cellophane-wrapped bed-sheet, duvet-cover and pillow-slip set. It had a pink-and-yellow floral motif.

'The feminine touch,' Cynthia said with a small, tight smile.

'Him don't like pink.'

'You'd know that, would you?'

Cutty shrugged. 'You is just like all women,' he said. 'Cyaan accept a man for what him is. Haffi change him. It don't work, Cynthia. It don't never work.'

Cynthia's mouth moved as if she was going to say something to that, but instead she turned and left the room without another word. Cutty stood in the kitchen sipping his beer and listened to her rip the cellophane packaging open and change the bedsheet and duvet-cover.

His mobile rang. He checked the number, hoping it would be Buju, but it was Spin. Gary must have rung him and given him his new number. Cutty slipped the cordless earpiece into his ear and answered it.

'Yo, blood.'

'So G fix you up with a phone then?'

'Yes, mi bruddah. So what I cyan do for you?'

'More what I can do for you, man.'

'Yeah?'

'Buju said to front you some merchandise, yeah? Like, on tick.'

'Aright,' Cutty said. 'Cool. Mek we hook up, yeah?'

'So where you hanging, man?' Spin asked. 'I got wheels.'

'Out and about, mi bruddah,' Cutty said vaguely. 'Here an' dere.' He didn't want Spin to come to Buju's drum while Cynthia was there: he didn't trust Cynthia not to start making sly remarks to wind him up in Spin's presence.

'In the Bush, yeah?'

'Yeah.'

'I can be at the Roti Hut in fifteen.'

'Cool. I dere.'

Cutty snapped his phone shut. He swallowed the rest of his beer and left the flat without saying another word to Cynthia.

Twenty minutes later Spin pulled up outside the Roti Hut in a black series 3 BMW. Despite the grey drabness of the day he swaggered in wearing Raybans and shot the girl behind the counter a wide smile that she shyly returned.

'Big Man's Wheels,' Cutty said as they touched fists.

'You know it, man.'

Spin went over to the counter and ordered jerk chicken and rice and peas to go. He was wearing a close-fitting white Nicole Farhi jumper, low-riding black Levi's and indigo Timb's. Away from Buju he had the manner of a don, and Cutty realised that Spin had ambitions. So far he had managed to veil those ambitions from Buju but now here he was revealing them to Cutty. Why? Did that mean he had a plan and he wanted to get Cutty on side? Or had he lost respect for Cutty as well as Buju while Cutty had been in jail? Was Spin scheming to supplant Cutty as Buju's general? Or did he want to take over from Buju as the click's leader and become a don? Cutty knew that Buju had lost his appetite for the role lately: for some time he had been talking about an exit strategy from the drugs business once he had made enough money to kick-start a legitimate business. Cutty looked Spin over and once again found himself wondering if Cynthia had been dropping sly hints to Spin about Buju and himself; if her words might be fuelling Spin's new-found desire for promotion.

Nothing stand still, he thought. He realised that his fantasy of picking up with Buju pretty much where they had left off had always been exactly that: a fantasy. He followed Spin out to his Bimma.

Cruising the streets in a flash motor was a totally different experience from trudging along on foot or waiting around on tube platforms, and it took Cutty back to the summer and better days, days of driving around with Buju in his Sportrak with the roof off, days of blue skies and sunshine. Everything had been sweet then. Except for Cynthia. And if Cynthia hadn't come up with her bullshit he wouldn't now be waiting on this dealing charge and the threat of more jail time, and deportation.

Dat gyal, she fuck up mi life.

They drove over to nearby Latimer Road and pulled up in front of a high-rise opposite the tube station.

'You wait here, yeah?' Spin said as he turned off the

engine. 'I know this geezer and you don't, yeah, and he's kind of on a hair-trigger, you know what I'm saying? He's expecting just the one of us and he don't like no surprises.'

Cutty shrugged. Spin got out of the car.

'Parking warden comes, move the motor, yeah,' he said, tossing Cutty the car-keys. It was a definite diss, but Cutty had no money and he needed the drugs, so he had no option but to take it.

For di present.

Spin crossed the street and disappeared into the tower-block. Cutty looked after him and wondered if he would have to beat Spin down. He knew he was harder than Spin and he hoped Spin was smart enough to know it too. But if Spin carried on dissing him and Buju then it would become become necessary to remind him who ran tings. Cutty didn't want to do that any more than he wanted to be a drug-dealer. He felt as if he was turning into his brother Joseph, the brother he had always despised for his lack of vision. The brother who was dead. Perhaps he should have brought the gun.

Spin was gone for over half an hour, and when he returned he smelt strongly of dope-smoke, but he had made the deal. Cutty returned the car-keys to him and Spin drove them to a deserted industrial estate next to Wormwood Scrubs. There Spin parcelled out the drugs. Cutty ended up with a paper packet containing a bag of Ecstasy tablets and a decent-sized chunk of cannabis resin. It was something, but he didn't reckon he could make more than £800 from the pills and dope combined, and that would almost certainly not be enough for his bail tomorrow. He wondered if Buju had meant for Spin to give him more, but there was nothing he could do about it if he had. Cutty bent over and pushed the folded paper packet into the top of one sock, then readjusted his track pants to conceal the bulge it made.

'So where can I drop you, man?' Spin asked as he restarted the car.

'Buju's block.'

Cutty no longer cared if Spin wanted to come in and found Cynthia there.

Spin evidently had other places to be, however: when he drew up outside the block he didn't even pull in but double-parked, flicking on his hazard lights. As Cutty got out he had a sudden last thought.

'Spin, man, mek you do I a favour?' he asked.

'What favour, man?' Spin's tone was neutral.

'Lend I a suit for di courtroom tomorrow.'

He and Spin were the same height. Cutty was broader-shouldered, but their builds were similar otherwise.

'I bring it by Buju's drum laters, yeah,' Spin said grudgingly.

Cutty nodded his thanks and pushed the car-door closed, and a moment later Spin was gone, brake lights flashing as the Bimma turned the corner sharply and raced off up towards the Westway.

Cutty turned to face Buju's block. Before climbing the stairs to Buju's drum he tried him on the mobile again. Again it went straight to ansaphone. Cutty left no message. He looked up at Buju's windows and imagined having some sort of confrontation with Cynthia that would resolve everything once and for all. He remembered the good feeling of Buju's lips on his. And he remembered Buju not offering to go surety for him.

His face hardening, Cutty turned away. What was between him, Buju and Cynthia would have to wait. Right now he had dollars to make.

The rest of the day Cutty hustled. He called in on a hair-stylist he had sold to before, a diminutive white

girl who worked in a salon just off Ladbroke Grove. She
wore thick black eyeliner, had peroxide-blonde hair
extensions that hung down to her arse, and always
wore platform boots that laced up to her knees. Ute was
her name. German or Dutch, he couldn't remember. He
managed to offload some pills to her for a decent price.
She was just going for a break when he arrived at the
salon, and they shared a joint in an upstairs store-room
to seal the transaction, and also so she could sample his
dope. She kissed him on the mouth but he didn't
respond. On his last visit she had offered him a blow-
job. That time he had almost said yes, but it wasn't her
lips he wanted on his dick.

Ute didn't want to buy the cannabis resin but she
thought that one of the queens she worked with, a fey,
shaven-headed Australian, had a friend who might. Ute
pestered the man into making a call, which he did,
rather grudgingly, Cutty thought. Clearly he didn't
much like Cutty or want to help him out. Perhaps he
was a racist, or perhaps he just saw Cutty as a macho,
most likely homophobic thug. Or maybe it was just that
the loud-mouthed Ute got on his nerves and any friend
of hers was no friend of his. But he made the call, and
twenty minutes later Cutty was in Queensway, making
his way along a dilapidated Georgian terrace to a flat
where a bunch of young Australians and white South
Africans were staying.

'The candyman's here,' a pretty, smiling white girl
said as she opened the door to him. He went inside.

They had the openness of those who don't believe
that the laws of the country they're staying in apply to
them, these young people. The flat they were living in
was either a squat or little better than one. After giving
out a couple of free samples Cutty managed to shift the
resin for a better price than he had hoped for. Not
enough for what he'd need for his bail tomorrow,

however, and since the backpackers weren't interested in his leftover Es he resigned himself to traipsing up to the West End later on to sell them in some bar or club queue. In the meantime he was content to kill time in the students' unthreatening company, and accepted the tins of beers they freely offered him.

'I was hitch-hiking in Morocco last year,' one of the girls was saying to her friends as she popped a can of Heineken and passed it to him. 'All by myself. Can you imagine?' She laughed and rolled her eyes. 'I know, I know, I was being *really stupid*. Anyway, these two Moroccan lorry-drivers pulled over and offered me a lift and I said yes. They asked me if I wanted to go with them to their dope farm up in the Rift Mountains and I said sure, why not. I mean *really*, how stupid can you get? But anyway I went up there, and I stayed there for a couple of weeks lying about in the sun and they didn't come on to me or anything, and then I asked them to drive me back down to the airport at Marrakesh. They asked me if I'd smuggle some dope for them and I said I didn't want to, which they were fine about. And they did drive me to the airport and I was so glad I'd said no because there were sniffer dogs everywhere.' She laughed again. 'Now I can't believe how completely stupid I was. I mean I could have been raped or murdered or anything, or got twenty-five years in jail!'

Cutty laughed too, slightly stoned and drunk by that point. The girl was fresh-faced and had never seen death or horror. He envied her her golden innocence. The other boys and girls sitting around the room now began to compete with her, offering up tales of their own reckless exploits. After a while one of them, a lanky Australian youth, turned to him with bright, if red-rimmed, eyes.

'You must have some tales, mate,' he said. 'Can you top Janie's?'

'Mi bruddah did shot on a streetcorner, downtown Kingston,' Cutty said heavily. 'In a gang cross-fire. Four years ago. Him was a drug dealer. Heroin and crack.'

'Did he die?' Janie - the Morocco girl - asked uneasily.

'Tree bullet to di chest, one in di skull.' He mimed a shooting motion, thumb and forefinger to his own temple.

The others fell silent. The atmosphere in the room changed. They were a little afraid of him now. He had become the raw centre in the middle of their steak, bloody and unwanted. Too revealing of the animal truth.

'Me haffi chip,' he said, struggling to his feet. Some home-training kicked in and the boy with the bright eyes got up too and saw him to the door.

'Sorry, mate,' he said. 'I didn't mean to – you know.'

'Is aright, man,' Cutty said. 'Is cool.'

By then it was 9.30 p.m. Cutty walked up Queensway and caught a bus to Leicester Square. He made his way along to Old Compton Street, wanting once again to see the battyboys parading uninhibitedly out in the open. He thought of going to Kudos to offload his remaining Es but was too self-conscious to go there on his own. Instead he went and sat in a nearby McDonalds for an hour, then sold them to clubbers in the queue for G.A.Y.

By eleven-fifteen he was done. He had made £930. It was a sizeable roll, not bad for a day's work, but it wouldn't be enough to keep him out of jail. But he couldn't think of any other way to raise funds. And he was exhausted: he hadn't fully recovered from yesterday's flu and the temperature had fallen steadily throughout the evening. He could think of nothing to do but get the tube back to White City.

He found Buju, Cynthia, Spin, Maxie and Gary in the lounge watching TV and listening to music. Another girl, Cookie, had come round with Maxie and was sharing the armchair with him. She was pretty, petite and, like Maxie, biracial, with short corkscrew curls. Spin showed Cutty the suit he had brought for him to wear in court. It was a smart pearl-grey, and still in its dry-cleaning polythene. Spin had also brought a white shirt and plain black shoes to go with it. Cutty thanked him and decided that his earlier assessment of Spin's motives had been unduly harsh.

Just another young bruddah trying to cut a dash an' stressing to impress.

As on other nights they all sat up drinking and smoking. This time Cynthia seemed determined to stay up as late as the rest of them, and ended up falling asleep on the sofa, her bare feet curled up under her, her head in Buju's lap.

Maxie and Cookie headed off around 1.30, but the others stayed interminably on. Once again Cutty had to give up on getting any time alone with Buju, and finally drifted off to sleep next to Cynthia on the sofa some time after three.

Chapter Twenty-One

Cutty got up early the next morning hung over and short of sleep. He showered, shaved and put on the shirt and suit and shoes Spin had lent him. Buju and Cynthia had gone to bed at some point while he was asleep, but Spin and Gary were still lolling unconscious on the sofa when he left to go to court.

He had £930 in a roll in his pocket.

There was no-one around to wish him good luck.

He met Jasmina Jalwar in the foyer of the magistrate's court, and she introduced him to his barrister for the day, Peter Levinson, a balding, round-faced man in his fifties who wore thick glasses and had a brisk, friendly manner. As they made their way to a seating area to wait to be called Jasmina briefed Peter Levinson on the previous charge against Cutty and how this charge came about as a result of it. That he wasn't being held in a cell this time around should have made Cutty feel hopeful but it didn't as he couldn't see any way of avoiding looming imprisonment: it didn't seem likely from what Peter Levinson said that his bail – if he even got it – would be set at under £1000.

After a wait of twenty minutes the list-caller called Cutty's case. Jasmina shook his hand and wished him luck, and he entered the courtroom alongside Peter Levinson. His palms were sweating as he stepped up into the dock, and the suit-jacket was slightly too tight across his shoulders.

The district judge was a large-boned Asian woman with bouffant hair who wore half-moon spectacles. She looked bored. Cutty found himself staring ahead like a zombie as the charge of possession with intent to supply was read out against him.

'Not guilty,' he said with an effort.

The judge then heard Peter Levinson's application for bail, and the CPS lawyer's objections to granting it. These, except for the part about Cutty menacing the key witness if he was left at large, were much the same as before: that Cutty was a foreign national who was likely to abscond if given the opportunity; that he lacked assets in, or ties to, the UK; and that he lacked even a fixed address.

'Your honour,' Peter Levinson responded. 'When he was informed by his solicitor that he was being charged with this offence Mister Munroe voluntarily attended his local police station to be charged, and he has voluntarily attended this court today. If he was likely to abscond he would have already done so, rather than risk coming before this court. He has pleaded not guilty and intends to vigorously dispute the accusation in court. Further, your honour, my client has recently spent almost four months on remand in connection with other charges which the CPS then dropped the instant the case came before the court due to lack of evidence. While I am not contending that the current charges against my client are purely vexatious, to refuse Mister Munroe bail in these circumstances would, I think, be unduly harsh.'

Peter Levinson sat down. The judge looked down at the papers in front of her and sucked in her teeth. The light caught on the rims of her half-moon glasses and made them flash and flare. Her brow puckered as she flicked Cutty's file back and forth. Cutty's entire body was locked with tension and he longed to shout something out. An anticipatory hatred began to surge up in him.

'I'm inclined to agree with you, Mister Levinson,'

the judge said after a long moment had passed, 'that to refuse bail would be unduly harsh. However, due to your client's uncertain address and lack of firm ties to the United Kingdom I'm setting the amount at £2,500.'

Sweat trickling coldly down his armpits, Cutty lent forward and whispered to Peter Levinson that he didn't have that much money.

'Your honour, setting my client's bail at that level for an offence of this sort seems punitive.'

'Nonetheless, that is my decision,' the judge said, looking over her spectacles at him. 'Which you may, of course, appeal.'

'But in the meantime Mister Munroe will be in jail.'

'I can pay,' a voice said.

Cutty looked round. It was Buju. He was in the part of the court set aside for visitors and observers, and must have slipped in after Cutty and Peter Levinson had taken their seats. He was standing, and shifting nervously from one foot to the other. His eyes were bright and his expression was hard and bold. He wore a red leather baseball cap high above a white bandana, his red and white leather biker's jacket, sagging jeans and dull red Timberlands on his feet. He had never looked more beautiful.

'And you are?' the judge asked.

Cutty quickly whispered to Peter Levinson. Peter Levinson got to his feet.

'This is Mister Brian Staples, your honour,' he said. 'Mister Munroe is currently living with Mister Staples, a contact of his in the music industry, a friend, and his *de facto* sponsor in this country.'

'I can pay,' Buju repeated.

'Thank you, Mister Staples,' the judge said. 'Please take your seat.'

Uncertainly, Buju did so.

'In the circumstances,' the judge continued, 'the

court will require the bail to be in the form of a security.'

'She means she wants cash,' Peter Levinson whispered to Cutty. Cutty twisted his head round and
mouthed 'cash' to Buju.

'I got the cash,' Buju said, holding up a roll of bills.

'Thank you, Mister Staples,' the judge said, apparently amused rather than offended by his nervy breach
of courtroom etiquette. 'You may arrange to see the
clerk afterwards for a receipt. Mister Munroe, you are
bailed to appear before the court on January thirteenth,
that is in just over two months' time. Do you have any
questions?'

'I cyan go?'

'Yes, Mister Munroe, you can go.'

Cutty thanked Peter Levinson. Then he and Buju went
to the Payments Office. At the counter of the Payments
Office Cutty pulled out his roll to pay what he could,
but Buju insisted he keep it.

'That's your seed money and survival stash, bruv,'
Buju said as he peeled off £2,500 from his own roll and
pushed the wedge of notes under the glass. The woman
behind the counter counted them off briskly.

'You understand that should Mister Munroe fail to
appear in court on the due date without sufficient
reason or excuse this money may be forfeit?' she
intoned. Buju nodded. The woman made out a receipt
and slid it to him under the glass.

'You're mine now, bruv,' Buju said to Cutty as he
pocketed the receipt, a suggestive smirk on his face.

They left the courthouse and went to find Buju's
Sportrak. It was parked just a street away, on a meter,
but there was a parking-ticket under the windscreen-
wiper.

'Didn't have no change, did I?' Buju said with a

shrug, shoving the ticket into the glove-compartment as he got into the car. 'Plus I was on a schedule, you know what I'm saying? Get in, man.'

Cutty climbed in on the passenger side and Buju started the engine.

'I got a trip to make,' Buju said, hitting the indicator and making a fast u-turn. 'You got anywhere to be the next X hours?'

'Anywhere but jail,' Cutty said.

Buju laughed and Cutty wondered if he was high on something. The sky had cleared and the sun was bright and although it was cold outside, inside the car it was pleasantly warm. Cutty didn't mind if Buju was high and he didn't much care where they were going: he was content to sit back and watch the streets pass by. He loosened his tie and unbuttoned his collar. Now he was free for at least a little while he felt connected with the rest of humanity again; with the minutiae of life; with human suffering and joy. Buju darted glances at him and kept on breaking out in small smiles.

They drove up onto the Westway. From its elevated curve Cutty caught glimpses of football and basketball courts flashing by below. He looked out at tube and railway lines and across the backsides of houses, at office blocks and multi-storey car-parks standing tall amongst the debris of Paddington Basin, the new pushing itself up forcibly out of the old, the living out of the dead.

Cutty had assumed they were going back to White City and Buju's drum but Buju didn't take the usual turning.

'Whey we a go, man?' Cutty asked him.

'The country, bruv,' Buju replied. 'Out west.'

'Yeah?'

'Yeah.'

The idea of not going straight back to Buju's drum,

where Cynthia and whoever else would be hanging around like a bad smell, was such a relief to Cutty that he was more than happy to roll along with Buju's wilful mysteriousness for a while. He even felt a little curious about what the English countryside would be like.

Soon the dual carriageway widened and became a motorway and the traffic sped up and spaced out. Twenty minutes later they were out of the city. Tracts of suburban housing tailed off into farmland. They passed green fields and fallow fields, and woods that were hazes of browns and soft greys. Where the great grassy banks that flanked the motorway fell away Cutty watched distant towns and villages wheel by. The pirate R&B radio station that had been playing when they began their journey faded out as they passed beyond the range of its signal and turned to static. Buju slipped in an India Irie CD.

'Brown skin, I love your brown skin,' he sang along.

Eventually Cutty raised the question that was uppermost in his mind. 'Where was you all day yesterday, man? An' why you no offer stand I bail when me arx you, an' why you avoid me so di last two days?'

Buju sighed and turned the music down. 'Cos I had to do some thinking, man,' he said. 'Some serious thinking. Like when you got out, seeing you that day like face to face, yeah? It made me realise I couldn't just carry on the way I was. Or even like *we* was, you know what I'm saying? You and me.'

Cutty nodded. Buju stared straight ahead. His grip on the steering-wheel was tight.

'The minute the feds got you banged up Cynthia was onto me like white on fucking rice, bruv. She was round my yard 24-7. She was into my business like she was on a mission. And when you was inside, man – when you was inside it fucked with my head, you know what I'm saying?' Sudden tears started at the corners of

Buju's feline eyes. 'It fucked me up. I couldn't fucking stand it and I was so fucking fucked up and I didn't know where to turn, you know? I ain't never felt that way before. And it weren't like I could talk to no-one about none of it. Not and like tell the truth. And I didn't wanna talk to her about it, but she was like nearest to who I could cos she knew some of it, and she was there. And I didn't wanna be with her, but - ' he shrugged irritably, and palmed the nascent tears away. 'She came on with this shit about you'd go down and then what?'

'You no tell shi drop di charge-dem?'

'Course I did, man.' Buju shot Cutty an angry glance. 'And she kept saying she was gonna go to the feds and drop 'em. But then she was coming up with this shit 'bout the feds would press charges anyway, and they'd got her statement and shit, so there was no point in her making me and her look bad by changing her statement. It didn't make sense, I knew that, but it was her way of keeping shit dragging along instead of getting it sorted.'

'But tell me true, man, was it you who fuck shi dat afternoon?'

'No, man! I don't know who the fuck that was. Still don't. But it ended up being yet another fuck-over, you know what I'm saying? Cos she used it to make out that was why the feds were gonna win the case, it don't matter if she testifies or not, cos it was forensic evidence of shit: that she'd been sexed that afternoon. So that turned into another argument how her dropping the charges wouldn't do no good. Plus I was feeling like a total fuckin' idiot for not realising she was cheating on me, and she was jerking my chain about that. And what all that shit meant was things got slowed up. And of course I weren't allowed to visit you or write to you or nothing. It was like totally fucked up and I'm sorry, man.'

'But yesterday?'

'I didn't wanna say I could bail you and then not have the cash, bruv. I sorted the deal so you could get something going through Spin, and for the rest of them twenty-four hours I was out hustling and sorting shit. Getting dollars in my hand. My mobile was fucked so I didn't get no messages, so I didn't know you'd even got a mobile sorted till the evening.'

'But you coulda tell I dat you 'ave di money.'

Buju nodded. 'But I didn't know you was even coming back to my drum, bruv.' He paused. 'Truth is, man,' he went on, and suddenly he looked embarassed. 'The truth is, just for once I wanted to play the hero. I wanted to rescue you, bruv. Stand up and be there for you in your hour of need, you know what I'm saying?'

Cutty smiled at that. Doesn't every man want to be a hero?

'The other thing, though,' Buju said. 'I only raised X amount of dollars, and I didn't know how much the bail was gonna be. So that way if it turned out to be this like fuck-off crazy amount I couldn't run to, well, I wasn't giving you this hope then letting you down. I'da sneaked out and you wouldn't of seen I was ever there. I know it's kinda fucked-up, bruv, but that's what I was thinking when I didn't tell you last night.'

Buju looked round at Cutty. Cutty reached out and placed his hand gently on Buju's thigh. Even through the denim he could feel the muscle tense as Buju inhaled sharply.

'Dat feel good, man?'

Buju nodded wordlessly and faced forward again as Cutty slid his hand over and down so his fingers were wedged warmly between Buju's thighs against his crotch. It felt so good to touch Buju again, and to know that Buju was taking pleasure from his touch.

Dusk was falling as they pulled into a service station

to refuel the car. Next to the petrol pump area was a small, featureless shopping complex that housed public toilets, several fast-food concessions and a newsagent's selling snacks, CDs, newspapers and magazines. Everyone in the place was white, but they took no particular notice of Cutty or Buju. Perhaps the suit Cutty was still wearing made him seem respectable, even though he had abandoned the tie. The white people here looked somehow more uniform than the white people in London, and less hard-faced.

They bought some popcorn chicken and fries and set off again. They had been driving for more than two hours by then, but Cutty didn't ask where they were going. It felt good just to be moving, and he was happy to let Buju make the decisions.

An hour later they left the motorway, and the roads became slowly narrower and windier until finally they were less than two cars wide, and when Buju and Cutty met something coming the other way then one or other or both vehicles had to pull over onto the soft grass verges and inch past each other to get by. By now it was night, and there were no streetlights except in the small villages they passed through, so Cutty saw nothing of the country they were now traversing except the dense, high hedge-rows that bounded the narrow lanes as they were illuminated in the sweep of the car headlights.

At a sign advertising a butterfly farm Buju slowed and turned down a single-track lane. A hundred yards along it he pulled up and got out. Cold air filled the car, making Cutty shiver. Buju moved out of the cones of the car headlights and became invisible. A moment later Cutty heard the clatter of a gate being pushed back. Buju got back into the car and nosed it gently onto a patch of grass next to a small cottage. He put on the brake, turned off the ignition and switched off the headlights.

'We're here,' he said. And he turned Cutty's face towards his and kissed him softly on the lips.

Chapter Twenty-Two

They got out of the car. The air was bitingly cold and it was country-dark, but above their heads the cloudless sky was bright with stars.

Buju looked up at the constellations riding high above them. 'Listen,' he said.

'Di sea,' Cutty said. He could hear the soft rush of the ocean on the still air and he was strangely moved by it. It hadn't occurred to him that they would find themselves somewhere by the sea.

'Through the field out back there's a path goes down to a cove,' Buju said, gesturing vaguely towards the darkness behind the house.

'What is dis place, mi bruddah?'

'Country cottage, bredren. It belongs to a friend of my mum's,' Buju said. 'This teacher. Middle-class white lady. She took a interest in me once, the only one what ever did. She and my mum kinda got to be friends, and she still lets us use it off-season. When I was a kid we didn't have no money so my mum'd bring me here for weekends, like for a holiday. This is the top of Cornwall, where we are now. The other end's Land's End. C'mon, man, gimme a hand with the bags, yeah.'

'Bags?'

'Food and clothes and shit.'

Cutty went and opened the back of the Sportrak and found two sausage-bags and several carrier-bags of groceries piled up in the boot. While he was lugging them out Buju went over to the front door of the cottage, reached up on tip-toe and groped along the lintel of the porch. A moment later he found what he was looking for – a bunch of keys - and got the door of the cottage open. Laden with bags Cutty followed Buju into the lightless interior. As he did so he felt a strange echo of the time they had first had sex. But that had been in a house they were robbing, and this time they were't burglars, they were, if anything, guests.

Just inside the front door was a small, low cupboard. Buju knelt and opened it and flicked a switch, and Cutty heard the sound of a meter beginning to tick. Then Buju stood and switched on the hall light. A weak yellow bulb lit hesitantly, illuminating a narrow hall with a swirl-patterned, rust-coloured carpet.

'Come to the kitchen, yeah,' Buju said, leading the way and flicking on lights as he went. Cutty followed him into a spacious kitchen with a large oak dining table with six chairs round it. Cast-iron pots and pans hung from hooks on beams and casserole dishes sat on shelves. On a Welsh dresser place-mats sat stacked and plates and cups and saucers were on display on the shelves above them. Along one wall a picture window looked out onto blackness. As Cutty stared at it Buju lowered the blind and shut out the night. Then he turned on the oven and all the rings on the cooker, and left the over door open.

'Heating's gonna take a while to kick in,' he said by way of an explanation, taking the bags of groceries off Cutty and putting them down on the dining-table. 'Mek I show you the rest, yeah?'

The cottage was a bungalow with three bedrooms, although one of these was a child's room with a crib you reached through the second bedroom, and was some sort of extension. The bathroom was separate from the tiny toilet. The air in the cottage was damp and chilly, and Cutty wished he had clothing to wear other than the suit Spin had lent him for his court appearance. But although the whole place was slightly run-down and tatty and cold, still it was somehow homely and comfortable. The sitting room was large and had two soft, chintzy sofas and two mis-matched armchairs, and a padded windowseat was set into a three-sided picture window. The room was lit by a couple of low-power standard-lamps. An old-looking TV sat in one corner on top of a dusty VCR and there was a large fireplace with kindling wood laid out carefully on top of balls of crumpled newspaper. Next to it was a basket full of logs.

'I'll get this going, yeah,' Buju said, kneeling down before the grate. He touched his lighter to the newspaper at several points until it caught. A few minutes later he carefully placed two logs across the by-now flaming kindling. The logs sputtered and crackled, and started to burn. The fire was instantly cheering, and even before it could have had any real effect it made the cottage feel less cold and damp.

Cutty watched as Buju moved around the rooms, putting his hand on the panel heaters to make sure they were working, running the taps in the kitchen and bathroom to check there were no air-locks, reverting for a little time to the almost-innocent boy he had been when he first came here all those years ago. Fleetingly Cutty wondered if Buju had ever brought Cynthia here, but he knew he hadn't: Buju would never have given this to Cynthia. And even if he had, she would never have accepted it. To her it would just have been a dump. She would have seen it as Buju robbing her of a proper holiday. She wouldn't have understood what Buju was giving of himself in showing her this. But Cutty understood.

'So what you reckon?' Buju asked, standing in front of him, the flickering fire-light glinting on the smooth browness of his face, his expression bold yet uncertain.

'I like it, mi bruddah,' Cutty said. 'Is *cold*,' he laughed. 'But I like it.'

Buju's lips split into a wide smile. 'Don't worry, blood,' he said. 'Cos we can warm it up, you know.'

He took Cutty's face in his hands and drew Cutty to him. They kissed deeply. It was the first time they had been truly alone together, with no-one knowing where they were, no neighbours to hear them through paper-thin walls, no click to come knocking on the door at any time of the day or night, no girlfriend to break into their business, no police waiting to make a raid.

'So how long we 'ere for?' Cutty asked.

'We got the whole weekend, man,' Buju replied, gazing into his eyes. 'Just you and me. Come with me, yeah.'

He took Cutty's hand and led him through to the kitchen, which was by now pleasantly warm. From the freezer-cabinet of the fridge he produced a bottle of champagne, and took two glasses from the Welsh dresser. Back in the lounge Cutty popped the champagne, and he and Buju toasted each other before the fire.

'To freedom,' Buju said.

'To us,' Cutty said.

'To us,' Buju repeated.

They touched glasses and drank. Then Buju fished out his iPod and speakers so they could have music. He set up the speakers, scrolled to a carefully-chosen playlist of mellow and romantic songs, and set it running. Cutty watched Buju's quick, deft movements and thought how much work he had put into all of this. He realised that Buju must have been working his way through to some sort of decision about what he wanted out of life, a decision that he maybe only came to yesterday morning. And once he had made that decision, he had had a thousand things to do if he was going to see it through.

The champagne quickly went to Cutty's head. He

rarely drank champagne, though he knew enough to know that Buju had bought the good stuff. Roberta Flack floated out from the speakers. *The first time ever I saw your face...* Cutty felt happy and peaceful, but the champagne on his empty stomach made him realise that he was also extremely hungry.

'Mek we eat, man?' he suggested, reaching over and touching Buju's cheek. 'You bring food?'

Buju nodded, and they pulled each other up from the cushions they had thrown in front of the fire and went through to the kitchen. Buju produced two swordfish steaks from the fridge, a bag of basmati rice and several plantains. He grilled the steaks, boiled the rice and sliced and pan-fried the plantains in olive oil, and soon he and Cutty were sitting at the kitchen table with steaming plates in front of them.

'Me na know you chef,' Cutty said as he put the first fragrant forkful into his mouth.

'I just see stuff on TV, man,' Buju said with a shrug, passing him half a lemon to squeeze over his steak. 'It ain't nothing special, you know what I'm saying? Cooking, I mean. It ain't rocket science. It's just choose this and do that. I don't get to do it much, though.'

'Ya too modest, star,' Cutty said. He remembered Buju grating ginger root that night when he had had the flu. How many gangstas even had a fresh ginger root in their kitchen cupboards? And cooking, he knew, was a matter of having someone you wanted to cook for.

With Cynthia it was always takeaways. Because Buju didn't want to cook for her. And she couldn't cook, and thought that lack made her a modern, independent woman. The rest of the click were afraid of any fish that wasn't served battered with chips.

As he ate Cutty found himself once again thinking of other lives, dream lives lived out in worlds where you could simply be yourself. When he was young he and his brothers would visit his grandfather, who was a fishermen. His grandfather would take them out on his boat and they would help him cast and draw in the nets. His grandfather would have been in his fifties then, a lean, hard-bodied man who was handsome in his straw hat, but had lost his teeth and his wife early, and had taken to drink. Looking back on it now the three young boys were probably more of a hinderance than a help, but Cutty remembered the excitement of dragging the net into the small, swaying boat heavy with wriggling red snappers. And he remembered the matter-of-factness of gutting the fish afterwards, just as he had learned from his mother how to wring a chicken's neck, and from his father how to butcher a goat. When he had told Gary, Spin and Maxie these things they had all said that they thought they couldn't kill a chicken, much less a goat. Strange how they found violence against another human being so much easier than wringing a chicken's neck.

Once Cutty and Buju had finished eating they went back to the living-room. There they kicked off their shoes and sprawled out together on the less lumpy of the two sofas, and gazed into the dying embers of the fire. It was only ten p.m., but they had both been up since early that morning and both of them had slept badly the night before, and the travelling and the emotional journey of the day had worn them out. Soon their eyelids were drooping.

'Let's go to bed,' Buju said after his head had nodded for the third time.

He got up with an effort and went and put the guard in front of the fire. Then he pulled Cutty up and led him to the bedroom. By that point they were too tired to make love, but knowing that for once time stretched in front of them unconstrainedly, they were content just to undress and slip under the covers together, and enjoy the simple delight of drifting off to sleep in each others' arms, lulled by the distant sound of the sea and the wind soughing in the trees.

Chapter Twenty-Three

Cutty and Buju woke early, feeling refreshed and extremely horny, their dicks jutting in readiness, their nipples and arseholes tingling, eager to make love. Buju had brought lubricant, and had sneaked it into a drawer in the bedside table when they dumped the bags in the bedroom the night before, so they barely had to break their rhythm to get hold of it. And that morning they did everything with and to each other that they had ever wanted to. Buju loved to chat, to name his desire, to let it burst out of him, and his voice, throaty with excitment, excited Cutty too, and he too named his desires.

They sucked and fucked and nibbled and bit and fingered and licked and tongued until their jaws ached, their dicks ached, and their arseholes were aching and slack. Their bodies were bruised all over from the passion with which they had slammed against each other, and their hearts were bruised by the sudden moments of tenderness that had broken out between the violent thrusts of that passion. They came in each others' mouthes, then kissed and shared the hot seed feeling outlaw and wild. Afterwards, sweaty and exhausted, they lay quietly for a time, side by side, staring up at the ceiling, hearts beating in unison, one perfect creature.

It was around one p.m. when they eventually got up. Buju had left the heating on override all night so the cottage was now warm enough even for Cutty. They shared a bath, then had a breakfast of tea and scrambled eggs on toast, both of them still naked.

Now it was daylight Cutty could see that the kitchen and living-room windows gave onto an expansive view of fields slanting down into a valley, through the V of which the line of the sea was visible. The sun was bright and the sky was a clear, cool blue. White caps dotting the waves showed it was windy out on the water. And there were several trees near the back of the cottage whose branches were grown out all pulled in one direction like a crazy hairdo caught in a sudden blast of wind, then frozen in place.

'You wanna go for a walk, man?' Buju asked, after they had finished their tea.

'It look cold, star,' Cutty said doubtfully, eyeing the twisted trees.

'Don't worry, star, I brought you some garms to wear. Come and see.'

Cutty let Buju lead him to the bedroom. There Buju unzipped one of the sausage-bags and unpacked it. He had brought Cutty a pair of new, dark-green Timberlands, a short, well-cut black leather jacket, socks, a Calvin Klein thong, a close-fitting white tee-shirt, a pair of silver-grey Levi's, a skinny-rib white jumper, a Burberry baseball-cap and a Burberry scarf.

'Oh yeah, and these,' Buju added, pulling a pair of black leather gloves out of a side-pocket in the bag.

'Man, dis too much, man,' Cutty said, intensely moved by the array of new clothes Buju had laid out on the bed for him, by the thought that had gone into the choices he had made.

'Couldn't let you go cold, star,' Buju said, looking shy and pleased with himself.

'You was on a mission di day before mi court appearance fi true,' Cutty said with a smile.

'Too right, star.'

They kissed and embraced tenderly, then started to get dressed. Cutty's new clothes fit him well.

'You know mi size,' he said, as he pulled up the jeans.

'Like I know the size of your cock up my arse, man,' Buju said. 'Cos I *feel* your size, you know what I'm sayin'?'

Cutty felt himself getting turned on again by Buju's brazenness. 'Yeah?' he said.

'Yeah.'

'Well, maybe you does need reminding, star.'

'So remind me.'

Cutty gripped Buju's shoulders with both hands, turned him around and pushed him face down onto the bed. Then he tugged down Buju's jeans and briefs and gazed at the smooth brown globes of Buju's large, muscular butt. Buju lay there doing nothing, excitingly passive and receptive. Cutty pushed down his own trousers and thong, slicked up his now-rigid erection with lube and mounted Buju from behind, pushing his entire length up Buju in a single thrust.

'Oh, yeah!' Buju moaned. 'Fuck me, star! Jook that arse!'

Cutty fucked Buju roughly, building with unexpected rapidity to his release. After he had come he kept his cock pushed firmly all the way up Buju so Buju could beat himself off while Cutty was still inside him.

Afterwards Cutty went through to the bathroom and washed his dick and his hands in the sink. 'You still want go for dat walk?' he called through to Buju, who was wiping himself down with a hand-towel in the bedroom.

'Yeah, man,' Buju called back. 'I'll be bow-legged, but I wanna get some rays.'

'Aright.'

About a hundred yards down the lane in front of the cottage they came to a finger-post that read 'Coastal

Path'. There they climbed a stile into a field of cabbages and followed a track that ran along one side of it. At the bottom of the field they climbed another stile, this one set into a stone wall, and a moment later came came out at the top of a cliff. The wind gusted strongly up there, setting the tussocky grass shimmering, and Cutty pulled his scarf tighter against it. The cliff-path ran off in both directions, following the undulations of the headland until it bent round out of sight to right and left. Ahead the cliff edge curved sharply down under a tangle of gorse and bracken before finally vanishing into a sheer drop beyond. Gulls were crying and, peering cautiously over the cliff's edge, Cutty could see them below him, floating on the wind.

Britain was an island like Jamaica was an island, he realised. It was just on the other side of the same sea. It was the reverse of his own homeland in many ways – its weather cold, its colours muted - and yet he could see there was a beauty to it. The wind was sharp but it buffeted care from him.

Buju took the cliff-path to the right, and Cutty followed him.

After a couple of minutes a middle-aged white man and woman in wind-cheaters and woolly hats appeared over the brow with a muddy golden Labrador in tow, and came along the path towards them. Cutty was curious as to how they would react to the presence of two black men in a deserted spot, but they passed by with a civil nod and a 'Good afternoon!' that was cheery, if perhaps slightly tight-lipped. Cutty glanced back to see if they were going to look back but they didn't.

The path forked, offering the choice of a continuity or a descent. Buju chose the smaller of the ways. It ran steeply down and down until soon he and Cutty were stepping out onto shifting pebbles at the bottom of a small, sheer-sided bay. Cutty looked around him. The slate cliffs that now surrounded them were striated with orange sediment. Little caves ran back into the cliffs, and these were vivid with emerald mosses. As well as pebbles underfoot there were large rocks, and these were pearl-grey, and their edges were softened by the passing of many thousand tides. In the centre of the bay stood two tall stone stacks, both of them fifty feet in height or more, that lent against each other to make a kind of pointed arch.

Buju clambered up onto a large, flat, slightly sloping rock. 'Fancy a smoke, blood?' he asked.

Cutty nodded.

Buju sat and produced a ready-rolled joint from his coat pocket and put it to his lips as Cutty climbed up to join him. Down here there was no wind and so it felt much less cold than it had up on the cliff-top, but they shared the joint huddled together, all but with their arms around each other, enjoying the intimacy the temperature seemed to justify. The sea was a soft grey-green, flecked with foam. Many of the pebbles were orange. The colours were unusual to Cutty's eyes, and he had the feeling of being on a film-set: nothing seemed quite real. And to be here with Buju was the most unreal thing of all. It was as if he was in a dream. He turned his head and kissed Buju on the lips.

To do such a thing out in the open was both exhilarating and frightening, even if 'the open' was somewhere where nobody could possibly see them or if somehow someone did see them, it would be nobody who Cutty cared about or was afraid of.

'I used to come here as a kid,' Buju said once they had finished kissing. 'Like on my own. I'd sit here and look out at the sea and daydream.'

'What about?'

'I dunno.' Buju picked up a pebble and tossed it in

the direction of the sea. It fell short, and clattered among the rocks. 'Not what I ended up with, though.' His brow furrowed. 'Maybe I dreamed about being rescued, you know? Some man coming along and rescuing me. Like a father, but not.'

'I cyaan rescue you, you know,' Cutty said.

'I know that, star,' Buju said. 'And I ain't no kid no more. I'm a man.' He stared out at the ocean. 'But I been thinking, man. 'Bout what I want. About freedom.'

'And what you reckon?'

'It's a complicated thing, star. Very complicated, you know what I'm saying?'

'I know.'

'I wanted to come out here, like away from everything, so I could work stuff out in my head. I mean like work out what I'm feeling. Cos back in my yard it's all distractions, you know? Business, dramas, worries, madness, bitches with problems, running the click. The thing is, what it is, what I realised is, I'm in love wit' you, man.'

He shot Cutty a glance. He looked achingly vulnerable, and afraid.

'Me love you too,' Cutty said simply. 'Cah my heart, it is yours.'

And they kissed for the longest time.

After a while the chill in the air began to seep into their bones, so they climbed down from the rock and made their way back up the track to the cliff-top. The wind was biting up there, and harsh enough to stiffen and tauten their faces, so they picked up their pace, and less than fifteen minutes later Buju was unlocking the front door of the cottage and they were hurrying inside.

Once the door was closed behind them they could shake out their arms and legs with a shudder and throw off their coats and hats and scarves. Buju relaid the fire and they stretched out on the sofa together and watched the sun set over the bay in a blaze of pink and orange as the logs flared and crackled in the grate.

'Is strange no-one call we,' Cutty said, idly flicking his mobile phone open to see if there were any messages on it for him.

'It's cos there's no reception down here,' said Buju.

'What, inna di whole a di countryside?' Cutty asked, closing his phone.

'If you go half a mile inland you get a signal,' Buju said. 'Why, blood? You got a call to make?'

'No. Is just - '

'What, man?'

'You no tell no-one 'bout dis?'

'That you and me was going away?'

'Yeah.'

'No, I didn't. Not Cynthia, not no-one.'

They fell silent then, and although they were easy in each other's company their thoughts turned back to the life they had left behind. Neither of them wanted to think about that life, or speak about it. Not now, not here.

Instead Cutty spoke about Sonny. He hadn't meant to, not really, but once he had started he was unable to stop. The words came pouring out of him as he got caught up in the ecstatic release of for once telling the complete truth about himself, about his feelings for Sonny, and about the terrible night that left Sonny dead and drove him, Cutty, from the country of his birth and landed him finally on Buju's doorstep, broke and almost broken, cold and friendless. Buju's arms tightened about him as he talked and eventually, when emotion overwhelmed him, Cutty wriggled round in Buju's embrace and buried his face in Buju's chest and let out the racking, convulsive sobs that were forcing their way up through his body so violently he was afraid he would vomit.

Afterwards he lay quietly in Buju's arms, too drained to speak or move, exhausted but purged. It was a good feeling. And now it was Buju's turn to speak, stroking Cutty's braided head as he talked as if Cutty was a cat, and Cutty closed his eyes and let Buju's words soak into his soul.

'What I been through ain't nothing to that, star,' Buju began in a soft, throaty voice that Cutty could hear had tears in it. 'Just, there's always the fear, you know? The fear that like whatever you do, it can all be taken away from you with just one word. Just this one fucking word. And what I been thinking these last couple months is that ain't a healthy way to live, star. You know it ain't healthy. But most of the time you take it cos it ain't like you want like strangers in your business anyway, or even your peeps, you know what I'm saying? Cos you know they ain't give you no re-spect. Not if you're kicking it with another man. You make out like you don't care and you even feel like maybe you're a outlaw. A man with a secret, and tough because of it. And you look at the gays in the streets and on the TV and they're like something else, like some other sex or something, nothing to do with you. And you take that bit of yourself and you put it in a box where it's just fucking and no feelings cos that's easy, you know? I mean, I been to them saunas, man. Got me some cock, got me some arse, whatever. It's like this sealed-off little world in there. Like the only people in there are there for the same reason you are, so - But even that ain't guaranteed safe, you know? Like say after we done over that house them queens lived in, yeah?'

'Yeah.' Cutty's reply was muffledly by Buju's chest.

'Even if you and me ain't connected that night I'd of had to give the saunas a break for a bit in case one of them turns up in there and recognise me, you know what I'm saying?'

'You tink dat mighta 'appen?'

'Sod's law, blood.'

'But dem ain't gonna call di feds after suckin' cock in a sauna.'

'Probably not,' Buju conceded. 'But it was a reminder, you know? How you can't keep nothing locked up in a box.'

'True.'

'And even if that don't happen still you drag back to your gates after getting a good jooking and then you got to sex some whiney bitch just so she don't go around casting no like aspersions on your manhood. And you got to chat pussy for hours on end to keep the click in line like Beyoncé does it for you and 50 Cent don't. And you smoke till your brain seizes up cos if you didn't your head's gonna blow.'

'Is what dem call di down-low inna America,' Cutty said. 'Or di Q.T.'

'Yeah,' Buju said. 'And you know what the fucked-up thing is? A lotta them queens think it's a turn-on. They think you're like this real man or shit, and they ain't, and you got this easy life or something as a result of it. Shit, man. They oughtta try livin' it.'

Cutty heard the clink of Buju's lighter and squirmed round so he was looking up at Buju, the back of his head resting in Buju's lap, as Buju lit up a joint. Buju dragged the joint into life, then bent forward and kissed Cutty on the lips, letting the sweet smoke pour from his mouth into Cutty's.

Later they cooked, and ate, and made love, this time in front of the roaring fire. That night Cutty slept better than he had in all the months he had been in England.

The next day the weather was fine again, and after

they had finally got up and bathed and had breakfast together they bundled themselves up in scarves, gloves and hats and went for another walk along the cliff-top. This time they took the opposite direction to the one they had taken the day before and, perhaps for no other reason than that the wind was less fierce, they walked much further and for much longer than they had on the previous day.

After three quarters of an hour of solid tramping, during which time they met no-one, they found themselves at the top of a set of steep steps that ran down to a sandy bay. The bay was fringed by a curving road along which ran a row of small shops, and houses were scattered up its sides in haphazard fashion. Cars were parked on the beach, and Cutty was surprised to see surfers in wetsuits riding the waves that rolled into the bay.

'Dem na cold?' he asked Buju as they made their way down the steps.

'They say you get a layer of water under the rubber and it warms up from your body heat and acts like insulation,' Buju said. 'They *say*. I ain't never tried it though,' he added with a shiver.

They watched as two wetsuited white youths, handsome, fresh-faced and blond-dreadlocked, loaded their surfboards onto the rack on top of a battered-looking station wagon. One of the youths noticed them watching and gave a cheery salute. Buju returned it easily.

'Less stress in the country,' he said by way of an explanation. 'Let's get something to eat, yeah.'

They found a fish and chip shop, and there Buju and Cutty bought battered cod and chips. A sign outside read, 'Local Catch', and Cutty was struck by the freshness of the fish: it tasted much better, much more real than the deep-fried fish he had sometimes eaten in London. Out on the street they bumped into the two dreadlocked white youths.

'Want some skunk?' one offered in a low, amiable tone.

'All home-grown,' the other added. 'Local produce. Good prices.'

'We're alright, man,' Buju replied. 'Got our own, yeah.'

'Cool, man,' the first one said. 'Enjoy your lunch, yeah.' He extended a fist. 'Peace.'

'Peace,' Buju echoed, touching his knuckles to the white boy's.

The two surfers passed into the fish and chip shop. Cutty and Buju wandered along the quay that bounded one side of the bay, eating as they strolled. Cutty felt ambivalent about the encounter they had just had. On the one hand being taken for a dope-smoker just because he was black and street-style – even though he *was* a dope-smoker – irritated him. On the other hand he found it surreally amusing to be offered locally-grown herb by a pair of white loxmen out in wherever they were in Cornwall.

At the end of the quay, recessed into the stonework and sheltered from the wind, was an unoccupied bench. Like a retired couple they sat down. The sun had warmed the wood, making them feel almost cosy. Buju and Cutty sat close together, and looked out at the sea.

'Is which way we look?' Cutty asked.

'North, I guess,' said Buju. 'Towards the bottom of Ireland. Look left and you'd be heading out towards the States. And the Caribbean.'

Cutty looked left, but his view was cut off by a bulge of headland. No land was visible across the horizon at any point.

'So is tomorrow we go back a London?' he asked. It was more of a statement than a question.

'Yeah,' Buju said, not sounding enthusiastic. 'We

better.'

And now they knew they had to talk about the future. They had to make some decisions, act on those decisions, and live with the consequences.

'I wanna get out the drugs business,' Buju said abruptly.

'Me also.'

'I know I've gone on about it before,' Buju continued. 'But it's like your life's a street, yeah, and there's a point where you come to like a crossroads. And you could carry on straight ahead the way you was going before.'

'Or you could turn a corner.'

'Exactly, man. And I wanna turn a corner. Being with you makes me wanna turn a corner. When you was inside it woke me up to that I weren't into what we was doing – me and the click, I mean – I weren't into that no more. And it's like if I don't make that decision now then I'm gonna get stuck on a path I ain't choosing.'

'I was a music producer back home,' Cutty said. 'Me come here fi promote mi label. And now me dealin' drugs.'

'Exactly, man. It's time we quit that bullshit and pooled our talents and did something else. Like soon I'll have enough to be like seed money for something. To start up some business like we used to talk about. Like promoting, doing events, whatever.'

'And di click?'

'Any of 'em wanna come along, that's cool. But they got to accept the new realities, you know?'

'And Cynthia?'

Buju kissed his teeth. 'I'm gonna get my keys back off of her an' tell her she ain't present herself as like my girlfriend or fiancée or whatever to no-one no more.'

'You cyan trust she?'

'Well,' Buju said uncertainly, 'I don't know, man. Truth is, I don't know. But what I do know is, she ain't happy like she is. And now you're back and she knows she ain't won, which is what she was aiming to do with them phoney accusations, she knows she ain't never gonna win. And she knows if I hear anyone implying any shit about you and me then I'm gonna assume it's her what told 'em, and she knows that won't make her position safe, you know what I'm saying? I don't wanna talk no ugliness, but she's smart enough to know that if she runs off at the mouth then ugliness will ensue.'

'Anyway she sweet 'pon Spin, you know,' Cutty said.

'Yeah?' Buju looked surprised.

'You no notice?'

Buju shrugged irritably. 'Probably, man,' he said. 'Actually, yeah,' he conceded. 'I suppose I did notice. I just couldn't think of how to deal with it, you know? I mean, yeah, I want rid of her, obviously, but I don't wanna lose respect, you know?'

'Well den, give she to him.'

'How you mean, man?'

'Tell Spin you know him sweet 'pon she and dat you givin' she to him as a gift,' Cutty said. 'Den go tell she official-like dat you want ya keys back and dat tings dem is over between you. She will run to him and he will be in your debt.'

Buju nodded.

'I don't reckon Spin's gonna want to get out the drugs business though,' he said, continuing his other line of thought. 'He's gonna want to carry on up that road for a good while yet. So when I say I'm quitting that makes a natural split.'

'And we?'

'Well, we can't be out in the open, can we, man?'

'Is too dangerous,' Cutty agreed.

'But I need you around, yeah,' Buju said, and his

voice was suddenly intense. 'I couldn't deal with not having you around.'

'Me also,' Cutty said simply. 'So?'

'We need to sort you out a place, blood,' Buju said. 'Make it our drum. Our place no-one even knows where it is, where we can be ourselves. And we keep on my old gates for business and whatever.'

Cutty nodded. He felt excitement rising up in him. To have hopes, to make plans again, set something soaring inside his chest. All of a sudden it was as if nothing was impossible. He had survived Jamaica. He had survived the burning of his business. He had survived the murder of his lover. He had survived jail. During his time inside the threat of a murder charge against him had receded, and his fear that the truth of what had happened back home would spread out across the world had not come true. He could use his music contacts here to get something going after all. And he and Buju could make a new life for themselves. He took a deep breath and felt the tang of salt on his tongue and lips.

That night neither of them slept well. Both of them were now wired, eager to get back to the city and begin their new lives as soon as possible.

Chapter Twenty-Four

The next three months saw many changes. The day they got back from the country Buju finally broke things off with Cynthia, first offering her to Spin as Cutty had advised him to do. Cynthia ran into Spin's arms, and as Cutty had predicted Spin was grateful, and also relieved at not having to admit that he had been fucking her behind Buju's back. And Cynthia's anger and bitterness and sense of failure was defused by being with a man who actually wanted and desired her.

Buju and Cynthia did have one last argument after he finished with her. She wanted him to have an AIDS test and he refused, arguing that even to risk being seen at the clinic came too near to threatening his rep. It was bullshit, and he knew it and she knew it, but he couldn't bring himself to change his mind. Eventually she stormed out. Later that day she went and had a test herself, a rapid-result one, and phoned him the following morning to tell him that although she supposed he didn't give a fuck, she had tested HIV negative.

'Of course I give a fuck, gal,' he said, relieved at the closure. But it set the worm of self-doubt wriggling in his mind. He knew he had been careless before Cutty and he knew he had had unsafe sex with Cutty. Before, that had seemed like it didn't matter because his life didn't matter. Now he was worried. It made him avoid sex with Cutty and things became tense between them. Eventually Cutty challenged Buju as to what was wrong and Buju told him.

'Well, inna prison dem did test I,' Cutty said.

'And?'

'Me negative.'

Buju was both relieved and stressed by this information. Cutty didn't pressure him to get tested but
Buju knew he couldn't live with the uncertainty,
couldn't risk Cutty's life as he had thoughtlessly risked
Cynthia's.

The fact that he had never loved her made his carelessness all the more nakedly contemptible to him now.
Shamefacedly he called her up and got the details of the
clinic she had been to, and for fifty pounds he got a
rapid-result HIV test.

He texted Cutty the result: '-ve.'

He texted Cutty but he phoned Cynthia. 'I'm
alright,' he said.

There was a silence at the other end of the line
then: 'I'm glad,' she said.

The doctor at the clinic warned him that if he'd become infected in the last three months the test wouldn't
show it but that didn't worry him much as he'd only
had sex with Cutty in that period, and he was sure
Cutty hadn't been with anyone else either. Neither of
them fucked women now they had each other.

The other big change in their lives was Buju and Cutty's
decision to stop dealing drugs. As Buju had predicted
Spin was determined to carry on dealing and keen to
take over as unofficial don of the click. Buju was
content to hand on his mantle. Soon Spin stopped
coming round to hang out at Buju's yard, no doubt
partly at Cynthia's request, and the others visited less
and less often. Although Buju and Cutty initially missed
the social buzz, the fact was that drinking less alcohol
and smoking less dope and having fewer late nights
meant they were able to think with clearer heads. With
more of a plan for the future they felt less of a need to
blot themselves out with booze or weed.

A week or so after their return to London they found and rented a flat off a private landlord. It was on the ground floor of a terraced Victorian house, and was in a quiet, tree-lined street just off the Uxbridge Road, on the opposite side from the White City estate, and had its own small, high-walled back garden. Buju and Cutty told no-one about it: it was their secret, private place. The other tenants in the house were mostly Australians and Spaniards, ephemeral guest-workers who came and went without getting in Cutty's or Buju's business beyond occasionally asking them for dope, which was irritating but inconsequential.

It was the first time either Cutty or Buju had ever really had a full private life, and both of them revelled in it. Unlike Buju's minimalist tower-block apartment, the flat he shared with Cutty quickly took on a cosy Jamaican clutteredness and colourfulness. They even found themselves making plans for what they would do with the garden when the spring came.

Cutty took a chance and began to re-establish his contacts in the UK garage and dancehall scenes. He found that those of them who were aware of the burning of his studio back home assumed it was either an attempt by a rival to wipe out the competition, or else an insurance scam. Either way they were happy enough to do business with Cutty in Britain, and that decided him: he and Buju would set up a recording studio in Buju's old drum, which Buju had kept on for just such a possibility. To make sure Cutty's name didn't get bandied about too much and lead to the revival of rumours Buju would be the front-man for the new studio, while Cutty would provide the technical know-how and promotional and managerial contacts.

As he had once intended, Cutty suggested their new business venture be called Refugee Records, and Buju, understanding him, accepted the name.

Maxie and Gary were keen to help with this new enterprise, excited by the idea of having friends in the music business, and it was gratifying to Buju and Cutty to be able to re-establish their comradeship with the pair on a musical, rather than a drug-dealing basis. Maxie and Gary also brought other friends along to help out at the studio and get the word into the street that a new record company was starting up with its own label.

Of necessity Refugee Records started off basic, but because Cutty knew what he was doing word-of-mouth was good and they were soon getting hired for sessions. Session money they straightaway reinvested into improving the equipment, and soon they had a convincing set-up. Buju, it turned out, had a lot of contacts on the pirate radio scene, and he used them to promote the artists he and Cutty were recording at a grass-roots level, as well as promoting the label itself. Cutty and Buju both worked at getting their artists onto garage or bashment bills, gaining them exposure.

There was no time or money left over for anything but work and more work, but Cutty and Buju were happy, happier perhaps than they had ever been in their lives, because when you're doing what you want, who cares about distractions? And finally Cutty could call his parents with some semblance of optimism about what he was doing in the UK. Making use of the rumours he had heard from his UK contacts, he hinted that the burning of his Kingston studio might have been the work of rivals, and that he had had to flee the country to avoid gangland retributions. His father, who had recovered fairly fully from his heart-attack, accepted this explanation, as did his mother: evidently his brother had decided not to tell them the truth.

Christmas came round. Cutty spent Christmas Eve with Buju, the two of them sharing a private seasonal night together, exchanging gifts of gold: a neck-chain and a bracelet. Earlier that week Buju had lugged a real Christmas tree back to the flat. It shed needles instantly but filled their home with the cool, sweet scent of pine. It was a scent Cutty had only smelt from air-fresheners before, and it was curious to him, but pleasant. On Christmas Day they went to Buju's mother's for lunch and spent the rest of the day and the evening with her, her new boyfriend, an aunt and uncle and some half-nephews and nieces. All of them were welcoming to Cutty, and Buju's mother was nothing but kind to the man who had led her son out of the world of drugs. Their warmth and friendliness drew much of the sting of the sadness Cutty felt at not being able to be with his own parents on that special day.

On New Year's Eve they went to a local blues to see in the new year, but despite having looked forward to going, when they got there they found it unexpectedly oppressive. In their own yard they could wind it up together to the music like it was the most natural thing in the world, but here they had to just stand or lean on the bar, or dance with girls they weren't interested in. Before, they would have accepted those constraints as life being what it was, but now it was harder for them because they had moved on in their heads. They came away sooner than they had intended to, but didn't speak of the reasons why.

It made Cutty realise that he now went to clubs only as a promoter, not for pleasure, and he felt at home in them when he did so only because he had a clear role to play. He wondered what it would be like to go to a black gay club – he knew there were several black gay club-nights in London - but something always made him hold back from suggesting it to Buju. It was as if going to such a club represented a step that, once taken, could not be gone back on.

*

It was on a grey, flinty morning in mid-January that Cutty's drug-dealing case finally came to court. He had managed to put it out of his mind until the new year had come and gone, but after that it began to preoccupy him, casting a shadow over what he was achieving with Buju.

He had a meeting with Jasmina Jalwar a few days ahead of the court-date, and she reiterated the plea-bargain she felt he should go for. After some discussion it was agreed that he would plead guilty to possession of cannabis and Ecstasy for personal use if the CPS would drop the dealing charge against him. He still hated the idea of pleading guilty to anything at all, but it seemed like the best he could make of a bad situation. Once again Peter Levinson was to be his barrister.

'I think they'll go for it,' Peter Levinson said cheerily as he shook the smartly-suited Cutty firmly by the hand on the day of the committal hearing, then extended his hand to Buju, who was wearing a formal striped blazer along with jeans and Timberlands. Ten minutes later the case was called, and Buju and Cutty followed Peter Levinson into the courtroom. Cutty went up into the dock while Buju found a place in the front row of the observers' seats. Peter Levinson went over to the CPS barrister. They shook hands and had a brief conversation. The CPS barrister, a grey, nondescript man in his forties, nodded several times, which gave Cutty hope. Peter Levinson came up to him where he sat waiting in the dock.

'They'll go for it,' he said in a low voice before returning to his desk. A moment later a court officer instructed everyone to be upstanding in court. They shuffled to their feet and the judge entered. This time it was an elderly and withered-looking white man with a stoop and a beakish nose. He sat, then gestured for everyone else to sit. He eyed Cutty with watery blue eyes that had a coldness to them that made Cutty uneasy. Could the judge refuse to accept the offer even if the CPS accepted it? He had no idea. A court clerk read out the charge.

'Before the jury are sworn, are there any matters arising?' the judge asked, looking down at the two barristers in front of him.

'If I may, your honour,' the CPS barrister said.

'Yes, Mister Sheppard?'

'Mister Levinson has given me to understand that his client is prepared to plead *nole contendere* to the charge of possession of a proscribed narcotic for personal use if the Crown is prepared to cease to prosecute the larger charge of possession with intent to supply.'

'And is this acceptable to the Crown, Mister Sheppard?'

'It is, your honour.'

The judge leant forward and whispered a few remarks to his clerk, then looked over at Cutty. 'Mister Munroe,' he said.

At a nudge from the court official sitting behind him, Cutty got to his feet.

'You are charged with the possession of a Class A prohibited substance, to wit two tablets of Ecstasy, and forty grammes of a Class C prohibited substance, that is, cannabis. How do you plead?'

Cutty froze. He found that he couldn't speak. His mouth opened but his tongue clove to the roof of his mouth and no words came out.

'How do you plead, Mister Munroe?' the judge repeated, more sharply this time.

With an effort he managed to force out the single word: 'Guilty.'

'Since the amounts of illicit substances discovered

at your place of residence were modest they may be considered as being purely for personal use,' the judge continued. 'Accordingly I sentence you to six months - '

Cutty heard Buju draw in his breath sharply behind him and his own chest tightened painfully.

'The sentence to be suspended for two years.'

Cutty allowed himself to blink and exhale slowly as the judge rummaged through his papers. *No jail. Tank God.*

'However, Mister Munroe,' the judge went on, still looking down at the file in front of him, 'your possession of in particular any amount of a Class A prohibited substance leads me to consider you to be of poor character, and accordingly I am recommending that you be deported back to Jamaica as soon as Immigration Services can authorise your removal.'

Peter Levinson jumped to his feet. 'Your honour,' he objected. 'Mister Munroe - '

'Mister Levinson,' the judge interrupted. 'Your client is of poor character and seems to me to have evaded charges of both rape and drug-dealing of late, and furthermore lacks a regular income or conventional employment.'

'Your honour, Mister Munroe is currently running a music recording business in partnership with Mister Staples - ' Peter Levinson gestured to Buju. Buju half-stood.

The judge looked Buju over with distaste. 'Nonetheless my ruling stands,' he said flatly. 'Mister Munroe is to be returned to his country of origin forthwith.'

'What the fuck was that, man?' Buju asked angrily. He, Cutty and Peter Levinson were standing in the hallway outside the courtroom.

'A racist judge,' Peter Levinson replied, his face flushing, clearly repressing his own anger at the ruling.

'But can he do that, man?' Buju's voice was getting louder. 'Get Cutty booted out the country? It's fuckeries, man. Pure fuckeries.'

'Calm down, bredren,' Cutty said quietly, touching Buju's shoulder. 'Well, man?' he asked the lawyer.

'Unfortunately yes,' Peter Levinson said. 'He can issue the order.'

'But what about the deal you was supposed to make?' Buju asked.

'The deal was that the CPS wouldn't pursue Cuthbert for the dealing charge, and that they wouldn't push for his deportation. And they didn't.'

'So why dem let me leave di court?' Cutty asked. 'Why dem no shove I straight back inna jail?'

'Bureacracy,' Peter Levinson said. 'Your sentence was suspended, so you were free to go. I know it seems crazy, but that's what happens when you follow procedure to the letter. What it means is that you're free to move about for the moment, until you hear from Immigration Services. And of course you're entitled to contest the application for removal in the meantime.'

'We fucking will, man,' Buju said, barely able to choke down his rage and frustration despite Cutty's steadying hand on his shoulder. '*Believe*.'

'So how we appeal?' Cutty asked.

'You'll need grounds,' Peter Levinson said.

'Grounds?'

'Why it would be injurious for you to be returned to your country of origin. For instance, if you were engaged in political activity against a repressive regime and your life could be in danger from that regime if you returned.'

'What about that the judge is a racist motherfucker?' Buju broke in.

'Very difficult to prove to a sufficient standard for it to achieve anything,' Peter Levinson said. 'And even then his ruling would probably still be allowed to stand. The establishment tends to protect its own; that's its nature. I recommend you get specialist legal advice as soon as possible. With the anti-asylum-seeker /economic migrant mood in the country right now Immigration Services will look to get things moving against you pretty fast. Your solicitor should be able to help you with that. And now I have to get to my next client. Sorry we've had such a frustrating outcome.'

Peter Levinson shook hands perfunctorily with Cutty and Buju, then hurried away.

'Fuckeries, man!' Buju spat the instant he had gone. 'What we gonna do, Cutty, man? This a fuckin' disaster!'

'First let us get outta 'ere,' Cutty said. 'Before dem get dem hands pon I.'

They hurried from the building feeling invisible fingers reaching for the backs of their necks, and made their way to where Buju had parked the car. They drove back to White City in silence, neither of them knowing what to say or do. They had no particular desire to return to the estate, but they had a recording session booked, and it didn't occur to either of them to cancel it.

'But you can't go back there, man' Buju blurted out eventually as he was parking the car behind his block. 'I mean, not with what went down. It'd be fucking *murder*, blood.'

'But dem tink I murder Sonny,' Cutty said wearily. 'When di authorities dem find out 'bout di whole fire business it will make dem *eager* fi deport I.'

'But you didn't murder no-one, man.'

'And how I cyan prove dat? Who will tell di truth? And even if dem find out di truth dem *still* deport I, nuh?'

'I don't know, star,' Buju said as they reached the

bottom of stairwell. 'I just don't know.'

They trudged heavily up the stairs.

Cutty got through the recording session on autopilot. Four youths were throwing down lyrics for a garage track they had been working on the week before. The Revolver Crew. They were full of energy and enthusiasm and ideas, and normally Cutty would have enjoyed working with them, but his mind was clogged with dread, and the time seemed to drag by with excruciating slowness.

Just as despair threatened to totally overwhelm him an unexpected thought broke through: he suddenly remembered stories he had read in *The Gleaner* back home, and in *The Voice* in London about gay Jamaican men who had claimed asylum in Britain just because they were gay, and had got it. At the time he hadn't connected his own situation with theirs because the impression he had picked up from the articles he had read was that those men had had to seek asylum abroad because their overt effeminacy made them targets of violence wherever they went within Jamaica, and he himself was not effeminate. At the time he had read the articles, he would not have considered himself gay either.

Now he wished he could remember the stories properly. Had they really just had to say they were battymen and look camp to get some sort of rubber-stamped unlimited leave to remain in the UK? Surely the immigration people would require some sort of proof of his homosexuality, and what the hell would that mean? Disgusting, degrading scenarios flashed through his mind. Even the thought of having to do no more than sit face to face with those people, those agents of the state, and utter the words 'I am a batty-man' for the public record made Cutty's gut twist with panic. He didn't trust the authorities – had less than no reason to trust them – and found it all but impossible to believe that his benighted sexuality could be his salvation under the law, but at that moment he had nothing better to go with.

He decided he had to speak to Jasmina Jalwar as soon as possible, and slipped out of the studio to call her office on his mobile. Peter Levinson had already told Jasmina the outcome of the trial, and she made an appointment to see Cutty at 5 p.m. that evening. Shortly after four Cutty told Buju he had to go and see his solicitor, and left him to finish up the recording session. Buju tossed Cutty the car-keys, and Cutty drove Buju's Sportrak over to Gray's Inn Road.

He would tell Buju his plan once he found out if it had a hope of success.

Jasmina Jalwar kept Cutty waiting nearly twenty minutes, during which time his whole body began to arch painfully as tension wrenched his shoulder-blades back and forced them together. Jasmina saw out the client she had been with, took Cutty through to her office, and gestured him to a seat.

'Sorry you're in this position,' she said. 'We're going through a time when the courts are encouraged to be heavy-handed with anyone who could be classified as an undesirable alien. Immigration's always a political hot potato anyway. Looking at the facts though, I can't really see any grounds to appeal the decision to deport you.'

'Di judge racist.'

'Yes, but the reasoning behind his decision was logical and consistent with precedent and policy.'

'Dat me a bad bwoi.'

'Yes, basically,' Jasmina said. 'The furthest we could go towards challenging his decision would be to argue that his dragging in your being charged with rape when the CPS dropped that charge, and him dragging in the dropped dealing charge was prejudiced. But of course you had by then pled guilty to possession of a class A drug, which in and of itself could be considered proof of bad character.'

'Dat was your advice.'

'Yes, I know.' Jasmina sounded tired. 'And I'm sorry. As you know our deal was that the CPS wouldn't push for deportation, and they didn't. Obviously we couldn't prevent the judge from reaching his own conclusion unprompted by them. I'm afraid Justice Rowe is known to be particularly hardline.'

'Racist.'

Jasmin Jalwar shrugged. 'One could perhaps demonstrate that by ploughing through his previous decisions. But whatever the reason why he initiated the deportation process the final decision will end up being made by Immigration Services. They're your problem now.'

'But dem cyaan deport I, man,' Cutty said, a tone of desperation rising in his voice.

'Why not?'

'Cah I-man life will be in peril.'

'Why?'

Cutty took a deep breath. 'Becah I am gay,' he said.

'You're gay?'

'I am gay.'

Jasmina Jalwar sat back in her chair and looked him over. She clearly didn't believe him. And why should she? He had first come to her having been arrested for raping a girl, and had never used the fact of being gay as a defence. More than that, he had actually chosen to go to jail rather than admit he was gay. As a consequence Jasmina Jalwar now saw him as a desperate criminal trying a desperate lie to avoid expulsion from the country for some shady reason of his own.

She sat forward again. She opened her filofax and flicked through it until she came to the page she was looking for.

'I recommend that you speak to this gentleman,' she said, jotting a name and telephone number on a card which she passed across the desk to Cutty.

' "Oliver Ross"?'

'Yes. He's a solicitor who specialises in immigration and asylum issues.'

'Aright.'

'Do you want me to ring him and arrange a meeting for you?'

'Yes.'

Jasmina Jalwar did so. 'Eleven o'clock tomorrow morning?' she asked Cutty. He nodded, and she confirmed the appointment.

After she had hung up the phone Cutty asked her for Oliver Ross's address and she wrote it on the back of the card she had given him. He recognised it as a street in Brixton, not far from the tube.

Buju was closing up the studio by the time Cutty got back to the block. Cutty told Buju that he had arranged a meeting with an immigration lawyer the next day, but didn't discuss the content of his meeting with Jasmina Jalwar. For some reason he was ashamed to tell Buju that he had admitted his sexuality to someone else.

That night he dreamed of Sonny for the first time in months.

Chapter Twenty-Five

'You want me to come with you, man?' Buju asked Cutty over breakfast the following morning.

'Nah, is alright, star,' Cutty said. 'Anyway, we 'ave a booking at twelve, nuh?'

'Yeah, we do.'

'Well, one a we mus' be dere.'

'True. But take the motor though,' Buju said. 'Cos I can walk to the studio, you know. Save you stressin' on the Tube.'

Both Buju and Cutty got a small thrill of pride out of referring to Buju's old yard as The Studio.

Soon it was time for Cutty to leave. He and Buju hugged tensely in the hall, and exchanged a brief, suddenly-passionate kiss.

'You sure you don't want me to come with you, man?' Buju asked. 'I can cancel the session.'

Cutty shook his head. 'Dem sessions is our future, star.'

'I know, man,' Buju said. 'But still I - ' He cut himself off before his emotions got the better of him. 'Good luck, star. Call me if you need anything, yeah. And be careful you don't go in the Congestion Charge zone. Or if you do, pay it right away.'

'Man, ya so law-abiding!' Cutty laughed.

'Model citizen, that's me,' Buju said, managing a smile in return. 'So get along with you, man,' he added, glancing at his watch. 'This ain't no soon-come kinda situation, you get me? Bell me laters, yeah?'

'Yes, I.'

*

Oliver Ross's office was tucked away in a backstreet off
Brixton Market called Beehive Place, in a small brick
block with smoked-glass windows. A brass plate by the
entry intercom listed several companies including
Oliver Ross, Solicitors. Cutty checked his watch. It was
10.40. He was twenty minutes early. He took a breath
and pressed the button by the name and a moment
later a male voice answered, 'Hello?'

'Is Cutty Munroe. I have an appointment wit' Oliver
Ross.'

'Come in,' the voice said. 'Third floor.'

The buzzer sounded and Cutty pushed the door
open and went inside. Ahead of him was a small lift. He
took it to the third floor. *Another solicitor*, he thought
wearily. He couldn't even diss the ones he had dealt
with up until now: as far as he could tell they'd done as
good a job for him as they could under the circumstances. But now here he was with another solicitor and
another battle ahead of him, and no idea if he had any
chance of winning it. Everything seemed stacked
against him. Again.

A dreadlocked black man was waiting for him as he
came out of the lift.

'Cutty?' the man asked.

'Mistah Ross?' Cutty asked in return, mildly surprised that his new solicitor should be a loxman.

Oliver Ross nodded, extending a hand for Cutty to
shake. He was in his late forties, Cutty reckoned, or
maybe early fifties. Grey twined through his locks and
flecked his goatee. He had a kind face, with large,
thoughtful eyes, sensitive lips, and raised freckles on
his Demerara-brown cheeks. Gold studs glinted in both
ears. He was short, maybe five foot seven, and wore a
white shirt with the sleeves rolled up and the collar
open, and plain but well-fitting black trousers.

'Call me Oliver,' Oliver Ross said. His accent was

English, neutral. 'Come in, Cutty. Would you like something to drink? Tea, yeah, or coffee?'

'Tea.'

Cutty followed Oliver Ross into his office. It was small and lined with shelves crammed with books and files. On the one free wall was a framed poster, an image of a black man's face, his eyes closed, his expression mask-like, beneath which was the caption: *Rotimi Fani-Kayode, 1955-1989, photographer*. Cutty wondered who he was.

A kettle sat on top of a filing-cabinet. Oliver clicked it on and fussed about fixing mugs of tea for them both, perhaps intentionally giving Cutty time to take in his surroundings. On a bulletin-board next to the poster were pinned up bills, flyers, postcards and articles. Cutty recognised the names Stonewall and Outrage. Some of the articles were about gay campaigns against homophobia in dancehall music. There was also something pinned up that had been printed out from a J-FLAG website. Cutty recognised that name as belonging to the Jamaican gay rights group, one of whose spokesmen, Brian Williamson, had been murdered the year before. He remembered the reports in the press at the time of the murder: the police had claimed it was just a regular burglary despite the hacked-up condition of Williamson's body. He remembered his brother's dismissive remark that, 'Hey, battymen get what them deserve.'

'Sugar?' Oliver asked him.

'Yeah, man. Two, please.'

'Sweet tooth.'

Cutty smiled a little and nodded. Oliver spooned the sugar in and stirred it before passing the mug to him.

'Now,' Oliver said. 'Come and sit down and tell me all about it.'

Rather than sitting formally behind his desk, Oliver gestured to the two easy-chairs that took up most of the rest of the space in the room in front of it, and they sat in those. Oliver watched Cutty over his steaming mug of tea, and waited for him to begin.

Despite Oliver's attempts to create a relaxed atmosphere Cutty found himself not knowing where or how to start. He sat there tongue-tied, feeling foolish. He knew Oliver was going to ask him about his homosexuality, and even though he knew Oliver already knew about it, still he felt ashamed and afraid of the inevitable disclosures. And what made it worse was that he didn't have much faith that Oliver would be able to help him.

'Okay,' Oliver said, once it became apparent that Cutty would need to be prompted. 'I'll start. Jasmina told me about your case -'

'Let me arx you someting, man,' Cutty interrupted him.

'Okay.'

'Are you gay?'

'Yes.'

'Aright, den.'

Oliver waited to see if Cutty was going to say anything else. When Cutty didn't, Oliver continued, 'Jasmina told me that the judge recommended deportation.'

'Yes.'

'And that it was then that you decided you would apply for asylum.'

'Yes.'

'On the grounds that you are gay, and in fear for your life if you get returned to Jamaica.'

Cutty looked over at the J-FLAG articles on the bulletin-board and nodded.

'But you didn't apply for asylum when you first arrived here.'

'No.'

'You applied for asylum only after pleading guilty to possession of a Class A drug.'

'Yes.'

'Okay,' Oliver said. 'Here's the problem. As it is the Home Office resists recognising gay men as potential asylum-seekers despite the House of Lords ruling that gay men and lesbians constitute a distinct social group and therefore qualify as refugees.'

'So?'

'So even though a number of gay Jamaicans have got asylum here because they fear homophobic violence back home, seeking asylum in the UK on the grounds of your sexuality is an extremely tough route to go. Despite the impression the media gives, it's not easy to successfully claim asylum here. There's still a hell of a lot of racism – and homophobia – in the system.'

'I am a black man, dread,' Cutty said with a shrug. 'Me used to haffi twice as good to get di same treatment as di rest, you know.'

'What's now complicating the situation,' Oliver carried on, 'is that there's claimed to be an increasing number of straight Jamaican men trying to pass themselves off as gay to get indefinite leave to remain here to escape criminal pasts back home.'

'And you tink I doing dat?'

'I think the Home Office will think you're doing that,' Oliver said. 'They'll certainly *say* they think that's what you're doing, whatever they really believe. Basically Immigration Services are a bunch of cold-hearted, hard-faced bastards. They're also hyper-sensitive to the political climate which, right now, is even more anti-immigrant than usual.'

Cutty drummed his fingers restlessly on the arm of his chair. He felt trapped by this shrewd, friendly, dreadlocked brother.

'So why you no believe I-man gay?' he asked irritably.

'Because you were previously charged with raping a girl.'

'Di charge was dropped.'

'But still, you were charged.'

'But me no rape she.'

'Well,' Oliver said. He reached round for a file that was sitting on the desk behind him, flicked it open and rummaged through a stack of photocopied pages until he found a phrase underlined in red. 'When asked if he had raped her,' he read out loud, 'client responded, "If it happened, she must have asked for it."'

'Ignore dat, man,' Cutty said, his chest tightening. 'It was just foolishness, you know? Just chat. I was fronting.'

'Immigration Services won't ignore it.'

'But me no say dat to di police. Only to mi solicitor.'

Oliver turned a page. 'You said to the police that the girl made a false claim of rape against you because you told her fiancée she had come on to you and you had turned her down.'

Cutty took a deep breath. He had wanted to keep Buju entirely out of this if he possibly could, and what he was about to say made him feel like a traitor, but what other choice did he have?

'You want di truth?'

'What is the truth?'

'I was – involve wit shi fiancé. On di day she accuse I she catch we – we was – 'aving relations pon di sofa.'

'Why didn't you tell the police this when they arrested you?'

'Man, ya crazy!' Cutty burst out. 'You 'ave locks an' you arx dat? You like man and you arx dat? You don't tell di authorities *nuttin'*, man! Mi bruddah, him a policeman, and me no trust he *one inch*. What you tink dem a go say, "Oh, you is chichiman, we understand, no problem: di gyal did lie, you free to go"? You tink I waan official records saying, "Disya man a battyman"?' Cutty found himself rising from his chair. His heart was pounding. 'Me cyaan do dat, man,' he said thickly. 'Disya, me comin' 'ere, it a mistake.'

Oliver half-rose as Cutty stood and caught him by the hand. 'Please, brother,' he said. 'Please, Cutty. Sit down, yeah?'

Cutty found the physical contact unexpectedly reassuring, and he let Oliver guide him gently back down into his seat. Where was he going to go, anyway, if he left here? If this man couldn't help him, who could?

They sat in silence for a minute or so, then Oliver spoke. 'I believe you,' he said.

'So why you believe me now?' Cutty asked warily.

A flicker of a smile played over Oliver's lips. 'Because we're still holding hands.'

Cutty glanced down and it was true, they were. He hadn't given it a thought, but a straight man would have. A lying straight Jamaican gangsta would have wrenched his hand from out gay Oliver's instantly, horrified by the contact. Oliver gave Cutty's hand a final squeeze, then let it go.

'Are you still involved with this man?' Oliver asked, and now he produced from a drawer a pad and pen to make notes with.

Again, Cutty found making such a bald statement of his gender preference difficult. But he managed to say, 'Yes. I am.'

'Does he have a name?'

'Buju.'

'And the fiancée? Miss - ' Oliver checked the file. 'Mitchell?'

'She has moved on.'

'Would Buju be prepared to testify to your relation-ship at the IS review?'

'Him haffi do dat?'

'It could make all the difference.'

Cutty didn't know what to say. He didn't know if Buju would be prepared to go that far for him. To have his sexuality made a matter of public record. For there to be the possibility it might end up in the newspapers or some other public forum that friends and family might become aware of. To have the state know, irrevocably, what he was.

'Well, think about it,' Oliver said, when Cutty didn't reply.

'Yes,' Cutty said.

'Okay.' Oliver scribbled a note on his pad. 'Well, let's move on to the next problem. The very few gay Jamaicans who have successfully claimed asylum here were mostly obviously gay, and you aren't. Anyone meeting you would assume you were straight.'

'Did you?'

'I really wasn't sure,' Oliver said. 'But the point is that you can't just say to the Home Office that you happen to prefer men and get asylum. They'll just say, so what? You have to show solid grounds for why you fear persecution if you're returned to Jamaica.'

'I 'ave grounds,' Cutty said. 'Oh, yes, bredren. Me 'ave grounds.'

And once again, and painful and difficult though it was, he told the story of the night when Sonny was murdered, when he too almost lost his life.

'To haffi run from friends an' neighbours cah dem does want fi murder you is a terrible ting,' he said finally, once everything was told, every soul-destroying detail exhumed and laid bare. 'An' part of me did dead dat night, you know.'

He fell silent. This time he shed no tears, but Oliver

lent forward and hugged him anyway.

'You were wronged,' Oliver said. 'And we have to make sure you don't get wronged again.'

'I did worry dat di police dem woulda frame I for di killing,' Cutty said. 'Is why me no claim asylum when me firs' arrive here.'

'You thought the British authorities would contact the police back in Kingston and be told you were wanted for murder there?'

'Exactly, man. I couldn't do it, you know? Dem woulda send I back. And den what? Dem woulda murder I.'

Oliver nodded. They sat in silence for a long moment. Outside the sky was darkening with thunderclouds. The office sank into gloom. Oliver reached round and switched on the desk-lamp. It threw out a low, soft yellow light. Rain started to lash the window.

'So you 'ave a man?' Cutty asked, needing to talk for however short a while about something other than himself and his situation.

'Yes,' Oliver said, and he smiled a warm smile. 'His name's Christopher. We've been together for nearly nine years now.'

'And your family, dem does know 'bout it?'

'They've known I was gay since I was a teenager.'

'And dem accept it?'

'Not easily,' Oliver said. 'And it took them years. My father longer than my mother. But they do now. And they accept Chris is my partner and that I'll bring him along to anything where you would usually bring a partner.'

'And his family?'

'It took them time too, but now they fully accept us as a couple. His mother even tells me I'm a good influence on him.' Oliver smiled again.

'You have a photo?'

'Sure.'

Oliver reached round for a framed photograph that was sitting on his desk and passed it to Cutty. It showed Oliver and Christopher on a sunny day, arm-in-arm in some park, smiling and shirtless with a blue sky behind them. Chris was taller than Oliver and younger, a handsome, clean-shaven white man with a sharply-defined blond box-cut and boyish features.

'You prefer di white boys den?' Cutty asked, some-how a little disappointed. He had imagined Oliver with another dreadlocked brother.

'Not particularly.' There was an edge to Oliver's voice, and Cutty realised that Oliver had picked up on the negativity in his tone.

'Ey, bredren, me no judge,' Cutty said quickly, hold-ing up a hand in a gesture of apology.

'Don't you?'

'Well, love strikes where it strikes, don't it?' Cutty said. 'And who am I to judge when dem does judge me just for liking man?' Cutty looked at the photograph again. 'Him good-looking, you know,' he added, trying not to sound grudging.

'Yeah,' said Oliver. 'He is.' But his expression was unrevealing.

'Is only since me come a England dat me check for white man at all,' Cutty said, by way of explaining himself more clearly. 'Back home dem di exploiter, yunno? Sex tourists an' dat. So dem no interest I den. Nine years, man!' he said. 'You must mean a lot to each other for true.'

'We do,' Oliver said. 'And he's had to go on a jour-ney with me. Because you can't be white and love a black man and stay white, you know? You have to give something up and take something on. It hasn't been an easy ride for him any more than it has for me. And I don't apologise for him or me.'

Cutty nodded. He had never had cause to give it much thought, but it seemed to him now that what Oliver was saying was inevitably true.

'Well, I do apologise,' he said.

Oliver nodded his acceptance, took the framed photograph from Cutty and placed it back on his desk.

'Okay,' he said, re-opening Cutty's file. 'Back to business. What we need to do is to make your asylum application as soon as possible. That means going down to the Asylum Screening Unit in Croydon tomorrow. I'll come with you. They'll register you and arrange an interview. That's when we'll have to state your case as effectively as we can, because the decision on your claim will be made on the basis of that one interview, plus any supporting documentation you can bring along with you. And I should warn you, they'll be cunts.'

Cutty almost laughed aloud at the sudden expletive.

'In the meantime,' Oliver went on, 'I'll contact J-FLAG and Amnesty International and see if I can get any information that tends to support your account of what happened to you and Sonny rather than what appeared in the press or the police reports. Hopefully there'll be some sort of time-lag between registering with the ASU and your case coming up to give us time to prepare.'

'We cyaan put off going dere in di firs' place?'

'No. You've got to apply for asylum before the deportation order is made against you or you'll end up being stuck in prison or a detention centre until your case comes up.'

Cutty nodded. He had no intention of ending up inside again.

Oliver rang the Asylum Screening Centre and made an appointment for ten the following morning.

'Come here for 8.30,' he arranged with Cutty after

getting off the phone. 'That way we can go down to Croydon together.'

'Aright, bredren.'

'Cool. Okay, well, I reckon that's about all our business for today. Do you have any questions?'

'Money,' Cutty said. 'Me na 'ave much, you know?'

'We can sort that out later,' Oliver said. Cutty nodded gratefully, and they got to their feet and shook hands.

'If you can try and get your partner to testify,' Oliver reminded Cutty as he saw him to the lift. 'I know it's a lot to ask, but it could be crucial to how your case goes.'

'I must reason pon it,' Cutty replied.

A moment later the lift doors opened and Cutty stepped inside. He pressed the button for the ground floor and the doors slid shut behind him.

As the lift started to descend Cutty's mind rapidly filled with questions he wanted to ask Oliver next time he saw him. Not legal questions, though: questions about what it was like to be a black gay man in England. It was strange – almost unimaginable – to Cutty to think that his future life might be here. That this land, this city, might really become his home. And he would be black in this white country, and he might also become something else here, something he could never even have imagined back in Jamaica.

The questions he most needed to ask he could not yet formulate.

Outside the rain had faded into drizzle, and the street-lamps were beginning to buzz and flicker into life.

Chapter Twenty-Six

C utty and Oliver sat side-by-side on the train to Croydon the following morning, Oliver's silence leaving Cutty alone with his thoughts. Buju had offered to come along but Cutty had told him that he didn't have to as this was just a registration session. Which was true, but the real reason Cutty didn't want Buju to come along was that he hadn't yet asked him about testifying to their relationship at the interview, and didn't want Oliver bringing the subject up before he had a chance to talk it through with Buju himself. Also the studio was booked, this time by a young girl from nearby Harlesden who was aiming to be the next Miss Dynamite. Shanazna Brown. She was good, Cutty thought: she had a chance to break big. Once again he was leaving Buju to supervise a studio session. But Cutty wasn't worried: Buju had picked up the technical side of the business remarkably quickly, quicker even than Sonny had done back in JA: he turned out to have a gift for it.

And yet, thought Cutty, if things had gone another way Buju could right now be rotting in jail, another ignorant, parasitical nigger banged up for dealing or burglary. Another young black man who would be seen as having nothing to contribute.

Croydon turned out to be not so much a place in its own right as just more urban sprawl, and Cutty had no sense of leaving London and arriving somewhere else. The only difference was that outside the station there were trams on tram-tracks as well as buses.

After a sappingly long wait out in the damp, cold air

a bus drew up. They got on. Twenty minutes later it deposited them in front of the Asylum Screening Centre. The Centre was on the edge of an industrial park and was a large, featureless box of a building that looked like a cross between an airport terminal and a mental institution.

Inside the Centre, in a lobby area, rows of defeated-looking and almost entirely non-white people sat waiting to be seen. Oliver led Cutty up to the reception desk to confirm their appointment. A pasty-faced but friendly white queen clicked on a screen, told them that they were booked in, gave Cutty a numbered ticket, and gestured for him and Oliver to take a seat on one of the rows of chairs and wait. They went and joined the other sufferers, most of whom were staring up like supplicants at an altar at a ticket-counter that was suspended on steel rods from the ceiling above the reception desk. The ticket-counter displayed the number 371. Cutty's ticket read 428. He felt instantly depressed.

They were seen after a forty-minute wait by a hard-faced young white woman with a bleach-blonde bob and a repressed Afrikaaner accent who introduced herself only as, 'Your screening officer'. Oliver had to ask her for her name, and she gave it, but grudgingly, as if his request was self-evidently unreasonable: 'Ms De Witt.' Cutty and Oliver followed her to a small interview room where Ms De Witt took Cutty's name, nationality and date of birth, and her male assistant finger-printed him. She also took Cutty's photograph with a small webcam camera. It was all unpleasantly similar to how the police had treated him when he had been arrested, and instantly made Cutty feel like a criminal, and worthless. Ms De Witt asked where he lived, and he gave Buju's old flat, now the studio, as his address. He wasn't going to give her his real address.

He wasn't having her or her snoopers in his true home, going through his and Buju's intimate things. She asked who he lived with, and he gave Buju's name.

'Relationship?'

Cutty hesitated. 'Friend,' he said.

Before Ms De Witt could enter Cutty's reply on the computer-screen in front of her Oliver put up a hand to stop her and said, 'Could I have a moment with my client before we carry on, please?'

Ms De Witt glanced at her watch to emphasise how very important her time was, then nodded curtly. Cutty followed Oliver into the corridor outside the interview room.

'What are you *doing*?' Oliver demanded angrily, the moment they were out of Ms De Witt's earshot.

'It ain't her business, man!' Cutty shot back.

'You're trying to claim asylum for being gay, Cutty! You can't do that and not tell anyone you're gay while you're doing it!'

'Fuck alla disya shit, man! She hate I anyway! Fuckin' white bitch! Me na have no chance!'

And Cutty started to walk away.

Oliver caught up with him after a few strides. 'Look,' he said. 'I know this is difficult. I know this is harder than anything you'll ever have to do. I know where you're coming from on all this. I know you've spent your whole life doing the exact opposite of what you have to do now. I've represented men who prefer men from Zimbabwe, Uganda, Bosnia and Iran, as well as Jamaica. The courage they had to find - ' He broke off and took a breath. 'Look, in the end the courage they had to find was a reflection of the need they were in. This, what we're doing now, it isn't worse than dying. It isn't worse than being beaten bloody in the streets. It's a bunch of bureaucrats, that's all. But there's no way round it: you have to do it their way.'

Cutty sighed. 'Ya right, man,' he said grudgingly. 'Ya right. Me know dat. But me cyaan tell shi 'bout Buju. Not witout him permission, you know?'

'So you haven't discussed with him about testifying?' Oliver asked, looking exasperated.

'No look like dat, man,' Cutty said, trying to force a smile. 'I will arx him. I promise.'

'But in the meantime you have to start laying your claim,' Oliver said. 'You have to say Buju is your partner or you have no case.'

'Still I will have to arx him first.'

'Let's go back to the interview,' said Oliver.

They returned to the room and finished the registration process, which only took a few more minutes, continuing on unchanged from Cutty claiming Buju as no more than a friend. Ms De Witt gave Cutty an Application Registration card, then arranged for him to be interviewed in three days time.

'Could we put it back a little?' Oliver asked. 'I'm waiting on information from abroad in support of Mister Munroe's case.'

'I'm sorry,' said Ms De Witt with a tight little smile. 'We have to comply with Home Office targets and Human Rights Act regulations for the speedy processing of applicants for asylum.'

'Look, you really do have to discuss it with Buju,' Oliver was saying.

They were on the train back to London. It was lunchtime and they had half the carriage to themselves, so they could talk reasonably freely without fear of being overheard.

'Me know,' Cutty replied.

'If he doesn't speak up on your behalf, and if I can't get some sort of evidence from J-FLAG or AI about what happened to you back in Jamaica then your case is looking really bad.'

'And if it fail?'

'Then we can appeal.'

'And if dat fail?'

'Then you'll be deported.'

'What you reckon di odds are now?'

'Right now you look like a drug-using heterosexual probable rapist who might be trying to evade a murder rap back home by coming up with whatever lie he thinks might swing it with the authorities in Britain.'

Cutty stared out of the window at the passing houses. Why did his life have to be so hard? All the people in those houses had their own problems no doubt, their own worries, but they didn't have *this*.

He left Oliver to chase up J-FLAG and AI and made his way back to White City by tube. When he reached the studio the session was cooking, and he threw himself into work just to escape his situation for a little while. Afterwards, when the day's recording was finished and Shanazna and her hangers-on had departed wreathed in ganja smoke, high on the weed and on the kicking track they had laid down, Cutty forced himself to speak to Buju about testifying on his behalf at the interview. Somehow it seemed easier to do it there at their place of work than it would have been to do it at their home, perhaps because in a way it was business. State business.

'Look, man, is a lot to arx, me know dat,' Cutty said awkwardly.

Buju looked down at the cable he was coiling. Cutty stared at the smooth line of his neck, the gold pistol in his ear, at his boyish features that were now in shadow. He felt that he was somehow doing Buju a terrible wrong in pushing him to do this.

'Ah, forget it, blood,' he said, trying to sound light.

"Llow it. Dere mus' be another way, you know?'

'Like what though?' Buju was still looking down at the cable.

Cutty shrugged.

They packed up, locked up the studio, and walked home, both of them tense and preoccupied, saying little to each other. The evening ground by with painful slowness. Buju avoided Cutty's eyes. Washing up he dropped and smashed a mug. Cutty came into the kitchen to find Buju kneeling and sweeping up the pieces. Buju looked up at him very directly then.

'I'll do it, man,' he said.

He got to hs feet and tipped the pottery shards into the bin. Cutty hugged him and Buju hugged Cutty back but their embrace was oddly stilted. Cutty should have felt relieved by Buju saying he would testify, but if anything the tension he was feeling increased.

The next two days crawled by in an agony of antici-pation for both of them.

Despite all that the day of the interview arrived with sickening suddenness. There had been little Cutty could do to prepare for it. Oliver had managed to get reports from J-FLAG of rumours that there was a homophobic component to the murder of Sonny Hilton and the burning of Cutty's Informer Sounds studio. They were unsubstantiated, but they were better than nothing.

In the meantime Cutty had taken Buju to meet Oliver. After an initial bullish evasiveness about his sexuality Buju had found himself getting on well with Oliver. Like Cutty he had never met a black gay man who saw being black and gay as a politicised identity to fight for.

'I ain't never met no activist before,' Buju said af-terwards. 'He knows a lotta history, that dreadlocks. He's got a lot to teach, you know? Kind of like a father suppose to be. Passing shit down. And he cares about his peeps, you know what I'm saying? He cares about you.'

Cutty nodded his agreement.

Behind them the backdrop of the world billowed and shifted: *The Voice* surprised them all by running a series of pieces sympathetic towards black gay men, even if the black gay couple whose commitment ceremony it reported on felt they had to hide their faces from the black world.

Still, it was progress. But back home in Jamaica a young man being chased by a homophobic mob was forced to jump from a pier into the sea to escape it, and drowned. In other incidents others were beaten and slashed.

And on Hampstead Heath a gay man was beaten into a coma by thugs. Some white man, but the story affected both Cutty and Buju very differently from how it would have done even six weeks ago. Cutty thought of Spin and Gary and felt depressed and appalled. It also depressed him to be stripped of any delusion that England was a haven for men who love men.

And so the three of them sat in the reception area of the Asylum Screening Centre, trying to keep their morale up as the minutes creaked by. This time they were kept waiting for over an hour, as if the authorities were deliberately trying to generate the maximum possible stress and anxiety.

Just as Cutty was deciding he really needed to go for a piss his number flicked up on the overhead counter. He, Buju and Oliver shuffled to their feet. The woman at the reception desk directed them to Interview Room 7.

'They're waiting for you,' she said with a smile that

tried to be kind. How much choking despair did she witness every day?

The interview room was spartan. Behind a grey plastic desk sat Cutty's inquisitors, a middle-aged white man and a middle-aged white woman, both of them pallid, unattractive and hard-faced. On the desk in front of them was an open case-file. On Cutty's side of the desk was a single hard plastic shell chair. Two other shell chairs were placed behind it against the wall next to the door. In one corner of the ceiling a surveillance camera was angled down on them, its red light blinking.

Cutty took the seat in front of the desk, Buju and Oliver the two against the wall. Buju tried to move his chair forward so it would be next to Cutty's but it had been bolted to the floor. He gave up and sat back, trying to look at ease in the suit he had chosen to wear for the occasion. It was by Paul Smith, and was navy blue. Back at their drum it had looked merely smart, but here in this dead grey room it seemed too stylishly cut, too fashionable for the serious business at hand. Cutty's suit was plainer but it too seemed somehow too much for the utter drabness of the interview room and its inhabitants. But maybe that was good? Maybe it could be read as somehow flamboyant or effeminate, and so fit into his interrogators' notions of how a battyman would present himself.

The interviewers introduced themselves as Mr Palmer and Mrs Cashmore. They informed Cutty that they were the ones who would decide his claim for asylum and added that, should he disagree with their decision, he had a statutory right of appeal. Also that he would be notified of the panel's decision via his solicitor within forty-eight hours of today's interview. If it was decided that he be deported, he would be required to present himself to Immigration Services forthwith for that purpose. Should he fail to do so, a warrant would be issued for his arrest. They then reconfirmed the information Cutty had given to Ms De Witt at his initial interview.

'Me have one correction to make,' Cutty said when they reached his address.

'Yes?' said Mrs Cashmore.

'When I say me live wit' Mr Staples - '

'Yes?'

'I did say we was just friends. But we is partners.'

He glanced round at Buju, who was now sitting bolt upright and looking sweaty. But Buju managed to nod stiffly when Mrs Cashmore and Mr Palmer turned their eyes on him. Mrs Cashmore made a note.

'Now, Mister Munroe,' Mr Palmer said. 'Tell us why you wish to claim asylum in the UK.'

'Cah me a gay Jamaican,' Cutty said. The phrase came out more easily than he had expected. 'Myself and a friend, we was attack by a mob back in Kingston. I manage to flee, my friend die. My business get burn down. Di police dem na investigate. Dem try to make it sound like I did burn it down. I am a known face pon di music scene in Kingston. Cah di rumour spread dat me is – gay – my life it is in danger. So me come a England, whey me have a few friends and business contacts.'

'In support of Mister Munroe's account,' Oliver put in, 'I have here reports from the website of J-FLAG, the Jamaican gay rights organisation, that there is widespread belief that the Kingston police did indeed cover up – and in fact collude in – this homophobic hate crime that led to the death of Mister Munroe's assistant, also a gay man.'

Oliver handed a sheaf of print-outs to Mrs Cashmore. She and Mr Palmer looked over them while Cutty, Buju and Oliver sat there in silence. Their expression was impossible to read. After several long minutes they put the print-outs aside.

'No official investigation has yet taken place into this allegation?' asked Mr Palmer.

'Amnesty International are looking into taking it up,' Oliver said quickly.

'But in the meantime?'

'In the meantime I checked personally with the Kingston police and they confirmed theat they are no longer actively seeking Mister Munroe in connection with the death of Sonny Hilton. Which is, at the least, extremely suggestive.'

'You have a conviction here for the possession of a class A drug, Mister Munroe,' Mrs Cashmore said, looking up from consulting his file. She wore large, half-smoked glasses that hid her eyes. 'Ecstasy.'

'Just for my personal use,' Cutty said, trying to make it sound inconsequential.

'A drug-dealing charge against you was dropped,' Mrs Cashmore went on, adding before Oliver could interrupt, 'as was a charge of rape.'

'Yes.'

'You *are* a homosexual, Mr Munroe?' Mrs Cashmore asked drily.

'Yes.'

'As a rule homosexuals do not rape women.'

'Shi lie.'

'That is a very heterosexual response, Mr Munroe,' Mrs Cashmore remarked, making a note on his file. 'I ask again: are you a homosexual?'

'What 'appen was - ' Cutty took a deep breath. 'Mr Staples and myself, we did become involve when I stay wit him in him yard. In his home. Him was also seeing dis gal and – well, she did come upon we.'

' "Being intimate"?' Mr Palmer asked, leaning forward slightly and running his tongue over his pale pink lips.

'Yes.'

'And what form did this intimacy take?'

Cutty looked at him with distaste. 'What you tink, man?'

'I don't know. That's why I'm asking.'

'We did what two man do when dem is being intimate,' Cutty said irritably. 'And dat ain't none a your business. But Cynthia come pon we, and she freak out and run over to di yard a shi best friend, and to punish we she tell di police dat me rape she.'

'Do we have a testimonial from this girlfriend?' Mr Palmer asked Mrs Cashmore. She shook her head.

'Di police drop di charge cah dere weren't no evidence cah nuttin' 'appen,' Cutty said, panic rising up in him at the thought of Cynthia getting involved in his situation, Cynthia describing him and Buju having sex to these cold voyeurs.

'It's true, man,' Buju burst in. 'What he told you, it's the truth.'

'Mr Staples?'

'Yeah.'

'And you, despite having this girlfriend, you also are a homosexual?'

'You gotta 'ave a girl on your arm, dontcha?' Buju said hotly. 'Or else people start saying shit. It don't mean nothing. It don't mean who you are for real.'

'But you don't have a girlfriend now?'

'I don't need no girlfriend. That's what I learned since – since being with Mister Munroe. That's how come I could come here, you know? Cos I want a life what's more truthful.'

'So do we, Mister Staples,' Mr Palmer said. 'Getting to the truth is our number one concern here today.'

'Well, *this* is the truth,' Buju said. And he got to his feet, stepped over to Cutty, tipped Cutty's head back and kissed him on the mouth. Cutty, although he was shocked and surprised, responded. After thirty seconds Buju broke the kiss and went and sat back down.

'That's what you wanted to see, ain't it?' he spat, his expression bold-face and defiant. 'So don't be coming out with shit about we ain't gay just cos we ain't shouting it all over the place or whatever.'

'Thank you, Mister Staples,' Mrs Cashmore said coolly. She turned to her colleague. 'Mr Palmer?'

'Why didn't you claim asylum on first arriving here, Mister Munroe?'

'Cah me na know dat being gay woulda give me grounds. And cah me tink di police a go frame I for killing Sonny so dere would be no proof I was in danger for my life.'

'So when did you realise you could claim asylum on grounds of your sexuality?'

'Well, I did hear back in Jamaica some time ago and also from what I read 'ere in di *Voice* and other newspapers. But it no occur to I dat I could - '

'So you *had* heard of being able to claim asylum if you were homosexual back in Jamaica?'

'Yes, but dem was always effeminate, you know. Obvious.'

'And you're not.'

'Which is how come it take me time fi tink tings tru, and see me is no different from dem.'

'But being not self-evidently homosexual, you could live your life in Jamaica without being in personal danger.'

'Until di night my neighbours dem try an' murder I.'

Mr Palmer made another note. He exchanged a look with Mrs Cashmore. 'Well,' he said. 'We seem to have covered everything. Is there anything else you wish to say at this point?'

'Yes,' Cutty said. 'When I arrive here me no have nuttin'. Buju – Mister Staples – cared for me. Now di two a we start we own business. I ain't no drug dealer. I ain't no rapist. I just want to live in peace.'

'Thank you, Mister Munroe,' Mr Palmer said. 'You'll be notified of our decision via your solicitor within forty-eight hours.'

'Tank you,' Cutty said uncertainly. He got to his feet and offered his hand for Mr Palmer to shake. Grudgingly Mr Palmer took it, then Mrs Cashmore. Then Cutty, Buju and Oliver left the room.

'How you tink it go?' Cutty asked Oliver once they were out in the open air again. His gut was spasming. Although he had managed to empty his bladder before leaving the building he was still left with a punctured ache below his navel. All three of them lit cigarettes.

'I'm not sure,' Oliver said, pocketing his lighter. 'But thanks to Buju's intervention - ' He gave Buju a smile – 'I'm pretty sure they believe you're gay.'

'I should think so too, man,' Buju muttered, dragging on his cigarette and looking around to make sure that what Oliver had just said hadn't been overheard by some passer-by.

'So now we haffi wait.'

'Yes.'

The following day Oliver received a letter from the Home Office: Cutty's claim had been rejected.

Chapter Twenty-Seven

'So we appeal,' Oliver said. He, Cutty and Buju were having an emergency meeting down at his office.

'But why dem turn I down?' Cutty asked, staring blankly at the Home Office letter, unable to focus on the actual words.

'They weren't convinced your life would be in danger if you were returned to Jamaica.'

'But that's fuckeries, man!' Buju broke in. 'They *know* his life would be in danger. What they mean is they don't give a fuck if a nigger battyman gets offed. Motherfuckers, man! Racist, homophobic motherfuckers!'

Cutty put his hand on Buju's and squeezed it to calm him. 'So we must prove it, star,' he said. 'We must prove di danger.'

'And how the fuck we do that, man?' Buju objected. 'We can't go there, can we? *You* can't go there, and I can't go there and play no battyman detective, and even if I did, and even if I found shit out, it wouldn't prove nothing cos I ain't no fed or nothing. And anyway no-one would tell me anything, would they?' He kissed his teeth in vexation.

'We'll have two months to get all the information together that we can for the appeal,' Oliver said. 'J-FLAG or AI may come up with more, and we can go over all the statements made in the press and by the police and see if any inconsistencies come up. That might give us something. Did Sonny's parents know he was gay?'

'No, dread,' Cutty said with a dismissive shake of

his head. 'Of course not. And if anyone arx dem, dem
will deny it.'

'Well, we'll do what we can,' Oliver said. 'In the
meantime there is another option we haven't discussed.'

'What's that, man?' asked Buju.

'Go public.'

'What you mean, go public?' Cutty asked.

'Get our case taken up by the press,' Oliver said.
'Start with the gay press and build it up from there with
the more liberal national papers. Amnesty International has at least started to take on gay, lesbian and
transgender rights in their campaigns. We get them
involved. Then there's the gay radical group Outrage
and there's a black gay group called Big Up. We could
try and get them to mobilise behind your case and
shame the Home Office into changing their decision.'

'Hold up, bredren,' Cutty said. 'Me appreciate what
you is saying, but alla dat, it na my world, you know?
Me na know nuttin' bout gay groups an dat. To even
call myself gay – well, it don't really fit, you know? I is
just – me.'

'I understand that, and I don't want to put you in a
place you're uncomfortable with,' Oliver said. 'But the
reality is you're already in a place you're not comfortable with: being sent back to Jamaica as a known
homosexual who might still get framed for murder.
And I know the idea of a gay community's a joke in
many ways. But within that there are people who do
care, who do want to make a difference, and who will
fight for your rights because you're gay too.'

Cutty found himself thinking back to the two white
gay men he had glimpsed so briefly in the house he and
Buju had burgled what felt like years ago. At the time
he had believed that he had nothing at all in common
with them, and yet if it hadn't been for the gay art on

the walls, the gay friends in the photographs, would he and Buju ever have taken that step beyond ambivalent flirtation into something real? Connection is a strange and sometimes unexpected thing.

But if he allowed himself to be taken up by the gays here then that would replicate the horrors he had faced back home: he would become a known battyman out on the streets, a target for any crazy motherfucker with something to prove. And Cutty wasn't afraid to fight but he needed a life where he could escape from fighting as well.

'If di appeal fail,' he said eventually with a shrug. His situation would then be so bad that anything would be worth trying.

Oliver nodded, and Cutty knew he understood.

Time passed. The fact that he was appealing meant that Cutty avoided being sent either back to prison or to a detention centre, but still he felt as if he was twisting in limbo. Suicidal thoughts were often in his head, though he kept these from Buju. He loved Buju and he loved their life together, but self-murder seemed like a way of thwarting both the control mechanisms of the British state and the baying killers waiting for him back home. Many days he stared at his face in the bathroom mirror and thought of cutting his wrists.

And however much Buju had become a home for him, still Cutty felt his exile as a pain that was never absent, only sometimes less intense. Because to choose to make your life in a new country is one thing; to be driven out of the country in which you've spent your entire life is another. And although Buju could share many things with Cutty, he couldn't share that. Cutty found himself having violently masochistic sexual fantasies that disgusted him even as they excited him. He thought of going to church, but then he remembered the sermons of the vicar at his parents' church on the destruction of Sodom and he stayed away.

One night he and Buju gathered their courage and went to a black gay club in Vauxhall called Bootilicious. They found it in the gay pages of *Time Out*, the London listings magazine. It was located in one of the arches under a railway bridge just south of the river near a mostly-white gay pub called the Vauxhall Tavern. Buju and Cutty were surprised by how long the line was outside, and how large and busy the club was inside, but both of them had to fight back a desire to bolt as they passed between the bouncers on the door, several of whom were black, seemingly heterosexual, and at least covertly contemptuous of their black battybwoi customers disgracing the race.

The Bootilicious clientele were mostly black gay men, along with some black women, both lesbian and straight, and a handful of white gay men. And for the first time as he wound it up with Buju on the dancefloor to the latest bashment tunes Cutty did feel at home in London. The black gay men around him ran the gamut from drag queens and the flamboyant to the gym-built and the down-low, from pretty-boy club kids to dreadlocked Rastas, and they hailed from the Caribbean, from Africa, from America, from all over Europe and beyond, as well as of course from the UK. He began to notice men who reminded him strongly of particular individuals he had known back home.

It was a liberating evening, but on another level it only increased Cutty's suffering: anything that made him feel more invested in living in London added to his dread at the thought of being forcibly deported. In that sense even his love for Buju, and Buju's love for him, was a sort of torture. And so his mood swung between surges of optimism that were almost euphoric and suicidal despair, and the pressure built up in his brain.

One time he heard a voice shouting out his name that he began to suspect had only happened inside his head.

But the studio was going well, and he and Buju threw themselves into work with even more determination than before. They lined up gigs and PAs for Shanazna, and she looked like she was on her way to becoming the label's first genuine star act.

In the meantime reports from Oliver were not encouraging. Kingston Police hadn't been forthcoming. The furthest they would go was to say that they considered Sonny Hilton to have been murdered by persons unknown, and that the attack on Cutty's studio had been in some way gang-related. Therefore Cutty was no longer a murder suspect.

'Which actually weakens your case from the point of view of your appeal,' Oliver told Cutty at one of their weekly get-togethers. 'Because it means we can no longer argue that the state is actively involved in oppressing or endangering your life. And without proof that they know you're gay and did nothing to help you when you were attacked we can't argue that they will definitely fail to protect you from homophobic violence.'

There was only one thing Cutty could do: he would have to call his brother.

Chapter Twenty-Eight

'You want me here when you call him?' Buju asked Cutty as Cutty sat on the sofa staring at his mobile phone. They were at home together. It was the middle of the week and it had gone midnight: over in Kingston it would be dinner-time. Robert would be home with his wife and children.

'I want you here,' Cutty said.

Buju bent forward and kissed him on the lips.

'But I cyaan do it wit you in di room, though,' Cutty added.

Buju nodded and got to his feet. 'Call me when you're done, yeah?' he said, and wandered off into the kitchen.

Cutty looked down at the phone in his hand. There was no point in putting the call off: letting more time pass would make no difference to how Robert would react to hearing from his battyman brother who had fled the country. He tapped in the international code for Jamaica followed by Robert's number and waited, his heart pounding as the tone sounded at the other end of the line.

'Hello?' a woman's voice answered. It was Robert's wife.

'Annette?'

'Cuthbert?'

'Yes.'

'Oh my God! How are you? Where are you?'

'Inna England. London town.'

'Well, my goodness!' Annette exclaimed. 'My goodness! Are you well?' Before he could answer she went on, 'I was surprised you didn't come home when your father had his attack, you know.'

'Well, I did want to but dere have been difficulties, as you know.'

'Yes,' she said blankly. 'And he is well, thank God. Making a good recovery. I was up there just last week and he was almost his old self.'

'So is Robert home?' Cutty asked. 'Mek I speak wit him?'

'Of course. Hold the line. Good to speak to you, Cuthbert.' He heard her calling to his brother, 'Robbie, is Cutty on the phone for you.' Then, 'He's just coming. Take care of yourself.'

'Hello?' the deep male voice at the other end of the line sounded unfriendly and suspicious. 'A who dis?'

'Robert? Is Cutty.'

'So what you want, man?'

'You tell Annette?'

'No.'

'Me haffi arx a favour, Robby.'

'What favour could you possibly want from me, Cutty?'

'Well, me need you to tell di truth, man.'

There was a long silence at the other end of the line. Cutty could hear Robert breathing. Then eventually Robert said, 'What truth?'

'You know what truth.'

'And what about our parents?' Robert asked coldly. 'You think about what that will do to them? Man, ya selfish. Never tink 'bout no-one but yourself.'

'Me no mean tell di whole world, you know,' Cutty interrupted. 'I just need a written statement dat tell wha gwaan dat night, fi show di authorities inna England.'

'Why?'

'So I can stay here. Otherwise dem a deport me back a JA.'

'And if I give you this statement, it means you don't come back?'

'Yes.'

'And how am I suppose to make such a statement without - ' Robert's voice dropped to a harsh whisper – 'Without compromising my fellow officers?'

'Compromise dem?' Cutty spat. 'Dem did left me and Sonny fi dead! Just drive off and left we!'

'And if you hadn't got into this rasclaat batty business,' Robert hissed, 'then nothing would have happen in the first place!'

'So you no care me almost lose mi life, den?'

Robert sighed exasperatedly. 'Of course I care, man,' he said, his tone sullen. 'I just wish...' His voice tailed off.

'Dat tings dem did turn out different?'

There was another lengthy silence at the other end of the line. 'So what you need me to say in this statement?' Robert asked grudgingly.

'Why di attack happen. How di mob did gather. How the police dem don't rescue we. How it get put down as gang violence - '

'But tell me true, Cutty,' Robert interrupted. 'You and this bwoi, this Sonny. Were you - ?'

'Yes.'

Robert kissed his teeth. 'Jesus Christ, man!' he said angrily. 'Is just as well Joseph dead, you know. If he'da been alive now he'd have popped you in the head, man.'

'Yeah,' Cutty said tonelessly.

'Promise me one thing though.'

'What?'

'If I do this for you, promise you won't spread it about. I mean, spread what you are about.'

'And why in hell me woulda go do dat, man?'

'I don't know, man,' Robert said. 'I used to think I knew you, Cuthbert. But I don't know you at all. So I don't know why you do what you do.'

'Just write down di truth, man,' Cutty said. 'Dat is all I arxin'.'

Robert grunted assent. Cutty gave Robert his address in London and then everything that needed to be said had been said. The two brothers exchanged perfunctory goodbyes, and the call was over.

Cutty slumped back and closed his eyes with a sigh. His palms were clammy and tingling and he felt wrung out.

'He said he'd do it?' Buju asked from the kitchen doorway.

'Yes,' Cutty said. 'He will do it.' Without opening his eyes Cutty held out his hand. Buju crossed the room and took it, then sat down next to Cutty on the sofa. He kissed Cutty's temple.

'Brave soldier,' he said.

'Mek we go to bed, man,' Cutty said thickly.

Buju led him to their bedroom. There they undressed and Cutty fell into bed. At first he felt sexless and drained, but as Buju slipped under the covers hot and naked next to him desire flared up in him, along with a great need to have Buju's dick inside his body.

'Fuck me, star,' he whispered as Buju slid behind him spoon-fashion.

'You sure, man?' Buju's voice was gentle.

'Yes, blood,' Cutty said. 'Fuck me.'

He felt Buju's dick stiffening between his buttocks and flexed his butt-muscles to encourage him, closing his eyes as he did so. He heard the soft sound of Buju fishing the bottle of lube out of the bedside drawer, then felt the thrilling intimacy of Buju's slick fingers sliding inside him. A violent shudder ran through his body.

'Yes, man,' he said hoarsely. 'Yes, mi bruddah.'

Chapter Twenty-Nine

Robert took a week to send his statement, but when it arrived it was lengthy and detailed, and contained enough information to substantiate Cutty's account of events. It was written as if Cutty was a person entirely unknown to the author: only their shared surnames suggested any connection between them. Oliver was very pleased with it, and straightaway photocopied it and – with Robert's name and any identifying details blacked out – sent it to J-FLAG back in Jamaica. This made Cutty feel somewhat guilty, but Oliver did it without consulting him, and did take care to exclude anything that could lead back to his brother.

As his confidence that he could win his appeal grew, Cutty started involving himself more in the new life he hoped would be his. He and Buju made more trips to South London to spend time with Oliver and the black gay men they met through him. And of course they met Chris, and the other white boyfriends a good many of those black gay men had. Some them, black and white alike, preferred partners of a different race, while for some it just happened that that was how things had turned out; that was just where cupid's arrow had struck. And for some of the black men their preference for a black partner was a political thing, while for others it was purely individual.

Cutty found Chris likeable enough, boyish, polite and considerate, and any impulse he felt towards distrusting Chris was held at bay by the nine years he had been Oliver's partner for. Because Cutty respected Oliver. Oliver was no fool, and Cutty knew Oliver would have seen through any white man with jungle fever in an instant.

Anyway, people were people, men were men, love was love, and there was good and bad in everyone.

After spending the evening with Oliver and Chris at a house party thrown by a friend of theirs, Cutty had asked Buju what he thought of these black men with white partners.

'So what, blood?' Buju shrugged. 'It's how you carry yourself, not who you fuck. Plenty brothers fucking brothers and ain't do nothin' for no-one. Let the bredren fuck who they choose. *Be with* who they choose,' he corrected himself. He took Cutty's hand and raised it to his lips. 'Like we all do,' he said, kissing Cutty's knuckles.

Being amongst these mostly black gay men was healing for Cutty and Buju, but it was still a schizoph-renic way of living. Out West they were two tough raggamuffins, bredrens running a business together. Down South they were partners, gay or same gender loving black men hanging out with other black gay men. Sometimes, occasionally, when they were with Oliver's friends, they would even allow themselves to camp it up a little – permit some of their fiercely-repressed flamboyance to burst out for a while, then guiltily push it way back down.

Despite the contradictions spaces were slowly open-ing in their lives that lessened the tensions that they had to live with. They bought a computer and got on-line and discovered a whole black gay world that neither of them had ever dreamed existed. They discovered jigsaw-pieces, fragments of an identity.

The day of the appeal came round. This time Cutty was better prepared and more confident. He was encour-aged by the fact that the adjudicator was independent of the Home Office, and had no particular vested interest in validating the ruling of the previous assessors.

The courthouse where appeals were held was in North London, so Cutty and Buju drove there. It was a large Victorian building with wide steps and pillars flanking the entrance. Cutty and Buju met Oliver in the marble-floored lobby. Cutty's appeal was being heard in Court Six. The set-up was more legalistic than the original interview had been, which meant that this time Cutty was allowed to have Oliver at his side to speak for and advise him. Buju sat just behind him, in the first row of spectator seats.

The adjudicator was a fair-haired, square-headed white man in his early sixties who wore small, gold-rimmed glasses. He listened patiently as Cutty and Oliver went through Cutty's reasons for seeking asylum. He nodded civilly when Buju stood up to identify himself as Cutty's partner, seemed attentive as Oliver briefly reminded him of the particularly vicious nature of Jamaican homophobia, and jotted down notes as Oliver read out Robert's statement.

Cutty found it strange to be in a court-room where there was no prosecutor trying to pull him to pieces. There was just the adjudicator. *Judge an' jury.* The adjudicator thanked Cutty and Oliver for their information, then pored over the Home Office reports he had spread out in front of him.

'Miss Mitchell,' he said, looking up from one of the documents on his desk. 'I see no statement from her validating your account of how the rape accusation came about.'

Cutty shot Oliver a worried look.

'The Home Office was convinced at the initial interview that Mister Munroe was telling the truth about his sexuality,' Oliver said quickly, 'and accepted that he was in a relationship with Mister Staples. We didn't think it would be necessary to furnish further proof for this appeal. Despite having obvious reasons to harbour resentment, I'm sure Miss Mitchell would be prepared to testify, however, if any doubt remains - '

'And what was the proof that the original assessors accepted?' the adjudicator asked.

'Well, Mister Staples kissed Mister Munroe on the mouth in the presence of both interviewers, and they felt the kiss to be sincere.'

A small smile puckered the adjudicator's lips. He gathered the papers before him into an orderly pile. 'Mister Munroe,' he said. 'It is my pleasure to inform you that your appeal has been successful, and that you will be granted indefinite leave to remain in the United Kingdom. Your solicitor will inform you of the necessary procedures you will have to complete, and of your entitlements under the law. Welcome to the United Kingdom, Mister Munroe.'

In the corridor outside the courtroom Cutty hugged Buju tight, tears squeezing from the corners of his eyes, and they kissed each other for the longest time, careless for once of watching eyes. Cutty felt reborn, and lighter than air.

After the paperwork had been done Cutty and Buju drove Oliver back down to Brixton. They stopped by his office briefly, then he invited them back to his drum, a flat in a block up Brixton Hill that he shared with his partner Chris, to celebrate the success of Cutty's appeal. Cutty and Buju were usually a little guarded around Chris, but that evening they were so full of joy that they let their guards down and cheerfully and spontaneously hugged him hello and kissed him on the cheek, which evidently pleased him: he produced two bottles of champagne from the fridge, and the four of them toasted Cutty's triumph, and Cutty and Buju's love.

Oliver and Chris's flat was on the tenth floor and had a small balcony off the living room. Although the night was cold Oliver threw the windows open and, glasses in hand, they stepped out onto the balcony and looked out over the glittering city that now belonged to all of them, and up at the stars that filled the cloudless indigo sky. There was a thin crescent moon riding high above their heads, a new moon, and Cutty thought how strange it was that the same moon looking down on all of this was shining on his brother and mother and father halfway across the world. He thought of the many journeys Africans had made across the Atlantic. He slipped his arm round Buju's waist and pulled Buju closer to him. Next to them Chris stood behind Oliver, his arms around Oliver's waist, resting his chin on Oliver's shoulder as they stared out at the view. Restless thoughts crowded Cutty's head. Would he be able to somehow see his parents again? Could they come here? What would he tell them if they did? Painful thoughts, but Buju was with him and that felt right, and it felt good, and the champagne was warming his body and that felt good too.

Everything was ahead of him now.

The End

Lightning Source UK Ltd.
Milton Keynes UK
UKOW050622110112

185154UK00001B/1/P

9 780956 971913